Pr...

"For unforget...
  remem...
  —Ga...

"Keep your eye on this author; one that go far."
  —*Huntress Book Reviews*

"Move over Stephanie Plum. Madeline Carter is
going to give you a run for readership."
  —*Writers Unlimited*

"If there's justice, many more people will be
finding out how good Richards is, and soon."
  —Sarah Weinman,
  Confessions of an Idiosyncratic Mind

Praise for *The Next Ex*

"Richards has a winning way with character and has
crafted a pleasing plot.... Readers craving a smart
heroine will find a lot here to like."
  —*Chicago Sun-Times*

"A solid whodunit and a quirky, fascinating character
who's good fun to spend time with...Madeline Carter...
is one of the best bets to invest your time in this year."
  —*Oakland Press*

"What any crime and mystery fan demands is great
plot. Richards delivers the goods...a refreshing
hybrid of hardboiled and chick-lit."
  —*Vancouver Sun*

"Be warned: this is one of those books that can
ruin your whole day. It's unputdownable."
  —*Gulf Islands Driftwood*

"Fantastic characterization, intricate plot,
spellbinding suspense... This was such a good book!"
  —*Fresh Fiction*

ISBN-13: 978-0-7783-2345-7
ISBN-10:   0-7783-2345-5

CALCULATED LOSS

Copyright © 2006 by Linda Richards.

All rights reserved. Except for use in any review, the reproduction or utilization of this work in whole or in part in any form by any electronic, mechanical or other means, now known or hereafter invented, including xerography, photocopying and recording, or in any information storage or retrieval system, is forbidden without the written permission of the publisher, MIRA Books, 225 Duncan Mill Road, Don Mills, Ontario, Canada M3B 3K9.

All characters in this book have no existence outside the imagination of the author and have no relation whatsoever to anyone bearing the same name or names. They are not even distantly inspired by any individual known or unknown to the author, and all incidents are pure invention.

MIRA and the Star Colophon are trademarks used under license and registered in Australia, New Zealand, Philippines, United States Patent and Trademark Office and in other countries.

www.MIRABooks.com

Printed in U.S.A.

CALCULATED LOSS

LINDA L. RICHARDS

MIRA®

Also by LINDA L. RICHARDS

THE NEXT EX
MAD MONEY

The loss of three souls dear to me—two human and one canine—rocked me while working on *Calculated Loss*.

The artist and designer Thea Partridge was mentor and friend. The world is a sadder place without her in it.

Chanook provided the blueprint for the canine character of Tycho in the Madeline Carter books. Though Chanook and Tycho looked nothing alike, no one who knew Chanook didn't recognize him from my portrayal.

The death of my ex-husband, Michael Leonard Richards, put me fully in touch with what it means to lose someone distant who was once dear. If, in *Calculated Loss,* Madeline's despair at losing Braydon resonates, it's because Mike's passing put me in touch—with more reality than I would have wished—with the idea of losing the co-caretaker of some of your memories, some of your dreams.

In all ways that matter, *Calculated Loss* is dedicated to the memory of these three vibrant spirits. I miss you still.

I'd like to thank my editor at MIRA books, Valerie Gray, for her careful and loving shepherding of *Calculated Loss.* Her input was both loving and significant, and Madeline and I both thank her.

Thank you once again to the men in my life: my partner, David Middleton; my son, Michael Karl Richards; and my brother Peter Huber. There are women who consider themselves lucky to have a strong, sensitive and deeply creative man in their lives. I am beyond lucky. I have three.

Thanks, also, to the early readers of *Calculated Loss:* Mary Beck (Madeline's official goddess of compliance), Michele Denis, Lang Evans, Andrew Heard, Carolyn Withers-Heard, Laura-Jean Kelly, Jackie Leidl, Patricia McLean, Betty Middleton, Linda Murray, Debbie Warmerdam and Carrie Wheeler. It strikes me sometimes that the members of this group are the soul and conscience of Madeline Carter. When she goes to put a foot wrong, they stop her in her tracks.

And, of course, thank you to Madeline's many fans. Your letters have provided many smiles, only occasionally a furrowed brow, but they've come to provide the backbone of my day. Thank you.

"Tell me what you eat and I will tell you what you are."
—Anthelme Brillat-Savarin (1755–1826)
French politician, gastronome and writer

One

The last time I saw Braydon Gauthier alive he was still my husband. We were in the bedroom of our three story walk-up in Chelsea. I was throwing clothes into a pair of battered suitcases that had seen more moving than traveling. He was perched on the end of the bed, worrying at the corner of our duvet—in the last possible moment that it would be *our* duvet—with one long-fingered hand. It was a habit he had—the fabric thing—and it didn't drive me crazy, but I knew it would if I hung around much longer.

"It's the car, isn't it," he said. "I know it's the car."

"It's not the car."

"Well, not the car. I mean, I *know* it's not the car itself. But the accident. You still haven't forgiven me."

I thought about it, though I didn't miss a beat in my packing while I considered his words. Finally I stopped, dropped onto the bed next to him and looked straight into his deep-set, hazel eyes.

"It's not the car, Braydon. And it's not the accident. More like what the accident represents."

He squinted at me and I could see he didn't get it. "We can fix the car, Mad."

I sighed. Tried again. "It's *you*, Braydon. Not the car. Or maybe that's not right. It's you and me. Together. We were just doomed from the start."

"Now you're being melodramatic."

I smiled at him then, because he was right. Which didn't actually make him more correct.

"Okay," I said, "melodrama aside, we're just too different, Bray. I mean, *look* at me," and I wasn't just indicating my pin-striped suit, or my careful chignon, but a whole lifestyle. Or, rather, the lifestyle I was, at twenty-five, just trying to put together. "When's the last time I left for the office later than 6:30 a.m.?"

He shrugged, yet we both knew the answer. It had been a *long* time.

"And you," I went on, "there could be a kitchen fire at Quiver and your sous-chef could get hit by a bus, but if it was your day off, you wouldn't bother going in."

"Oh, come on," he chided, "if Arnie got hit by a *bus*, maybe I'd go in."

He saw me, I think, notice the light in those eyes when he smiled at me. And notice the way the skin at the corner of his eyes crinkled slightly when he did. He covered my hand with his own, and I enjoyed, for a second, the warmth of his strong, soft touch. A touch as familiar to me then as the touch of my own hand. It wouldn't have taken much, in that moment, for me to let go of my resolve. I moved his hand. Gently. Got up. Addressed myself again to those suitcases.

"Okay. I get what you're saying. You're all about work and I'm...not. Isn't that our balance, though? Isn't that what we bring to each other?"

"I thought so for a while," I said, tossing a sweater into one of the suitcases. "For a long while, really. But it's more than that, Braydon. It's not just work, it's life philosophies. It's how we approach the world. And, like I said before, it's *not* about the car, yet you could have killed yourself that day. You could have killed both of us. And Curt for that matter, too."

"There's that melodrama again."

I stopped my packing for a moment. Looked at him. "I don't think so. What was it I overheard you say to Curt the other day? You said, 'Madeline lives for work.' You said it critically, but it got me thinking, Braydon. I'm not so sure you were wrong."

"Madeline, c'mon. I didn't mean it that way."

"But Braydon, you were right. I do. I live for my work." And here I pulled myself to my full height, which at five feet eleven inches is not inconsiderable, and looked right into his eyes, my back straight. "I want to be the best stockbroker in the city of New York, ergo the known universe." I was twenty-five, so I was able to say this completely without irony. And mean it. "I *will* be the best stockbroker in New York. I am prepared to do whatever it takes. Work all the hours necessary. Step on whoever gets in my way. You laugh," I said, "but I'm serious. And hearing you say that to Curt crystalized it for me. It's what I want, Braydon. It's all I want."

"It didn't used to be," he said, somewhat petulantly, I thought.

No," I said gently, "it always was. It's just that, for a while, I thought there was a place in my life for that balance you mentioned. That is, I thought we balanced each other. But we don't, Bray. And we never will. I *will* be at the top of my profession." Later I wouldn't be proud of it, but I met his eyes and said, "And you'll just hold me back."

Thinking about it now—thinking about his face— it was like I'd kicked him in the solar plexus, or some other highly sensitive spot. I'd hit some kind of mark. Maybe one I hadn't even known was there.

"I can change," he said, but there was no real resolve in his voice.

"We don't change, Braydon," I said from the wisdom of the quarter century I'd been granted to that point. "No one ever changes. We are what we are."

Sometimes, now, I wonder about it all. I wonder about what would have been different in our lives if I'd stayed. If, that day, he'd offered me some compelling reason not to go. When you see where it ended up, it's like we changed places. And I have to claim my part in that, I guess. I have to acknowledge at least some small edge of responsibility for what, in the end, happened to Braydon Gauthier. My husband. If only for a short time.

But that was New York, in the long ago. Now I live in L.A.—in Malibu, actually—and my life is very different.

The phone rings a lot at Tasya and Tyler's house. She's a busy actress, he's an important director and, to top the whole deal off, there's Jennifer, Tyler's teenage daughter. I can't imagine another house where the phone would have so much reason to be ringing all the time.

The phone doesn't ring that often for me. I'd been staying in the guest room at Tyler and Tasya's Malibu cliff house for three months. Before that I'd been renting a cute little apartment fitted neatly under the main deck of their house. That ended when the apartment—with all my stuff inside—was blown up by a madman. My car got blown up around the same time. Both of those things are a different day's story. But on *this* day I was homeless and carless and pondering my options.

While being their tenant, I'd become as close to Tyler, Tasya, Jennifer and their dog, Tycho, as family. Since they have a big house with a lot of empty rooms, Tyler and Tasya insisted I stay with them while I contemplated my next move. Living there was not a permanent enough arrangement that I'd added my own phone line, but my best friend, Emily, had surprised me with a mobile phone when she'd given up on me ever breaking down and getting one for myself.

"At least this way," she said when she presented me with the tri-band cell, her dark eyes flashing with pleasure when she gave me her gift, "you'll be able to redirect your personal calls to your very own phone. And I won't have to bug Tyler or Tasya every time I want to talk to you."

I'd been half pleased, half irritated. She was right, of course. I *did* need a phone, and it really hadn't looked as though I was ever going to get one on my own. I seldom admit it, but I can be a bit of a Luddite. *Still*, I'd thought. *Still*. Sometimes it seems as though I spend my life being a little sister. Even when I'm not.

So the ringing of the house line did nothing to alert me. And, since I'd made some friends since moving to Los Angeles from New York, it didn't even alarm me when Tasya let me know the call was for me. Not everyone had my cell number yet. I took the call on the land line in my room.

I *did* become alarmed when I heard the voice on the phone. And even though it was one I hadn't heard in a while, I could detect the distress in it instantly.

"Maddy, it's Anne-Marie." Anne-Marie is a very nice lady. She lives in Canada and is my ex-sister-in-law. I would have been less surprised if my caller was the president. Well, maybe not, but you get the idea.

"Anne-Marie, what is it?" We hadn't spoken since Braydon and I split up close to a decade before. Anne-Marie and I exchanged cards at Christmas and sent each other the occasional joke in e-mail, but we didn't talk as we had when I was her brother's wife. It just hadn't fit the program. So hearing from her, after all this time and sounding alarmed as she did now, I knew right away it wasn't a social call.

"It's Bray, Maddy," she said without preamble. "He's dead."

I sank onto my bed without realizing I was doing it, vaguely aware that I was glad the bed was there to grab me. It wasn't that I fell, exactly, but my legs had just suddenly ceased being interested in holding me.

"Oh, no, Anne-Marie. I can't believe it." I could almost feel her nod, but she didn't say anything. "When did it happen?"

"Three days ago. Oh, Madeline, it's terrible." Emotion choked her voice. I had the feeling that she'd used up her current supply of self-control in calling me. That whatever reserves she'd had were now gone. "He killed himself."

I got through the balance of the conversation with Anne-Marie with surprising calm. Some type of otherworldly calm, really, because all of it is still so clear in my mind. I didn't feel anything, but every other sense seemed to be working overtime.

It was midafternoon and the stock markets had been closed for only a short time. I'd had a good session and had been chewing on the satisfaction of a day's work well done when Anne-Marie's call came.

Tasya, an international film star of unsurpassed beauty, was in the kitchen. Tasya was born in a Soviet Bloc country when there was still a Soviet Bloc. She was making some sort of soup that day—some homeland dish—heavy on the onions and cabbage. The smell of it—warm, comforting, reassuringly homey—was all around me. To this day if anyone says the word *suicide* I think of cabbage soup. And vice versa.

Sunshine was slanting through the half-open blinds in my room. Partially filtered light illuminated the dust motes that trailed through the air. The sun that reached me warmed evenly spaced bands on my forearm.

Anne-Marie was telling me my ex-husband was dead. Dead by his own hand. Yet it wasn't the least bit real to me. When I tried to make a picture of it in my head, all I could see was Braydon laughing. It's still difficult for me to imagine him without a smile on his face.

I made myself focus on Anne-Marie's words: she'd said something that required a response.

"You can stay at my place while you're up here." She made a sound that came out half laugh, half sob. "I've wanted to invite you so many times. I wish I had...before."

"Anne-Marie, that's lovely of you. It's touching that you thought of me at all. But I don't think it would be appropriate. Me coming for the funeral, I mean. Maybe I could come up some other time for a visit." I knew Braydon had remarried, for one thing. I couldn't imagine Braydon's new wife would be very receptive to having me there.

"Oh, Madeline," Anne-Marie said, "you just have to come. Mom and Dad told me especially to ask you."

"They did?" Oddly, knowing that my ex-in-laws expected my presence brought me closer to breaking than anything else so far in the conversation.

"Yes, they did. They always loved you, you know that. And, anyway, Madeline, there's a bequest."

"A bequest?"

"Yes, there's something Bray wanted you to have."

"A bequest," I said again.

"I think it's Old Stinky," she said, as though I'd asked.

Old Stinky. I hadn't heard the name for so long, it brought me up short. And suddenly I was back nearly a decade—a time machine in the form of a phone call—and Braydon and I were at the Jersey shore. I could almost smell the salt air, taste taffy, laughter and Braydon's love for me on my tongue.

On the trip out there we'd fallen in love with a sports car, of all things.

It was a ridiculous car to fall in love with. Neither of us had any money—certainly not for a car—and this wasn't even a good car. I mean, it was a *great* car, but it was all about a glorious past and potential. It was a 1962 Sunbeam Alpine Mark II with right-hand drive. The vehicle had a darkly cancerous flank and holes in the passenger seat. With the top up, the entire thing exuded the vague and unsettling odor of damp and nasty, old, unused automobile. It ran, but not without billows of smoke at distressingly irregular intervals. You never knew when one would come. Hence Old Stinky. That and the damp upholstery, anyway. Where the paint was whole, you could see that the car had once been the color of the sky, and the parts of the interior that were still intact were red leather.

Possibilities.

We didn't need a car. We hadn't been looking for one. We lived in New York City where transit is good and private cars are next to impossible to get around in, never mind park. At least, for regular people.

"That's just it," Bray said with a laugh when I pointed these sensible things out. "This isn't the sort of car you drive around. Not right now. This is the sort of car you buy today and fix up tomorrow, when you have the money. And by the time we have the money, we'll be able to afford to run a car!" He looked so pleased with himself at this bit of reasoning that I had to smile. It was like he was asking for a puppy. Or maybe like he was one.

"See, Madeline," he said, "it'll be our dream car. We'll know our dreams have come true when we can drive this car."

And now, if Anne-Marie was right, Old Stinky was about to make a reappearance in my life. And none of the dreams Bray and I had held together had come true.

Before I got off the phone I told Anne-Marie I'd make arrangements to arrive in Vancouver the following day, the day before the funeral.

When I turned back to my computer, I discovered I couldn't focus on my work. The death of dreams does that to me, I've found. It's one of the things that makes me sadder than anything.

I was somewhat surprised to get through the balance of the day without incident. Braydon Gauthier was dead. I felt as though there should be some sort of misstep in the world. Like some earthly pulse or heartbeat should be out of whack. And, of course, nothing was.

For a while I curled up on a lounge chair on one of the big decks. The skies over Malibu stayed a pale and empty blue. The warmth of the day was cooled by a breeze off the ocean. That ocean seemed calmer to me today. From the distance of the vantage of my canyon, it seemed positively placid.

I was so deeply focused on the calm quality of the coming evening that I didn't actually see Tyler until he dropped into the lounge chair next to the one I occupied. Even then it was more the feel of his presence than seeing him that let me know he was there.

"You've been quiet tonight," he said, his tone gentle and observational. From Tyler, and also from my friend Emily, I've come to understand that really good directors tend to be keenly aware of the nuances of human emotion. It's how, I suppose, they get to be really good directors. It is also a trait that can be irksome when you feel the need to just be reflective and unobserved.

"I am, I suppose, contemplating the nature of human mortality," I said after a while.

"Yikes," he said, a smile in his voice. "I'll admit, that's more than I bargained for. What brought this on?"

"I heard from my ex-husband's sister today."

"I didn't even realize you'd ever been married."

"I was," I replied. "A long time ago. Eons."

He nodded sagely. "Eons happen when you're as ancient as you've become."

I couldn't resist returning his smile. "All right. Eons might be an overstatement. I was twenty-five when we split up. When I left him."

"Eons." He nodded again. "And the sister called today?"

"Oh, Tyler. He's dead. And it was an unnecessary death." I found myself suddenly and oddly reluctant to tell Tyler flat out that Braydon had killed himself. Like it was a detail too private to share, at least for now. "It was unnecessary and…and…unexpected."

"And you're feeling sad. That's understandable."

"Is it?" I said, looking him full in the face for the first time since he'd joined me. "I'm not so sure."

"You're not sure about what? That it's understandable that you feel sad?"

I nodded. "I guess," I said. "See, it was over for Braydon and me a long, long time ago. I really don't have any feelings for him anymore. I mean…really."

Tyler smiled. "I get that already."

"I haven't even thought about him in…I don't

know. A long while." It was the first time I'd articulated it, even to myself. But it made more sense once I had. "And we haven't had any kind of relationship since we split up. We didn't have kids or even any property together, so the divorce was straightforward. Everything was handled by our lawyers. Just papers to sign and legal bills to pay, nothing even to fight about. It was over and done with. I thought so, anyway. But now…"

"Now you have more feelings than you thought you would and you're not sure what to do with them." It wasn't a question.

"I guess." I hadn't thought about it that way, but I realized Tyler was right.

"I think I understand. When Karen—Jennifer's mother—and I split up, it was the biggest mess imaginable. It was *ugly*, Madeline. With a capital UG. Teams of lawyers, the kid, property, the works. And that was just at the very end. Getting to that place was a nightmare in itself. There were times—I'll admit this to you, but I'm not proud—there were times through all of that when I honestly felt that if someone had told me Karen was dead, I would have been glad." His eyebrows seemed to form a single straight, bushy line with the seriousness of his thoughts, of what he was trying to convey. "But that was then. I'm happy with my life as it is. I wouldn't wish for anything different and I adore Tasya, but there's a part of me that will always care very deeply for Karen. It's different though, right? It's complicated. I wouldn't put things back the way they were—I don't wish Karen was my partner. Not ever. But a part of me will always love her for the things we were to each other. The things we'll always share."

I nodded. "I think I understand what you're saying. That Braydon and I had a special bond and that it's okay for me to love the memory even though I didn't love the man anymore."

"That's the thing with loss, I think, Madeline. Whatever you're feeling is okay. Maybe that's something you already know. Like, you were out here contemplating when I saw you. That's the right thing. Just giving yourself permission to feel any old thing you're feeling. Not questioning too much. You once had something special with this man. And now he's gone. That's a sad thing, no matter how you look at it. And whatever comes up for you around that is the right thing for you, then."

"He was a chef," I told Tyler, though he hadn't asked. "A pretty famous one. Television shows and books and all of that."

"Did you spend any time together? After you split up, I mean."

"No. He called me pretty regularly for a while, wanting to get back together. Told me things were different. That he was different. I just kept telling him people didn't change. But they do, don't they, Tyler? People change all the time."

Tyler just smiled at me, kind of sadly. "Like I said, Madeline, just feel what you're feeling. Nothing else matters right now."

We sat then for a while in companionable silence. Me with thoughts of Braydon, now gone. Tyler perhaps with thoughts of Karen, now a fairly accomplished potter in New Mexico. After a while he reached over and squeezed my hand before he pulled himself to his feet. "You'll be okay, sweetie. I know you will. But holler if you need anything. You know where I am."

I smiled up at him, shielding my face from the last of the day's sun with one hand. "Most of the time."

That night I called my mother in Seattle. She needed to know, I thought. She'd had a stake in it all, too.

"Mom," I said as normally as possible when she answered the phone brightly.

"Madeline, what's wrong?" I didn't try to figure how she could have detected the least amount of distress in the single syllable I'd uttered.

"Mom." I couldn't think of a way to soften it. Better just to get the words out. "Bray is dead."

My mother didn't say anything for a moment, and I let her be. I couldn't know what was going through her mind, but I had a rough idea. For a time, she'd thought of Braydon as part of our family. Once my mom makes an emotional commitment, she doesn't let it go so easily. Maybe we're even alike that way. Had she stopped entertaining the notion that Bray and I would get back together at some point? I think so. She never mentioned it anymore. But you couldn't really be sure.

"Oh, kitten. I'm so sorry," she said finally. And I could tell that she was. "How did it happen?"

The tears on my cheek surprised me. I hadn't felt them coming. Or maybe I had. Maybe they'd been coming all day. My mom's concerned voice smoothed the way for them. If you can't cry in front of your mom…

"He killed himself."

My mother went quiet again. I imagined her in her too-bright kitchen—overdesigned for her by my sister when she was in her interior design phase. "I'm so sorry, kitten," she said again. "Is there anything I can do?"

I shook my head, then realized she couldn't see me. What she'd said was typical Mom. I knew she probably had many questions, but she saved them. She knew they'd keep. Her first thought was of how she could fix it. And, of course, there was nothing for her to fix. She'd know that, too. But she had to try.

"No, Mom. But thanks. I'm going up there for the funeral tomorrow."

"Oh, the funeral. Oh, Maddy. Poor Jess and Bob." Jessica and Robert Gauthier. Braydon's parents. Of course, Mom's mind had gone to them almost right away. They'd been related, in a way, by my marriage to Braydon. And my mother would be thinking of how horrible it would be to lose a child, even one who hadn't been an *actual* child for a long time. "Madeline," she said now, "do you want me to come with you? I can get the time off work if you'd like me to be with you."

I have friends whose moms are very different than

mine. They tell me about them. They talk about relationships where every exchange is like an invisible jousting session. Where there is nuance in every syllable and you have to watch where you step because there are land mines in each conversation, each family exchange.

My mom isn't like that. She doesn't tend to say things she doesn't mean. And she doesn't say them for effect. I knew that, if I felt the need for her presence at Bray's funeral, she wouldn't hesitate to come with me, no guilt involved. And I knew she wouldn't be hurt if I turned her down. It's not that she didn't care either way, it's that she didn't have a stake. Or rather, she did, but the stake in this case was what I needed. Knowing all of that, it was easy to answer her.

"Thanks so much, Mom. That's really sweet of you. But I think I'm going to do this on my own. I want to see you, though. I'll probably swing by Seattle for a visit on my way back to L.A.," I told her. "I...I think I'll be driving home. Anne-Marie says she thinks Braydon left me a car."

"Old Stinky," my mother said. It wasn't a question.

I nodded again and smiled through my tears. "Yes," I said. "I think that's what it must be."

When I got off the phone, I felt better for having talked with my mom, but only just. Braydon and I had not been in love—had not even been married—for a very long time. We'd been apart far, far longer than we'd ever been together. But his absence in the world was suddenly unbearable. Much more unbearable than his absence from my life had ever been.

It seemed inexplicable, but as I struggled for sleep it came to me. The thing that Tyler had only suggested. The act of having been married—of having tried our hand at this sacred bond—had created a kind of pact between us. The pact was one I hadn't been aware of when Braydon was still alive. But now it occurred to me that he and I had created memories we'd never shared with anyone else. Memories we'd held together.

No one, for instance, would remember my twenty-fifth birthday.

Uncharacteristically, and at Braydon's behest, I'd taken the day off work. Braydon got up early, before even I—a habitual early riser—had stirred. He'd slunk quietly into the kitchen in our little apartment and made me a quarter century birthday feast. Chocolate-dipped french toast with real maple syrup and a glass of champagne and orange juice. Chocolate, Braydon used to say, is forever.

He'd brought this to me in our bedroom, little burning candles stuck in the French toast, singing the birthday song as he went. I'd felt something as close to pure joy as I've ever felt: being honored and coddled and feted all in one. I'd felt immortal.

I'd felt loved.

I remember eating some of my French toast, and feeding some of it to Bray. I don't know how much we ate, but I do recall the lovemaking that followed, the syrup spilling and some of the chocolate melting and adding their own sweetness to our coupling.

I remember the way the room looked afterward. The mess on the floor. The mess in the bed! Syrup and champagne and sweet sweat. And we laughed. We laughed while we loved. And after.

The look on Braydon's face. Sometimes it's difficult to imagine that anyone will ever look at me that way again.

This memory—so many other memories—were things that Braydon and I shared. Memories we held together.

And now Braydon is gone. How long can I hold them alone?

Two

I woke up early, even for me.

It was still dark and it was so early the North American stock markets weren't yet open. And, though I wanted to, I couldn't get back to sleep. I fluffed up my pillow, then tossed and turned for a while. I folded the pillow in half, then tossed a bit more. I added a second pillow, as though I felt my head needed elevation in order to relax. None of it worked. There was a lot, it seemed, on my mind. Pillows wouldn't help with that.

A while ago my world came apart at the seams. For one reason and another, I'd not done much yet to repair it. Sometimes you need to heal before you can recover. Sometimes you just need to sit and think and try to be peaceful for a while. I seem to have that sort of personality. And grief, as Tyler had suggested, is sometimes best left just running its course, like a cold. You can try to make things better, but time is the only thing that will make it right in the end.

So, I hadn't bought a new car. I hadn't found a new place to live. I hadn't yet replaced all my clothes and other personal items. But I'd made a single necessary major purchase: a gorgeous little laptop computer with a sleek finish and a lot of round edges. It had cost me twice as much as the desktop computer it had replaced, but was four times as powerful and probably a tenth of the size. Since I no longer had a desk, a computer that didn't require one had seemed like a sensible purchase. Especially since, at the moment, I never knew where I'd be working from one day to the next.

Now, in the dark in Tyler and Tasya's guest room— my temporary home—I pulled the computer out from under the bed where it lived, cracked the lid and let the light from the screen provide the only illumination in the room.

While I logged on to my trading account I considered how my life had changed. I'd spent over a decade as a stockbroker at one of the largest brokerage firms in the world. I had an M.B.A. from Harvard and my career had been on the fast track: there was no corner office at Merriwether Bailey I couldn't have aspired to. It turned out, though, that my aspirations weren't to do that aspiring.

I'd been having doubts about the quality of my life even before my best friend was killed on the job. Jackson's death sent me into a tailspin that ended with me changing everything recognizable in my existence, but I'd been asking myself those heading-to-midlife questions already when it happened. You know the drill: sixteen grueling hours a day on the job, for what? A bonus at Christmas and a key to the executive washroom? It's like, one day you wake up thirty-five and wonder what the hell you're doing. You wonder if everything you've worked for is enough. Once you start asking that kind of question, it usually isn't. Enough, that is.

I had no relationship, no kids, no cat. I had a career I was proud of, doing work I was good at and that I loved, and it was almost as though I woke up one morning and said: Okay. Good. I've done what I set out to do. Is that everything? So? What now? Money and...

It just wasn't enough.

Becoming a day trader had *not* been the first thing to enter my head. How could it have been? From where I'd been sitting, being a day trader would have been as natural as a priest leaving the church in order to sell plastic Jesus statues at flea markets. I mean, the two things are kind of connected, but from the priest's position, the world is probably better off without more plastic Jesus salespeople.

A broker at a venerated firm like Merriwether Bailey is a pretty well elevated animal. We're not talking about the petty life-forms you see in movies, preying on old ladies in Iowa and Kansas. These are the dudes— and dudettes—on whose fortunes the most fortunate rise and fall. My clients—the people whose portfolios

I controlled—consulted me the way they might an oracle. Except I was better paid. They trusted me the way they trusted their doctors. And well they should have; more often than not, their financial health was in my competent and expensively manicured hands. And the way these things are structured, the more money I made for them, the more money I made for me. Commissions, like a car salesman. Only, in my world, everybody won or everybody lost. It wasn't us against them, but rather us and them against the magical numbers of the market. And may the best oracle win. And I was pretty good.

Day trading is different. In the first place, day traders use their own money and, under ideal conditions and as the name suggests, they do what they do in a single day: in and out, with a tidy profit in between. Buy low, sell high and get out before the rest of the market has even realized a shift is afoot.

Brokers at big houses like Merriwether Bailey—brokers of the sort I used to be—look down their noses at day traders, if they even acknowledge their existence at all. And they don't have to; day traders are a fringe element. Brokers need a license to do what they do with other people's money. Day traders can be anyone at all…and frequently are. You probably know a day trader. You just don't know who they are, if you follow.

There's not even really such a thing as a day trader. That is, you won't find it on any job description or those offers for vocational courses found inside matchbooks. And no one has it printed on their business card. But there are a lot of us. For various—and perhaps obvious—reasons, we tend to keep pretty quiet.

And so I looked at myself, this early morning, with my pillows stacked behind my head and the laptop where it belonged: on my lap. I was in my jammies, my hair not yet brushed, the sleep still in my eyes, while I downloaded my e-mail and read the first of the morning's news releases.

Prior to the wide acceptance of the Internet, doing what I do in exactly the way I do it would have been nearly impossible. But one of the things that happened in the early days of the tech revolution was that brokerages got online and a large portion of the way stocks are traded—at least at a certain level—underwent a radical change.

There have probably been day traders as long as there have been stock markets. People who look for market fluctuations and make short-term investments for their own advantage. But the Internet—and with it self-directed trading—has meant that anyone can do it anywhere and with a minimum of equipment. All you need to direct your own trades is a trading account, an Internet-connected computer and a Web browser. Everything beyond that and a trader's own acumen is just icing.

Self-directed trading means exactly what it says: you make your trades in a very hands-on way. Back in the day, when John Q. Public wanted to interact with the stock market, he'd call his broker and place an order:

buy or sell. Along with the phone call, there might be some advice. "Don't buy that, John. That's a sucker's bet," or, "You know, that company doesn't look bad on paper, but the word on the street is not so great."

Self-directed trading via the Internet is mostly cheaper, but sometimes you get what you pay for. With the advice of your—hopefully caring and well connected—broker out of the picture, you're on your own. And you know what they say about being your own lawyer—fool for a client?—you can just about double that when it comes to the stock market, and your personal financial well-being is at stake.

See, here's the thing: Let's say in your greenhorn glee you ask to buy 600,000 shares of a company trading at a dollar per, when you *really* meant to type in 6000. *Oops*, you think. *No big deal. I only have ten grand in my trading account.* Except there's no room for "oops" in the stock market. Depending on how your trading account is set up, it's often possible for the buy you ordered to go through. In which case, about three days later—on the settlement date—you get a call from the brokerage—and it'll be an actual call from an actual person—asking you—politely at first—to please deposit the five hundred and ninety-something large required to settle your account. And since most people who call themselves John Q. Public don't have six hundred thousand dollars sitting around with nothing to do, the shit can very suddenly hit.

You laugh. You say, *that would never happen to me.*

And you're probably right. It probably wouldn't. But stuff like that happens a lot. More than anyone involved would likely care to admit. And that's when you get it—too late—that as much as all of this can look like a game, at its core it's a deadly serious business. And please pass the half million dollars and change, please.

Now, me? As much as the paraphernalia I use for my online trading looks just like John Q.'s—maybe even less sophisticated—and despite the fact that I'm no longer connected to a brokerage and therefore have no formal status, I *am* an expert. Most of my adult life has been spent on the business end of a computer screen or a phone, crunching numbers and likelihoods and possibilities. Living and breathing and feeling the market. To say that the market is my life would be cliché, but it would also be true, at least in part. And I'm very, very careful when entering a buy order on my computer.

The upshot? In reality I do have a very special bit of equipment that John Q. does not have: over a decade of experience at one of the top brokerage houses in the world. And it's that bit of experience on which I hang my livelihood and, in some respects, my future. It's mostly been working out okay so far.

On this morning, before the Malibu sun had even begun to poke its nose over the horizon, and with the prospect of a sad trip I wasn't looking forward to ahead of me, I knew it would be best if I could cram as much of a workday as possible into the little bit of time I had available.

I spent some of that time going over news releases in both my e-mail inbox and on various sources of news I rely on on the Net, including my favorite blogs. This is an important part of my daily routine. It keeps me tuned to the pulse of the market.

By the time I'd finished my reading, I'd made notes on several companies in my trading journal and figured it was time for coffee and a bit of movement.

With the scent of dripping coffee perfuming the house, and dawn creeping over the canyon, I pulled on my running gear. While I sat on the floor of my room lacing my sneakers, Tycho appeared like a very large puff of smoke. The shoes get him every time: he knows what it means when I put on shoes that are designed for running.

"How do you even do that?" I asked him. The large dog didn't answer, but wagged his tail at me hopefully. It made a dull thud when it connected with the door.

Tyler's dog is huge and ungainly in appearance. He weighs well over a hundred pounds and looks something like a cross between a cairn terrier and a great dane, which is to say that he looks pretty strange. He adopted me not long after I moved into Tyler's house, and accompanied me on all my morning runs.

When I lived in the apartment under the deck, Tycho was pretty much a fixture at my place, especially since, with their lifestyles being what they are, the family was seldom in residence, especially at the same time. I was home a lot. Tycho didn't take very long to notice this and he moved right in, often sleeping on my bed while I worked. He weighs nearly as much as I do, so I didn't get much say in the matter.

Since I'd started staying in the guest room, however, things had shifted again. Tycho bunked in with Tyler's daughter, Jennifer, when she was staying in Malibu with her dad. When Jennifer was at her mom's place in New Mexico, Tycho preferred a small carpet in the living room that afforded him a view of the canyon while he snoozed. Dog TV. But he always seemed to keep at least one ear on me and my activities, as I quite often do things that are interesting to dogs.

As we let ourselves out the kitchen door I noticed the sun coming up a dull red over the horizon, flooding the canyon in a glow that would have looked almost threatening if it wasn't so beautiful. It had been hot these past few weeks but, like most early mornings, it was still cool now, the breeze from the ocean having long ago swept away any heat that might have remained trapped in the canyons from the previous day.

Malibu in the morning is, to me, a beautiful irony. You have to remind yourself that, just down the coast, one of the largest cities in the world is just starting to wake. Or, rather, coming more awake because, like most big cities, there are parts of Los Angeles that never, ever sleep.

In the early morning Los Flores Canyon feels light-years from that. You can hear birds calling and lizards scurrying and insects scuttling. You can always taste the eucalyptus in the air. And sometimes the smell of orange blossoms or other flowers that seem positively tropical to me join with the eucalyptus and the barest whiff of salt and the sea to create this intoxicating scent that I can't imagine anyone ever duplicating. Bottles of Malibu in the Morning? Now *that's* a company whose stock I would buy and actually hold on to.

Depending on the weather and the wind, quite often you can hear the buzz of traffic from Pacific Coast Highway or, later in the day, the sound of the kids playing at the school on Los Flores Canyon Road near Pacific Coast Highway. But other times—and I like those best—you don't hear any sound at all. At least nothing that isn't about nature. Nothing that hasn't been heard in these canyons for thousands of years. At those times, it's hard to imagine how close you really are to nearly ten million people. It's hard to imagine anything at all.

This was one of those mornings. And as Tycho and I pounded up Rambla Pacifico heading for Castlewood Drive, I tried to free my mind of everything but the pavement under my feet and how the air felt touching my face, lifting my hair. It worked for a while. Running almost always does that for me: the cobwebs get whipped away. Or maybe washed away in the bath of perspiration and elevated heart rate. There's not room for anything extra, I've found, when you ask a lot of your body.

But the mental peace I craved was illusive. With the deserted canyon road snaking away from me, and

Braydon close to my mind, another early morning came back to me. Another stretch of road. Another lifetime, maybe? It felt so long ago; like someone else's memory, not my own.

I don't remember the road we were traveling, but I do recall our destination: Curt had a girlfriend whose family had a house in the Finger Lakes region, near Trumansberg in upstate New York. The plan was for the three of us to drive up from the City and meet the girlfriend there. It was a holiday weekend and both the stock market and the restaurant were going to be closed. We were anticipating massive quantities of fun.

Bray and I were in Old Stinky, Curt in a champagne-colored rental. We could have all fit in the rental, but Braydon insisted on taking Old Stinky, which was a two-seater. We'd decided to make a little convoy with Curt, though, since Old Stinky was unreliable, at best. Come to think of it, the convoy might have been my idea. Walking to the nearest service station from a broken-down car is so not my idea of a good time.

We left the city early to avoid traffic, something like four in the morning. I snoozed for an hour or so, and woke up on some clever shortcut Braydon had taken in order to snip off a few miles or minutes by avoiding the stretch of I-80 that leads to Del Water Gap.

I woke to find us traveling too fast on a ridiculously empty piece of rain-spattered back road. Bray, who was not a small man, was hunched over the steering wheel in intense concentration, as though willing the little car to go faster. It would have been funny had I not realized instantly what was happening: beyond Bray, I could see Curt in his rental, similarly focused. The two men—one the owner of a restaurant, the other his head chef—were racing.

"What the hell are you doing?" I asked, the sleep banished instantly from my voice by equal parts of outrage and fear.

Bray took his eyes off the road for a split second and tossed me a sheepish grin. "He told me he thought this thing was gutless." There was a mild yet wild exaltation in his voice. My mouth fell open when I heard it there, because he didn't sound anything at all like the Bray I thought I knew. Braydon didn't notice. "That's what he said— 'That piece of shit is gutless.'"

"When?"

"What?" His attention had refocused on the road.

"When did he tell you that Old Stinky was gutless?"

"Always. Every day. Ha," he shouted in Curt's general direction, though there was no question that Curt would be able to hear him. "Who's gutless *now?*"

There was, to my mind, absolutely no question about who would ultimately win this race. Sure, Old Stinky was a sports car, but not one intended for flat-out American-style racing. The kind of "sports" intended by the car's British designers were probably more like who could get to the next hamlet in time for a pint. On the other hand, Curt's economy rental car hadn't exactly been designed with speed in mind at all. Rather, who could get to the airport with the most luggage *and* passengers. No matter where you were standing, it was a pretty silly race.

Unfortunately, neither driver seemed the least bit aware of this silliness. Or, if they were, they'd chosen to ignore it, for whatever testosterone-laden reasons. Whether or not the reasons they had were good—and I had no doubt that they were *not*—I wanted no part of it.

"Let me out. Now."

Braydon shot another glance at me, maybe to see if I was kidding. And even though his eyes went back to the road in an instant, it would have been easy for him to see that I was not.

"I'm not going to let you out, Madeline. This is your journey, too, you know." He said it between gritted teeth.

"What kind of bullshit are you talking? Stop this car *now*. You can endanger yourself all you want, but you've got no business involving me in your stupid man games."

He gave no sign of hearing me, so intent was he on the road, and on Curt in the other car. I could see the other man's hands gripped tightly on the champagne-colored steering wheel.

We were on a simple two-lane back road: one lane going in either direction. Except, at the moment, our Finger Lakes–bound vehicles were taking up both lanes, neck and neck, Curt slightly ahead and hugging fast to the lane normally reserved for northbound traffic; Old Stinky gaining increment by increment, as though fueled by nothing more than Braydon's solid will. This was a side of him I'd never seen before. I didn't like it.

Because Old Stinky was right-hand drive, Braydon could peer over his right shoulder and look more or less directly into Curt's face. I watched in a sort of horrified fascination as this face-to-face interchange took place. It really was frightening. The veins on both men's faces stood out in places where I hadn't known either of them had them. What was worse, though, was this sort of vacant mania I saw there. It looked to me like TV crazy-guy faces, only worse, because I was in the car with one of them, not safely home on a sofa, happily munching microwave popcorn.

What came next was sort of predictable, even though it took a running together of circumstances to make it happen. First, the rain got worse. Or maybe we ran right into a rain cloud. Either way, the slight drizzle deepened into something more ominous, and I could see that the road we were covering at such an alarming pace looked suddenly slick and dark. Next—and I could see this first because of my position on the left-hand side of the car, where drivers normally sit in North America— we entered a long and fairly gentle curve and— finally—we were alone no longer. I was the first to see the headlights coming at us. Heading, in fact, to the place that I, Braydon and Old Stinky were currently occupying. And at the pace we were going, they were heading toward us fast.

Later I'd wonder if, had I just kept my mouth shut, things would have come to a happier conclusion. But why do we even ever bother with such musings? The fact is, I *did* scream, and Braydon *did* see the oncoming car very suddenly, resulting in him tugging on the wheel too hard, which—in a car that was thirty-plus years old and probably well beyond the time when new tires should have been applied—caused us to lose control.

Look at those words on the page: *caused us to lose control.*

That's what happened, but somehow it just doesn't cover it. From where I was sitting, it felt like limbo. Limbo and vertigo combined. I could see Braydon hauling at the wheel, but whatever hauling he was doing seemed to have no effect; we spun in circles that felt tight and controlled—but were probably anything but—and the only thing I was aware of was the squealing of the ancient tires and the absolute silence of my mind. People talk about your life flashing before your eyes. That was not my experience. It was quite opposite. When I think back on that moment on that rainy morning, all I can conjure up is this sort of bubble of absolute quiet, absolute calm. As we spun I actually noticed and registered the first light poking above the horizon, and I can still recall the ghostly glow that light gave to a line of trees: deciduous. The memory still holds a certain ghostly beauty.

How long did we spin? I don't know. An hour? A minute? A lifetime? Enough. But when the car hit an embankment with a painful scream of injured metal, it was sweet relief and deadly fear all rolled into a single tidy package.

The car, again, was ancient, and there was nothing as fancy as a three-point harness available when it was new, and none had been retrofitted. I guess we were lucky that the Alpine even had lap belts. I was wearing mine. Braydon—as filled to the top with testosterone as he'd ever been in his life—was not.

When the car stopped its elegant circling—very suddenly—I was thrown painfully against the lap belt, but stayed pretty much where I was, held more or less in place when the car ended up on its side: the passenger side, which in this case was the left. I sort of dangled there, not far from where the earth had come to meet us, while my brain kept spinning. It seemed to take a while for it to catch up with my body.

Braydon was thrown clear. I didn't see it—as deeply concerned as I was with my own mortality in that instant—but later I'd discover that, when the car came to its final stop, Braydon went through the convertible's soft roof, the skin of his face and unprotected arms inadequate to slowing him down.

The first thing I was really aware of was Curt. Or, rather, Curt's voice, reaching me somehow through the rain.

"Gee-sus, Braydon. Oh my God." Was he weeping? "Oh my God," again. "Sweet Jesus, Braydon. Try not to move."

"Curt?" My voice, when I found it, was disturbingly weak. It was the first time in my memory that I'd called on it and found it reluctant to answer. "Curt!" I said again, more firmly this time. "Curt, help me, please."

And yet he didn't. If I extended my neck completely to the left, I could see Curt, bent over the place where Braydon had fallen.

"Curt," I tried again. "*Please* help get me out of here. I'm trapped."

My voice had so little effect that, for a moment, I wondered if I really *had* spoken aloud. Curt was hunched over Braydon, his thick, dark hair falling forward over his face, a face that had gone pale with fear and perhaps a touch of guilt. Or maybe the guilt was my own invention. Something supplied by my anger.

I told myself at the time, as I scrabbled futilely against the lap belt that had saved me but now held me captive, that I'd never forgive Curt for not helping me. The anger was ill-placed, I know. But it kept me conscious, kept me focused, until help arrived.

I think it was a paramedic who examined me quickly—"Can you feel this? Please move that…."—and finally cut the lap belt, then helped me unsteadily into the back of an ambulance. The ambulance carrying Braydon was already gone. And Curt was nowhere in sight. I'd find out later that he'd ridden to the hospital with Bray.

As things turned out, the greatest injuries had been

to the car. The biggest injuries that could be seen, that is. Sometimes things get broken in places that are hidden.

Now in Malibu, as I slowed for the cool-down portion of my run, I pushed these thoughts away. I would be flying to Vancouver today. Meeting again with Braydon's family and probably even some of the people I'd once called friends. There'd be plenty of time for Braydon thoughts later. Later, I suspected, there'd be no running away from them.

Three

When Tycho and I crept quietly back into the house after our run, Jennifer was perched at the kitchen counter, a mug of coffee steaming away in front of her.

"That stuff will stunt your growth," I said with a smile. The lanky seventeen-year-old smiled back at me. We both knew that she'd added close to four inches to her height in the last year.

"I hope!" she said, pouring me a cup. "You know those Versace pants I bought last month? I don't want them turning into capris while I'm not looking."

"Yeah, coffee will help with that," I said sarcastically, pulling out the stool opposite her and plopping myself onto it. "What's up?"

"Up?" she said, the morning light picking out the red in her smooth dark hair when she tossed her head in indignation. "Why does something have to be up?"

"Umm, let's see," I replied. "Maybe because it's, like, the crack of dawn and I can *see* you."

She smiled at that because it was an obvious thing to notice. As I said, Jennifer is seventeen. Getting up early is not something she generally does.

"Dad told me you were going to Vancouver today. That you were leaving early."

I nodded.

"He said you were going to your ex-husband's funeral."

I nodded again.

"And, I don't know. It got me thinking, I guess. I started thinking about how I'd feel if Corby died."

"You're still seeing Corby?" I asked, surprised. I hadn't seen him around for quite a while.

"No, we broke up *ages* ago." Which I knew, from a seventeen-year-old, could mean anything from two months to a year. "But that's what I mean. I started thinking about how I'd feel if he died. And I haven't seen him for *forever*, but I knew I'd be really sad. So I thought, you know..." She looked deeply into her coffee mug as she spoke. Embarrassed. "I just thought, with your family being so far away and all, I should check in with you. Make sure you're okay."

This so touched me, I almost didn't have words. Anyone who has spent time around a seventeen-year-old girl—or ever been one—could understand how touched I was. Seventeen-year-old girls are notoriously self-involved. It moved me that Jennifer had found space in her heart and her incredibly hectic life to think about how a death that was semi-near to me might make me feel.

I told her this. That her concern made me feel really cared about. And I thanked her. But she wasn't so easily put off.

"No, really, Madeline," she insisted. Less embarrassed now that it had all been blurted out. "Are you okay? How are you feeling?"

The sincere concern, I decided, demanded a sincere answer. Which was actually slightly problematic. I'd been very carefully avoiding emotion around Braydon's death. It hadn't been that difficult. Our relationship had been old news; it wasn't hard to submerge my feelings about him. In a way, had I not been doing that for years while he was still alive?

I reached for the coffeepot and added fresh java to my cup while I thought, absently stirring in sugar and cream while I considered Jennifer's words.

"I guess," I said finally, "I've been trying not to think about how I feel. What I feel doesn't matter. How could it? We'd been apart a long time. We didn't have a place in each other's lives anymore."

"Still," Jennifer insisted, her dark eyes stern. She would not, I could see, be put off that easily.

I smiled at her. "Still. Yeah, it's funny. It bothers me more than I would have thought. He killed himself," I said softly.

"Dad didn't tell me that."

"I didn't mention it to him. But it makes me wonder about who Braydon had become." Saying all of this aloud and to another human was making these emotions feel more clear. "Because the guy I was married to would never, ever have killed himself. He was so up, Jennifer." I looked directly into her eyes, suddenly feeling it was important that she got this part. "He was the most optimistic person. Everything was sunny to him. Everything was...possibilities. And I guess it just makes me so sad that, I dunno, I guess that he lost that somewhere along the way. That he became someone who *couldn't* see the happy warm things in life so much that he just didn't want to do it anymore."

Jennifer didn't say anything for a moment, as though she was considering my words. "You're saying that you thought he was one way and, in the end, you discovered he was someone else?"

"Something like that," I said. "Not that exactly, but something close."

After a shower, and with another mug of coffee in my hand, I got back to my computer with fifteen minutes to spare before the open. I don't have to be in position when the opening bell rings on the floor of the New York Stock Exchange. It's not like, at home in Malibu, I can actually hear the bell. But when I'm able, I like to be in a position to monitor activity when the market opens.

It has always seemed to me to be magical. Mystical.

Maybe some of both. Minutes before the opening bell, it's as though this incredible buzz—or maybe it's a hum—is building toward that open.

In the right head space, you can feel it. When the orders first start to come in they aren't executing yet, just stacking up waiting to be filled. A trader with her eye on the ball—and all the screens necessary to monitor a lot of stocks—can get a feel for the way the early part of the trading day will go just by watching. But only a feel. It won't be an accurate portrayal. Rather, it can give you a hint of what's going to follow.

I got that hint this morning on a security I'd been watching closely for a few days. It was a fairly new online gaming company whose share price had been climbing steadily since their IPO at the beginning of the year. Then, a few weeks earlier, a change in regulations had put the corporation on shaky ground and, right around the time I became aware of the company, their stock had tumbled.

There is no hard and fast rule when something like that happens. The whole online gaming thing is still relatively new territory. But the market likes numbers, and online gaming has the full menu in that department. Numbers of people visiting their Web site. Numbers of credit cards on the barrel. And, most importantly, number of dollars rung up over secure order lines.

This company had IPOed with all the right numbers. What was different now was the possibility of a new rule that would make a portion of what they did illegal in a lot of regions where they now did business. Obviously, the outcome of all of this would affect their numbers in the long run: fewer people, less money, fewer credit cards. For the moment, however, nothing had actually changed…except that the company's stock was now trading roughly seventy-five percent below the level it had been selling at the month before.

I didn't know where all of this would lead but, in the short term, I had a pretty good guess. The first few days after news got out about the possible regulatory changes, a number of stock analysts had changed their position on the company and a lot of people had sold, sold, sold their holdings, which is where the tumble had come from. It had been a two-day freefall where no one was asking a lot of questions, just shouting, "Sell and sell now." And if everyone wants a market sell—which is a selling of shares at the price the market is currently offering—the stock declines accordingly.

There is a place, however, beyond which a security that has actual value behind it is not likely to fall because, at that point, people say, "Hey! Good deal!" And they start buying again. Plus, of course, the vultures—in the form of day traders like me—start to emerge and buy.

This is the sort of action that calls us. Solid company, unfortunate turn of events, possibility of great change in the coming days. It's the change that brings the day traders out from under their rocks. A nice, slow steady growth is of no interest. For the most effective results, day traders need flux.

On this particular morning, I could see it was going to be a day of great flux for this particular company. Fifteen minutes before the market opened, there were close to 400 sell orders and only 17 buy, which looked like another day of plummeting. Despite what the numbers were telling me, my gut said different. I put in a market buy for three thousand shares that would execute at the open. I was banking on the large number of sell orders pushing the opening price down from the previous day's two-dollar close. Then, with the backlog of sell orders dealt with and the damage done, I was predicting that the price would recover enough during the day for me to sell my early-morning purchases at a couple of thousand dollars in profit. Pretty much the textbook day trade, if there was such a textbook. Which there is not.

I was aiming to sell at $2.50 per share, which I knew was a bit ambitious but certainly not an impossibility. And it didn't have to even go that high for me to make a bit of money.

Not long after the open I got my three thousand shares at prices varying between $1.89 and $1.96: the total cost to me was $5700.

As soon as my trade had been executed and confirmed, I put in a sell order on the same shares for $2.50 for all three thousand shares which, if all went as planned, would net me around $1700, which would make for a pretty good showing on the day and contribute nicely to my monthly expense fund.

I was quite sure it would take several hours for the stock to get to that price, if at all. But I wasn't taking any chances. The trouble with doing things that way was that if the stock price went up steeply during the day, I wouldn't be in a position to notice and respond by holding on a little longer. However, this wasn't a day for watching the ticker. I had places to go. My holdings would just have to take care of themselves for a bit. I popped my laptop into its travel case with some reluctance and started throwing things into a suitcase.

Vancouver. I planned for rain.

Four

When I'd let Tyler know about my travel plans, he'd told me he had to go into West L.A., and offered me a ride to the airport. Since taking a taxi from Malibu to the airport would be expensive and not much fun, I took him up on his offer.

"I sincerely have to get a car," I commented while we tootled down the Pacific Coast Highway in light traffic. From the car window, the ocean looked calm again. Teeny little whitecaps broke the surface of the water. The day was warming up, but the breeze off the ocean was keeping things cool for the moment. It was a glorious day. Tyler didn't have the air-conditioning on and we hummed along with the sunroof in his SUV open, enjoying the feel and sound and scent of the warming day while we could.

"L.A. is *not* a city where you can do without a car."

Tyler grinned. "I'm surprised you've lasted this long already."

It hadn't been long. Or it hadn't seemed like it. But I'd spent some of that time moping and some just working and some of it dealing with insurance companies and really not very much of it wishing I had wheels. I had lost more than a car and an apartment: I'd lost someone very special to me. But the world keeps turning even if we don't always feel like turning with it. I knew that, at some point, I was going to have to get a life again. I also knew that it didn't have to be right now. And, as it happened, it looked very much like the car thing was going to take care of itself. For better, as they say, or for worse.

As we drove, I remembered that Emily and I had penciled each other in for dinner in Santa Monica the following night. When I opened my cell to call her, I once again ogled the phone's tiny color screen and the teeny little lens that would allow me to take bad digital photos. I hadn't even wanted a cell phone. Not really. And if I did, I'd only wanted a phone. But it turned out that "just a phone" was a little too much to ask. I suspected this one did a whole lot of things I wasn't aware of. That disturbed me a bit. Like my phone was keeping secrets.

"Your ex-husband killed himself?" Emily said when I told her. "That's awful, Mad. How?"

How? It was a good question. One I hadn't thought to ask Anne-Marie the day before. Though truly, I wondered, did it matter? The key thing was, Braydon had suddenly not wanted what he'd built.

I told Emily I wasn't sure how long I'd be in Vancouver but that, even with a stop in Seattle to visit with my family, I figured I'd be back in Los Angeles by early the following week at the latest. "Let's do that dinner as soon as I get back, okay?" I told her. "I'll have so much to tell you."

"No kidding," she said, her voice warm but her concern for me apparent. "You'll need a complete debriefing."

LAX was unchanged from my last visit: a large cluster of identical buildings with identical parking structures filled with people identically intent on getting to their various destinations as quickly and painlessly as possible. Identically.

I like airports. I keep promising to drive myself to one at some point when I have no place to go. I'd like to spend a few otherwise empty hours sitting among people, watching them and their mini-dramas unfolding. Let's face it, reality TV still has nothing on...well, reality.

I like airports, but I don't like the contortions involved in modern-day air travel. I *understand* all those precautions, but no one says you have to *like* them. And these days air travel—especially international air travel—means that you have to stand in a lot of lines.

I'd gotten to the airport at ten in the morning and by the time they boarded my flight it was after lunchtime and I was hungry. Nowadays, however, a not-quite-three-hour coach class flight between Los Angeles and Vancouver doesn't merit anything that I consider to be real food. I cursed my lack of foresight—some sushi or a fish taco grabbed in the terminal between my endless lines would have been a seriously good idea, but I hadn't had it in time. Instead I had to make do with an in-flight bag of nuts, a cup of coffee so bad I thought it should be entered in a competition and, eventually, a sandwich containing some sort of mystery meat. The sandwich looked as though it had been made off-world somewhere. A science fiction sandwich. Lovely.

The lackluster meal didn't hold my attention for long. It was fuel, and not very satisfactory fuel at that. Along with not bringing a fish taco, I hadn't thought to bring a book or magazine to read and I wasn't interested in what they had on offer on the plane. I made a valiant attempt at reading the financial section of the *Times*, but my mind kept wandering. I tried hard not to think about the purpose of my trip—just to go with the flow of the idea of travel—but thoughts of Braydon kept crowding my brain. I hadn't had much sleep the night before and I was tired, but I don't sleep well on planes at the best of times and this wasn't one of those.

Braydon. Two days' growth and a smile on his face. That's generally how I think of him.

Braydon. I had to remind myself about why I'd left him. The reasons had seemed important at the time but, when I looked back—now that it was really too late—I had to admit ending things with him had possibly not been my best course. It had been, at the time, the only course I could see. But was it the right one? I'd never really know.

The thing is, there are no wrong decisions in life. Not really. We all do the best with the information that's available at the time. This, at least, is what I tell myself whenever I'm tempted by regret. There have been times when I've found comfort in that thought. Times when I could have beaten myself up looking over my shoulder, but I sheltered under the idea that the thing I decided was the only thing I could have done given available information.

And all of that is true. I know it is. But is it *right?*

Two bad ideas don't make a good one. Not exactly a bolt from the sky. Yet how often do we do exactly that in our lives? Pile not-so-great ideas on top of worse ones until we end up with a big ol' pile of stuff that isn't working?

This is fact: Braydon and I should never have gotten married. It might also be a fact that I should never have gotten married at all. Ever. Though I'm not quite willing to concede that point yet, officially hooked up was just something Braydon and I shouldn't have bothered with.

So, bad idea one: thinking that we could wrap our incredibly disparate lives into one cohesive whole. Bad idea two: well, really, all the others are just themes on bad idea one. There was simply no way Braydon and I could have worked. Ever. In a million years. At least, not at the place we were then. And does anything else matter? Not so much, I'm thinking.

At the time I was a *machine*. I wasn't yet twenty-five years old when we met, and I was pretty new at Merriwether Bailey. I was still learning the ropes and practicing my chops. I was in the office every morning three hours before the opening bell—read that 6:30 a.m.—earlier if I had trades that would be affected by the international markets.

Bray was always wanting me to take it easier. Doing stuff so that I'd ease up. Pathetic stuff, occasionally. Like the time he turned up at the office at lunchtime with a picnic basket, having planned some romantic hour-long break. What would have been in the picnic basket? I've wondered about that sometimes, in the years between. Because, of course, I didn't find out on the day. It would have been things that were subtle and sublime—that was Bray's style then. It would have been nouvelle, obviously. But not so nouvelle it made you gag.

So let's see: a half bottle of something wonderful and appropriate, like a youthful gewürztraminer or a Riesling so sharp and young it practically crackled. There would perhaps have been herb-encrusted chicken legs fried in olive oil and stuffed with marscapone or goat's cheese, and maybe a Tuscan bread salad or a Provençal potato salad—heavy on the lavender because he knew it was my favorite—and, of course, a baguette so crusty it almost cut the inside of your mouth. Then grapes, maybe, or pineapple spears—perhaps dipped in chocolate—or pears with more goat's cheese, just because he knew how much I loved the stuff. How much I couldn't get enough.

Here's the thing, though: I never found out. I already had my usual lunch on my desk—a nice, yummy mug of Maalox—when I saw Braydon come into the bullpen, pale hair a little too long, spilling over his collar, covering one hazel eye. He was a big man, but there was a softness about his physique then. He wasn't fat, not Bray, but his edges were blurred somewhat, both physically and emotionally. I couldn't imagine he'd ever sliced even a tenderloin without a twinge of guilt.

And all of these were things I'd liked about him when we'd first hooked up. He was so *different* from the men in my world. All hard edges, solid lines and no shades of gray other than their suits; buy low, sell high and don't take any shit in between.

Bray was the kind of man who'd make love to you gently in the evening, then get up early to make you an omelette because he knew you'd do without if he didn't. Thoughtful stuff. Generous stuff. How could you not fall in love with a man like that?

So the picnic. Bray arrives in the office and I catch sight of him right away, just like the forty other brokers and traders in the room. I'm on the phone—of course. I was always on the phone in those days—but I could feel this cringe straight up my trade. And he had this beautiful childish expression on his face—like pure anticipation—and I just felt embarrassed. I'm not proud of it now, but right then I just felt like I wanted him to go the hell away. A brokerage was *not* the venue for softness, affection. And, at the place I was in my career, plus the fact that I'm blond, five-eleven and—like Sal, my boss, used to joke—"not hard on the eyes" all the while fighting for a toehold in a field still chillingly testosterone-dominated, well…let's just say I didn't figure that Bray showing up with a picnic basket was going to do my career or my rep any good.

Hey, like I said: I was young. I was insecure. And later, I'd feel mean. But right then I got him out of there as fast as I could. And I wasn't gentle about it. Two weeks later—and a whopping fourteen months into our marriage—I left him in Chelsea. Not without regrets but—hell!, I told myself—I had my priorities straight. I knew where I was going, what I wanted. Braydon Gauthier had as much ambition as a salamander. Six years out of the Cordon Bleu and, sure, he was head chef, but for a good but equally unambitious restaurant in Bed-Stuy. We were *clearly* unaligned stars. Just *what* had I been thinking?

Sitting on the plane out of LAX bound for Vancouver a decade later, with the intention of saying my last real goodbye to my ex-husband, I wondered at how much difference a few years could make. At the time of our divorce I'd thought the marriage had not been significant in my life. And not, ultimately, significant in Bray's. But looking at how things had turned out, you had to wonder at the ways we'd affected each other, the impact we'd had on each other's lives. In the end, it hadn't taken much more than a single afternoon to chuck the career I'd sweated over. Belatedly, I'd thought, getting hold of my priorities.

Bray, for his part, had thrown himself into his work after I left him. He'd turned into a reflection of the machine he'd married. I got hints of this in the year or so between our separation and the time the divorce was final. He'd call me. Every few weeks at first, then the time between calls got longer.

"You were wrong, Maddy." I remember the call. He'd had the sense to wait until after the markets had closed for the day, but I was still at my desk, moving papers around and already preparing for the next day's opening.

"What was I wrong about, Bray?" I tried to sound disinterested, as though my thoughts were elsewhere. It had only been a few weeks and I was trying to make sure that the distance between us was real.

"You said people don't change. But I'm changing, Maddy. I can feel it. I've changed."

"Uh-huh," was all I said, or something equally noncommittal.

"No. Really. I'm…I'm not at Quiver anymore."

"You're not?" This surprised me.

"I think you were right all along. About potentials and stuff. What was it you said…?"

"Talent, Bray. It was about talent. You've always had gobs of it. And you'll never fully realize it at Quiver. It's too small. Too out of the way."

"Well, I think you're right. Now. Now I think you're right. And I'm putting things in motion…."

"I'm pleased you're getting on with your life. I really am. But don't do it for me. It has to be for you."

"Well, I'm working really hard. I have these great ideas, and—"

"Look, Bray, like I said, I'm glad things are working out for you. But you don't need to tell me any of this. Just, you know…" and more sanctimonious stuff.

The fact was, I was only half listening and I was listening with none of my heart. I'd moved on. Not to another man, but to my work. Later—much later—I'd discover I should have been saving some advice for myself. But, Bray? I guess I didn't believe him. People don't change, I kept saying.

I stopped hearing from him a few months later, about the time he moved back to his hometown, Vancouver. Within a year he'd started a little bistro that almost instantly became one of those hot spots that people stand in line for and that take reservations six weeks in advance.

His timing was good and he was pretty enough. A food network had just launched, and one of the network cheeses was one of his patrons. Next thing you know, they offer him a show and—overnight—he's the host of *Haute City Food*, where he cooked up a storm in front of an audience, his set a stark modern restaurant kitchen with the city skyline—perpetually sunset—behind him.

Haute City Food launched him, and within a year he started doing *Gauthier's Gastronomique*, as well. GG, as it was known, had an entirely different pace than *Haute*. Where the earlier show was all glam style—complete with the show's own band, the Haute Boys—

GG was more intimate. Just Bray in a stark white kitchen making the kind of food he'd courted me with. When I was still in New York I'd watch it sometimes when I came home from work, salivating over his beautiful edible creations while munching on a peanut butter-slathered rice cake and thinking about what might have been.

I was glad for him. I really was. And I didn't have any regrets. Not really. But part of me watched his meteoric rise and recognized what had happened: he'd internalized the part of him that was mine. He'd plowed it all inside himself and used the loss to fuel his latent ambition. I wouldn't have said it aloud because it made me feel very self-centered even to think it—it's all about *you*—but what else could explain this sudden reversal? Sure; he'd always had talent—loads of it—but to do something so focused with it and, ultimately, so successful? That took something more.

By the time GG was a hit, he'd opened three new restaurants in U.S. cities known for their cuisine, written a couple of bestselling cookbooks (with co-writers, sure. But his name and mug were on the cover: all that mattered) and established his corporate headquarters in Vancouver.

After a while, I tried to stop paying attention, but it got more difficult when his company went public along with a whole lot of fanfare and the launch of Bray's magazine, *Haute Gastronomique*. Of course, all this haute stuff—along with huge dollops of success—

had made him irresistible on a number of fronts. A line of frozen foods (Haute at Home) added to the diversified nature of his business, and the wheelbarrows of money he was presumably making added to his allure. About the time *People* magazine did an article on him—predictably entitled "The Hautest Bachelor in America"—I tuned right out. That was self-preservation. In the article he'd been quoted as saying that he owed a great deal to his ex-wife, who'd taught him a lot about prioritizing your life. I'd laughed at that. The kind of "ha!" where a smile never enters your eyes or your heart. I'd laughed and felt like crying.

But that was then. Before my life in New York—all I'd worked and sacrificed for—had come to an end. Before I'd come to realize that a decade of sixteen-hour days and having practically no personal life had gotten me exactly two things: a fair-size bank account—I wasn't rich, but I was certainly comfortable—and a decent but empty co-op apartment. I had chucked it all, moved to L.A. and, basically, started anew. And somewhere in all of that I realized that—by the hand of a god who loves irony—Braydon Gauthier and I had, in a sense, changed lives.

"Oh Madeline! I can't tell you how good it is to see you." I was buried in a hug the size of Nebraska in the ample arms of a woman I had once called sister: Anne-Marie, who looked unchanged and completely altered.

I'd forgotten how much she looked like Bray: kind hazel eyes and good light chestnut hair. The generosity of her spirit was almost something you could touch. I guessed that she was over forty now—Braydon had been her little brother—but her skin was smooth and youthful. And not with the manufactured youth I'd gotten used to in L.A.—so often accompanied by the trout lips produced by too generous a helping of collagen, or breasts so high and firm they looked as alien as my airplane sandwich—but with the youthfulness that accompanies a healthy lifestyle and a bright outlook. But for the sad shadows under her eyes and a chase of gray at her temples, Anne-Marie looked just as I remembered. I told her so.

"You look great, Anne-Marie. You've hardly changed at all."

"Well, *you* have changed, Maddy. You look sensational. Look at you—you look like a movie star." I laughed at this and she went on. "No, really. It's partly your height, I think. And that glorious hair of yours." She looked at me appraisingly. "Those things are just the same. But last time I saw you, you still had this sort of coltishness about you. That's gone now. You've grown into yourself. You look like a woman now."

I smiled at this and thanked her, but I thought about what she said. Was that perhaps the difference? Was that what had been wrong? Had it simply not been the right time for me and Braydon? Had the girl not understood what the man had offered? I pushed this thought away and, with my single suitcase retrieved and my laptop case and messenger bag slung over my shoulder, followed Anne-Marie out of the airport and out to the car.

The airport had grown incredibly since my last visit almost ten years before. I stopped right outside the doors ostensibly to admire it, but also to inhale deeply of the British Columbian air.

This is a thing I do, have always done: this testing of the air when I get off a plane. I love that moment, when you first ingest the local air, when you taste it, roll it around on your tongue like a fine wine. It's only at that moment—when you've just left an air-conditioned airport after getting off an air-conditioned plane—that you can truly taste the essential being of a place. Taste it right down to its constituent components. On this day I tasted earth and things growing richly, and I tasted salt and the sharp tang of the sea.

Anne-Marie watched me and smiled. Then she hugged me again and I could see her eyes were moist. "I take it back," she said. "You really haven't changed at all."

I enjoyed the drive from the airport in Richmond into the city. Despite my apprehensions, it wasn't raining, but I could tell it had been recently. You can say what you like about the rain in Vancouver, but when you live in Los Angeles and visit cities in the Pacific Northwest, you realize that all that rain keeps things very clean. There was a sharpness to all of the lines that you don't get very often in L.A. On this day, the sky was the sort of clear blue you usually only see in children's picture books, shot through with black-edged puffy white clouds that looked no more real. The air felt sharp and clear and almost touchable. It was glorious.

As we drove, I could see tufts of grass everywhere: strips of it next to sidewalks, plots of it in front of houses and sometimes even stores, in small parks. There was so much grass, and all of it looked startlingly green to eyes that had grown used to brown grass. Even shopping malls seemed to sport the obligatory well-tended green space. Everything looked beautiful to me.

The airport is in the suburbs, the drive between mostly neighborhoods and secondary shopping areas. But there is a moment when you're on that path between the airport and the downtown core when you get your first view of Vancouver proper. And if it's a clear day and you haven't seen it for a while, it's so lovely it takes your breath away.

That doesn't really cover it, but it's a start: Vancouver is a breathtaking city. Like Seattle in some ways, certainly, but more so. It's all about location, location, location. Vancouver's downtown core is islandlike, surrounded on three sides by the sea. It hosts one of the largest city parks in the world—larger, even, than New York's Central Park—and all of this is backdropped by real, honest to goodness mountains that are so tall that some of them sport snowy peaks nearly year-round.

When we were together, Braydon had occasionally amused me by spouting interesting facts about his hometown. Now that I was back here, an alarming number of those facts were coming back to me. More than I thought I had retained.

Looking towards downtown, for instance, I recalled that he'd told me about an aesthetic code the city had in place to keep things looking lovely. Only certain types of houses could be built in certain neighborhoods and there was a clearly defined limit on how tall a skyscraper could be: the view through the buildings to the mountains needed to be preserved at all costs.

"I'd forgotten how beautiful it is," I said to Anne-Marie as we drove.

She pulled her eyes away from the road for a second to smile at me. "It's funny how you can forget things like that." I could feel her hesitation before she spoke again. "You haven't asked me where I'm taking you," she said finally.

"I knew you'd get to it. And it doesn't really matter to me, does it?" I smiled. "I'm at your mercy."

She sighed. "I really do wish we'd stayed in touch, Maddy. In person, I mean. There was no reason for us not to, was there?"

I shook my head, but of course there had been. I had rejected the baby brother she loved. And, in doing that, had I not indirectly rejected the love she'd extended to me? She hadn't made me feel that way, but I'd felt it on her behalf. That's the thing about a marriage. You make plans. You get all enmeshed in each other's lives and families. In fact, you make each other's lives and families your own. It's one of the rules.

When I'd left Braydon it wouldn't have mattered what we told our families. They knew. Braydon had been besotted with me. No less so when I left him than on our wedding day. You couldn't look at him look at me and not see it. I was—well, again, I was in my mid-twenties—but I was *cordial*. I was *polite*. I was occasionally even *accommodating*—not something I've been often in my life. But I was never—not even for an hour—besotted with Braydon. I never looked at him and saw anything other than what was there. For a while I just thought that's what love looked like. For a while, it was enough.

Anne-Marie had known this. She hadn't told me she knew, but I saw it anyway. As time passed, I thought Bray's family had probably stopped minding. He was a big success, after all. CEO of a public company, the face on numerous cookbooks, a television star in foody circles. And when had he started his little empire? Not until after I'd dumped him, that's when. If anything, I'd thought, they probably would have thanked me.

Not now, though. Now Braydon was dead. Dead changes things. It can wash hurts away or make them stand out, and I wasn't yet sure which way this creek was going to flow.

I was thinking all of these things—about families and creeks—when Anne-Marie broke into my reverie. "You're not ever going to ask, are you?"

"Hmm?" I said.

"Where we're going. Don't you even want to know?"

I smiled at her. "I'm not curious, Anne-Marie, because I know I'll find out."

"You're right about that," she said, swinging into a long driveway on a wide, tree-lined street. "And we're here. Come on, Mom and Dad are expecting you."

Jessica Gauthier greeted us in the foyer.

"Madeline." When she embraced me I fought the urge to support her on her feet rather than hug her back. She was alarmingly frail, and her fine, pale skin seemed to be stretched too tightly across the delicate bones in her hands and those in her face. After a few moments she stood back from me and looked into my eyes, then touched my cheek gently with fingers that felt like the wings of a bird. "Madeline," she said again, "I knew you'd come."

This was not the house I'd visited when Braydon and I were together. That had been a comfortable three bedroom family home in a good but not expensive part of the city. This was a palatial home in lower Shaughnessy, one of Vancouver's oldest and priciest neighborhoods. I'd recognized it because Braydon had driven me through the area on one of our visits, a part of the city that, he'd said, visitors must always see. We'd driven around and admired the stately old neighborhood, but we'd not coveted. At that time, Vancouver hadn't been in either of our plans.

Jessica saw me notice the house and smiled sadly. "Isn't it beautiful? Braydon bought it for us. Two years ago next month." She ran her hand across the highly polished surface of a table in the foyer. I tried not to hear the whispery sound her skin made on the wood. "We fought about it." A weak smile. "Gently. Of course."

"He won." I smiled back at her.

"Yes. He insisted. He said it was a thing he'd always dreamed about—buying us a big, beautiful house. It wasn't really what we wanted, but..." Her voice trailed off.

"You never could deny him anything," I said softly.

She looked up at me and smiled through the beginning of tears. She shook her head. "No, you're right. I never could." She collected herself and led us deeper into the house. "Come along then and say hello to Robert. He'll be glad to see you, too."

The living room was large and imposing enough that it had probably once had a different name. It had probably been called the "lounge" or the "parlor" or the "receiving room." But with Jessica and Robert in residence, a living room it had become. Though some of the furniture looked expensive, antique or both, I thought I recognized the sofa from their old house, along with a familiar oak coffee table with a glass top and some other pieces they'd probably had since their kids were young. They'd brought the suburbs into Shaughnessy.

Robert sat near the center of this design cacophony in what had probably been his favorite recliner for the last twenty years. As diminished as Jessica seemed to me, she was the picture of robust good health compared with her husband. When I'd last seen him, Robert Gauthier had been the sort of big, blustery man you imagine perpetually fixing his house on weekends, the thought of a beer and a game—any kind of game—not far from his mind. When Braydon and I had visited, there had been much backslapping and general joviality. At our wedding, Robert had made the sorts of toasts designed to make the groom avert his eyes and the bride blush. He'd been successful on both counts.

I could barely see even a shadow of the Robert Gauthier I remembered in this man. He did not get up to greet me. This alone I found telling. A decade ago he would have twirled me off my feet. Now, he looked up as we entered the room, but his eyes didn't light with interest or curiosity and he didn't return my greeting when I said hello.

"The doctor said it was a mild stroke." Anne-Marie answered the question I hadn't wanted to ask. She lowered her voice, as though to avoid disturbing her father. "When he heard about Braydon."

"Shouldn't he still be in the hospital?" I asked quietly, concerned as much by the lack of interest in his eyes as I was by his pallor.

"It was very mild," said Anne-Marie. "He visits the doctor every other day, and he has a private nurse here at the house who's with him when one of us can't be. They thought he'd recover better here at home."

Jessica went to her husband and rubbed his shoulder gently, as though willing the transfer of her energy to him. Maybe she just didn't have enough of her own. "Not so mild, maybe, Anne-Marie," she said softly. "It's not gotten any better." And then to me, "Thank you for coming, Madeline." She indicated we should sit, then selected a chair near her husband for herself. "I wasn't sure you'd agree under the circumstances. But we couldn't think who else to ask."

I was confused. I looked from her to Robert, whose expression didn't alter, then to Anne-Marie, who I was surprised to see flinch guiltily under my glance.

"I didn't ask her, Mother," she said now.

Jessica's mouth opened in a surprised "O," and her hand reached up quickly to cover it. "Anne-Marie," Jessica said warningly, but her tone was mild.

"Didn't ask me what?" I was genuinely puzzled. The two women exchanged a glance, then Jessica looked at her husband, as though for support. Finding none there, she looked back at me, and once again at her daughter.

"How much does she know?" Jessica asked finally. I was growing increasingly alarmed.

Anne-Marie shook her head. "Almost nothing. Just the very basics."

Jessica sighed audibly as though not quite sure how to proceed. Finally, with another unrewarded glance at Robert, she said, "I don't know what to do." She looked at her hands, then rubbed them together gently. I could see her pondering how to begin. I curbed my impatience and let her gather the threads. I didn't have anywhere to go, anyway.

"Forgive me," she said finally. "I still have difficulty wrapping my mind around all of this. So that I don't cover old ground, please tell me what you do know."

I tried not to notice how, despite the studied air of casualness about them, both women seemed to lean imperceptibly forward in their seats while they awaited my reply.

I spread my hands helplessly. "Braydon—" My voice broke slightly, and I cleared my throat, then started again. "Braydon…ended his life." I was prepared to go on, but stopped when I realized I really didn't know anything more than that.

"Do you know why?" Jessica asked, watching me closely.

I shook my head.

"It was because he lost one of his stars," she said matter-of-factly.

"He what?" I asked, not comprehending.

"The new Vulcan guide was published last week," Jessica said. I knew from having been married to a chef that the stars handed out annually by the Vulcan guide's editors are the holy grail to people at the higher strata of the restaurant business. Six stars is the maximum: there's nothing better. One star is abysmal. It's pretty much worse than not getting mentioned at all. Two stars is barely a nod, three is an invitation to a private club: you can look, but don't touch. Four is very good indeed and five, of course, is even better. Internationally, only a handful of restaurants have six stars. Even in cities like London, New York and L.A. there are only ever three or four restaurants with six stars. WhyVeeAre, Braydon's flagship restaurant in Vancouver, had been given six stars right out of the gate the year it opened. Even I had heard that and acknowledged it; I could remember thinking how pleased he'd be. How proud. Money and fame were one thing, but the acknowledgment of respected peers is something entirely different. I'd thought about how much work it would have taken to get there. And that maybe, I remember thinking, he really *had* changed.

"And what happened when the guide came out?" I asked.

Anne-Marie shook her head. "Nothing. Nothing you'd notice. I mean, he was upset but not unduly so. Just what you'd expect."

"He had so much going on in his life," Jessica broke in. "The television shows, the magazine, a new book coming out. The restaurants were all doing well and he was hoping to open more. So many good things."

"And Haute at Home was really taking off," Anne-Marie said. Jessica nodded agreement. "*The Robb Report* called it his ready-to-wear line. They talked about him like he was a fashion designer." She sighed, then sat back sadly before continuing, settling herself more deeply into the elegant wingback chair. "He and Mimi seemed to be getting along really well," she said, though I thought her tone held reservation.

"Mimi?" I asked.

The two women exchanged a glance. "You didn't know he'd remarried?"

"Yes, I guess I did. But I didn't remember her name."

"They got married two years ago," Jessica said. "Just a few months after Braydon gave us this house."

I was getting too much information. My head was almost swimming with it. I tried to bring them back on track.

"You said the Vulcan star thing didn't bother him. But you also said that's why Braydon killed himself."

Jessica and Anne-Marie looked at each other before either of them answered. I caught the look and the small shake of her head that Anne-Marie aimed at her mother. No, I surmised from the look, this was another thing Anne-Marie had not told me. "It's what it said," Anne-Marie said finally. "It's what *he* said. In the note."

"A suicide note?" I asked quietly. Both women nodded. "Can I see it?" I asked.

"Mimi has it," Jessica said.

Of course, I thought. That was the kind of thing a wife would be given. I tried to ignore and dismiss the pang I felt at this thought. The cause of it wasn't something I wanted to think about. "But," Jessica went on, "Braydon's note said that he felt the Vulcan people had undone all of the work he did."

"'With the withholding of a single star.'" I could tell Anne-Marie was quoting.

"Would it really have meant that much to him?"

Both women shrugged almost in unison. One could

see their relation in that simple gesture. "There are people who say it would have," Anne-Marie said finally.

People. I thought. But didn't say anything.

"Yes," Jessica agreed. "That it would affect reservations at the restaurants, that it would affect the stock—"

"It would definitely have affected the stock," Anne-Marie broke in.

Jessica acknowledged her daughter's words with a gesture I read as "perhaps."

"I wouldn't have thought it would mean so much," I said. "Not really. I mean, maybe to Braydon personally, but not to the business end."

Jessica executed her small shrug again, but Anne-Marie put a voice to it. "We'll never know, of course."

"And I would imagine that his death has affected everything very much." I stopped when I realized what I'd said. "I mean, beyond his family, beyond here. All of the things one would have feared at the loss of a star will have certainly have come true with his death."

Jessica sighed. Nodded. Then sighed again. "That's why we wanted you to come, Madeline. It's beyond what we would have thought. And I'm so glad you've come to help."

I looked at Anne-Marie, but the younger woman avoided my glance. At her mother's words she'd risen and gone to her father. He hadn't moved, and seemed oblivious to our conversation and perhaps even to our presence. Anne-Marie fussed with him now, nonetheless. Adjusting his sweater, smoothing his hair. I tried to rouse a wave of anger at her for whatever omission she'd omitted, but found I didn't have the heart for it. I could read her love and concern in her every gesture. This was, I reminded myself, Anne-Marie. If there had been an omission on her part, its reason would make itself clear to me soon enough.

Jessica, meanwhile, had followed my glance and read my look. She took umbrage on my behalf. "Anne-Marie," she admonished, "did you not even tell her that?"

Anne-Marie shot a glance at her mother and shook her head. "I'm sorry. I…it just seemed easier to tell her you wanted her here for the funeral. Less… I'm sorry. Less crass."

Jessica seemed taxed by her daughter's words, but not beyond endurance. I remembered anew the gentleness that had always marked my dealings with her.

She propped her fingertips together and seemed to look very closely at her nails. I followed her glance. They were simply manicured, the hands smooth and long-fingered. She seemed to be gathering herself, thinking where to begin. My heart went out to her. How could it not be a difficult time? Which reminded me. "My mother sends her sympathy, Jessica. And she sends her regards."

Jessica smiled at me. A sad smile. "Of course she would. Dear, dear woman. Thank her for me, will you, Madeline? And when next you see her, give her a hug. All right then," she said finally. "We've left you in enough suspense. It's not intentional, I assure you. But finding the right words can be difficult and I'm not sure which of them are important. You understand?"

I nodded to indicate that I did. And I pressed myself again for patience, not always my strongest suit.

"Right, then. I'll tell you as it happened, as I remember it, and Anne-Marie can correct me if I go astray. But in the telling, I think, you'll see why I wanted you here. Beyond, of course—" and here she favored me with her most gracious smile "—beyond the welcome comfort of your presence."

I smiled back at her, still willing the patience to sit there and keep quiet. Everything, I told myself, would be revealed in good time.

"The Monday after...after..." She stumbled as though for a word.

Anne-Marie supplied it. "The Monday after Braydon was found."

"Thank you, Anne-Marie. Yes: the Monday after Braydon was found—Monday of this *week*, mind—the board of Gauthier Fine Foods called a special meeting. They replaced him, Madeline." She looked at me, stricken eyes wide, as though willing me to see how wrong this was.

I was as gentle as possible. "That's normal, Jessica," I said softly. "I know it's hard, but how a company responds when...when something like this happens can have an enormous impact on a publicly traded company's stock. It can make all the difference. Who did they name as CEO?"

"Doug," Jessica said. "Mimi's brother." She looked at her daughter for support. "What was Doug's title before?" Anne-Marie indicated she didn't know, so Jessica went on, "He's the financial expert on the board of the company. Not the accountant. The finance something?"

"CFO?" I offered. "Chief financial officer?"

Jessica nodded. "Yes, that's it."

I smiled at her. "But that's good then, isn't it? He knows the company well and is even a member of the family." I honestly couldn't imagine a better situation. From where I was sitting, everything sounded as perfect as it could be under the circumstances. As I'd told Jessica, in times of great transition it's imperative that a publicly held company move quickly if for no other reason than to maintain shareholder confidence. It's important that the shareholders at least have the feeling that the company they've invested in is handling a bad situation in the best possible way. A board that sat on its hands in this case would look rudderless and vulnerable, and the appearance of either of those things—and certainly both—must be avoided at all costs.

In the case of a company where—because he was a celebrity and his face was very visible—the CEO was very much the brand, this would be even more important. "Yes," the board would want to be seen as saying, "it's a very bad time. But look how prepared we are to weather this calamity."

Perhaps understandably, Jessica was not seeing things from that perspective.

"Doug is *not* Braydon," she hissed. The abrupt departure of her gentleness surprised me.

"No, no, of course not, Mother." Anne-Marie beat me to the words. "No one is saying that he is."

"Then how can Doug even try to replace him?" Jessica looked from me to her daughter, then back again as though willing us to see things from her position.

I once read somewhere that there are seven stages of grief. Understandably, Jessica wasn't very far along the process yet. Somewhere between stage one, disbelief, and stage two, denial. Bringing me here might even be the threshold to stage three: bargaining. I hoped I wasn't around for stages four through six: guilt, anger and depression. The way the situation looked now, things could get ugly for a while before Jessica reached the seventh stage of acceptance and hope.

"Mother's concern is a little deeper than that, though," Anne-Marie said.

"How so?"

"When he took the company public, Braydon saw to it that the family had a large chunk of stock," Anne-Marie said, "to be administered by Mother and Father throughout their lifetime. Even when Braydon was alive, the corporation owned by our family was the largest single shareholder."

I nodded. It likely reflected not only Braydon's affection for his family, but respected his earliest investors. I had no doubt that his parents—and perhaps other family members—had ponied up the dough so that

Braydon could open his first restaurant. And to be worthy of six Vulcan stars right out of the gate, there would have been a lot of dough to pony.

Sometimes people who have never been close to the restaurant business think it's an easy way to make a living. Some even go for it. I mean, how much could it cost? Rent the space. Buy some kitchen gear and a bit of food. Hire some help. Then charge thirty bucks for a steak and ten for a crème caramel. Ka-ching. But there is so much more to it than that. I knew this from both Braydon and from the clients in the hospitality industry I'd worked with in the past. The cash outlay to open a decent restaurant can seem endless, and the execution and service of really sterling food is an expensive business.

"Braydon and Mimi held another chunk of stock." That too made sense. "And Doug—even though he's Mimi's brother—held his own. Upon his death—" Anne-Marie said these words evenly, as though trying not to think about what they actually meant "—Braydon specified in his will that he wanted the family—that is, really, Mother and Father—to receive another fifty percent of his personal holdings and that another member of the family representing *this* chunk of family stock be given a place on the board."

Here Jessica took over again. "And *that's* not happening, Madeline. They are putting roadblocks to that happening."

I wasn't sure I understood. "Why?" I asked.

"I think they're afraid Mother will stop plans from moving ahead, now that Braydon is gone."

"And would you?" I asked.

Jessica looked distressingly close to tears. "Maybe. I don't know. But it's not been a good week." She smiled thinly. "Honestly, I've not been in my right mind. But that's not the point, is it? The point is what's right. And even if I didn't cooperate this week… Well, it's just not the point."

"As Mother said, Madeline, though this is a very difficult time for everyone, we just want what's correct. We want what Braydon would have wanted."

Jessica nodded her agreement. "The trouble is," Jessica said, "I'm not really sure what I *should* want. Part of it is grief, yes. But, if I'm very realistic—very honest—it's also because I've never done any of this sort of thing myself."

"What sort?" I asked.

"You know, business things. Braydon always handled company business that affected us. And had people that helped with that. And Robert has always handled our household affairs." She looked toward her husband, still sitting placidly in his chair. "And he can't. Not just now."

I sighed. To my completely untrained eye, it didn't look as if Robert would be doing those sorts of things ever again.

"What Mother had hoped was that you might…look into all of this while you're here."

I could feel my face scrunch up in consideration. I couldn't help it. I didn't know where this was leading, but I was pretty sure I didn't like it. "Look into what?"

"We'd hoped," Jessica said, suddenly more brightly, "you would represent us—this block of the family shares—within the company for the moment. That you could just, you know, look into things and tell us that everything is as it should be."

The suggestion came to me so far from left field, it nearly hit me in the head. I just wasn't expecting it. Had I been, I certainly would have run. Or at least dodged more gracefully. Instead I floundered, like a big, stupid fish.

"I couldn't do that," I said hastily.

"Of course you could. We'll sign papers so that you can, if necessary." Jessica had clearly thought this through and decided it was the best course. All she had left to do was convince me, something she figured she had enough cards to do. I wasn't sure she was wrong.

"You don't need me, Jessica. It really sounds as though you'd be better off with a lawyer."

She made a shooing motion with her hand. "Of course we have a lawyer. That's how I know about the signing part. But he isn't *family*, Madeline."

I studied my shoes. "Strictly speaking, Jessica, I'm not family anymore, either."

That shooing motion again. "It's not the same. He is an impartial non-family member. He bills us by the hour, so the more hours the better."

"He's very good," Anne-Marie assured me. "Very

trustworthy. And for aspects of this, his thoughts and opinion are all we require."

"But what we want," Jessica took over again, "is for you to examine everything from the *inside*. On our behalf. Just perhaps spend a day at the company and look everything over, then tell us all is what it seems to be. Or not, as the case may be. Please say you will, Madeline. It would do so much to ease my mind."

My first reaction, when all of their words had sunk in, was an unexpected wave of resentment. They had a high-priced lawyer, they'd said. But here I was. And I could perhaps be coaxed into doing it for free. After a couple of beats, though, I realized that wasn't it at all. It wasn't about relative dollar values. Not this time. It was about convincing me to be their window into a world that was confusing to them, a world they knew I was comfortable in and understood well.

Viewed in that light, I realized that what they wanted wasn't so much, not really. And I could understand their concerns. Jessica and Anne-Marie had suddenly been plunged over their heads into a financial stew not of their creation. What they were really asking for was reassurance. It seemed pretty likely to me that I would, as Jessica had suggested, spend a day at the corporate headquarters of Gauthier Fine Foods and discover that everything was just as it appeared to be. And I knew that I could plan on spending *another* day explaining that to Jessica and reassuring her, as well as perhaps coaching her about what she could expect in the future. Another two days out of my life. I looked at the gentle, bereft woman and thought of my own mother. I thought also about Braydon and I knew that, had our situations been reversed, he would have done this for my mother in a heartbeat.

I sighed. And then I shrugged. And then I gave in.

"Okay," I said after a few minutes of consideration. "I'll do it. But I'll be honest with you—I totally expect to find everything just as it should be."

Jessica looked unconvinced but disinclined to argue. She'd gotten what she'd wanted, after all. There was a lasagna in the oven—the sort of offering, I suspected, that friends and family bring by in times of extreme emotional distress. Covered casseroles made with love and offered in hope for the best in a bad situation. Jessica moved us to the dining room, but food didn't seem to be what any of us were in the mood for. We pushed the lasagna around on our plates for a bit, but conversation was suddenly difficult. I was tired from a long day and perhaps Anne-Marie and Jessica were just tired of dealing with their current reality. In any case, I found myself thinking about where I was going to be laying my head.

"We thought you could stay at Braydon's apartment," Jessica said when I asked.

"It's very comfortable and you'll be close to the office," Anne-Marie added. "You can even walk from the apartment if you feel like it. Braydon often did. It's just a few blocks."

"But his wife...?" I let my question go unasked, while quelling the rise of panic I felt. After all, I told myself, I could always go to a hotel.

"Mimi and Braydon lived in the Valley. They've got a lovely home on an acreage out in South Langley," Jessica said. "An estate, really. After they got married, Bray kept his apartment in town for when he didn't feel like driving all the way home when he worked late."

"It was never Mimi's place," Anne-Marie assured me. "And she doesn't go there."

Part of me felt like arguing. Jessica and Robert's huge house, I reasoned, would surely have a corner free for little me. And, on the telephone, Anne-Marie had said I could stay at her place, though she now told me she hadn't realized at the time that her place would be full of her husband's family, in town from all parts of western Canada to pay their final respect to their famous in-law.

As things were, I was tired enough that the thought of an apartment all to myself was appealing, even if it had until recently belonged to the person I used to be married to.

At the door as she bid us good-night, Jessica gave me a hug, then took my hands in hers and tilted her head back to look directly up into my eyes. "Thank you for doing this, Madeline," she said, squeezing my hands with more strength than I had thought she was capable of. "It really means a lot to me. To all of us."

In the car on the way to Braydon's apartment, Anne-Marie apologized for not filling me in more deeply. "I...I just didn't know what to say."

"It's okay, Anne-Marie. Really," I said. Meaning it. "I understand. You guys all have had so much to deal with."

She smiled at me gratefully while negotiating a busy thoroughfare and explaining further about the sleeping arrangements. More apologizing.

"Stop saying I'm sorry, already," I joked, trying to lighten the mood. "You're sounding *way* too Canadian."

"I can't help it." She smiled back. "I *am* Canadian."

She told me again that both she and Jessica had guests arriving from out of town for the funeral. "I wanted you at my place—we could have put someone else at Bray's—but, honestly, Garth's family are a fairly loud bunch. You'll be happier at Bray's." She hesitated before going on. "Plus, Mother thought it would be good to get you in line with the business stuff right away. Bray did some work at the apartment. He kept a desk there."

"She's thinking I'll poke around?"

Anne-Marie grinned. More herself, I noted, away from under her mother's eye. "Hoping, more like. Anyway, you'll like it. And you'll get more peace there than you would have at my place. It's kind of a zoo right now. Here we are."

Anne-Marie had pulled her car in front of a sleek, modern building I was quite sure hadn't existed in Vancouver on my last visit. It was concrete, three stories high, with a waterfall dominating a central courtyard.

"It's amazing," I said, not bothering to hide my admiration.

"Braydon loved this place," Anne-Marie said. "He bought his suite almost before they broke ground."

At street level, the building housed tony shops and art galleries. Anne-Marie led me to a small elevator that shot us up a single level to where an open gallery led to each of the condo units. "The building isn't very old," Anne-Marie explained as we walked, "but it was built in a loft style."

"Postmodern quasi warehouse?"

"Something like that. And Granville Island is practically across the street," she said, pointing toward downtown. I knew Granville Island fell on the edge of the water that separated the west side from the downtown core. I even remembered taking a charming water taxi from the market area on the island practically to the financial district. At least, that was how it had seemed to me.

"Bray loved going to the market and surrounding himself with fresh ingredients. He said being around food in its purest form inspired him."

Braydon's apartment seemed utterly unlike the Bray I remembered. The front door opened onto a room two stories high. Nearby was a kitchen so modern it looked as though you could fly it to the moon, and I could see a small but efficient workspace with a tidy desk and computer adjacent to the kitchen. A good-size guest bathroom claimed one downstairs wall. Upstairs was a single huge bedroom with still another bathroom, this one with a jetted tub. A stairway led up from the bedroom, and when I looked at Anne-Marie questioningly, she explained that it led to a roof deck.

"Please make yourself completely at home, Madeline," she told me. "You'll find everything you need." She pointed to a multiline phone on the little desk, "Let's make line two your direct line while you're here. Feel free to give out the number." She had thoughtfully written it out for me on a card. "No one would use that line to call in, so you don't have to worry about intercepting callers who don't know…"

"Anne-Marie, thank you. It's enough." And it was. It had suddenly occurred to me that, even though I was unsettled, Anne-Marie had been running interference with her mother all day. That was, when she wasn't picking me up at the airport or playing tour guide at her late brother's apartment or playing hostess to Garth's noisy relatives. She was outwardly calm, but I had no doubt she was frazzled.

"Everything will be fine for me here. You go on home now. I'm sure you have lots to do. Try to rest. Maybe call me in the morning with, you know, a schedule. I'm installed. Tell me when to be where and then don't give me another thought." I hugged her quickly. "I'm a big girl and you've got enough to deal with."

She smiled, but I could see her eyes swim with pain

and perhaps fatigue. "I do, don't I?" she said, hugging me back. "Well, if you're sure you're okay…?"

"I am."

I could see her hesitate before taking her leave. "There's one more thing, Madeline." Another hesitation. And then a rush of words, as though she were trying to put them all in place before they flitted away. "Mother and I have talked about it, but only to each other. And it's probably stupid. It's probably nothing. And it's certainly nothing you can help with. I just thought it should be said between us. It's just that…"

"What…?" I said gently and, I hoped, encouragingly.

"Well, Braydon. Braydon dying the way he did. Mother and I…well, we don't really believe it."

"You don't believe he's dead?" I asked, trying to comprehend.

"Oh, no. We believe that, all right." She looked stricken. And more sad than I'd yet seen her. "No. We *know* he's dead. What I'm getting at is *how* he died, Madeline." She pushed her hands through her hair, then dropped onto the sofa, as though the sudden weight of it all was more than she could take. "Please, please tell me you won't laugh."

I sat down next to her on the sofa and touched her shoulder with a gentle hand. "Anne-Marie. Please," I said gently. "No matter what it is, I won't laugh."

She smiled gratefully, then went on. "See, it's just that, well you *knew* Braydon. He was capable of a lot of things. But killing himself?"

"You and your mother are thinking he didn't kill himself?"

She nodded. "It sounds silly out loud like that but, yes—that's what we're thinking. But it *is* silly because what, really, are the options? So we think that it's quite possible it's the grief, clouding what we see, you know? But, Braydon? I just think...well, I just keep thinking there would have been some clue, some sign. And there wasn't, Madeline. We didn't see anything in him altered. He was just Braydon. And then..."

I regarded Anne-Marie evenly for a moment, digesting what she'd said. "Has anyone suggested...?"

She shook her head. "No. No one. And, like I said, it's probably just us." She tried a smile that didn't quite work. "Maybe thinking about other possibilities helps us get through all this."

"Denial?" I asked.

"Something like that."

"So why are you telling me? Is that something you wanted me to look out for while I'm looking into the other stuff? The possibility of motivation for foul play?"

"Oh, no." Anne-Marie shook her head adamantly. "And when you put it that way, it really does sound silly. In order for that to be the case—for Braydon *not* to have killed himself—it means someone must have wished him ill. A *lot* of ill. And I just can't imagine that. Even then, there would probably have been some sort of hint, right?"

I just shook my head. Really, what could I say?

"Listen, Madeline, I'm sorry I even brought it up."

Anne-Marie got to her feet, the briskness back in her voice and manner. She was ready for another round of the business of getting on with life. "I know it's just me and Mom being silly. We…well, we just loved him so much, Madeline. *You* know how much we loved him. And maybe imagining…other possibilities makes it just a little more bearable for us. Otherwise…" Her voice trailed off for a second and I could see tears glittering just below the surface. "Otherwise…well, we loved him. Shouldn't we have seen something? Shouldn't we have known?"

Anne-Marie's pain was fresh and raw; it grabbed at me like a living thing. I wanted there to be words—a string of words—I could say that would make everything right. But there wasn't. How could there be? Nothing could take this away, make it better.

"I'm so sorry, Anne-Marie." Were there ever words more limp? More lame? It wasn't enough. But it was all I had.

"Oh, Maddy, *I'm* sorry. I'm going to go now. And I'm sorry I brought all this other stuff up. Forget I said anything. My number is on the card I gave you. Mother's, too. Call if you need any little thing."

Once I was alone, the thick concrete walls seemed to settle around me in a blanket of quiet. It was a little disturbing.

I walked around for a bit, poking here and checking there, trying to catch a glimmer of the Braydon Gauthier I'd known. I couldn't. The smooth, cold gray walls, the dark postmodern art, the stark Danish modern furniture: nothing twigged a recollection for me. Nothing told me this was the home of a man I had once loved and known well.

But, of course, it wasn't his home, I reminded myself. The place he called home was nearly an hour to the south in a pastoral community filled with large houses and rolling fields. That, at least, was all I remembered of Langley from my previous visits to the area. There was more to the place than that, but I didn't doubt it was this part that Braydon had occupied. Presumably venting his softer side—the side I'd known—at the home he shared with his wife.

I moved through the rooms aimlessly, pulling open a drawer here, peering into a cupboard there, but nothing gave away much of anything about the apartment's former occupant. Well, he was neat, I could see that. Or he'd had a housekeeper. Maybe both. But, mostly, the apartment seemed oddly devoid of personality.

An armoire in the bedroom held chef's whites with Braydon's name embroidered on the breast pocket in a tidy script. The same armoire held neatly folded T-shirts, jeans and chinos, and carefully pressed suits, all in dark colors and expensive fabrics.

The bathroom held rows of men's toiletries—only the better brands. I unscrewed a few tops and tried to get a whiff of the Braydon I remembered. He wasn't there.

I had better luck in the kitchen. This was another room that didn't look as though it belonged to Braydon

as I'd known him. To me it looked more like Braydon
as he'd aspired to be. This made sense to me.

A very good set of All-Clad cookware gleamed from
its rack over the six-burner cooktop. One cupboard
held oils and vinegars only: white truffle oil, pressed
grapeseed oil, extra virgin olive oils of various descrip-
tions, as well as balsamic vinegar in three varieties—
good aged, infused with fig and another infused with
maple syrup. I hadn't known there were so many types
of such basic things.

One drawer was given over entirely to knives, mostly
with ceramic blades, all astonishingly sharp. I closed the
drawer quickly. Seeing them there—neatly and potentially lethally laid out—had made me realize that, so far,
no one had told me how Braydon had died. Suicide, of
course. But that, I thought, was a label that could be
stuck on a wide variety of deaths. But maybe the how
didn't matter. Maybe the only thing that counted was
that Braydon had suddenly wanted it over with. He'd
wanted it over with badly enough to do something
about it. And part of me still couldn't believe he wasn't
just out there somewhere. My own denial.

The condition of the All-Clad—perfect yet with
signs of wear—as well as the knives and the varying
levels of fullness of the oils and vinegars told me that,
unlike many kitchens in posh apartments, this one had
seen some cooking. It made me wonder if Braydon had
done some of the test work for his cookbooks and his
television shows here. Though restaurant kitchens are

ideal for the preparation of beautiful meals, they're less than perfect for working with a recipe you want beginners to be able to replicate in their own kitchens. That would have made his in-town apartment an extension of his workspace, which explained the little office area and all of those good suits.

I can never resist an unguarded refrigerator, and this one—commanding as it did all of the space between floor and ceiling—was no exception. Unsurprisingly, Braydon's Sub-Zero was a sonnet to good eating. It held a mind-boggling array of condiments as well as a full complement of fresh fruits, vegetables and even some packaged meats. These last would need throwing out at some point, but I found I didn't have the energy for it and, in any case, it wasn't my place. And they hadn't started to stink yet. That would come with time.

Near the front of the refrigerator I found a small plastic container of something that looked spreadable. I sniffed it suspiciously, but it smelled okay. Some sort of artichoke and cheese dip or spread from the look of things.

Further investigation led me to an unopened box of gourmet crackers and a few bottles of wine. I was suddenly starving. Between my mystery-meat sandwich on the plane and the grief-soaked lasagna at Jessica's, I remembered I hadn't eaten much all day. Alone now and relaxing slightly, hunger washed over me in a big wave.

It was easy, in Braydon's perfectly organized kitchen, to find a corkscrew and a wineglass. I opened a bottle of an inviting-looking Chianti and poured myself a glass. I cored and sliced an apple I found in a fruit basket on the counter, put the slices on a plate, then smeared some of the crackers with the artichoke spread I'd found in the refrigerator, added them to the plate, then headed up towards the roof deck Anne-Marie had pointed out earlier.

The night air seemed chilly to my L.A.-acclimatized body, but the day had been warm and sunny and it felt good to be outside. Better still when I drank in the view of the city the roof deck afforded.

I'd expected Braydon's deck to be party appropriate, and I was right. The outdoor furniture I found there was tough enough to stand up to Vancouver's damp climate, but so carefully chosen it looked like an outdoor living room, albeit one with a spectacular view. I chose a comfortable-looking chair at a patio table that looked out over the city and sat there while I munched and thought.

I was not looking forward to the following day. The fact that Jessica hadn't wanted me in Vancouver just for the funeral, but rather to help look after her business interests, had come as a surprise. I toyed with the idea of not going to the funeral service, rather just attending the reception that would follow.

After a while, though, I decided that not going would be a nod to goodbye, only. Not a proper farewell. And I'd come such a long way.

With that decided—and with a little food and nice wine inside me—I felt somewhat better, more in control. More ready to face whatever might come my way.

The sheets on Braydon's bed looked perfectly clean. I stripped them off anyway, unwilling to lose any sleep wondering if my dead ex-husband's cooties were mingling with my own. The very thought made me shudder. I found replacements in a small closet in the bathroom, along with towels and other clean linens. The new sheets smelled like lavender and I smiled. It was the first strong sign of Braydon I'd gotten since entering this private space.

This thought made me take a seat on the half-made bed. Because that, really, was one of the things that had been bothering me on a day so filled with small things it had been difficult to isolate a single one. There was little of Braydon anywhere in his life, that I could see. At least, not the Braydon I'd known. For that matter, the Braydon I had been married to would have had a difficult time running a restaurant on his own, never mind a corporation. I had no doubt that it *had* been Braydon; I'd seen him on television and recognized him. I'd flipped through a few of his cookbooks, seen his distinctive mug. Seen that smile. But there is a central ingredient required for success in conventional things, a single-minded sense of drive and purpose, and I had a difficult time imagining my ex-husband possessing either of them in large enough quantities to create and then administer a mega-successful corporation like Gauthier Fine Foods.

Now, understand: that's not a bad thing. There are corporate animals. And there are others. Braydon had clearly always been in that "others" category. Gentle, as I've said, creative, thoughtful, sensitive: not qualities you think of when corporate success comes to mind.

Which meant…what? That someone else had been running things, out of the public eye, or that Braydon had changed vastly since I'd known him? I looked again at the cool gray walls, examined the crisp black sheets in my hand. Changed a *lot*.

I was still thinking about it when I turned off the lights. As I fell toward unconsciousness, the soft city sounds of Vancouver lulling me toward slumber, I thought of Braydon—*my* Braydon—who was nowhere in evidence here.

Five

I once saw a movie with a girl—a woman, really—whose life inexplicably splits into a couple of alternate realities. In one, she'd missed her connection with some sort of conveyance—a bus, a train, a taxi—and went back home to find her lover in bed with another woman. In the other reality, she manages to make her connection, and goes blithely on with her life not realizing that her boyfriend is getting his cookie deliveries from another location.

Our heroine was sweet of face and nature and, ultimately, both realities conclude on a happy ending. It was Hollywood, after all, and it was a date movie that was determined to send us on our way smiling and with a warm feeling deep in our hearts or stomachs or wherever it's appropriate to feel such things. But it made me think about the crossroads in our lives and how we never see them when we're standing right at them, which is bothersome, really. I mean, shouldn't there be some kind of sign at crossroads? Some sort of special marker? Neon lights blazing: This Way Now.

These are the types of thoughts I was having as I opened my eyes on the morning light hitting Braydon's steel-gray walls and black linens. I thought again about Braydon. About our duvet. And I thought about the crossroads he must have passed to get to this place—the place he was at today. Owner of this coldly beautiful apartment. Bestselling author. Acclaimed chef. Television apartment. And, from this day forward, inhabitant of a specially purchased plot at a Burnaby funeral park.

My thoughts were dashed by the electronic bleating of the phone. I rolled over on my elbow and looked at the beast: line two. I picked it up.

"Good morning, Madeline. How did you sleep?"

Anne-Marie. Probably not searching for honesty right this second. I didn't give it to her.

"Fine, Anne-Marie. How are you?"

"I'm just calling to see if you have everything you need, and to synchronize our schedules." Her joviality was forced. Not real. Both of us knew it. And yet. Her brother was being buried later in the day. What were our options?

"Okay." I matched her tone as brightly as possible. "Synchronize away."

She told me that the funeral was at two and the reception would follow directly. "But how will you get there?"

"Like I told you last night, I'm a big girl," I told her. "I'll find my way."

"Oh! You know what we forgot yesterday? Old Stinky. There's underground parking in Braydon's building. The car is down there. And the keys are there at Bray's. It's your car now, Madeline. You could drive yourself."

She told me where to find the keys and gave me directions to the funeral home. I told her I'd see her there at two.

Back in the kitchen, I rummaged around until I found the coffee grinder. It didn't even occur to me that Bray might not have one, and I was right. Then I struggled with Braydon's espresso machine until I had something that vaguely resembled an Americano. There was no way I was beginning this day without something bracing and caffeine-laced. Braydon's very good roasted-in-Italy beans supplied both once I'd had my way with them.

I was pleased to see that Braydon had wireless Internet access in his little office, and I managed to get my laptop up and surfing the Net in a pleasingly short time.

It took some focusing to get my mind deeply into work mode, but I didn't have a lot of options. I had time on my hands and, hopefully, there was money to be made. I crammed my workday into the next couple of hours, pleased to see that the sell orders I'd made the day before had executed pretty much as I'd planned. The few other securities I'd been monitoring hadn't quite reached the point where I wanted to act on them and, with so much else on my mind, plus being in a strange city, I didn't feel like researching anything new.

I was just getting ready to log off my trading account when something occurred to me. I initiated a search on "Gauthier Fine Foods" by name rather than trading symbol. As I did it, I realized that I'd never done research on Braydon's company before. I mean, I'd read a few articles and I'd seen him on TV, but I'd never tried to get information on his company once it went public. I wondered why that was—some subconscious thing?— but I didn't wonder long. The search didn't turn anything up.

Thinking I'd typed it in wrong—Gauthier had never been my last name—I did it again. With the same result. Which, for the moment, made no sense to me.

I pulled open one of Braydon's desk drawers and found his business cards exactly where I would have thought they'd be. Then I carefully typed in the URL of the company's Web site.

The Web sites of most publicly traded companies differ slightly from outfits that are privately held in that they have two very clear and separate missions. The public mission is the same as everyone else's: to sell as many widgets as the traffic will bear. But look more closely at the publicly traded company's Web site. Somewhere—usually slightly out of the center of traffic—you'll find an area meant to appeal to investors. And, despite the low profile from the main page, there's quite often more juicy stuff in the investor area than anywhere else. That's because companies want potential investors to know their widgets are the coolest, and they want current investors to know they sell their share of widgets. But they don't necessarily want the widget buyers to know that bits of the company are floating around awaiting purchase. It's a funny sort of double standard, but it tends to hold.

I found the investor-relations area on the Gauthier Fine Foods Web site without much trouble. From there it was an easy matter to find the area where stock quotes would normally be found. This is something almost all publicly traded companies have made easily available since the advent of the Web. I'm not sure what the rationale is, especially in the case of companies that are having a bad quarter or a bad day, but they do it anyway. Mostly it's a delayed quote—it costs a lot to get a live one—but they all have some version of stock quote on their Web sites. Except the page where Gauthier's quote would have been was "currently disabled," which made no sense at all to me. In fact, it was vaguely alarming.

Though the exchange the security traded on wasn't mentioned, the company's trading symbol was shown. When I saw the symbol—GAFFF—alarm bells started to go off. It was, quite simply, too many letters. I looked around the posh apartment, the skookum computer, thought about the big expensive life and tried to make sense of it.

That trading symbol—GAFFF—could only mean one thing: Gauthier Fine Foods was being traded on the

Pink Sheets. From everything I knew, Braydon's company had been doing very well and had been since long before his IPO. I remembered reading about said IPO when it happened, and though I'd avoided doing anything that felt even vaguely research with regards to Braydon's company, I knew it hadn't been on the Pinks at the time. I would have remembered—and scoffed—if it had.

I know I should backtrack here slightly and explain the Pink Sheets and why I'd scoff at them. But I almost can't. It's like stock purgatory. The place where securities go when they've been bad and the place securities can't get out of if they're not good enough. And neither of these are truisms. Neither of these are written in stone. And yet.

Let's say a very young company with lackluster financing and a less-than-sterling approach wants to go public. Maybe it's even a *good* and promising company. But not *that* good. Not *that* promising. Good, but not good enough. Or good, but with shady management: people doing things not quite the right way. If that company just couldn't quite cut it on the stringent listing regulations of the NASDAQ or the NYSE, they might still cut it to trade on the Over-the-Counter Bulletin Board—the OTCBB. But if they weren't even up to *those* standards, they could definitely trade on the Pink Sheets. It is probably not true that a child could take her lemonade stand public on the Pinks. But it might be. And it's definitely the place she'd have the best shot.

On the other hand—and this was what I feared might be the case here—let's say a company starts out superpromising and gets all the right breaks and manages a solid IPO on one of the respected North American exchanges. But, say, the stock price slips really low and stays there, or there's something funky with their structure or their paperwork or both. After a while—after a few warnings and opportunities to do things better or right—that company will get busted down to the Pinks.

When that happens, it's not officially a death kiss but that's pretty much the reality. A kind of: you can't play with the big boys, but we'll still let you play. For now.

When I was a broker with a large firm I never did trades with companies that traded on the Pinks mainly because the money I was trading with wasn't my own— it belonged to clients who trusted in me to do the right thing by their investments and, to the best of my ability, I always did. Securities that trade on the Pink Sheets tend to be riskier propositions, in part because the companies that play there aren't compelled to the same level of accountability as stocks that trade on the NASDAQ or the Exchange. And part of that account-ability—or lack thereof—means that it's just more dif-ficult to get information on a lot of the companies that trade on the Pink Sheets. They're not required to share as much information and so, in a lot of cases, they don't.

To my dismay, this seemed to be the case with Bray-don's company. Dismay because, from what I'd seen, there was no reason for him to have been trading on the Pink Sheets in the first place. From what I knew, Gauthier Fine Foods was a real company with a strong product line and good financials. Granted—and as I was beginning to realize—I didn't know a lot. But the profile didn't fit with the way things were as I understood them.

One thing was suddenly amazingly clear to me: Jessica's instincts might just have been right. Perhaps she did, after all, have cause for concern.

Six

It had been one thing to think about taking Old Stinky—now *my* Old Stinky—for a cruise around Stanley Park when the thought was an abstract. Me sitting in Braydon's apartment—suddenly wanting to be *out* of Braydon's apartment—and thinking about being at the wheel of this old dream of a car. Standing there looking at her, I realized it was going to be a different proposition altogether.

First of all, though, I gasped at her new beauty. I remembered the charming little rust bucket Braydon and I had found, how he'd exclaimed at her lines, and at the hint of blue he could see beneath the rust.

"Imagine it, Madeline." His enthusiasm was a catchy thing. We were, perhaps, a block from the ocean. Mid-July on the Jersey shore—is that a song?—warmth on my shoulders, sunshine on his hair.

"Close your eyes and imagine what this car could look like. *Will* look like. A little sky-blue cloud scudding along the highway. Still have your eyes closed? Good. Now, see me in the driver's seat, you beside me, shotgun. And you're wearing that dress I like so much—the paisley one?—and you've a hat on your head, but the wind keeps fighting you for it. And you laugh. Oh, you laugh! While you hold the hat to your head."

I remember opening my eyes and looking at him like he was mad, but with a smile on my face. "You're crazy," I'd said.

He'd nodded. "Yes. Of course I am. Now close your eyes again."

I did so, obediently. And I can almost feel the kiss of the sun on my face as I think of it, all these years later. And the flutter of something warm in my heart.

"There's a picnic basket in the trunk."

"Who packed it?" I asked, my eyes still squeezed tightly shut, enjoying the game.

"Who do you think?"

"Okay. That's good. As long as it wasn't me."

"No Spam sandwiches and rice cakes, sweetheart."

"So where are we going on our picnic?"

And so on. What was I then? Twenty-four, perhaps? Twenty-five? I had all the time in the world. Well, right that second I did. Right that day. The markets were closed. I remember that clearly, as well.

At any rate, the game was not to be resisted. Braydon had made me see it. Really, he'd had me with the little blue cloud. And now here it was, just as he'd said. Our dream was mine to drive. But I'd forgotten one very salient thing. Something that came home to me with a thud now that I stood next to her and contemplated actually taking her out for a spin: our little blue cloud was right-hand drive. And something else came back to me, as well: the last time I'd driven in this car, things had ended rather badly.

Even with Braydon and Curt's ridiculous race pushed out of my mind, the right-hand drive seemed, for a few minutes at least, quite insurmountable. I'd been *in* right-hand drive cars before, of course. Aside from the times I'd driven in this very car with Braydon, I'd been a passenger in right-hand drive cars in the U.K., where everyone else is doing it, too. But I'd never *driven* a right-hand drive car. And if I'd ever thought about doing it, I'd never thought about doing it in North America, where all the other drivers are sitting on the left side of the car.

So, you think, what's the big deal? Left-hand drive? Right-hand drive? The principles are the same, right? Well…sorta. Except for most of my life and all of my personal driving history and training, when I'd sat in the driver's seat, I'd sat on the left side of the car. That's what my brain was geared for. Plus, to complicate things further, the Sunbeam Alpine is the windiest-in-your-face kind of wind-in-your-face sports car and, therefore, it is, of course, a stick. And I can handle a manual transmission just fine, thank you very much. My dad made sure all his daughters could drive a stick as soon as they were old enough to drive at all. He reasoned that, if a pesky boyfriend was doing some cruising-time bothering, he wanted *his* little girls to be able to take the beast's car and drive herself home, no matter what. (Practical man, my dad.) But I was conditioned to shift with my right hand while sitting on the left side of the car. Even contemplating doing it from the right-hand side gave me something like the vapors. It was a whole new thing.

And so I sat there in the underground car park for a while—probably not a long while, but it certainly felt that way. I sat there in the little blue cloud formerly known as Old Stinky and thought about the fact that it would probably be a pretty simple matter for me to go and find myself a rental.

While I sat, I admired Braydon's work. Or, more probably, the work he'd had done. Old Stinky truly was no more, inside and out. The car was, as they say, in showroom condition. The leather seats and dashboard gleamed with health and vitality, the carpeting was perfect, the gearshift knob was a gleaming blob of chrome but for the Sunbeam logo on its crown. I stopped then and thought about what that meant and why a logo seemed inappropriate here.

"The shift pattern," I groaned. Modern cars have a shift pattern printed on the gearshift knob. At least, sensible ones do. This was something else I'd have to figure out on my own. And I was practically in downtown Vancouver. On a weekday. It would be nothing like L.A. traffic, but it was traffic, nonetheless. And it was a pretty good bet that I'd be a bit of a hazard at least for a while.

I was almost disappointed when I turned the key in the ignition and the car purred painlessly to life. A pleasantly throaty little "grrr." It would have made things a lot easier if the car hadn't started and I'd been forced to go out and rent one.

While Old Stinky idled and with the clutch pushed in, I played with the gearshift, determining where all four gears plus reverse were located. With that out of the way, I inched the Sunbeam out of its slot, feeling an almost uncontrollable wave of oddness as the car started to move with no one sitting where I knew a driver was *supposed* to sit.

Once I was in traffic and had managed a few blocks without either stalling the car or colliding with anything, I started to relax a little. Maybe this wouldn't be so bad. Then, stopped at a light in four-lane traffic, I looked out the driver's window to see the driver of the next car looking in at me from just a few inches away. The disorientation caused my stomach to do a mean backflip, and I refocused on the road and all my current distractions.

By the time I got to the other side of downtown and the entrance to Stanley Park, I felt like I had everything under control. I didn't think I'd ever be truly comfortable driving on the "wrong" side of the car, but at least it looked like I'd be able to manage it without killing anyone or myself.

Stanley Park is amazing, a thousand acres of near virgin timber adjacent to the downtown core and mostly surrounded by water. The park hosts a world-class aquarium, several venues for outdoor theater, a yacht club, a rowing club, a cricket club, a lighthouse, a lake with ducks and geese and maybe beavers, some really great restaurants, several amazing gardens and historic markers, a suspension bridge, a mounted police force and so many miles of trails you could get lost in the forest without ever being out of hearing distance of the city.

None of this was what I was here for today. My twofold purpose was the Stanley Park Drive, the one-way road that circumnavigates the park's boundaries. My purpose was twofold because, on one of our trips to Vancouver, Braydon had taken me on the park drive and I'd loved it. I wanted to see it again now with eyes that were older and more appreciative of natural beauty. My larger purpose was more immediate: the park drive would afford me a more or less peaceful space and pace in which to get used to the peskier aspects of the new Old Stinky.

And the park was beautiful. I stopped a few times to get out of the car and approach the seawall, a Vancouver feature I'd forgotten and that had been enhanced since my last trip. This was thirty-something kilometers—I don't do conversions well and Canadians think metrically, but I know it translates to miles and miles and miles: something like eighteen of them—of paved roadway at the water's edge suitable for walking and biking (but not driving) that stretches from Stanley Park to the other side of the water and the city where the University of British Columbia has its lovely campus.

At various points on the Stanley Park Drive the seawall was accessible from a car park, and so I stopped and parked and walked short stretches, enjoying the sea air and the ocean vistas so different from those I enjoyed of the same ocean back in Malibu.

After successfully negotiating the park, I felt a little more confident about the car. More as though I was approaching some sort of uneasy partnership with it. Confident enough, in fact, that when I cruised up Robson Street toward the Burrard Street Bridge, and a parking space opened up right in front of me, I grabbed it instantly, pleased to find myself safely parked in the middle of one of the best shopping areas in the city.

And I needed to shop. I'd lost most of my clothes in the same other story that had claimed my apartment in Malibu—the one that landed me in Tyler and Tasya's guest room. I'd been replacing things slowly, but an hour on Robson Street would help put things right in that department.

I am not a clotheshorse. Never have been. But there is something pleasing about power shopping. Something that pleases me about having made several successful purchases and being laden with heavy bags from elegant stores to prove it.

Shopping, I think, appeals to the hunter-gatherer instinct in me. My ancestors scraped animal hides and laced their clothes together with leather thongs. But do you think they would have done that if they'd had Mastercard back then? I'm thinking maybe not.

"Who died?" The salesclerk was so tiny and delicately built, I wouldn't have credited her with the baldness of the question. Looks are almost always deceiving. I'd bought a Marc Jacobs suit—pants and jacket, severely discounted but still expensive—at another store and had pulled out the jacket to hold against the black of the blouse I was considering purchasing to wear with it to Braydon's funeral.

"Very severe." The pewter-skinned clerk nodded approvingly, her carefully painted lips puckering into a smirk of approval.

"I'm going to a funeral," I'd explained needlessly. Needlessly because perfectly coiffed sales assistants in expensive stores almost never care about details like that. And maybe I was right, but it prompted the girl's question, anyway.

"My ex-husband," I said, almost without thinking about it, wondering if black on black on black might be a little *too* much. "He's a chef here in town, actually. Braydon Gauthier."

"Get out," the clerk said, surprising me with her easy recognition of his name. "And you're his ex-wife? Too weird."

"What's weird about it?" I asked, bridling slightly.

"Not the ex-wife part." I noticed with interest that she'd dropped the cool and disinterested facade and was regarding me with frank curiosity. "It's just that I'd heard so much about Braydon Gauthier for so long. And seen him on TV. Then I meet him. Then I hear he's dead the very next day. Now I meet you. Weird, right? Like we're connected somehow."

I nodded agreement but I was still digesting her words.

"Where did you meet him?"

"At Au Bar." I knew nothing about Vancouver nightlife, but I was pretty sure that with a name like Au Bar, it was bound to be a club.

"Who was he there with?"

"He didn't seem to be with anyone," the girl said thoughtfully. "Not that I noticed, anyway. But he left with my friend Desiree."

"He left with her? Like…you know…*left?*" I asked. The girl nodded. "But he's married." The words felt naive even as they came out of my head.

She gave me the kind of smug, superior look that can only be properly handled by women between the ages of sixteen and twenty-four. "I think I might have known that. But let me tell you, he wasn't acting very married."

"What do you mean?"

"He was pretty much partying. Him and Dez were dancing. And he was buying Möet like it was going out of style."

"He was drunk?" Women *and* booze? Could we be talking about the same Braydon Gauthier?

She gave a sort of half nod. "I guess. I didn't really think about it. He had some E, too."

"E?"

That look again. "Ecstasy," she said carefully, as though fearful she'd have to explain the drug, as well. "He was pretty free with it at our table."

"And the next day he was dead?"

Her eyes narrowed suspiciously. "Not the very next day. What are you trying to say? Desiree had nothing to do with it. He killed himself in his restaurant, right? The night *after* we met him. They said on the news that they found his body in the morning. She was pretty broken up about it, too. She kinda thought they might be going places."

As I headed the car toward the Burnaby funeral home I couldn't get the girl's words out of my mind. So much about what she'd said didn't feel right. Braydon the heavy partier. Braydon the adulterer. Braydon the user of recreational drugs. None of that fit with my picture of the man.

When I thought about it, though, maybe the pieces the girl in the store had unwittingly given me shouldn't have surprised me that deeply. The Braydon Gauthier the woman described sounded like a man about to self-destruct. Twenty-four hours later, he was dead.

Seven

Maybe because of my history with Braydon—and despite what I'd recently learned about him—I'd expected his funeral to be a quiet family affair. Private. Small. Understated. What I hadn't taken into account was his celebrity. With a smattering of local and national news crews and a small phalanx of fans standing outside the funeral home, Braydon's send-off was a minor media event.

Arriving a little early, I found the mission-style building awash in a small throng. You could tell Braydon's fans from the invited guests at a glance.

The guests were dressed as though, well, as though they were going to a funeral.

Behind the reporters, the mostly middle-aged female fans stood outside the building in casual clothes, watching with somber yet somehow expectant expressions.

What, I wondered, did they hope to see? What would they accomplish by being here? When I thought about it, though, I realized I already knew. It seemed likely that, to most of these women, Braydon had seemed like a friend. Someone who visited them in their homes five days a week, a couple of times on Sunday if the food station was showing reruns. Most of these women probably owned at least one of Bray's books. Perhaps they sometimes picked *Haute at Home* up at the supermarket after the office and, on special occasions, prevailed on loved ones to take them to one of Braydon's restaurants.

The scene wasn't a circus. Braydon hadn't been a rock star, after all. But he *had* been loved. I could see that in the sad and patient faces of the women who watched us enter the funeral home.

I wondered if Braydon would have been warmed or irritated to see this gentle display. Then realized that, most likely, it would have depended on his mood. Something I'd forgotten until now. Something that all of this proximity to Braydon's life was, no doubt, bringing back.

Braydon could, I remembered, be extremely outgoing or intensely private, and both things might come within a half an hour of each other with little or no warning. I pushed the thought away. I was here, after all, to help celebrate his life. Unbidden thoughts of character traits I *hadn't* enjoyed were unwelcome right now. Out of place.

Though the mission style of the architecture was oddly incongruous here at the heart of the rain forest, the old building had been gracefully designed and lovingly maintained. An archway led to a corridor where an oversize entry door opened onto a huge foyer. Beyond the doors, the wood floors gleamed warmly and large antique furniture brought the huge room back to scale.

There was a faint taste of must in the air—oddly not unpleasant—and the barest hint of incense, but above both of those the most present odor was that of flowers. Roses, gardenias, lilies and lilies and lilies. Why, I wondered, are death and flowers so strangely linked? The life of the flowers, perhaps, a metaphor for the fleeting beauty of human life? Or is it the mere prettification of something that most of us don't care to think about?

Thoughts like these were pushed away when I caught sight of a carefully lettered sign outside the open door of the largest of three chapels in the funeral home. "Gauthier Funeral," it announced in appropriately somber letters. I entered on a wave of trepidation that vanished at the sight of Braydon's casket, front and center in the big, tastefully decorated room.

Was there music playing in the room? I think there must have been. Something quiet. Classical, maybe. Or traditional jazz. I've thought about it since and I can't recall. That bothers me on some level; I'm usually so good about details. I can't remember any of it. Not who was in the chapel when I entered and, of course, not what they were wearing. It was as though, for me, the black-and-chrome casket, the legs that supported it cleverly disguised by still more flowers, was the only thing in the room.

That's not strictly true. The casket itself wasn't what focused my attention, despite its jolting finish. But the contents of the casket. That was a different matter.

I knew from occasionally catching his television shows that, in the ten years since I'd last seen him, Braydon had aged, though not badly. A decade will do that. As I slowly approached the casket, though, I could see that in some odd way, death had erased those years.

Carefully composed in embalmed slumber, his head resting on a silken steel-colored pillow, Braydon looked eerily Braydonlike. Eerily because it was a pose I remembered well. My husband's profile at rest, his lashes thick on his cheeks. Too thick. The kind of lashes women have to work at and that men are often given without asking or even noticing.

I stood at first a few feet from the casket, thoughts and memories coming so quickly I was choked by them. Choked helpless.

"Do you really have to go to the office today?" He hadn't opened his eyes, just heard the alarm and felt my response to it. I was still in bed, but I wouldn't be for long.

It was not yet light out. Most people would have said it was still the middle of the night.

"You know I do." The floor was cold on my feet; I remember that, as well. It wouldn't have taken much for me to crawl back into bed. It would have taken too much.

I looked over at him then—I don't know why this is so clear to me. I looked over at him and saw him lying there peacefully, as though he slept, though I knew he didn't. It was three o'clock in the morning and I hadn't turned the bedside lamp on with the alarm, but the city light that seeped into the room illuminated him clearly. His eyes were closed, his breathing regular, his features that morning beautiful in his peaceful partial slumber. I reached out, traced the contour of his nose with the tip of my finger, allowed my hand to trail along his lips. I smiled when he kissed my fingertips.

"Would Sal really care if you were late one single morning?"

It was early in our relationship. If I heard the slight whine in Braydon's voice, I ignored it. Instead I took back my hand.

"Sal would care. And it's not that kind of job, Braydon. You know that. It's not like I'm a secretary or I sell stereos, and someone will cover. People *depend* on me."

"The world will sink if you don't go in, is that it?" I'd taken my hand back and begun preparations for my day. Braydon had gone back to peaceful mode, his eyes closed, his head flat on the pillow. Only the slight tic at the corner of his eye betrayed his irritation.

"I'm not saying I'm indispensable, Bray. I'm saying I'm trying to *make* myself indispensable. I *want* to be indispensable. Scratch that—I *need* to be, if I'm going to get what I want."

"You'll get it," Braydon said as he rolled from his

back onto his side. The side that didn't face me. I tried not to hear the cold in his voice. "You'll get it because you'll do whatever it takes."

A human touch brought me back into the present, to Braydon's funeral. An arm draped softly round my shoulders. "He looks unbearably alive like that, doesn't he?" It was Anne-Marie, in a dress with a color that could only be described as ashes of roses. Under her makeup, her face matched the rose-gray of her dress. She looked drawn and tired, like she was coping the way a dog copes with being kenneled. Like her heart would break. Like she'd get through all this in the end. Like she just didn't have any options but was dealing with them, anyway.

"He really does, Anne-Marie. I...I kind of hate that."

"I know what you mean," she agreed.

"Like, do you remember the little eye thing he had when he was annoyed? I think...I think I was just looking for that. Silly, isn't it?"

Anne-Marie shook her head. "Not silly, no. Just part of everything, I guess. Like, I think I expect to see his chest rise and fall. Seeing him here like this, I want to put my hand over his heart. Stupid tradition," she said, indicating the open casket, her emotion heartbreakingly close to the surface.

Now it was my turn to circle her shoulders with my arm. "It's for us, sweetie," I said soothingly. "Not for him. You know that. It's meant to show us that it's really true, so we can deal with it. So we can go on."

She turned and looked straight into my eyes for a moment, and what I saw there was wrenching. A pain so raw and sincere, I had to look away. I realized, then, that I had no idea what she was going through. Thankfully. I thought of my sisters, Miranda and Meagan. Losing them was something I couldn't bring myself to think about. Anne-Marie didn't have that choice.

"I'm going to go and make sure Mother is all right," she said after she'd pulled herself back from the brink of tears. She indicated the place at the front of the room where Jessica had taken a seat. Dressed in a plain black skirt and suit jacket, the frill of her white blouse accentuating her pallor, Jessica looked even tinier than usual. She sat primly, hands folded on her lap. I got the impression that the only thing holding her together was self-discipline. That she felt as though if she relaxed her guard for even a second, it would all come apart.

Robert sat next to her, nattily dressed in a dark suit and tie, closely shaved and with his hair neatly combed. His expression looked unaltered from the day before. He was like a Robert mannequin, I thought. He seemed almost to not be there at all. A neatly dressed woman with severely styled hair sat right behind him. I guessed that this was Robert's private nurse, nearby in case the emotion of the day became too much for her patient, though I doubted he was currently in a place where emotion could touch him.

The chapel was beginning to fill. There were a lot of people and, as I took a seat, I avoided looking at the

black-and-chrome oblong that dominated the front of
the room, instead surveying the space and scanning the
crowd lightly for familiar faces.

The walls were dark and oak. Somber. The ceiling
was coffered—more oak there—and the lights sus-
pended from it were in the arts and crafts style. On one
side of the room, windows faced out onto a private
garden. The curtains were drawn back and I could make
out mature trees and multicolored flowers beyond. It
was a pleasant room with a pleasant view. Inappropriate to my mood. And inappropriate to the situation.
But lovely.

It was a large room that I gauged would seat two
hundred, and the way the room was filling, we'd hit
that number easily on this day. Mostly beautiful people,
dressed in clothing both somber and expensive; we
might have been on a location shoot for a movie about
a successful man cut down in his prime. "Cue the
mother. Cue the ex-wife. Bring on the mourners. Right.
Quiet on the set, please! And *action*."

There were several in-laws and cousins and other
family members I vaguely remembered but would have
had a hard time naming. Though I'd never met her
before, as she moved through the crowd to take the seat
that had been saved for her, I had no such trouble with
Mimi. She wore black on black, as did I, but her dress
looked like couture and she wore a small hat with a
little veil like a 1940s movie widow. Though the veil
obscured her face, it did so only slightly, and I could see

she was beautiful in the way that a greyhound can be beautiful: otherworldly and exotic. Perhaps warm if you got to know her, yet on the surface, anything but.

I decided that the man who held her elbow must be her brother, Doug Withers. Since this was the man Jessica was so suspicious of, I watched him closely while he took his seat.

Though Mimi looked to be in her mid to late twenties, her brother had to be a good decade older. He was almost as slender and as delicately drawn as his sibling. However, where her hair was a gold so pale it was almost white, his was sparse enough that the color was difficult to determine, though his pale eyebrows and light blue eyes made me guess that at some time his hair had been as light—and possibly as abundant— as that of his sister.

Their features were similar, as well. Though what on Mimi was a cold but delicate beauty appeared weaker in the masculine version. Something that wasn't helped by an almost total lack of chin.

I am opinionated. And I tend to make decisions— about people and situations—very quickly. Too quickly sometimes. I just can't help it. And right now, based on the teensy bit of (completely biased) information I had on him, and on his lack of chin, and the way he held his sister's elbow—as though she were a possession, not a sibling—I made a judgment now. I decided I didn't like Doug Withers, for what I admitted was no good reason at all.

When the widow took her seat, it seemed to be a sort of sign, because the service started almost as soon as she sat down. And here, finally, I became aware of the music. The Chopin seemed to swell over the room, the notes mournfully reminding any who might have forgotten what our purpose was here today.

The service made me wish I had not come. It was long and dreary and, as people spoke lovingly or admiringly or respectfully about Braydon, I felt increasingly uncomfortable. They might, I thought, have been talking about someone I didn't know at all. What had I been thinking? I wondered. What had led me to come to this celebration of the life of the man I'd divorced a decade before?

Afterward, at the cemetery adjacent to the funeral home, my discomfort didn't go away. I watched with a feeling of disconnection as they lowered the black-and-chrome box into the ground. I'd come to say goodbye, but I'd realized something back in the chapel when I'd seen those lush lashes against his cheek. I couldn't say goodbye. Braydon Gauthier was already gone.

I started out following a procession of cars from the cemetery back to Vancouver for the funeral reception, but it seemed like a long drive. I was still shaky with my skills in a right-hand drive car and, before we'd gone very many blocks, I got separated from the little convoy and became hopelessly lost.

When I saw a Starbucks sign I decided I'd rather

have a latte than a bad case of anxiety. A quiet fifteen minutes, I reasoned, would restore my sense of normalcy. It didn't, but the coffee tasted good, anyway, and I felt some of the oddness that had been creeping up on me drift away.

The reception was being held in a venerable old home just off South Granville that had long been a private club. After I got back on the road, I found the address with far less trouble than I'd anticipated. In the foyer, the concierge informed me that the Gauthier party had all of the garden level for their event, a description that was so cheery I had to suppress a shudder.

The family was in a receiving line at the entrance to a large banquet room. Robert and Jessica looked as fragile as they had earlier, though Anne-Marie seemed to have managed to quell the aura of urgent tragedy that had been with her at the funeral home, and was now back to being as forcibly cheery as she'd mostly been the day before, though I could see the redness around her eyes.

Part of Anne-Marie's apparent calm might have come from her husband. Garth stood next to her quietly, nodding to people as they passed, but I could see the hand he kept firmly on the small of his wife's back, as though he were transferring some of his blustery good energy to her. It was a simple gesture, easily overlooked, but the sight made my eyes swim ever so slightly. Love is made of and from so many things, and it takes a different shape for everyone. But this—

the reassuring hand, steadying quietly—*this* was what
sent us out to nightclubs and on blind dates and out to
dinners and movies with almost total strangers. The
thought that somewhere—maybe in the most unlikely
place—we, too, might find that special someone to
stand next to us when things are dire as well as when
they are beautiful. I did not envy Anne-Marie what she
had, but what I felt was something very like that.

Mimi stood at the head of the receiving line, with
her brother still at her elbow. When I finally approached, I did so with trepidation that had nothing to
do with Withers and his sister and everything to do with
the family I had once been part of. There was no doubt:
even though I knew some of these people and had cared
deeply about a few of them, I was the outsider now.

On hearing my name, Mimi greeted me frostily. I
didn't blame her and wasn't really sure I wouldn't have
done the same in her position. No one likes to be
reminded they weren't the first.

Doug didn't bother meeting my eyes, for no good
reason that I could see, other than he was perhaps
scanning the line behind me to see who was more important. His hand, when he offered it to me, was un-
pleasantly cold and ever so slightly limp and clammy.
I let go of it as quickly as possible, suppressing the urge
to wipe my palm on my Marc Jacobs pants.

Jessica and Anne-Marie were warm, of course.
And I'd forgotten that Anne-Marie's husband, Garth,
was as hail and hearty as his father-in-law had been

until recently. Up close I could see that not only had his hand not left its reassuring place, it moved ever so slightly, as though gently massaging the place between Anne-Marie's lower vertebrae and her coccyx, sending her strength, perhaps, and a small measure of comfort.

With the receiving line behind me, I entered the room proper, noting two tables laden with beautiful food. Grief, I've discovered, is a hungry business. And Braydon had been a professional chef; I'd had no doubt that this event would boast good eats, even if, for once, I wasn't in the mood for them.

"Appropriate, isn't it?" a man said to me, following my glance and echoing my thoughts. "Braydon would have approved of the food, I think. It looks quite wonderful."

He was perhaps four inches shorter than me, though he had the bearing of a much larger man. He held himself with a kind of rough dignity and, though he wore a suit of an excellent cut, I got the feeling that this wasn't his usual uniform.

"Madeline Carter," I said, sticking out my hand.

His grip was firm, but not overly so. You could tell that a show of his superior strength would have embarrassed him. "Simon Carrier," he said, matching my businesslike tone. "I am…was…Braydon's producer."

I sort of think funerals are barbaric and archaic, but Simon's lapse reminded me of one important purpose for the ritual: it helps place the deceased firmly into the realm where they now belong. It helps move them from the now into the then. I could see that Simon was just working through this.

"His producer?" I asked.

"Right. I produced his television shows. How did you know him?"

And how was it, I wondered, that no matter where I went these days, I always seemed to end up talking to people who were somehow in show business? I said none of this.

"We were old friends," I said, feeling at first that this was enough. Simon's face told me it wasn't, and I decided to come clean. "I am his ex-wife."

Simon registered a sort of "aha" look. I could tell he'd heard about me, if only in the abstract. Not a feeling I was entirely comfortable with.

"You live in New York, don't you?" he asked politely.

"Los Angeles these days, actually. I did live in New York, though, when Braydon and I were together."

"That's what I thought. You know, I *have* heard about you," he said.

"Don't tell me."

He smiled. "No. Seriously. But it was all good things."

"Ha!" I said, only half joking.

A small group of people greeted Simon then. People he worked with, I gathered, in the television end of things. He introduced me, but I knew I had no hope of remembering their names, so I didn't try very hard. A girl with severely cut hair and black glasses to match, who carried a purse shaped like an alligator. A gangly young man whose suit jacket cleared his wrists by a good two inches. Another man whose girth seemed to match his height precisely, and who took in a great wheeze of air with every second breath.

After they'd moved on, Simon explained that they did most of the editing and computer graphics for Braydon's television work.

"Where did you do the show?" I asked, unsurprised that the trio were computer types. They'd worn their geekiness like a badge.

"We have a studio at Gauthier Fine Foods. It was one of the reasons Braydon wanted the new building." New building? This was another thing I hadn't known. "You know how he was," he said. I nodded, though I wasn't sure anymore that I did. "He wanted as much control of the entire operation as possible. Having everything under one roof helped with that. He seemed to think it did, anyway."

"Who owns the shows?" I asked, thinking I might as well use this time to start my research for Jessica.

"Gauthier Fine Foods," Simon said. "I think the company owned everything. Braydon used to joke that they owned his soul." He smiled at his comment, but the smile washed away as quickly as it had come when he realized what he'd said. I could see his pallor heighten under his tan.

"Nice to have met you, Madeline. I think I'll go off and stand in a corner for a while before I start chewing on my other shoe."

I put up a hand to stop him. Simon had looked mortified, yet what he'd said wasn't really so bad. I might have stopped him, too. But just then I noticed a woman across the room. A woman no one would have missed in any crowd. And she was staring right at me.

On first contact I didn't like Sonya Foy. It wasn't just how she looked, though that could have been part of it. She was scary beautiful. Magazine girl beautiful, with delicate little features, a porcelain complexion and a shimmery curtain of blue-black hair that hung almost to her teeny waist. Seriously, who wouldn't hate someone who looked like that?

Her suit was a pale maroon and beautifully cut, but there was a childishness in that cut. If I looked at her closely, I could see she was well past thirty, but there was something girlish about her, something she knew about and wanted to exploit. The way she did her makeup and the choices she'd made about her clothes told me that. It would have been easy to be fooled. Easy to think she was closer to twenty than forty, but there was something in her eyes. Whatever the rest of Sonya Foy's demeanor and dress said about her, the eyes gave her away.

She was predatory; I knew that the second I saw her. Predatory like a sleek but hungry cat. And from that first glance across the room, all of my instincts shouted a warning. And I tend to listen to my instincts. It was curiosity that sent me in her direction.

"So you're the ex-wife," she said when I introduced myself, something inexplicable in her tone. It would have been an inappropriate enough comment at the best of times, but considering where we were, it was, to me, unthinkable. So much for the politeness of Canadians.

"I am," I said pleasantly enough, though Braydon, had he been there, would have understood the tone and crossed to the other side of the room.

"Hmm," she said, fingering the wineglass in her hand thoughtfully, "I can't say I expected to see *you* here."

"I hadn't expected to see *you* here, either," I said levelly.

She looked me straight in the eyes then, and I could see that my assessment had been right: maybe almost forty, but workin' it. But I saw something that surprised me, as well—my barb had hit an unexpected target. She was suddenly uncomfortable, though I had no idea why.

"What do you mean?" she said, confirming my guess. "I didn't know you and Braydon were still in touch."

"You didn't?" I said, as naturally as possible because, of course, we hadn't been. But did she have a reason to know that? I didn't think so.

She confirmed my guess by shaking her head.

"Ah," I said.

She narrowed her eyes at me, something that made the facade of deep youth fall still further. "You're a broker, aren't you?"

I nodded, but said, "I was."

"Ah," she said back. I got the feeling she wanted to

ask something but couldn't figure out how to redirect the conversation. I took it out of her hands.

"Braydon never mentioned you," I said flatly. I knew it contradicted what I'd said before, but that was partly my intent. That instinct again. I wanted to keep her off balance. And it wasn't a lie. He never had. I didn't bother telling her I hadn't spoken with him in almost a decade.

Her eyes widened then, though if she was surprised by my words, she covered it well.

She shrugged. "To be honest, he didn't talk much about you, either."

This did not surprise me. Nor, really, did I care. I shrugged back. "Tell me how you knew him."

Her hand fluttered to the collar of her blouse, right above the plunging promise of her melonlike breasts. I saw her gently edge aside the single strand of pearls she wore to touch her collarbone delicately. It was, I could tell, a nervous gesture. "Oh," she said finally, her free hand described a dismissive motion. "You know."

I shook my head. I did not.

"We had some business dealings. Nothing very official."

Business dealings. I couldn't imagine. Yet, unless he'd changed a great deal since I knew him, she wasn't his physical type—all those breasts—and she didn't look like a candidate for a casual affair. Business dealings.

"Were you his broker?" I hazarded. I didn't really believe she was. And yet there was something about her I recognized. Not about the her that she was, but the her she represented. It was almost as if she gave off an odor, which admittedly, she did not. But I suddenly realized that looking at Sonya Foy was almost like looking into some weird magical mirror. As though, when I looked at it, an evil me was looking back.

"No. Not a broker." That dismissive gesture again. "Nothing like that."

And then I knew. Something in her tone or maybe in the cadence of her denial. "You're a promoter," I said quietly, willing my voice to not make it sound like an accusation. "You were *his* promoter."

Her eyes widened then. I saw it: a direct hit, even while her mouth formed words of denial. It didn't matter. I knew what I'd seen. "I can't imagine why you'd think that, Madeline. It was such a successful company. Why would they even need a promoter?" Her words held no weight with me. But for one.

"Was," I said.

"Excuse me?" I could tell she didn't see what I was getting at.

"You said *was*. Yet it is, of course. The company still *is*, even with Braydon gone."

"I didn't say *was*."

"Of course you did. That's exactly what you said. What did you mean?" I felt as if there was something important I wasn't grasping. Something just out of my reach.

"I didn't mean anything." She caught herself, though I wondered if she even noticed she'd also taken a half step back, away from me. "Whatever you thought you heard, you were mistaken. Listen, it was lovely talking to you, lovely finally to meet, but this has been very tiring for me. I'm afraid I have to go now." And without waiting for my answer, or even checking my response, she took herself off. The receiving line had dispersed, and Doug was walking among the guests and chatting solemnly. I watched as Sonya caught his eye and motioned him over to her. I saw her whisper something to him quickly, then leave the building, cross the parking lot and get behind the wheel of a car: something dark and expensive looking, though I wouldn't have been able to identify it beyond that.

After she was gone, I secured a glass of white wine and found a quiet corner. I felt as though I needed to think, and the mourning going on all around me was getting in the way of that.

Something significant had just happened. I was just having a hard time determining exactly what it was.

"Madeline?" The voice brought me back with a thud. "Madeline, is that actually you?"

I had to look at the face for perhaps a full minute before its identity came clear. In part, the Vandyke beard threw me. That and time. I knew it was a face I hadn't seen in a while.

He was perhaps forty-five, with a full, dark head of hair—and that funny little beard. His eyes were the color of horse chestnuts: warm and liquid and, right this moment, welcoming. The eyes did it.

"Curt!" I said finally. He was so out of place to me here. So far from Chelsea and Bed-Stuy. "It's *so* good to see you."

It's possible that the last of these words didn't get uttered aloud, because I found myself enveloped in a sturdy hug. Then he pushed me away from him, his hands still on my upper arms, and looked square into my face. "Gosh, girl, but you look good! Sight for sore eyes and all of that." I waved his comments aside with a smile, but he said, "I'm *serious*. And I can't decide if it's because you look so great or because it's so great to see you, or both. Maybe that's it, then—both."

"I've got to say, Curt, that I'm flat out amazed to see you here."

"You didn't know I worked for Braydon? He never mentioned it?"

"It's not like we stayed close, Braydon and I. It's not like we even stayed in touch."

"I know." He nodded. "Braydon would talk about you sometimes. Before…"

"Before Mimi?"

Another nod.

"Ah, well," I said. "I'm glad he found someone."

"Did you?" he asked quietly.

"Curt!" I replied. "This is hardly the place to talk about my love life. Seriously. But I want to know— what are *you* doing here? Did you guys keep in touch all this time?"

"We didn't for a long time. Then, when everything

really got going, he contacted me. His timing was great for both of us. I'd had to close Quiver and I wasn't sure what I was going to do with myself."

"You had to close Quiver? That's so sad, Curt. It was such a great place."

"Honestly? I think it was a little ahead of its time. And it was never the same once Braydon left. But, yeah, it was sad. I have a great gig with Braydon, though." He seemed to pull himself up when he remembered where he was, and drop a mask of mourning over his face. "Until recently, of course. We've all been very sad since Braydon died."

"You said you worked for Braydon, but what do you do?"

"Braydon hired me. But I work for Gauthier Fine Foods. And I run the restaurant," he said. "I run all the restaurants."

And this, I realized, made perfect sense, after a fashion. Curt had been the lackadaisical owner of Quiver, the good but unambitious restaurant Braydon had cooked at in Bedford-Stuyvesant. Curt had been confident that the beautiful nineteenth-century architecture of the Brooklyn neighborhood, as well as its relative proximity to more pricey Manhattan, was sure to bring gentrification. He'd been right, too. Though not in time, it seemed, to save Quiver.

Curt had been a frequent visitor to our apartment on the nights when both men were off work at the same time. In the blink of an eye it came back to me. Nights when I'd gone to bed—because my rising time came early—and the two of them would sit in our living room, glasses of red wine and excellent snacks between them, the sound of their quiet chatting lulling me to sleep, short bursts of laughter occasionally pulling me back.

They were weaving dreams together, I knew. Plotting and planning beautiful restaurants where people lined up for food that would be remarked upon. Another dream of Braydon's that had come true, I realized.

I smiled at Curt now. "That's so right. That's so perfect. I always knew you two would make beautiful restaurants together. But what happened to Quiver?"

"Ah, it's a tough business. And we were right about Bed-Stuy, Madeline."

"Yes, I know," I said. "I thought about you guys when I was at a gallery opening there a few years ago."

He smiled back, but I saw the cloud fall across his face. "Yes, we were right," he said, only a touch of bitterness in his voice. "But not soon enough." A second later, though, I wondered if I'd been right about the bitterness, because he sounded like his usual cheery self. "Never mind any of that now, Madeline. It's been too long since I saw you. Please tell me you'll come by the restaurant while you're in Vancouver. I'll give you some wonderful food. You look starving."

I laughed at that, because it was something Curt had always said about me. That I looked hungry. And, of course, he'd been right. I'd been hungry: for money, for status, but mostly for success. A lot of the time, I'd also been hungry for food, simply because I'd often been too busy to stop and eat.

"That sounds lovely, Curt. Is the restaurant even open right now?"

"Not today. All of the Gauthier Fine Foods restaurants are closed today. In memory of Braydon. But you know the industry—tomorrow it's business as usual. And it's a sad thing, but half our customers won't even make the connection. You know how it goes."

I nodded. It was true. "Well, I think I have a busy day tomorrow. But maybe I'll stop by WhyVeeAre and look in around dinnertime? I'd love a tour, Curt. I'd love to see the restaurant that you and Braydon built."

"Braydon built it," Curt corrected. "I just helped him keep it all together. But tomorrow evening would work very well for me. I'll be cruising in and out pretty much all day. When you get there, tell the maître d' who you are. I'll make sure you're expected. And if I'm not there, he'll know how to reach me."

After a while Curt excused himself, saying there were a few people he needed to touch bases with. Almost as soon as he'd moved off, I found Simon Carrier at my elbow, as though he'd been lurking nearby waiting for the chance to come back and chat with me again.

"I decided I'd had sufficient self-flagellation," he told me solemnly, but with a light in his eyes.

"That's good," I said, returning his smile. There was a warmth and openness about him that I liked.

"And I thought, since you probably don't know many people here, I'd come and keep you company for a bit."

"I know Curt. He and Braydon were friends back in New York. Do you know him?"

"I do." He nodded. "Though not particularly well. Our branches of the business don't have much overlap. Who else do you know?"

"Well, the family, of course."

He nodded. "Of course."

"But it's a bit awkward," I admitted. "Old wife, new wife, you know."

"I can imagine." He cast his voice lower. "Mimi's not one to be overshadowed."

I looked at him closely to see if he was teasing me and decided that perhaps he was.

"Anyone you want to meet?" he asked. "I can introduce you."

"Not really. It's not that kind of thing, is it?"

"Perhaps not," he agreed.

"I'm really wondering if it was a good idea for me to even come," I said with more candor than I'd intended.

Simon smiled at me and touched my hand, a gesture I knew was meant to be reassuring. "Of course it was, Madeline. Never mind the politics. It's not about that, not really. I mean, that may be an aspect of what you feel here—how could it not be?—but remember the spirit in which you came."

I looked at him quizzically. "I don't understand."

"'Course you do," he said evenly. "It's Braydon. And it's the same reason I'm here. You came to say goodbye."

Eight

Despite what Simon told me, I probably did not stay as long at the reception for Braydon's funeral as I should have. Appearances, you know. And I'd come such a long way, too. Presumably, everyone in attendance had known and loved Bray. And I loved him, too—or at least, I'd once imagined this to be the case—but it suddenly seemed so long ago. A time out of memory. A time out of time.

After chatting amicably with Simon for a while, I fended off a couple of well-meaning Gauthier cousins, then decided I'd had enough. Whatever I'd come for, it wasn't here.

Before I left, I sought out Jessica to give her my respects and let her know I was going.

"Thank you for coming, Madeline," she said quietly. Mimi was nearby and I wondered if Jessica was trying to avoid having her daughter-in-law overhear. "I think it would have meant a great deal to Bray that you made the effort." She dropped her voice further. "And thank you for what you've agreed to do. Let me know how it goes."

I told her I would, then saw myself out, trying not to think about how good it felt to be out in the air as I walked back to my car. How good it felt just to be alive.

On my way back to Braydon's apartment, I drove past Gauthier Fine Foods. It was after hours and the building was closed, but it was still impressive. Six stories high, all steel and glass and everything bright and shiny and new. In an area dominated by very old buildings it stood out in a weird sort of relief.

I sat in my car—in Old Stinky—in the empty parking lot and looked up at this imposing structure and thought about our—mine and Braydon's—third-floor walk-up in Chelsea.

We'd looked at a lot of apartments, but Braydon had been insistent on taking the one we eventually lived in. As I sat in the car in Vancouver, craning my neck up to look at the office building Braydon had created to house his company, I thought about him admiring our apartment's original moldings and the chipped but still graceful pedestal sink in the bathroom.

"I dunno, Bray," I'd said when we went to see it. "It sorta looks like the Cramdens should live here."

He'd laughed at that, but said, "I know. But that's the beauty, Mad. It's the real thing—the real New York. It's just as it should be, don't you think?"

And the thing was, it hadn't really mattered that

much to me. It was quite close to my office and in a neighborhood that wasn't bad and that was getting better and, in the end, I'd given in without much of a struggle. Don't Sweat the Small Stuff was my motto then. Maybe I already knew that some of the big stuff would be, for me, insurmountable.

But how could *that* man—enthusiast of original hardwood floor and supporter of archaic turquoise tile—how could he have commissioned this…this—I struggled for the word, trying to avoid *monstrosity*, but coming back there again and again nonetheless.

I was still thinking about that as I continued my drive, pulled the car into its stall underground and let myself into Braydon's ultramodern apartment, which just intensified the feeling.

I was so deep in thought that when my purse started making a loud, demanding shriek, I dropped it on the floor. I recovered quickly, though. It was the cell phone's voice, so infrequently used so far that I hadn't had time to acclimatize myself to its insistent little bleats.

"Hello," I said into it cautiously, almost expecting the call to be for someone else.

"Madeline? Are you okay? You sound funny."

"Gosh, Emily, *you* don't sound funny at all. It's great to hear your voice."

"Guess why I'm calling," she demanded.

I smiled into the phone. It was amazingly good to hear a friendly voice. A voice from my real—my current—life. I was surprised to find that I suddenly missed L.A.

"There's a play opening on Melrose and you wanted to see if I could make it?" I said, taking a complete shot in the dark.

"Nope. Not even close. Try again."

"Umm… Okay. You're thinking about putting in a hot tub?"

"Where? Where would I put a hot tub? That's just dumb. Another try, please."

"Clearly, I'm going to need a hint of some type. Start with something simple."

"Okay, here's a hint," she said. Giving up the game. "I'm coming to Vancouver."

"Get out. When?"

"Tomorrow morning. You got time to hear how this happened? It's a good story."

"Sure. Shoot." While Emily and I talked, I directed myself to a nearby chair. It was a midcentury modern metal-and-leather contraption that looked decidedly uncomfortable, but when I dropped into it, I found it fitted me nicely.

"Well, you know that feature I was working on in Prague? We're in postproduction now and we needed some ADR with the female lead."

"ADR?" I'd been picking up movie lingo at an alarming rate since moving to L.A. and finding myself ankle deep in film people, but this was a new one on me.

"Additional dialogue recording," Emily supplied. "It's stuff you record after you've finished filming to fluff up the dialogue."

"Like voice-overs?"

"No, not really. Like when there's a shot of one actor, but you hear another actor talking? Stuff like that. Or, sometimes, the sound levels were off in the first place and you need to get it right. Actually, with this one, there's some of both."

"So...you're going back to Prague by way of Vancouver?"

"No. *That* would be funny. But that's not it. Latencia—the female lead—lives in Vancouver."

"Latencia?" I said. "What the hell kind of name is that?"

Emily, who is used to me, continued as though I hadn't spoken. "Normally we would have gotten her to fly to L.A. for this, but she's expecting a baby in a few weeks and can't fly. I *could* have sent someone else..."

"But you figured, since I was here anyway..."

"Exactly! I get a free trip *and* I get to look like I'm stepping up. How fun is that?"

"Very fun," I said. "You want me to pick you up at the airport?"

"No, it's cool. I've got a car reserved. Vancouver is like L.A.—nothing is close together. At least, nothing I need. How long are you still in town for?"

I thought about Jessica's request and realized I didn't really know. "I'm not sure right now," I said. "A couple of days, anyway."

"Excellent! I can make this last that long."

We arranged to have dinner the following night.

Since Curt had invited me for dinner at WhyVeeAre, it seemed like the perfect place to meet. I didn't have the address, but I gave her the name of Braydon's flagship restaurant and told her it was enough of a landmark that almost anyone would be able to give her directions.

"Your timing was great, Emily. I can't even tell you. It was just super to hear your voice. The right moment."

It was true. After I got off the phone, I felt lighter than I had when I'd first gotten back to the apartment. I hadn't realized what a toll thoughts of death and dying had taken on my psyche. It is Emily's nature—her special gift—to breathe light and life into everything she touches. And I knew that seeing her would help put my assigned mission in Vancouver into its proper place. She not only always has good advice, she also has a tough time keeping it to herself.

It was seven o'clock in the evening. The stock market had been closed for hours, so serious work was out of the question, and it was way too early for me to think about sleep. As much to kill time as anything, I decided to try and get a jump on research for Jessica by poking through Braydon's desk at the apartment. Since in some ways the condo gave off the vibe of office extension, it seemed likely to me that he would have kept business stuff there.

A thorough inspection of the desk proved me right, but was also disappointing. I could tell that, just as I'd surmised, the condo was used for work as much as for living, but the work Braydon had done here wasn't very different from what he'd done in our apartment back in New York, only now he had better gear.

The files in the desk were all food and restaurant related. He had carefully filed histories of the menus of each of his restaurants. Reading them made my mouth water. He had ingredients lists and the names of suppliers in each of the cities in which one of his restaurants was located. He had files of restaurant reviews. A lot of them, I noted as I thumbed through, glowing. He had files of article ideas. A shelf behind the desk held student notebooks filled with his works in progress; the food-stained pages indicated to me that he kept one of these notebooks at his elbow at all times while he was in the kitchen, jotting notes to himself while he worked on his foody creations.

The computer on the little desk yielded more of the same. Folders of recipes—these in more finished form than those in the notebooks. Chapter notes for books in progress and books proposed, as well as comments on details: possible food stylists, preferred food photographers, and notes on Braydon's philosophies on food, presumably to add content to the books.

All of this reading about food started making me hungry in a way that only Braydon ever could. With visions of cookbooks dancing in my brain, I made my way back to the kitchen, intending to put together a little snack, washed down with a glass of the Chianti I'd opened the night before.

On my way to give the refrigerator another close inspection, I discovered something that stopped my trek in its tracks. Wedged between the sauté pans, I noticed a student notebook of the same type that I'd found in Braydon's office. Somehow I hadn't seen it the night before. I pulled it out and flipped to the latest entry. It was a recipe for braised ribs, obviously Braydon's most recent concoction. And in the refrigerator, when I went to inspect, among the packages I'd noticed the night before and thought to throw away, there were short ribs. They'd been put away in the packaging in which they'd been purchased. I picked up the package of short ribs and felt their heft. I turned them over and noted the cost of the package—$22.50—and the date they'd been packaged—the very day Braydon had killed himself.

I plopped the package back in the Sub-Zero as though I'd been burned. Closing the refrigerator door with a solid *whoosh*, I allowed myself to sink onto one of the bar stools at the kitchen island, feeling the hot push of tears before I could even isolate the reason.

Clearly, there was something wrong with this picture—though, considering how long I'd been out of said picture, it was difficult to isolate.

I flipped open the notebook again and looked over the ingredients list in Braydon's careful hand. Carrots, onions, shallots, fresh mushrooms, dried lobster mushrooms, Chianti (two cups), heavy cream and butter.

I went back to the refrigerator. In the crisper I found carrots, onions, shallots and button mushrooms as well as a still fresh container of cream and a pound of good quality butter. I had no trouble at all finding a plastic bag in the cupboard that contained dried lobster mushrooms, but by the time I did, tears were beginning to stain my cheeks.

Before I gave way to the things I was feeling, I went back and double-checked the date the meat had been purchased. And, of course, I found that what I'd surmised was correct: on the day Braydon had killed himself, he'd been deep into the process of developing a recipe for short ribs in a mushroom sauce.

Now, here's the thing: anyone can develop any old recipe they want any old day of the week. But does anyone, I reasoned, go out and purchase $22.50 worth of short ribs—not to mention a host of complementary ingredients—on the very day one intends to exit this life? While I guessed it was possible, on the whole I was thinking: Not so much.

I wondered about what I would be doing on a day I intended to make my last. Honestly, it's not something I think about. I like this planet and, in a lot of ways, it's been good to me, so I think more about prolonging my life than ending it. But, seriously, if I did? I'm pretty sure buying short ribs would not be one of the things I'd do.

Now, Braydon? He'd always been a foodie. His mind just worked in ways that were different from mine. But I was pretty sure that, if he were thinking about making the grand exit, short-rib shopping would not be near the top of his list, either.

So all of this gave me reason to pause and ponder. Despite what Anne-Marie had said to me on the night she dropped me off at the apartment, this was the first instant in which I thought, Hey. Is this really what it seems to be? And in the next instant I chided myself. After all, I thought, sometimes a duck is just a duck is just a duck. Sometimes all really is as it seems. It was true that my most recent history had been full of things that were other than what they had at first appeared. *"Items in mirror may be closer than they appear."* But that, I said to myself, didn't mean I should become a conspiracy theorist.

So, I thought, Braydon gets up one fine morning after partying at Au Bar until late the night before. He walks to the market, stocks up on vittles—including a package of short ribs—comes back to his apartment, puts everything away carefully and then…

And then…

It came to me that I still didn't know what the "and then" might be, other than he'd made himself dead. Thinking to correct that, and with my hunger forgotten for the moment, I went back into the little office, booted the computer again and got Google on the line.

"Braydon Gauthier," I typed, "+suicide." I was flatly amazed at the number of responses the search phrase brought back. I had only been thinking of him as Braydon, the sweet but slightly goofy young man I'd married. Just as the mass of mourners at the funeral home in the afternoon had done, now the depth of international grieving I caught a whiff of on the Internet put things more in perspective for me. In a lot of circles, it seemed, Braydon Gauthier had been a star.

Thinking I'd get a better take from the local papers, I tried there first, then realized, as I did so, that I probably should have made this search before I left L.A.

"Celebrity Chef Takes Own Life after Loss of Status," trumpeted the online edition of one of the local newspapers. When I scanned the piece, I realized they must have reproduced the whole article that had appeared in the print edition. It was sad stuff. Sad by every definition of the word.

"Food icon Braydon Gauthier was found dead in the kitchen of WhyVeeAre, his flagship restaurant on West Sixth Avenue in Vancouver.

"'We are deeply saddened to lose Braydon,' says Douglas Withers, spokesperson for Gauthier Fine Foods of which Gauthier was CEO. 'He will be widely mourned and deeply, deeply missed.'

"Withers reported that when Gauthier heard that WhyVeeAre had been awarded only five Vulcan stars in this year's guide, rather than the six the restaurant has been awarded annually by the guide since opening, the restaurant's owner and executive chef became despondent.

"Says Withers, 'Obviously, we had no idea of how badly he would take the news. We've had no indication—before or since the publication of the guide—that business would be affected. Clearly, Braydon took it in a personal way, rather than one relating to the business.'"

As befitted Braydon's hometown newspaper, the article was thorough: part news item, part obituary for a beloved and famous son of the city.

Braydon, the article said, had ingested large quantities of *Cerbera odollam*, a deadly poison from what was commonly known as the suicide tree. The article reported that, though the drug is difficult to detect on toxicology panels, crushed kernels from the plant were found in a vial near the body, making it possible to isolate the substance in Braydon's system.

The suicide note that Jessica had told me about was mentioned here, as well. Not what the note said, just that it existed and had been found. The article also mentioned that the body had been discovered in the kitchen of the restaurant by staff arriving for work in the morning. Medical examiners determined that Braydon "had been dead for several hours" by that point. The police had been called right away but, with "irrefutable evidence" of suicide so close at hand, they'd ruled out foul play.

When I was finished reading, I surfed a little further, but didn't find anything that added to this basic knowledge. I knew the bare facts, and that was enough: Braydon had started his day brightly enough that he'd anticipated working on a new recipe. By the end of the day, however, he'd been so gloomy he couldn't imagine going on. I put the short ribs out of my mind. After all, they meant nothing. Nothing, that is, but the obvious: I was now in the second stage of grief. Denial. And who, really, could blame me for that?

Nine

Vancouver is in the same time zone as Los Angeles, so I had no convenient jet lag to blame for messing with my personal clock. Still, the next morning I came awake to full light. A glance at the clock at bedside confirmed what I already knew: I'd overslept. It was 9:00 a.m. and, though I couldn't imagine how it had happened, I'd slept far beyond the 7:00 a.m. target I'd set for myself. Which is another thing I've come to learn about grief: it wears you out.

I opted not to mess with the espresso machine, but headed for a coffeehouse I'd seen down the block. Once there I inhaled a grande latte and most of a cheese scone while I pondered the balance of my day.

I'd told Jessica I'd look things over for her at Gauthier Fine Foods, but neither she nor I had given much thought to what that might look like. And, with the mission this close at hand, I found I was *not* relishing the idea of poking through things that weren't my business. I sighed and soldiered on; I'd promised Jessica and I didn't really see how I could get out of it.

Anne-Marie had suggested that the company would be a doable walk from Braydon's apartment and, since the day was fine, I decided on this option.

It was not a fast walk. In fact, it was a couple of miles. But I hadn't had a good run—or any type of exercise, for that matter—since my morning run in Malibu with Tycho on the day I'd left for Vancouver. I looked forward to pushing my body, even if it was only a little bit.

And Vancouver is a gorgeous city for walking. Emily had said it was like L.A. in that nothing is very close together. In some regards that's true; Vancouver is a city that's very spread out. But the downtown core and many of the nearby business areas are close together, and Braydon had clearly intended that his apartment be walking distance from work.

I was surprised when, about halfway to the office, I saw a sign for WhyVeeAre. It hadn't occurred to me that the restaurant would be en route, though this, of course, made sense, as well. Braydon's whole life had been walking distance. At least, it had until he got married.

Though it wasn't yet lunchtime, I could see that the restaurant was stirring. There would, I knew, be all sorts of work to be done before the doors opened. I remembered *mise en place*, the prep work that goes into the food that keeps a fine restaurant running. Stocks would be simmering, vegetables would be in the midst of being chopped, and every station in the restaurant would be getting attention, ensuring that everything was "put in place." A process that, in really good restaurants, goes down with the precision of a military operation.

"Yes, Chef! Right away, Chef! Of course, Chef!" Though I didn't know who Braydon's lieutenants would be addressing this way now, I figured there'd be someone. The kitchen hierarchy is military in that respect, as well. There's always a general.

Unlike the office and his apartment, the building that housed the restaurant struck me as very Braydon. It had once been some sort of industrial shop—a garage, perhaps, or a widget manufacturing company. Braydon had transformed the previously utilitarian space into something wonderful; I could see that even from the outside.

Garage bay doors would open, I could tell, onto a beautifully landscaped patio. Inside, the ceilings were high and, through the mullioned windows, I could see that many of the original fixtures were still in place but had been painted out in white. A long mahogany bar dominated one side of the room and, aside from careful floral arrangements and large works of modern art, provided the only color in the place. The tables were clothed in white, the napkins were white, the floor was white, as were the walls. Simple elegance and a non-elegant venue. How perfect, I thought. How *Braydon*. It made me sad to think I'd never taken the time to see it while he was alive.

* * *

The balance of my walk was uneventful. Strikingly beautiful. Pleasant. But without incident. When it isn't raining, Vancouver is a gorgeous city for walking, and it wasn't rainy today. The streets are clean, the natives are friendly and the air feels sweet and good filling up your lungs. There might be nicer cities than Vancouver but, on my long walk to Gauthier Fine Foods on that day, I had trouble imagining where they might be.

All visions of provincial beauty were banished the second I entered the glass-and-steel encrusted foyer of Gauthier Fine Foods. Everything I'd felt on the previous day when studying the building from outside was intensified once I'd passed through the front doors.

Black marble floor. Exposed glass elevator. Visible steel construction. Slabs of concrete, raw and imposing. And glass and glass and glass. I decided it must take a team of cleaners a case of Windex every day just to keep all that glass so pristine.

Even the receptionist looked cold and polished and expensive. She was tall and slender and blandly friendly, as though extruded from some top-of-the-line reception factory. Even features. Perfect hair. Clothes you forgot the second you looked away.

When I announced myself to her, she said politely, "Yes, Miss Carter. You are expected. If you'll just follow me, I'll show you to Mr. Withers's office."

After riding the elevator up two floors, it did not surprise me to find Doug Withers ensconced in a seriously imposing corner office. The black marble, glass and steel theme was carried on here, as well. Doug sat behind a desk made of all three materials. I didn't like it—working surrounded by all of those cold materials all day would have left me feeling cold, as well—but I knew the desk had probably cost a mint. For some people, that's enough.

Doug reclined in a huge, black leather chair. Its slightly smaller twin sat in front of the desk. He indicated I should sit.

"I wonder what you expect to find here, Miss Carter," he said without much preamble. I remembered the cold clamminess of his hand from the day before and was glad he hadn't offered it to me when I entered his office.

"I don't actually expect to find anything, Mr. Withers." I suppressed my instinctive dislike of the man and tried my best at a warm smile. This would all go better, I knew, if I wasn't ruffling feathers the second I walked in the door.

"Doug. Can I call you Doug?" He nodded his head almost imperceptibly, and I went on, still at my warmest and most engaging. "Jessica is an old friend, as you know. The death of her son has left her understandably upset," I said, aiming for candor. "Personally, I think she's jumping at shadows." That smile again. "But, under the circumstances, I didn't see how I could say no to her when she asked me to look in on you."

I could see a barely concealed snort from Doug as I

said this. "Look in? That's not exactly why you're here though, is it?"

"What do you mean?"

"She's in the middle of a million conspiracies. She's already had her lawyers all over ours, did you know that?"

I shook my head. I hadn't actually known. Though, from what she'd told me, it was not a surprise.

"That's right. Her son's not been dead for a week and all she seems to worry about is the company."

I tried for a conciliatory tone. "Look, Doug, I'm not here to dish dirt. Jessica is *bereft* right now. I doubt she's even thinking clearly yet. She asked me to come here and I told her I would. And I'll tell you what I was thinking—I expected to come here, spend the day poking through a few things that you're going to give me—" he looked as though he wanted to interrupt, so I held up a quelling hand and soldiered on "—and then I expect to go to her tomorrow and tell her that she's worrying for nothing. I mean, that's what I *want* to tell her, okay? That's what I *hope* to tell her. I just want to help lay her fears to rest. Will you help me do that?"

He looked only half-convinced. But we both knew that, with the lawyers circling, he didn't really have much choice.

"What do you want me to do?" he asked grudgingly.

"I'd hoped to spend a little time with you now, then spend a few hours in Braydon's office, looking over whatever you care to give me to look over."

"I guess I can do that. Where do we start?"

I took a deep breath. He was cooperating now, but I knew that the first question I had—the question that *had* to be first—was likely to set him back on the defensive.

"How long has the stock been trading on the Pink Sheets?"

"About six months," he said carefully.

"Since the beginning of the last fiscal?" I guessed. He nodded.

"Are you going to tell me how that happened?" I asked, because we both knew that, since it was a publicly traded company, it would be easy for me to find out.

He sighed deeply. Then he cleared his throat. *Then* he took a sip of water. I noted all of this, but didn't say anything. "We had…we had some accounting problems." Then with more strength, he added, "We had some trouble with an accountant."

"And…" I prompted, deciding that, for the moment, it would be best not to mention that I knew he'd been chief financial officer of the company at the time, which would have meant that, ultimately, the responsibility for any "accounting problems" would be his.

"We were late with some SEC filings. Not all of them," he said quickly.

"Ah," was all I said. Because you don't get delisted for being a little late with your filings to the Securities and Exchange Commission. You get delisted for being chronically late, ignoring all the warnings and then, for good measure, maybe fudging some figures besides. But I didn't pursue it with him then. There was no point. It would just get him back on the defensive and, anyway, as I'd told him—and as he had to know—it was all stuff I could find out easily enough on my own. Instead I went in a different direction.

"I'm sure you already know Jessica's greatest concern."

"She's very upset that I was named CEO," he said, no hesitation at all this time. "Especially so soon after Braydon's death."

"Right. I've already told her that moving quickly on that was a good move on your part."

"You did?" He softened visibly at this. I could see it in his pale eyes.

"I did. I told her that it was important you do that so that the company continues to look strong and in control even in the face of extreme adversity."

"That's right!" he said quickly. "That's exactly right. And she just can't see it."

"Of course not, Doug. She was his *mother*. Her heart is broken right now."

He nodded. I could see I'd mollified him somewhat.

"I can understand that part, Madeline. Truly, I can. But I've been very focused on saving this company that we've all built. You can see that, can't you?"

I nodded. "I can. But you have to help me make Jessica see that, Doug. She's not ever going to get off your back unless you do."

I was pleased to see a small smile. "That would be

wonderful. Getting her off my back, I mean. We've got enough to think about at the moment without trouble from that quarter. How can I help?"

"Well, for starters, she feels that Braydon's wishes are not being adhered to. She said that it was Braydon's wish that a family member—from her branch of the family—be named to the board upon his death."

I stopped without asking a question when I heard him sigh deeply and saw him run his hands through his sparse hair. "Not that again," he said. "I've already heard that from her lawyers. I'll tell you the same thing I told them. The same thing I told her, for that matter—we have every intention of respecting Braydon's wishes. But everything must be done in due course. Madeline, you understand the corporate end of things. And, obviously, since she's sent you here, she respects you. Maybe you can make her see this. As you probably know, we called a special meeting of the board directly after we discovered…what had happened to Braydon. It's all so…unfortunate. All so unexpected. But, from a purely business angle now, he was CEO and we could *not* leave the company without a rudder." He indicated himself. "Even if the measure was temporary, it had to be done. The other matters that concern Jessica—the family board member and the dispersal of funds or shares—that must wait until a regularly scheduled board meeting. No matter what this has meant to us— and I won't kid you, Madeline, losing Braydon has been a blow—but no matter what that means to us personally and privately, everything we do at present must be done properly and in due course, for the sake of the stock and the long-term health of the company, if nothing else."

All of this made perfect sense to me. I told Doug as much and indicated I'd pass it on to Jessica.

"I'd appreciate it, Madeline," he said, looking relieved. "Does she have any other concerns?"

"It would be great if you could brief me on the company's status at the present time. I think it might make all the difference to Jessica if I could offer her a more or less outside and unbiased opinion. I'll go through the paper later, but I'd like to hear it from you first. Your own assessment in your own words. What's your take on the company's condition at the moment?"

Another sigh. "Well, losing Braydon has been difficult, as you can imagine."

I nodded, encouraging him to go on.

"He was such a visionary. So much of all of it was his energy. But we have a very strong base, even without him. The restaurants don't rely heavily on his presence. Sales of the books are up, of course. For the moment. The magazine's readership has been growing and our indicators show that will continue. We're rethinking the television series right now, seeing if we can plug in another host."

I suppressed a shudder at his choice of words. The thought of plugging in a host in Braydon's place—like an electrical appliance—was distasteful to me. I didn't show any of this. Instead I pasted a small smile on my face and nodded encouragingly at him to go on.

"We're projecting that the fast-food line will continue to grow with Braydon's name and face on the box, even without his actual presence. It's sold in supermarkets," Doug explained earnestly. "And in a world where cake mixes and syrups have been sold throughout modern history with names and faces that don't even exist…"

He trailed off and I nodded. I could see the reasoning behind that.

"So there are a lot of very good points. A lot of positives. On the negative? Well, you'll see it as soon as you sit down with the financials." He held up his hands. "With all of the expansion, we're cash poor."

I nodded. As he'd pointed out, a lot of companies are in that position.

"I was always trying to get Braydon to slow down. Just build on what we had. But there was always some new thing he wanted to be involved with. Like this building, for instance." He indicated the glass and marble and steel all around us. "And the studio he built." He rolled his eyes heavenward. "State of the art, but *so* expensive. Then there's a full staff working on the shows. And the staff of the magazine. It seemed like every time he'd go out of town, he'd meet a new celebrity editor that he wanted to put on retainer. And he was researching opening more restaurants—he wanted Atlanta and he wanted Austin. Which, yes, are both great cities for restaurants—we've got all the data on that. But it would have spread us so thin."

"You were against it?" I asked.

"Oh, absolutely. I was encouraging him to open another Vancouver location or, failing that, Seattle, because it's close. Which would have meant our initial overhead would be lower. The more distant the location, the more it costs us for R & D and just setting up new supply chains and so on. But he said we already had Vancouver covered and he wanted important *food* cities, whatever the hell that is."

"That's…that was Braydon," I said noncommittally.

Doug nodded enthusiastically. "Absolutely. And he was researching a cookware line. Which would have been fine, but he didn't want just any old cookware line. It had to be top-of-the-line stuff. The best. The kind of stuff that's so expensive, most retailers won't even carry it. So that was gonna be a nonstarter for me. At least in the foreseeable…" He seemed faraway for a moment. As though he were thinking about something. "What else… He was six months behind delivering his latest cookbook to his publisher. He had enough *stuff*, you see, but he said he wasn't happy with it. Said a lot of the new recipes were bloodless. That was the word he used. And not up to the caliber his readers expected."

"Was that a problem for him?"

"Not really. I didn't think so, anyway. His books have done extremely well and his editor had pretty much given him carte blanche. I mean, they wanted it six months ago. But it was Braydon, so they gave him extensions. And he was pretty enthusiastic." Doug had brightened visibly. "Said he had some really great ideas…."

I could see the light of enthusiasm click off without warning. I didn't question it; I thought I knew the source. Doug had just remembered there weren't going to be any more cookbooks. Not, in any case, from Braydon.

He shot a quick glance at his watch and I grabbed the hint. "Doug, thanks for your time. If you could just direct me to Braydon's office…."

"Sure, Madeline. I'll have Stina show you the way." Stina. Of course. "Just get her to bring you anything you need—water, espresso, juice—and I'll send over things I think might be of interest to you. Will that work for you?"

I said that it would. He told me he had a couple of meetings that would take him through lunch. "I'll be back here at 2:00 p.m. at the latest, though. Maybe 2:30. I've always got lots to do, but I'll be available should you have questions or whatever."

Braydon's office was as different from Doug's as could be imagined. The exposed concrete had been painted a deep suede color, and much of the concrete floors were covered by Oriental rugs that didn't take an expert eye to identify as antique. A huge oak desk beckoned invitingly from the far corner of the big room, while a comfortable-looking sofa and a pair of club chairs occupied the space nearest the window. A coffee table was piled with all types of reading material. Cookbooks and various food and lifestyle magazines appeared well-read, while a two-year-old Gauthier Fine Foods annual report looked pristine.

Braydon's desk yielded a similar mix. The obligatory late-model computer perched on one corner of the desk, as well as a couple of framed photos of his wife and family—Jessica and Robert looking ebullient in happier times—but a cursory inspection of the desk's contents showed mostly food-related notes and files.

When Stina entered with my latte and an armload of files and found me snooping through her late boss's desk, I jumped guiltily, but she didn't look perturbed.

"It's pretty much a mess," she said with a smile.

"How so?"

"Oh…Braydon," she said, not without affection. "He wasn't the most businesslike of businessmen."

I nodded inwardly. Maybe he hadn't changed so much, after all.

"What do you mean?" I asked anyway.

"Well…" She placed the files and my coffee carefully on the wood desk and flicked an imaginary piece of lint thoughtfully from her black skirt. "He was always very friendly," she offered. "But not *too* friendly, if you know what I mean."

I nodded. I'm tall, slender, have an overabundance of blond hair and have always worked in male-dominated fields. Plus, I'd known Braydon. I knew exactly what she meant.

"And he was *unconcerned*, you know?"

I didn't and I said so.

"Well, that's not quite right, either. He was *very* concerned, but about Braydon things. Did Los Angeles get the order of lobster they needed? Did the new linens arrive in New York all right? What about the shipping of the frozen foods? Did the trucking companies absolutely guarantee that everything would get where it was supposed to go without the slightest bit of thawing? It seemed to me he was very concerned with the things other bosses would think of as details, things they would have other people do for them."

I nodded. "You're saying he was very concerned with the things that had to do with the day-to-day running of the restaurants and the stuff that related to the quality of the food."

"Right. But shareholder and board meetings? Press conferences? Other things to do with running this place? That didn't really hold his interest. It could sometimes be hard to get him to show up for those."

"Was that a problem?" I asked, knowing as I did so that I was likely risking asking one question too many and having her clam up. But it was a risk I was willing to take. I knew her view on the operation would be as unbiased as I was likely to get inside these walls. Her job looked secure. She had nothing at stake in talking to me, nothing to lose or gain. And it felt like a quiet day.

"A problem?" she said thoughtfully. "Not really. Not for me, anyway. Like I said, he was easy to deal with.

Now, him…" She grimaced as she pointed one slender index finger toward Doug's office. "He's different. I mean, don't get me wrong," she said loyally. She did have *some* things at stake. "He's a very nice guy. But his priorities aren't the same. He didn't always *get* Braydon, if you know what I mean." I saw her eyes slide over a photo of Mimi on Braydon's desk while she added, "Not everyone did."

"Mimi?" I asked.

"She's very nice," Stina said mechanically. And I understood something as she did so. Behind every successful man, they say. And where was Mimi now?

This feeling was confirmed by Stina's body language. Clearly, as the conversation had gradually come around to Mimi, Stina decided she'd said enough.

I saw her straighten slightly as she prepared to go. "I better get back to work."

"Does someone else do the phones when you do stuff like this?" I asked, because I hadn't heard incessant ringing.

"No phones, really. Well, not much. We've got voice mail. Around here reception pretty much means the extra stuff no one else is assigned to do." She smiled. "I'm kind of like everyone's personal assistant's personal assistant."

"Sounds like fun."

"It really pretty much is. Most of the time." She smiled weakly as she headed toward the door. "It's been a rough week, though. Dial nine if you need anything. You'll get me."

The latte was good, as I'd known it would be. Braydon would not have been Braydon if he hadn't made sure his office was supplied with the best coffee he could get his hands on. It was likely his restaurant patrons paid five bucks a cup for the same brew his lowliest assistant bookkeeper drank every morning. The thought was reassuring, somehow. That, over the course of years, so much about a person could change, but some essential things always stayed the same. I liked the thought of that. And I liked the coffee.

There is a place I go when I read financial reports. It's difficult to describe. But the place is probably the largest reason I have stayed slender all of these years, despite a diet that isn't always as health-infused as it should be.

I lose track of reality when I get very deeply into reading about the guts of a company. I know it's ridiculous. And I suspect it's the same feeling a lot of people get when they're deeply into a novel. I've not often had time for that type of reading in my life, but I can't imagine getting any more joy out of reading long fiction than I get from learning about all the intricacies of a publicly traded company's financial situation. How goofy is that?

I forget to eat. I forget to sleep. I forget about everything but the words and the numbers in front of me. This habit has saved me countless pounds—that not-eating thing—and cost me several relationships, but I've not ever tried to change it. Why would a bird decide not to sing? Or a pig decide she likes the ocean instead of a mud bath? Sometimes in life we just know where we belong.

So time passed me by as I sat in Braydon's office— first hunched over his desk, then curled up on his couch—with all of the details Doug had seen fit to furnish me with regarding Gauthier Fine Foods International, Inc.

I knew I didn't have everything. I could, I think, almost smell the holes where information should be: the places where Doug had withheld. It didn't matter. If he'd included everything, but put red flags on the things he didn't want me to notice, I couldn't have drawn this picture more perfectly. Oh, after I'd read, I knew there were still voids, but I have the knowledge: I know how to fill in the holes.

The picture that emerged was slightly patchy and not entirely in keeping with what my eyes had seen. The company had, as I'd known, gone public five years earlier in the sort of style that most corporate entities can only envy.

Braydon's first television series had only been on the air about a year at the time, but he'd been the kind of hit that inspires the phrase "overnight sensation." In a heartbeat he'd gone from respected but little-known Vancouver chef to international cooking sensation. His book made all the bestseller lists, his face was in all the magazines. He was a star.

From what I could glean, Doug had already been in

the picture, though Mimi, apparently, had not. Doug had been the money guy, the one who put the deals together, shook the shakers, moved the movers and packaged everything up into something that would sell. He'd sold Braydon, and he'd sold him at a premium. The IPO had been sterling and the new stock had closed its first day at $45 per share—fully double what the IPO price had been.

It had, according to the reams of paper in front of me, been all smooth sailing from there. For a while. The well-capitalized company had climbed ever higher, the restaurants had started opening in key cities throughout North America, more books had followed—all bestsellers—the second show, the magazine, the frozen foods. There had been no ceiling in sight.

From where I was sitting, I knew that—looking over all of this information a year ago—I would have figured that here was a company that could keep growing throughout Braydon's working years and beyond. Braydon had—with Doug's help—built something that was larger than the sum of all of its parts.

The hiccup had come just over a year before and, for most of Gauthier Fine Foods' investors, it really would have looked like only a hiccup. The press release Doug had thoughtfully included with my reading material had put a thoroughly delightful spin on the fact that, after deciding not to meet one of the New York Stock Exchange's core requirements for continued listing, stock in Gauthier Fine Foods would be traded on the

Pink Sheets effective pretty much immediately from the date the release was issued. Understandably—since treating investors with kid gloves is pretty much standard practice no matter where you trade—they'd made it sound almost like changing where you get your hair cut or where you buy your twist ties. They'd made it sound like something casual that would, in all likelihood, be better for their investors in the end, anyway.

The reality, of course, was quite different. No one—and I mean *no one*—would swap their spot on the New York Stock Exchange for the lineup on the Pinks any more than someone would trade their Manhattan Beach condo for a tract house in Simi Valley. And it's a pretty good analogy, too, because while both of those are places to live, there are intangible benefits attached to living in the former that are absent in the latter.

The NYSE is where stocks wanna live. The Pinks are sometimes where they go to die. No one who knows anything will tell you any different. Not, at least, if they're telling the truth.

And I knew that the supersmooth transition that Gauthier Fine Foods had accomplished with this move wouldn't even have been possible prior to 1999, when the Pink Sheets went from being the actual printed pink pieces of paper that brokers got sent—and reputable brokers barely glanced at—to the high tech, highly visible, easily accessible entity the Internet had allowed them to become. Though the Pinks were more visible now, at heart nothing had changed: this was the

Wild West, honey. No regulation means that, potentially, just about anything goes.

No regulation also means that securities that trade on the Pinks can be more difficult to analyze. In the first place, a more shallow paper trail is necessary. In the second, even if there is a reasonably deep paper trail, with no one keeping score, the numbers on those papers are sometimes only worth the paper they're printed on. Not even that, I guess, since, once it's been printed, it's just used paper.

So I knew that, after Gauthier Fine Foods was delisted, everything I read about the company had to be taken with a grain of salt. Oh, they'd supplied their shareholders with figures, all right. But were the figures accurate? Maybe they were. But without the Exchange breathing down their necks, they seriously didn't have to be.

What surprised me most was that the stock price hadn't gone down since the delisting. In fact, it had continued to go up in a way that, when I looked at the charts, made me suspicious of its regularity. I knew this was possibly due to my cynical nature. And due to my background, as well. They don't go around handing out securities licenses to young brokers who haven't had the value of SEC regulation whapped soundly into their brains. Without the smile of the Securities and Exchange Commission, I felt as though I was working without a net. And I'm a brave and athletic girl, but there really are some things I just won't do.

While I found all of this interesting, perhaps beyond the realm of normal human understanding, I began to wonder if any of what I'd read and learned would help me answer the questions Jessica was asking. On paper, everything looked just as it should. But from my perspective, and with all the facts I had available, it was unsupported paper. Still—I looked around the posh offices, thought about all the cool toys—things really didn't look bad.

As Doug had said, the company was cash poor, but there was a lot of equity in *stuff*. This building, for one, as well as the valuable real estate it stood on. The income generated by the television shows. The licensing deals in place. The books. The magazine. The restaurants. The frozen foods. The empire was certainly generating cash flow and, despite Braydon's death, it showed every sign of generating even more.

Why then, I asked myself, did I—like Jessica—have this feeling of unease?

A light rap on the closed door disrupted my thoughts.

"Come," I called, then smiled when I recognized Simon Carrier's face. He was more comfortably dressed today, in chinos and a golf shirt. He looked more relaxed. Probably, I mused, the clothes weren't the only reason.

"What a nice surprise," I said. "I've been buried in here for…" I glanced at my watch. "Three hours! I don't believe it."

"Stina told me you were here so I thought I'd come

up and say hi, and see if you'd like a tour of the studio."
He grinned sheepishly. "Thought I'd see if I could make
you think I was less klutzy, too."

I smiled back at him. "I didn't think you were klutzy,
anyway. But I'd love a tour of the studio. It sounds like
a nice break from what I've been doing here."

I'd imagined that the studio would be in a sub-
basement somewhere in the new building. I was wrong.
In the elevator we went up from Braydon's third-floor
office, not down.

The top two floors of the building had been designed
for Braydon's production and publishing concerns.
Simon referred to these as the floors where "creative"
was housed. This seemed like a lot of space to me and
I said so. Simon nodded in agreement, but explained,
"The penthouse level is where we do most of the actual
production work. It has the permanent sets for both
shows, plus an editing suite and half a dozen production offices. My office is up here and Braydon had an
office here, as well."

"He did?"

"Sure. Just a small one, so he'd have a place to make
calls and just be at home without having to whip back
down to the corporate level every time he wanted to
take a load off."

That made sense. "What about the floor underneath it?"

"More production offices—the more junior people—and the art and editorial offices of the magazine.

The ad people are mostly in New York and Toronto, so there are only small sales offices here. But on this level we also have test kitchens and another studio. That studio is small, though, intended only for shooting stills. Mostly of food for the cookbooks and the magazine."

"Stills?" I asked.

"Sorry. Still shots as opposed to motion," he said. "You know—regular photos. Like I said, we mostly do cookbook stuff there, as well as annual reports and things."

"I don't know much about all of this, Simon. But I would have thought that kind of thing would be done in a photographer's studio. Somewhere else."

Simon laughed. "Well, mostly, you'd be right. But Braydon was very concerned with quality. Of everything. You probably knew that about him."

I nodded.

"We were making do in the old building, in Yaletown. It was very cool and very convenient to everything, but we'd really outgrown it. Then Doug got the idea to have something purpose-built. He got his hands on this land and really pushed for the new building. Once he got into the idea, Braydon was all over it and made sure we had more than everything we needed."

"It was Doug's idea?" I was pretty sure that Doug had left me with the thought that it had been Braydon's passion for Gauthier Fine Foods to have a skookum new building.

"Pretty much, yeah. Braydon wasn't so keen at first.

He told me he thought the constant expansion was diluting the company. That it was time to sort of stop and reevaluate."

"Doug won, though?"

"Absolutely. I think Braydon was glad about it afterwards, though. He really loved that we had more than enough space to do everything we needed."

I tried to turn off the alarm bells in my head. It was hard. *Braydon said. Doug said. Simon said.* It wouldn't really, in the long run, have made any difference whose idea it was. Would it?

The elevator had stopped on the fifth floor, the one beneath the studio level. "Come on," Simon said, "we'll start with the test kitchens and work our way up."

He led the way along a well-lit corridor with doors heading off in both directions. At the end of the hall, I could see a large, bright room with huge windows that looked out over a nearby soccer field. In the distance, the city was glorious in full sun.

"He wanted control of all aspects," Simon said as we walked. "And he reasoned that, in this way, the food could be prepared for the shoot in the test kitchen, the stylists could have their way with it and the photographer could do his magic, all in a pretty controlled way. He was right, too. His books didn't only sell well, they won all the awards they were eligible for, including photography and design."

Simon stopped in the large room. I surmised this was

the photo studio, even though he had told me it was small. Small, like everything else, is a relative matter.

The walls were painted white. Various bits of complicated-looking lighting equipment lined both sides of the room, ready for action without much notice. Simon pointed out a heavy curtain, currently pulled back. "It's a blackout curtain," he said, following my glance. "Braydon wanted the photographer to have natural light available if it suited him, but to be able to shut the light out completely if the lighting situation needed to be totally controlled."

I didn't understand a lot of what Simon was telling me, but it all looked and sounded impressive and I said so.

"Yeah," he agreed. "It is. Pretty much state of the art. In fact, for cookbook shoots this is the best setup in the city. Maybe the whole country. Since the facility was completed, we've actually done several other chefs' books here, as well."

"Braydon rented out the facility?"

"When he wasn't using it. It made sense, since the gear was all here, anyway. Braydon said it allowed him to build relationships with photographers before he committed to having them do a book or work on the magazine. He was always scouting talent. Now, wait until you see the kitchen."

I'd noticed we'd passed hardly anyone on these two floors. In fact, when I thought about it, the whole building seemed underpopulated. "It seems very quiet," I commented. "Are there usually more people around?"

Simon nodded. "Yeah, this place is generally hum-ming. But with everything that's happened this week, and Bray's funeral yesterday, pretty much everyone who usually works on these floors has the day off."

"What about you? You're here," I commented.

"Yeah. And not the only one, either. There's always stuff that needs doing. I thought I'd just rather be here than somewhere else today. Some of the others felt the same way. And it isn't like the work stops, anyway. I'll show you what I mean," he said, opening the door on a computer-filled room. The overhead lights were off and in the dimly-lit space I almost didn't notice the girl working at a row of monitors, their light providing the only illumination in the space. She looked up as we came in, acknowledged our presence with a nod of her head, then turned back to her work.

"You'll remember Gwen," Simon said. I must have looked blank, because he added, "From the funeral yes-terday. Gwen, remember Madeline?"

"Oh, of course," I said, remembering now the heavy-rimmed glasses, the alligator-shaped purse. "Hi, Gwen." She acknowledged me with a nod, but didn't turn her face from the screen again.

Simon looked at Gwen as though he wanted to say something more, then sighed and turned back to me. "This is the editing suite," he explained.

He walked over to the bank of computers opposite those Gwen was working on, flicked a couple of switches and pushed some buttons. Braydon's face flooded half a dozen screens. Simon's face reflected a kind of proud sorrow.

"This is what we're working on right now. It's going to be very difficult. We still have four episodes each of both *Haute City Food* and *Gauthier's Gastronomique* that need editing."

"What's difficult about it?" I was vaguely aware of Gwen, who was either so deeply involved in her work she didn't hear us, or was pointedly ignoring us and hoping we'd go away.

"Oh. I've been in here most of the day and I feel like—well, look around—I feel like I'm working with him. I feel like he's alive. And I keep expecting him to pop his head in the door like he always does when he's in town. 'Hey, Simon,' he'll say. 'You making me look good?' Stuff like that."

Gwen nosily pulled a Kleenex out of a box and blew her nose, but didn't say anything. When she went back to her work I looked at her more closely and decided her eyes were redder than they should have been. And puffy. I didn't think it was a cold.

"I can see what you mean," I said to Simon. "It's actually a little bit creepy."

It was. Braydon speaking cheerily at the camera while beating eggs for a soufflé. Braydon laughing with the Haute Boys. Braydon adding olive oil to a sauté pan. Braydon at a location shoot in a market, explaining various cuts of meat. Braydon, Braydon, Braydon.

It was hard to see how Simon and Gwen could avoid going mad. At least, while everything was still so fresh.

"Maybe you should wait awhile," I suggested, including Gwen in my comment, though she ignored me. "Maybe it won't be as difficult when a bit of time has passed."

"You're right, you know. We've talked about that. But, honestly? I think this is a little therapeutic for me right now. Maybe for Gwen, too. I really do feel an awful lot of sadness. And, I wonder if you can understand? Somehow, immersing ourselves in all of this—" he indicated the many images of Braydon "—sort of allows me to wallow in sorrow and get on with my work at the same time. If that makes any sense."

I nodded. It made a kind of sad and perfect sense.

Gwen didn't say anything or even look up again from her work, but a couple of sniffles seemed to speak volumes.

From the editing suite, Simon led the way to the kitchen that adjoined the studio. It was remarkable on several levels.

The appliances—two cooktops, a couple of large refrigeration units, a dishwasher and two double wall ovens—were all white and top-of-the-line household grade. The counters, the ceiling, the floor and a large island in the center of the kitchen space all were white, as well. The total picture—the kitchen and the large studio space beyond it—reminded me of a clinic. I said as much to Simon, which made him laugh.

"That's funny, Madeline. Because, around here, we called Braydon 'Dr. Food.' And it had as much to do with the prep space he designed here as anything else."

"So what you're suggesting is that I'm not the only one who thought it was somewhat clinical?"

"Exactly. Though, in truth, I think that's pretty much what Braydon was going for. An almost sterile environment in which to prepare and present almost perfect food. Here, though, let me show you something."

He led me to a bank of cabinets built against the far wall and laid a hand on one of the cabinet pulls before he opened it. "Okay," he said. "Sterility everywhere, right? Everything white. And then…" With a flourish he pulled open the cabinet on a riot of color so bright that, after all that white-on-white-on-white, it caused you to step back, almost. And to blink.

It took me a few seconds to understand what I was seeing. For the bright islands of visual hilarity to sort themselves into the useful objects they were. Plates and bowls and chargers of every description were stacked neatly within the cabinets. From ultramodern to Danish modern to art nouveau, arts and crafts and beyond to deep antique. There were Japanese serving dishes as well as place settings that I could only think to describe as baronial. The dishes were painted with flowers and birds and in deep golds and bright maroons and just about everything in between.

I looked a question at Simon.

"I thought you'd guess," he said in answer to my

look. "He used these for the photo shoots. For the food. And I don't think he ever used the same plate twice. A lot of cookbook authors get stores or manufacturers to let them use whatever they like from their lines for plating. It's kind of a promotional consideration. But Braydon felt that wasn't honest enough."

"How do you mean?" I asked.

"He felt that, since each recipe he created was meant to be unique and distinct from anything that had gone before, he wanted the food showcased in a like fashion. So he collected these." Simon indicated the plates, closed the door and opened another. This time I was looking at myriad cups and saucers and mugs. "And these." Simon closed the door and opened two drawers at once. I could see wildly different place mats and cloth napkins and tablecloths and napkin rings....

"I could go on," Simon said. "But you get the idea."

"Amazing," said I.

"Absolutely," he agreed. "It got to be like a collection with him. Wherever he traveled—and he traveled a lot—he kept his eye out for places he might find something new and different. He hardly ever came back empty-handed. Oh, oh, oh!" Simon said. "You're crying. I'm so sorry. I didn't realize...."

I hadn't realized, either, but I pressed my fingertips to my cheeks and found that Simon was right: there was moisture there. Not a lot, but enough.

"I'm sorry. My fault, not yours. I stumbled across...well, a memory, I guess. I'd forgotten it was there."

A memory. Nothing more. A memory of the infancy of this collection. Another day. Like the one of the car. Only this time we were less carefree. Or I was. I don't remember. I *do* recall an antique shop on East 60th Street and a ridiculous teal serving platter that didn't seem to fit the Victorian profile of the store at all.

"It's from the 1930s, actually," the proprietress had informed us. "It *is* rather a plain piece. I'm not really sure why I brought it in." She'd touched the dish thoughtfully, running her index finger around its scalloped rim. "It spoke to me somehow. Not terribly valuable. Nor shall it be, I think. Not for a long time, anyway. But a bargain at the price."

The price was fifty dollars. Not so much, really. And Braydon had coveted it. But I'd coveted something else that fifty dollars could buy. I don't remember what anymore. A dress? Surely not that. A dinner somewhere? An electric bill? It doesn't matter. What *did* matter was that we left the store without the plate, and I'd reasoned that, had he *really* wanted it, Braydon would have insisted. But he hadn't.

I'd felt mean, though. I'd seen how much Braydon had wanted it. And the next day, I'd taken an actual lunch break from work and returned to the shop to buy it.

Now, in Braydon's clinically white studio kitchen, I opened again the first cupboard Simon had shown me, and there at the bottom of one of the stacks of large plates, I found it. I took it out. Felt its weight. Turned it over, examined the unexceptional hallmark, and was glad I'd gone back on that day. Things hadn't turned out at all as we'd planned, but it was good to be able to stand here now and know that, for all the wrongs I'd done him, there'd been one right thing that had mattered, that had lasted. And today I could hold it in my hand.

The television studio on the penthouse level took my breath away. I had little idea of what I was looking at, but I knew it was good. Properly done. And it was fun to be able to walk through the space of the show I'd seen on television.

"I don't understand, though," I said, looking at the permanent sunset behind the set of *Haute City Food*. "I thought the building was pretty close to brand-new. Yet I'm *sure* I saw Braydon on this set something like six years ago."

Simon grinned smugly and nodded. Obviously this was a point of pride. "You're right. It's a bit of technological magic. We had the set recreated here, exactly as it was."

"Seriously?"

Simon nodded again. "Yeah. Braydon was adamant that all of the details be exact. He said he didn't want to mess with something that had done so well. He didn't want to upset the formula."

Seeing the studio reminded me of something else.

"Doug told me earlier that it was possible you might find a new host for the shows."

"We've talked about it," Simon said. "Only briefly,

mind you. We've not been without Braydon for very long."

"Do you have anyone in mind?"

"Actually, Doug has put forward Mimi's name."

"Mimi?" I asked, thinking, I suppose, of myself and how ill-equipped I would have been for hosting a hit cooking show by virtue of having been married to a chef. I mean, I can order from a restaurant menu with the best of them, but cut an onion or attempt a sauce in public? Forget it. "Is she a chef?"

"Not at all. But Doug feels that, as Braydon's wife, she'd bring an element of recognizeability with her. You know—carrying on in the tradition of, that sort of thing. And she's not hard on the eyes." He smiled at me warmly. "Braydon seems to have had a penchant for marrying beautiful women."

I accepted the compliment as gracefully as I could—I'm not the best at taking compliments about the way I look—and allowed him to move us to the next leg of our tour. But I stored away the information he'd given me for future examination. Mimi Gauthier as Braydon's public replacement. From a straight-up financial viewpoint, it wasn't such a harebrained scheme. But how Jessica would feel about it was another thing altogether. I hoped she already knew. I didn't want to be the one that had to tell her.

Simon showed me the offices next. Simon's own was medium in size but maximally functional. It was the office of a man who had a lot to do. A few other offices were attached to people whose names meant nothing to me. There was a conference room that would allow twenty people to meet comfortably and, finally, at the far end of the corridor, Braydon's studio-level office. Small and simply furnished, I figured that going through the paperwork here was going to be a waste of my already dwindling time: likely just more recipes and creative outlines.

A corkboard above the desk caught my eye, though. Photos of Braydon and a lot of people I didn't know. But for one. In truth, I recognized the cleavage before I put a name to the face: Sonya Foy. Her face was cozily close to Braydon's, her teeth looking pointier and more predatory than they had in real life.

"Sonya," Simon pronounced when he saw my interest. I wasn't sure, but I thought I heard a hint of distaste in his voice.

"You know her, then?"

"Sure. We all know her." I'd been right: distaste. "Hard to miss her. She's here a lot. She does some sort of consulting work for Doug."

"Doug," I said. "Not Braydon?"

"Doug." Simon nodded confidently.

"What sort of consulting work?"

"I'm not really sure." He looked as though he were trying to remember. "Some financial thing, I think. Funny, now that you mention it, I'm not even sure I've ever heard exactly what it is she does."

"Why don't you like her?"

He smiled at the question. "What makes you think that I don't?"

"Something in your voice, when you talk about her. Something in your face."

His finger traced a pattern on the desk blotter. "It's just that…" He shot a glance over my shoulder, as though making sure no one was within hearing distance. "She and Braydon had…I dunno. Some kind of weird connection."

Ten

Weird connection. I thought about what Simon had said as I walked from the Gauthier Fine Foods offices to WhyVeeAre. Weird connection. What did that mean? And even though I'd tried to prod him for more, Simon wouldn't budge any further. He told me he'd probably already said too much.

I didn't know why Simon's choice of words should disturb me. But it did. It made me feel uncomfortable in a place that I recognize but have no name for. The place where instinct lurks and thought seldom does. Or certainly logic. It bothered me and that was enough. I am a creature of instinct. It's something that's kept me safe and gainfully employed all my adult life.

Yet instinct was not enough here. Jessica had asked me to come and inspect, and I had. I wasn't quite sure yet what I would tell her, but I knew that, whatever it was, it probably wouldn't be what she wanted to hear.

As I walked through the dwindling daylight to meet Emily at WhyVeeAre I pondered all that I'd learned. When compiled into a mental list, it really wasn't much. But then, what had Jessica hoped I'd be able to see that no one else could? Even if there'd been something, the stock trading on the Pinks created an impenetrable smokescreen. And maybe that was the point. It was all pretty much their word against their word; without regulation, there was no place for me to check that what they said was true.

I thought about calling Sal, my boss at Merriwether Bailey and the closest thing I've had to a father figure in my life since my own father passed away. Sal can often be counted on to find information on publicly traded companies when there's nothing much available. However, I knew that, with Gauthier Fine Foods trading on the Pinks, there wouldn't be much for even him to find.

I'd already told Jessica that I thought creating Doug as CEO wasn't a bad move. On the contrary, it had possibly been a necessary one. In terms of getting what Braydon had wanted his mother and the rest of the family to have, as Doug had said, the company was cash poor right now. And, in any case, tabling the matter for the next regularly scheduled director's meeting wasn't out of line. In reality, too, cash flow situations being what they are, by the time that meeting rolled around, the company's cash situation might be more sunny. In short, the whole thing might resolve itself without outside intervention.

I decided I'd tell her exactly what I believed: that though things *looked* good at Gauthier Fine Foods, there was no way for me to really know that at present. In my opinion, she'd be best served by doing two things: one, supporting her daughter-in-law's brother in his running of the company and two, working closely with her own lawyers. Not to block Doug, but to be as sure as possible that everything was progressing as it should. In short, she should be supportive and diligent. Supportive because, *if* Doug was doing what he should, the last thing he'd need right now was a bereft mother blocking his way. And diligent because, if things were *not* what they seemed, Jessica would want to make sure she was first in line to get what she had coming.

Either way, I felt it was the most I could do and, as much as it was occupying a large part of my brain at the moment, I knew that once I was on the road back to L.A., I'd let go of what I'd seen here in Vancouver.

I was fifteen minutes late arriving at WhyVeeAre and Emily had already been seated. I'd seen her the week before in L.A. but, with all that had happened and with so many miles between us and our homes, it seemed much, much longer.

It was almost ridiculously good to see her, sitting— as Curt had promised when I had called earlier to tell him she'd be joining me for dinner—at a very good table. She was near enough the open kitchen to watch the dinnertime show of staff preparing beautiful meals, but far enough from the noise and bustle for us to enjoy a quiet conversation.

She rose when she saw me and enveloped me in a warm Emily-style hug. "You don't look so great," she said.

"Thanks," I said wryly.

She executed a pooh-poohing motion with her hands. "You know what I mean. You look great, of course. You always look great. And you look…I dunno. Not tired, exactly. But kind of worn down, I guess."

I sighed as I took a seat on the banquette across from her. "It's shaping up to be that sort of week. And I'll tell you everything later. Really I will. But right now I want to know about you. *You* look great. And you look *smaller*. Have you lost weight?"

She grinned. "I think I have. I'm going to write a self-help book, Madeline. Because I've found the secret. I'm going to call it *The Film Industry Diet.* I've discovered that if you eat enough airline food and grab enough meals off the catering truck you can't help but lose weight."

"Ah." I smiled back, settling into the comfortable banter that had marked much of our friendship. "So the secret is to eat a lotta crap food?"

"More like, the secret is to eat *only* crap food. Food bad enough that you don't even want a lot."

I laughed and felt more relaxed than I had since before I got the first phone call from Anne-Marie. A waiter arrived and we gave him our drink order. A couple of cosmopolitans seemed like the right way to begin a meal in this elegant spot.

After the waiter had left, I turned back to Emily. "So tell me again why you're in Vancouver?"

It was all of the opening she needed. She launched into stories about the lead actress on the film she'd worked on in Prague. The Prague stories led to Emily's subsequent need to come to Vancouver to do the ADR for the movie.

"Okay, honestly? I didn't *need* to be here myself. I could have managed the whole thing from L.A. just fine. But since you were here anyway, and it ends up being, like, a free trip…well, how could I *not* come? And I like Vancouver. I come up here every chance I get."

I was glad she'd pulled whatever strings she had. It was great to see her. "How long are you in town?"

"Another couple of days for sure. You?"

"I'll be through everything I need to do in Vancouver tomorrow. Then, guess what? I'm *driving* back to L.A."

"You're driving?" Emily was clearly surprised. "Why?"

I told her about Old Stinky—she found the story touching, as I'd known she would.

"From Vancouver, I'm driving to my mom's in Seattle. I'm planning on spending a couple of days there with Mom and my sisters, then I'm going to take a couple of easy days driving home." I had a thought. "Why don't you make the trip with me?"

"What? Mom and sisters and everything?"

"Well, if you wanted, you'd certainly be welcome.

I've told you before, she's that kind of mom. But I was thinking, you could finish what you have to do in Vancouver, then fly to Seattle and we'll drive back to L.A. together."

"A road trip?" Emily laughed. "How positively *Thelma and Louise*. We could do the wine country and a bit of the coast. Make a little trip out of it. How fun!"

We got so deeply into thinking about what that road trip might look like and how Emily could adjust her schedule to make it happen, that we didn't notice Curt until he was standing over us. Emily saw him first and broke off speaking in midsentence to greet him.

"I don't know who you are," she said in a sultry voice, "but I think it might not be an accident that you're standing there."

"It's not," he said, matching her tone and picking up her hand and pressing it to his lips. "I saw two lovely ladies alone from across the room. It seemed to me that such roses needed the balance of a boyish thorn."

I thought I'd better step in before they got out of hand.

"Emily Wright, this is Curt Foster. Emily is a friend of mine from Los Angeles," I explained. "And Curt is an old friend of Braydon's."

Emily smiled and sighed. "Ah, well…and here you had me thinking it was love at first sight."

"But of course it was, madam," Curt said with a courtly gesture.

"Yeah, yeah," I said. "Take a load off, Curt. And join us if you have the time."

"For you, Madeline, there is always time."

"When did you get to be so full of sap?" I asked him.

Another smile. "I have always been full of sap, Madeline. You just never noticed. But I will join you, just for a while," he said, while taking a seat on the ample banquette, "before the restaurant fills up for the evening service."

Emily looked at me questioningly and I said, "Curt manages Braydon's restaurants." I shot a glance at him, knowing that wasn't quite right. "Or something like that."

"That's close enough," he said with a dismissive gesture. "It's not important. What *is* important is making sure you lovely ladies have a memorable meal here in Vancouver. If I may be so bold, I'd like to order for both of you? And the meal, of course, is on the house." I made to protest, but Curt insisted. "No, no. I'll not have it any other way."

He excused himself and went to the kitchen to give our order directly to the chef. On the way back to the table, he stopped off for a brief chat with the sommelier, who arrived, just after Curt rejoined us, with a bottle of red wine and three glasses.

"It is the 2002 Sandhill gamay noir," he said while the sommelier opened the bottle and poured a small amount into Curt's glass. "I thought you might appreciate a fine British Columbian wine."

He made a show of tasting it carefully, pronounced it superb, and had the waiter pour each of us a glass.

"A toast to my lovely companions," he said in an expansive way, lifting his glass. Then, more quietly, "And to absent companions. Your presence is missed."

The wine was rich and full on the palate. I said as much.

"You've grown up then, Madeline. I can remember a time when, for you, the purpose of wine was washing a fishy taste out of your mouth."

I laughed, remembering the incident he was referring to. A special staff dinner at the restaurant in Bed-Stuy. The first—and only—time I'd eaten frog's legs. I'd taken a mouthful of the—probably superbly prepared—amphibian casserole, then grabbed my wineglass and drank deeply, trying to erase the taste.

"It was swampy. Not fishy," I corrected.

"Either way, it was a sixty-five dollar bottle of wine. Meant to be enjoyed, savored, not used to banish tastes one finds unappealing."

I laughed. "You're right, Curt. Of course. But my taste buds have matured. I was a *lot* younger then."

"We were all a lot younger then." Then, thoughtfully, "Well, perhaps not so much younger. What was it? Eight years ago? Ten? We have changed, of course. But not beyond recognition. You know," he addressed me after a pause, "I'm very relieved that you're speaking to me."

I smiled at him, not understanding. "What do you mean?"

"That business," he said, waving a hand as though

by way of explanation, "with the cars. You resolved never to speak to me again."

"I did?"

"You did. I remember I was crushed at the time. How would you say it? Flattened. To think you would not forgive me."

"I'm starting to remember the sap now," I said dryly.

"It's true, though. And I can see in your eyes that you *do* remember. I feel as though I should explain...."

"Curt, for heaven's sake, how long has it been? Whatever it was, I forgave you long ago. I don't think I've even ever thought of it." Though this was, of course, not quite the truth. "And Braydon is dead. Why would any of it matter now?"

"You see," Curt began as though I hadn't spoken, "there was a part of me that was aware of you that day, Madeline. I could hear you calling me. I've never forgotten it. I really wanted to go to you, to see if I could help you but...I can't explain it...."

"It was a long time ago, Curt. It doesn't matter now."

"Still. I've always felt I owed you... It was just seeing Braydon there, as he was...I just couldn't make myself *leave* him, Madeline. It was like...it was like he needed me...."

And I didn't need you? I thought, but did not say. As I'd told him, it was all so long ago now.

"I thought he was going to die." And there was something very like anguish in his voice as he said this. It brought me up short because it really had been a long time ago. So much had happened since. And, of course, Braydon had not died that day. Not even close. He'd been stunned and had just about the worst case of road rash I've ever seen, but after a night spent at a local hospital under observation, they'd let him go. Curt, I remembered, had not left his side.

"Curt, please, I understand. Really I do. It's done and, like I said, so, so long ago. I don't think we really need to go there anymore. Not after all that's happened."

He reached across the table and took my hand, squeezed it and smiled at me. "Let's drink, then. To Braydon." He included both me and Emily in his toast. "He would have appreciated this company."

I smiled and sipped and saw Emily do the same. Both of us were, I think, anxious to help the conversation skate back to more neutral territory.

"This place really is incredible, Curt," I said, taking in the large dining room that was now beginning to fill for dinner. "You couldn't have imagined this all those years ago."

"It *is* incredible," he said, nodding. "And special somehow, because it was the first. But you should see Nineteen, in Manhattan. Breathtaking. And Too Haute in Los Angeles. It is just as we dreamed."

"Do you spend much time in Los Angeles and New York?" I asked.

"I try to spend an equal amount of time at all of the locations. It's difficult, but I manage. I try to do a lot on the phone and on the Internet but, for some things, my presence is required."

"No Mrs. Curt, then?" Emily asked.

Curt smiled at her and looked full into her eyes. "No. Where would the room in my life be for such a luxury?"

"What I don't understand," I asked, "is the reason WhyVeeAre lost its star. Did something change? The place looks wonderful to me."

"Its Vulcan star?" Curt clarified.

I nodded.

"No, nothing changed," he said, looking around the room. "Not here. But these things happen. A chef's popularity rises and falls. The business of the stars? It can be a bit of a popularity contest or something of a political thing. I think that, after several years of being the enfant terrible of the food industry, Braydon just got overexposed. They don't like that, those Vulcan people. I warned Braydon about it."

"You did?"

Curt nodded. "To be a truly great chef in the eyes of the guides, one must be like Barbra Streisand."

Emily and I exchanged a glance. Curt had lost both of us on one quick turn.

"I don't get it," Emily said.

Curt smiled. "She has always been elusive of the media, not really letting anyone know what was coming next. And never, ever overexposed. And Braydon? It was fine when he was opening restaurant after restaurant. Fine even with the books, because they were good books, books with dignity. But the television? That was pushing it, though not the final straw."

"There was a final straw?" I said.

"Oh, yes, Madeline. Can't you guess?" I shook my head and Curt went on. "The fast food, Madeline. The *frozen* food. When Braydon told me about it, I was opposed to it so strongly, you can't imagine. Because I feared it would be his undoing." He spread his hands helplessly. "And I'm sorry to say, I was right. So sadly, however, because it was beyond even my expectations."

The three of us were silent for a moment, each with our own thoughts. I broke the silence. "Do you really think that's...that's what happened? That he killed himself over the star?"

Curt stroked his beard thoughtfully. He seemed to ponder what I'd said. "Interestingly enough, no one else has asked me that. And I've thought about it a lot. Would Braydon, *our* Braydon, do such a thing for such a reason? And I think our Braydon would not have done. However, so much had changed in recent years. *Braydon* had changed so much, I don't know if you would have recognized him. He worked so hard, Madeline. He wanted so much. He played very hard, too, of course. Sometimes too hard, I think."

"What do you mean?" I asked.

He averted his eyes, looking slightly caught. I wondered about it. "There were parties. He was a celebrity. A star. There were...women." He cleared his throat. "I'm sorry, Madeline. I think I've already said too much. It's best, sometimes, not to dwell on the things that were…less than perfect. But perhaps losing the star seemed like the final setback? I don't know. I have no answers."

"The note," I said quietly.

"I'm sorry?"

"Jessica told me he left a note."

"Ah, yes, the note. I haven't seen it. But, yes—I understand it mentioned the star. There, then, from the horse's mouth, as it were. And, honestly, if not that, I don't know what else. He didn't seem unhappy."

We sat in silence for a while. I mean, what could you say to that? He hadn't seemed unhappy. Everyone had told me variations on the same theme. Yet he had been. Apparently, dreadfully so. Enough that he'd taken his own life.

I was glad when these sad thoughts were interrupted by the arrival of our appetizer: seared scallops in a truffle butter sauce, served with a garlic parsnip mash.

Curt oversaw the placement of our food, then excused himself to get some work done while we ate our dinner. He told us he'd rejoin us for coffee after the meal.

The food looked and smelled amazing. To my mind, more like something to be framed than consumed. But though I'd been hungry half an hour before, I suddenly found I didn't have the spirit for it. Emily saw my hesitation and admonished me. "For God's sake, Mad, try one of those scallops. They're *amazing*."

I did as she suggested and discovered she was right.

"But why are you eating them, Em? You're a vegetarian. Scallops aren't a vegetable."

"They're not?" she said, eyes wide and innocent.

"Ah, you thought they grew at the bottom of the ocean?"

"They *don't?*"

"Never mind," I laughed. "If you're going to be difficult."

"I *am* going to be difficult 'cause, check it—someone brings me a plate of anything that looks that good? I'm going to stick it in my head." She grinned at me before making another scallop disappear, as though to demonstrate her point. "It's not like it's *veal* or something."

The balance of the meal was just as wonderful. Plate after small plate arrived at our table, each one more remarkable than the last. It seemed as though we were consuming vast amounts of food but, as Emily pointed out, the only things vast were the steps being taken to bring it to us. Curt had ordered us a tasting menu, and that night Emily and I tried a small amount of almost everything that WhyVeeAre had on offer. In deference to Emily's—tonight somewhat lapsed—vegetarian status, I ate the really meaty things and left larger shares of the vegetable matter for her.

Almost as soon as the last plates had been taken away, Curt reappeared. "Did you leave room for dessert?" he asked as he took the seat he'd vacated earlier.

We both shook our heads. "Not really," Emily said.

"Fine then," said Curt, addressing our waiter. "We'll just have the pear and apple tart."

Emily and I groaned but shared a smile. The wonderful food had done much to restore our mood.

And we didn't just have the pear and apple tart. Well, we had that, but also a cheese plate and a bottle of ice wine. "A British Columbian specialty," Curt pronounced. "You can't go home without having some."

"We can get it in L.A.," Emily pointed out.

"Of course you can," he agreed. "But you can't drink it in British Columbia when you're in L.A." Since the illogic of his logic was inarguable, we sipped while we nibbled, and though we talked of inconsequential things for a while, by the time the food had been cleared and we sat with coffees in front of us, the conversation had turned back to Braydon. Perhaps it was inevitable. I have eaten in wonderful restaurants, some that included stars on their bragging sheets. But I had never before that night—nor have I since—had a meal as wonderful as the one Emily and I shared at WhyVeeAre. The combination of flavors, the preparation, the presentation—everything was perfect. I'm no expert on food, but I've eaten a lot of it, and this seemed to me to be as good as it gets.

Yet if Curt was right, the food hadn't contributed to the loss of the star.

"You said before that you hadn't seen the note Braydon left. But I thought he was found here, at the restaurant."

"He was, but I wasn't here."

"You were out of town?"

"No, actually. I'd taken a much needed day off. I was in the country. I didn't come in that morning at all. Not until after I'd heard."

"One thing I don't understand," I said. One thing? "Why here? Why not at his apartment? Or at home? Or even at the office? Why in this restaurant he obviously loved so much?"

"I think maybe that's why, Madeline. That and because this was the restaurant that had lost the star, so in a way, it was perfect."

"But wouldn't he have been afraid of compromising the restaurant's reputation?" I asked.

"I think it's possible the fate of the restaurant—or anything else, for that matter—was not so much on his mind."

"How did he do it?" Emily asked quietly.

I found myself waiting for Curt's answer. The newspaper article had given a rough sketch but, despite the fact that he hadn't been here, Curt's view would be more personal.

"Poison," Curt said simply. "He poisoned himself."

"I read that in the newspaper. It said it was *Cerbera odollam*. I made a mental note because I'd never heard of it before."

Emily obviously had, because she was nodding. "The fruit of the suicide tree," she said. "I've seen a few things about it in the newspaper recently. It's very common in places where it grows. Like India. Not so much here. Well, not so much in the States, anyway."

"Nor in Canada, either, as far as I know," Curt said. "But it's an unregulated plant thus far." I looked at him closely. The fact that the plant was unregulated seemed an odd tidbit to hold. But Curt looked...well, like Curt. If he was hiding anything, I couldn't see it. "And I'm told it has beautiful, scented blooms," he was saying. "I wouldn't imagine it would be difficult to get it into either country, in one form or another."

"How did anyone know that's what it was?" Emily asked. "I've read the drug is next to impossible to detect."

"There was a bottle at his elbow when they found him," Curt said. "Filled with more of the stuff. It apparently made determining cause of death much more easy."

"I guess," I said.

"But the taste. I've read it has an awful taste."

"Emily," I said. "You're startin' to scare me. How do you know all this stuff?"

"All those international flights," she said. "Then sitting around in hotel rooms. I've been doing a *lot* of reading."

"I don't know about the taste," Curt said. "I don't know as much as you about this. But I do know he put the drug in his food."

"Food?" I said.

"Yes," Curt said. "Didn't you know? He made himself a last meal."

Eleven

Between us, Emily and I had consumed most of a bottle of red wine, a half bottle of ice wine and a cosmopolitan apiece. It had been over the course of several hours and we were far from intoxicated, but when we left WhyVeeAre, neither of us felt that driving Emily's rental would be a very good idea.

She said she thought we should call a taxi, but the night was clear and not too cold, and I suggested a walk. "We're not far from the seawall. We can walk back to Braydon's and, if we're feeling up to it by then, I'll drive you back to get your car. It'll give me a chance to introduce you to Old Stinky."

Neither of us could believe the clarity of the air that night. It seemed almost otherworldly, especially when, once on the seawall, the damp night air brought a kiss from the ocean. But it wasn't just the air. I felt as though

I could see more clearly, as well. And not just things at a distance. Even the hand in front of my face seemed more distinctly outlined than it did in L.A. I wanted to enjoy the sensation for as long as possible.

"There's something not right about Curt," Emily said as we walked, surprising me.

"I thought you liked him. I mean, it *really* seemed like you liked him. I thought I was going to have to call Tristan the way you were behaving."

Tristan is Emily's boyfriend and has been pretty much since I introduced them a while ago. Introducing them is how I like to say it, though it's a bit of an overstatement. I was there on a sort of date, and Emily and Tristan were there as sort of air bags, in case of a test-date crash, I guess. And, of course, *Emily* was the one that ended up with sort of a boyfriend.

Emily waved a dismissive hand at my evoking Tristan now. "Oh, please. That tonight was nothing. A little flirting. Just because we're in the provinces doesn't mean you have to act provincial." She looked pleased with herself at the joke. "And I didn't say Curt wasn't attractive, I said there was something not right about him. It's not the same thing."

"How do you mean? 'Not quite right'?"

She looked thoughtful. "Hard to say, really. Just, sometimes, I thought he was saying things he didn't believe. Did you have that feeling?"

I shook my head. "Not really. But I'm listening." I've learned that listening to Emily is a good idea. There are certain things my instincts are infallible about, but people isn't one of them. That's pretty much Emily's department. She understands about people: about why they are what and who they are. It's one of the things I love about her.

"He kept saying how wonderful Braydon was. How much he admired him. But sometimes it just felt, I dunno. It was all a little hollow, I guess. Like he'd said all those words too many times before."

"I didn't get that," I said thoughtfully.

"It was subtle," Emily said. "Like, well, like when we're on set and having a not-so-great day. And we've done a scene twenty-five times. After a while, the actors aren't really feeling their lines anymore, they're just saying the words. And they're acting, but you stop believing it because *they're* not believing it anymore. Curt was like that. And all that stuff about the car. What was that, ten years ago? More? I thought it was a bit much, him going on the way he did. It made me think…oh, this just sounds silly. But it made me think he had a purpose."

"What purpose?"

"See," she said, "I told you—it sounds silly. No purpose. Forget I said anything."

We walked in silence for a while and I pondered what Emily had said but, truly, it didn't make much sense to me. I had to acknowledge, though, that when I looked at Curt I saw not just the man he was, but I felt the portion of history we shared. It made clarity difficult. It polluted it, like the air in L.A.

"He said something that bothered me," I said after a while.

"What?"

"That last meal business. He said that, for his send-off meal, Braydon made himself a braised duck breast with caramelized pear and orange sauce and Moroccan couscous risotto."

"Right," Emily answered. "Honestly? If I were going to do a thing like that, I would only be able to *hope* for a meal that wonderful." She thought for a second, then added, "As long as it was a tofu duck."

"Yeah," I agreed. "I mean, the meal sounds great, right? Only there's just so much wrong with it."

"What do you mean?"

"Well, in the first place, Braydon hated duck, at least when I knew him. He was always the guy that preferred the white meat from the turkey or the chicken. And duck is nearly all sort of like dark meat. So he generally just avoided it."

"Not a great favorite, in other words."

"Hardly. And duck and *orange*? I can still hear him rant about the cliché of that. 'Sure, I'll prepare a duck in my kitchen, just don't make me eat it. People like duck, so fine. But if I ever serve duck with *anything* orange, you may as well kill me because my soul will be dead already.' Stuff like that."

Emily had stopped walking and stood facing me. "Get out," she said.

"Seriously," I said, nodding. "Or words very much to

that effect. I mean, he would have preferred your tofu duck. But wait!" I urged her forward again. "There's more. That business about the Moroccan couscous risotto? Sounds yummy, right? But—unless he'd changed a *lot*—that's not something he would ever have considered food, let alone put in his head."

I'm almost still embarrassed when I think about our visit to a very trendy East Village eatery. *The* restaurant of that particular week. They had a bulgur risotto and my usually gentle Braydon kind of went ballistic. He was *all* over first our waiter and then the kitchen manager. (The waiter couldn't pawn him off quickly enough.)

"Risotto is a rice dish." I still remember him over-pronouncing the words. "Arborio rice, specifically. Bulgur. Is. *Not*. If you mean bulgur, then say bulgur. But if you're going to call it risotto, I will expect something else." And so on.

I remember blushing and skootching down farther in my chair. Hey, I was twenty-five. My skin had yet to thicken. It would be years before I came to realize that it's a waste of time to feel embarrassed around people you will never, ever see again. As it was, I just remember pushing some type of greens around on my plate uncomfortably while Braydon alternately sighed and fumed. It wasn't our best ever evening out. Braydon was a gentle guy, yes. But there were certain things that got his goat. What he saw as the deliberate misrepresentation of food was one of them.

I gave Emily the short version of all of this and she

stopped again and kind of squinted at me. "What are you saying?"

I propelled us forward again. "I…I don't know, really. I just thought it was funny, that's all. I mean, I've been trying to think of a meal he would have found less appealing—based on what I remember, I mean—and I just can't."

"And…?"

"And nothing. Forget about it. Just thinking out loud, I guess."

We'd been walking for a long time by now. It would have been impossible for me to say how far we'd walked, but we'd been hoofing it for around forty-five minutes.

We'd passed through various types of terrain and past different landmarks, some of which I even recognized. We had, for instance, while never leaving the seawall, walked through a charming little square with a central fountain, some shops and several great-looking restaurants. We'd walked right through the middle of an off-leash dog park. We'd walked under the Granville Street bridge and seen the entrance to Granville Island. The seawall had begun to really meander then, and we'd passed many beautiful waterfront condos before walking under yet another bridge, after which the seawall led us to an expanse of green, which was where we now stood.

"I'm pretty sure we overshot Braydon's apartment. We've gone too far."

"Pretty sure? How sure?" Emily asked.

"Hmmmm…maybe ninety percent."

She nodded. "That's pretty sure."

I shrugged.

"Should we go back?" she said.

"Well, we *could* go back. But we're not exactly lost. We know what's behind us. And I'm enjoying this a lot. Do you want to keep moving ahead? Find out what's over the next rise, so to speak? Or are you tired?"

"I'm good. And all this walking is probably helping to work off the liver."

"You *ate* some of that? Man, were you ever a bad vegetarian tonight. And it wasn't exactly liver. Well, it was more than liver—it was fois gras, but—yeah, I'm sure it is."

"Is what?"

"I'm sure the walk is helping to work it all off. Including the pear tart. And the cheese."

"No meat in that," Emily said, sounding pleased with herself. I figured that, if it *had* been made out of meat, she probably would have eaten it anyway. She'd just been in that sort of mood.

The ocean was slightly wilder here than it had been at the beginning of our walk. Not wild in the way it gets in Southern California—all of the lower West Coast of Canada is protected from the open ocean by a large island—but the water seemed a little more…enthusiastic, and the wind, when it touched us, was more direct. Here the seawall meandered through a large green space, and though it was quite dark now, we met joggers, bikers and other walkers as we went.

After a while the seawall straightened out again and a wide, paved path led us away from the water's edge and into a small neighborhood filled with shops and cafés and restaurants. A few blocks into the neighborhood a sign told us we'd arrived at the Sunset Grill. We looked at each other and smiled. This far from Sunset Boulevard and with full dark upon us, we couldn't resist what seemed like some sort of signal or perhaps an invitation. We agreed that, after all that walking, a nightcap was in order. Maybe even a snack.

Inside was a surprise: more Irish pub, less L.A. rock diner. The room was warmly lit and intimate, the space dominated by the sort of dark wood bar with brass accents that's become synonymous with places of this nature—establishments where a welcoming atmosphere goes hand-in-hand with beer on tap and the kind of food that fills you up happily. Entirely different from WhyVeeAre. Entirely what we needed.

Emily smiled at me while we found a table. "I think I'm home."

It was a weeknight and there was apparently no sporting event going on because the televisions were off and the place was half-empty. Or maybe it was half-full, depending on your perspective and your mood.

A fortyish man with intelligent blue eyes and not a lot of silver hair presented himself at our table with an air of repressed joviality. His presence was strong and friendly. I took him instantly to be the proprietor.

"And what can I bring you ladies tonight?" he said in a clear, deep voice.

"What's good?" Emily asked.

"Is it your first time here?"

"It's my first time in the city," she said. "We live in Los Angeles."

"Ah, well, you're in for a treat then. Everything here is good. What are you in the mood for?"

After a bit of negotiating, we decided we were, after all, feeling a bit peckish as well as thirsty. The proprietor, who instructed us to call him Fred, advised us that the establishment's tap beer was very good—a local microbrew. Emily ordered a pint and I got a smaller glass. As well, Emily asked for a veggie burger, "with salad, though. Not fries." And I opted for half a dozen chicken wings with a side order of blue-cheese dressing—not Roquefort, since we were in Canada—for dipping.

"Good choice." Fred nodded approvingly before he went off to get our drinks.

"I can't believe we're planning on eating again," I said when he'd gone.

"All that walking," Emily said. "Besides, tasting a city is a big part of visiting one, don't you think?"

"That's funny," I said. "Braydon used to say that. Or something like it. That you could measure a place by the food it put into the world." I sighed. Braydon. It had been years since I'd thought of him regularly, but at the moment I didn't seem to be able to get him out of my head.

"It's not surprising, you know," Emily said, looking at me closely.

"What isn't?"

"That you can't stop thinking about him."

"Did I say it out loud?"

Emily laughed. "No. I could just see something in your face. But seriously, Madeline, it shouldn't surprise you. He used to be your *husband*, for crying out loud. And you're staying at his place, we ate at his restaurant, you spent the day at his office, you went to his funeral yesterday and you now own his car. Of course you're thinking about him. How could you not?"

"It's not that, though," I said. "Well, I guess it is a bit. But it's more, too." I paused. How could I explain the feeling of unease I'd had growing ever since, really, I'd discovered the short-rib recipe at Braydon's apartment in the morning? I told Emily about that now.

She looked at me carefully before she spoke. "Madeline, what are you suggesting?"

"Nothing. I don't know. Nothing."

"No. Something, I think. I mean, you tell me about the short ribs. You told me about the mismatched food. You're doing some calculating. I know you well enough to see it."

"Well, those things, sure. But…it's hard to describe what I'm feeling. Everything feels absolutely as it should be. And everything feels wrong."

"Tell me what you mean," she said solidly.

"Well, the company, for starters." Saying these things aloud was making me realize I was more concerned than I'd let myself believe. "On the surface, it all looks just as it seems. There's this gorgeous new building with all kinds of high-tech gear. Musta cost a bundle, too. There are balance sheets that seem to balance, a stock that's trading more or less as it should be. A new CEO responding well in a crisis. All…correct, I guess. All right, you know?"

Emily nodded, prompting me to go on. "And yet…?"

"Well, the fact that the stock is trading on the Pink Sheets *really* alarms me." This statement was out of the blue enough for Emily that I had to stop and explain the whole concept of the Pinks. But she's a quick study and, like me, knows when she doesn't have to understand all the details. She got the concept quickly and told me to go on.

"And then—" I shrugged, feeling lame "—then all the food stuff. It's just… I don't know."

"Madeline, are you thinking he didn't kill himself?"

"Like I said, I don't know."

"Has there been any hint of that?"

"What do you mean?"

"Well, what about the police? Is there an investigation?"

"No." I shook my head. "Not as far as I know. His mom and sister maybe think it, but that's natural, right? They'd want to think that. Other than that, there's been no hint. Just, you know, suicide. I don't think there's been any question that it wasn't." I hesitated.

Watched Emily's face closely. And then, "you think I'm crazy, don't you?"

Emily took her time answering, then surprised me when she did. "You know, I don't. I'm not saying you're right, mind you. But…well, something is bothering me, as well."

"What?"

Our beers had been delivered during my explanation of the Pink Sheets, and the proprietor took this moment to bring our food.

"I'll show you," she said to me, in answer to my question. And then, as he was putting our food on the table, she addressed our server. "Fred, you own this place, don't you?"

"That's right. I'm one of the owners. Have been since we opened in 1987."

"Then tell me, hypothetically—and please don't take this the wrong way."

I looked at Emily closely, wondering what she was up to.

"I'll try not to," Fred said with an easy smile.

"If you were to kill yourself, where would you do it?"

"Emily!" This was me. Of course.

Fred smiled again, a patient one I suspected he kept for potentially irritating customers.

"Well, I don't know that that's something I'd do. I got married not long ago. I love my wife—she's beautiful and funny and smart. I've got great friends. Business here is pretty good and—"

"No, I mean..." she interrupted. "Let me put it another way. If you *were* to kill yourself, where's the last place you'd do it?"

"Emily!"

Fred looked perplexed, but not overwhelmingly so. "Can I get you ladies something a little milder to drink?" he asked hospitably. "Something maybe non-alcoholic. Coffee? Tea? Some orange juice, maybe?"

"No, no. The drinks are fine," Emily said with an impatient wave. "We're not drunk."

I snorted.

"Well, not *very* drunk, anyway. And that's not why I'm asking. Just bear with me for a second. Let me try again. If you *were* to kill yourself, would you do it here? In the kitchen?"

Fred chuckled. "I guess I could pretty much say that would be the last place. If that's what you were getting at, you're right. And I can say that right off, because I had cause to think of that a week or so ago. When that television chef guy offed himself? They said on the news they found him in the kitchen of one of his restaurants, right here in Vancouver. And I thought, well, just like you said. I thought that's the last place I'd ever do that. You know—a chef doing that in the kitchen of his own restaurant? That just didn't seem right somehow."

"What do you mean?" I asked, getting into the game. "Not right?"

"Well, it's a *kitchen*, isn't it? And what chef doesn't love his kitchen? I mean, I'm not a chef. I'm a restaurateur." He sniffed, then smiled. "A bar owner, sure, but food is a big part of everything here. And we're very proud of our food. And we're very careful about how everything is prepared. And I *bought* all the stuff in there—the ovens and the Hobarts and everything—it's good, expensive gear. And you work on your reputation all the time when you have a restaurant. You put *everything* into it and it's everything to you."

"So what you're saying," Emily said, "is that even if you weren't planning on being around, you wouldn't want to risk doing anything to hurt the restaurant."

"Right. There's that. But it's the *kitchen*. Come on. Like I said, it'd be the last place. For sure."

Twelve

After we picked up Old Stinky, I drove Emily back to WhyVeeAre—closed now—to get her rental car. We hugged goodbye and Emily told me she'd call me in Seattle when she knew for sure when she'd be joining me.

"It's gonna be total *Thelma and Louise*," she said with a pleased smirk. "Only without the guns and exploding tanker trucks."

I laughed but didn't contradict her. The two of us *could* be kind of dangerous when left in each other's company for too long.

I headed back to Braydon's apartment with nothing more than the soaker tub on my mind. The day had seemed endless, and so much had been packed into it that I could barely remember what I'd had for breakfast: it seemed like it must have all happened a week before.

I started a tub going, then hit the kitchen with the

idea of grabbing another small glass of the Chianti I'd
been sipping at for the last few nights. But once in the
kitchen, I stopped in my tracks. Something wasn't
right. I could feel myself squinting and scanning
around, trying to spot what had given me the feeling.
It was difficult; it wasn't my place. Yet the idea of some
sort of wrongness persisted and even intensified.

While I went back upstairs to turn off the water, I
kept my senses tuned for anything that might be
amiss. I knew that the door had been locked when I'd
come in; I'd had to use my key and I would have
noticed if it had been tampered with. It hadn't been.
Though it seemed unlikely that anyone could get in
through the secure roof deck, I checked that entrance,
as well. Locked.

In the bedroom I had the feeling that my things
were somehow different from the way I'd left them.
Was it only a feeling? I tried second-guessing myself, but
it only added to my confusion. Had I really left that
pashmina there, just so? And what about the shoes I'd
worn to Braydon's service? Hadn't they been over there?
And my trading journal. I'd left it near the computer
in the office. Hadn't there been some notes stuck
between the pages? And so on. I moved from room to
room, using the same nonscientific approach, and it
seemed to me that much was different. But I couldn't
put my finger on what, and nothing actually seemed to
have been removed. Nothing I noticed, at any rate.

By the time I'd covered the whole apartment I was

feeling silly and even annoyed with myself for the paranoia. Obviously, I told myself, the way I'd started thinking about Braydon's death—as though there might have been more involved than met the eye—was having an effect on me. Now, apparently, I was jumping at shadows. More, I was making shadows where there weren't any.

I went back to the kitchen to get the wine I'd poured earlier, then headed up the stairs for the bath I'd promised myself. Halfway up the stairs I stopped and went back down to check that the door was fully secured. I knew I was being silly. But it still didn't seem like a bad idea to be safe, as well.

In the morning I tidied up the little bit of mess I'd made in the few days I'd been staying at the condo, packed up my stuff and stowed everything in the car. When I made a last walk around the apartment to make sure I hadn't left anything behind, I realized that, despite the fact that it was a lovely space, I wasn't going to miss it. In fact, I wasn't going to miss this whole episode of my life. Standing in the living room, having a last look around, I could almost hear a door closing. The end of another chapter in my life. The one with Braydon in it.

I had thought that the Braydon chapter was over years before, back in New York. I realized now that it had never truly been over. Until now. I felt a little sad. But I was also relieved to have gotten through my Vancouver visit and the stirring up of all of those old emotions and ultimately had survived.

I'd called Jessica when I first got up to let her know to expect me, and she'd invited me for lunch. So when I pulled up to the venerable house in South Granville, I wasn't surprised to see Anne-Marie's car ahead of mine on the driveway. When I got out of the car, Anne-Marie came out the door herself to greet me.

"What a gorgeous day!" she called from the stairs. "I wish I had time for a walk."

"Where would you go?" I asked lightly, getting out of the car.

"Spanish Banks, I think. I love it down there on a day like this. The ocean, the forest—it's beautiful."

"Is that near Stanley Park?" I asked, joining her on the stairs.

She shook her head. "No. Out near the university campus. Actually, if you keep walking up the beach from Spanish Banks, you're more or less *on* the campus after a while."

Up close, she looked better than she had when I'd seen her a couple of days before. More rested. I told her so.

"Thanks," she said, ushering me into the house. "I actually got a decent night's sleep. Partly because our houseguests are finally all gone. And partly because…well, I'm still sad, but the funeral helped. I guess I feel a bit more at peace about everything."

"That's good," I said, shushing the voices in my head that had been plaguing me since the day before. Short ribs. Wrong food. Girls and drugs in bars. There's instinct and then there's insanity. It's possible the words are related somehow. But I don't think so.

Once inside I was struck again by an almost inappropriate awareness of opulence. The house was lovely, but I sensed that its present owners had never felt quite comfortable in the space.

This feeling was intensified when I saw Jessica, dwarfed by the sheer height of the ceiling in the foyer and by the vastness of the room itself. And, unlike her daughter, she didn't look better than the last time I'd seen her. If anything, she looked worse: smaller still and more diminished. I tried not to let my face betray a hint of this.

Both women bustled me into the dining room, where the table was set for three. Robert was nowhere in evidence. Seeing my questioning glance, Jessica said, "Robert is resting just now. His nurse is with him."

"Is he…is he any better?"

Jessica tried a wan smile. "It's hard to say, really. He seems a little more peaceful today, at any rate."

Lunch was lovely. I'd forgotten that Braydon had inherited some of his natural skill, and Jessica was a terrific cook. I had the feeling she'd thrown herself into the preparation of the food for this lunch, perhaps as a way of staunching the pain she was feeling.

She'd made us a classic eggs Benedict that included a perfect hollandaise that I could tell at first bite was homemade. She served the bennies with beautifully golden home fries and—just to show this was brunch and not breakfast, I guess—blanched white asparagus tips and a delicate green salad with her own raspberry vinaigrette.

"This is amazing," I said, attacking the food cheerfully. I hadn't realized how hungry I was. Halfway through making my bennie disappear, I noticed the other two women weren't really eating. They were making eating motions, but I had the feeling that neither of them was doing much beyond pushing the edible material around on their plates. I felt like a pig, but I also felt compelled to carry on, it was that good.

After lunch—and I tried not to look longingly after Jessica and Anne-Marie's barely touched plates as they were whisked away—Jessica led us out to a terrace where a table had been set with tea.

"You really shouldn't have gone to so much trouble," I told her, noticing the madeleines on the table and knowing they would be freshly baked. She smiled at me when she saw me notice and I returned the smile. I had never been in her house when she had not made madeleines.

"In your honor, of course," she said.

"Thank you."

Not wanting to disappoint her, as soon as I had a cup of tea in front of me, I tucked right in. After all, I couldn't imagine where—aside from Montreal or Paris—I was likely to get a madeleine like this: fresh from the oven, the richness of the butter causing the cookie to almost melt on the tongue.

I managed to eat quite a number of them while telling Anne-Marie and Jessica about my visit to Gauthier Fine Foods. They hadn't known about the stock trading on the Pink Sheets, but both women could recall some kind of upset with the stock that had changed things drastically less than a year before. Braydon had been upset about it, they reported, but not inconsolably so.

"That was probably it," I said. "See, the thing is, no matter what Doug said, the Exchange doesn't just dump you on a whim. You have to actually have done something—or, in this case, not done something—in order for them to delist you. And the trouble is, too, with Braydon...with Braydon...out of the picture, it's more difficult to track."

"How so?" Jessica asked.

In the nick of time, I stopped myself from blurting out that Doug Withers wasn't the first CEO in history to blame a dead man for his troubles. It was true, but it would also have been an insensitive thing for me to say. And potentially misleading. I didn't *know* Doug was blaming Braydon for something he himself had done. But I did suspect it. And, truly, a lot of people would have done the same in his shoes. That didn't necessarily mean he was doing anything strictly *wrong*. It might not be the most chivalrous thing to do—to blame someone no longer around to defend himself. It might not be the most noble. But for a lot of people, it would certainly be the most convenient.

"With the stock trading on the Pinks, I'm a lot less useful to you than I might otherwise have been. The best thing for you to do is have your lawyers stay in close touch with the company. I don't think it will hurt Doug to know you're watching him. Chances are he really *is* doing his best. But, see, in either scenario, your help and support will be the most beneficial to *you*. If Doug has not been as forthcoming as he should be, being helpful puts you in a position to watch him. Keeps you closer, if you follow, than if you were being adversarial and he wanted to keep you at arm's length. And if your suspicions are correct, you'll see it quickly—or your lawyers will—and you'll be in a position to move."

This wasn't the best advice I could give the two women, it was the *only* advice, because dissension among family members at this point wouldn't do anyone any good. I wished there was more I could do—I really did—but the fact was, theirs was going to be a waiting game for the next little while. There just wasn't anything for it.

When I said goodbye, all three of us promised to keep in touch and perhaps visit at some point, but I wondered if even we knew how hollow the words probably were. I liked Jessica and Anne-Marie and, on a certain level, having been so enmeshed in their lives again for the last few days had not been uncomfortable, except for the most obvious reason: Braydon's absence. It was that very absence that now made me doubt we'd ever keep in touch. That ending chapter, again. That closing door. Something was different. Something would never be the same. For all of us. Forever.

From Vancouver, I headed due south on Highway 99 and was surprised—as I always had been—at how quickly almost all traces of city were left behind. The land between Vancouver and the Canada-U.S. border is exceedingly fertile. You don't need to be an expert agriculturalist to know this; it's apparent in the field crops that grow just off the freeway, the tall silos bulging with their contents on the farms next to the highway and the happy-looking horses and cows that watch the cars speed past their fields.

I wasn't surprised to find that, once the city was behind me, I felt a certain tension leave my shoulders. A tension that, on a conscious level, I hadn't even realized was there.

The day was cool, but fine and clear. I made good time out of the city and was flatly amazed when I saw a sign that announced I was approaching Peace Arch Park.

I knew from a previous visit that the park was jointly maintained by the Canadian and U.S. governments. There are gardens and picnic areas, but the central monument—a huge concrete triumphal arch that straddles the border—is a lovely symbol of the continued peace that both countries have enjoyed for a long, long time.

It's pleasant to stop the car near the monument and stroll through the gardens—Braydon and I had done just that the first time he'd brought me home to meet the folks—but that wasn't part of the plan for me today. I had a few hours of driving before I got to Seattle and, since I was still struggling a bit with the right-hand drive, I just wanted to get it over with.

As I approached the border, however, I could see that things weren't likely to be as straightforward as I'd hoped. I'd never been through this crossing when it was anything other than cursory. Not much more than "Where are you going?" and "How long were you out of the country?" and "What was the purpose of your trip?" Braydon had told me that this was the norm. However, he'd also said that, if timing was important, you had to allow for more than cursory inspections. According to him, sometimes there would be more than standard vigilance in place. Braydon had said it might be because the border guards had been alerted to look for something specific, or it might even be because some new mandate had been handed down from on high.

Whatever the case, as I got close to the U.S. Customs building, I could see that this was going to be one of those days. There seemed to be no cursory crossings happening today; all of the drivers in front of me were being asked to get out of their cars, and a light but time-consuming inspection of each interior was taking place.

I groaned inwardly. I didn't have anything to hide, but I didn't relish the extra minutes this would take.

It was already awkward to maneuver the right-hand drive car up to the left-hand drive window and have to lean across in order to roll down the window. (And while I did so, I made a mental note to avoid drive-through restaurants when driving this car.)

The border guard was polite but not especially friendly. It wasn't, I reminded myself, a job where friendliness was highly prized or even desired. I saw him compare my passport photo to my mug while he asked me the routine questions. And even though I'd expected it, when he said, "Please step out of the car," I felt a little surprised. Surprised and guilty. Like I'd done something.

The search itself went quickly: the car was small and I didn't have a lot in it. And it's probably true that I did not look much like a drug smuggler or a gun runner or a terrorist or whatever it was they were looking for on this particular day. Plus the paperwork for the car was all in order. Since I was basically import-ing a vintage automobile into the States, to avoid possible delays, I'd looked into what was required be-forehand. So the search was all pretty routine and surface, and my paperwork spotless. Up to a point.

When the border guard bent to look under the driver's seat and said, "What's this?" while reaching underneath, my heart gave a good lurch. I hadn't looked under the seats and I cursed myself for it now. Who knew what Braydon had kept in his car? If it was something incriminating, I was going to be the one in-criminated. I felt a damp sweat spring up on my skin.

The border guard looked over the papers he found

under the seat closely but, apparently satisfied with what he saw there, he closed the folder and handed it back to me. "Looks like you lost this," he said pleasantly enough.

I was aware that my hands were shaking slightly as I took the folder. A ridiculous reaction, I knew, but I didn't seem to have much choice in the matter. As I got back into the car, I gave the folder a perfunctory glance and recognized Braydon's handwriting. Beyond that, I just wanted to get the hell out of there.

Once safely through the border, however, I couldn't get the folder out of my mind. At the first exit, I pulled off the freeway and followed the road into the tiny hamlet of Blaine, Washington.

I stopped the car at the far edge of a big gas station parking lot. The folder was back in my hand even before the car had fully stopped.

There were four pages of handwritten notes—Braydon's hand—plus various photocopied documents. While I read, my heart started beating faster.

No single thing in the folder was incriminating in itself. I narrowed my eyes as I read, willing a pattern to emerge from the various pieces. There wasn't one—not one that I could discern, at any rate—but together they created a picture that begged to be made sense of.

The photocopies were of invoices from various companies I'd never heard of, all billing a single company I'd also never heard of—DW Investments—for what seemed to relate to many aspects of a construction project. DW Investments listed an address on West Broadway in Vancouver and, oddly, no telephone number and no Internet address.

There were handwritten notes on the photocopies. Braydon's hand—I had no trouble at all recognizing his distinctive scrawl. I did, however, have trouble deciphering the notes; he'd obviously written them for himself and he hadn't felt the need to write carefully so his notes could be read by others or transcribed. I could make out occasional words. "Check this," had been written next to an invoice item for 2500 square feet of laminate floor. "Purpose?" was scrawled next to an entry for 6000 meters of rebar.

I had little more luck with the pages of notes. Here again, Braydon had obviously been writing for his own benefit. What I could decipher, though, made me think he had a lot of questions relating to what I presumed was the construction of the new Gauthier Fine Foods building on West Sixth. And he had a few ideas for answers, but these were so shorthanded, it didn't take me long to give up hope of figuring out what he'd meant.

The last two sheets looked to me like printouts of PDF files. They were for some kind of pre-promo relating to a television show to be hosted by "Mimi Withers Gauthier." It was not a cooking show, but some type of lifestyle effort—design, food and style were mentioned specifically—but what caught my attention—and what had caught Braydon's, as well, because he'd circled it three times in his usual brown ink—was the production company listed: DW Entertainment. The same address as the construction supplier, and the same odd dearth of information that I noted with relation to DW Investments.

Had I found any one of these things by themselves, it would perhaps have aroused my curiosity, but not inspired my involvement. So Mimi was checking out options—so what? So there had been bills from construction companies, of course. So Braydon wrote himself mostly indecipherable notes—was that supposed to be a news flash? But together in a file under the seat of a car probably no one besides Braydon ever drove? This meant something. I wasn't sure what, but I sensed it meant something really big.

I was barely aware of getting the car in motion again, of pointing it back toward Canada. I don't recall making a decision about where the car was taking me. Nor did I fully understand why. Yet I drove without hesitation. And, other than clearing Canada Customs to cross back over the border, I didn't stop even once before I got where I was going.

Thirteen

The neighborhood—if one could call it that—the street and the house were all almost exactly as I'd imagined they'd be. The little estates in the area each seemed to command the better part of ten or twenty acres. Country estates. Large houses perhaps best described as small mansions. Beautiful tree-lined driveways flanked by white board fences and expensive looking equines munching on beautiful green grass. Heaven just off the highway.

The Gauthier home was a palatial single-level heritage-modern structure with mature landscaping that made it look as though the house had been in place for a hundred years. Expensive, I knew, to get a house to look like that. It costs a bundle to get new money to look old. I think that's why a lot of people with new money don't bother to make the attempt.

The four-car garage was attached and the doors were closed, so I didn't know what might be in there. There was a late-model Chrysler on the circular drive and no signs of activity anywhere within eyeshot. It wasn't the kind of place where you might expect to encounter a security guard or even a maid, just the country home of simple people with a lot of money. In other words, anything was possible.

I pulled Old Stinky directly up to the front of the house and marched right up to the front door and hit the doorbell. The strains of a metallic version of something by Pachebel could be heard above the coo of nearby birds and the gently rushing aquatic sounds of a water feature. I wrinkled my nose. Pachebel in a doorbell, I thought, was a little over-the-top.

When no one answered, I went around back. Here the U shape of the house protected a perfectly coiffed courtyard. In the center of the courtyard, an amoeba-shaped swimming pool had center stage, while all the accoutrements for perfect entertaining flanked the edges of the water.

Trying not to feel like an intruder—though what else was I?—I walked up to the French doors at the back of the house and rang another bell. Still nothing. But from here, I could see into some of the rooms through the glass panes in the door. It looked—all of it—like a spread for *Architectural Digest*. Vases placed casually—just so—next to paintings leaned against walls near shelves filled with beautifully bound books near tall candles on elegant pedestals. To me, it didn't look like a place for living as much as a place for looking at and perhaps for showing.

A tidy stable was not far off, and when I approached, all looked quiet there as well. The scents brought me straight back to the girls' camps of my youth: summer-cured hay and the gentle pong of horse dung and all of the things that together say "horse" to your nose.

The inside of the stable was as predictable as the house had been. Not necessarily a barn, but a designer's idea of a place where horses should live. A wide and well-lit central aisle connected six roomy box stalls, each fitted with rubber mats and automatic waterers. There was a large tack room and lounge at the far end of the barn where a full array of saddles and bridles—for both English and Western styles of riding—were hung carefully against one wall. A couple of sofas, a coffee table and a small kitchen area took up another part of the space.

The stalls were empty just now, the horses that occupied them presumably the ones I'd seen in the paddocks that flanked the long driveway. It was all so lovely. A picturebook idea, really, of the way a life should be. For a second—or maybe only half of a second—I thought that this was the life that *could* have been mine if things had gone a different way. Back to Braydon morose on the bed. Back to that duvet. The life that *would* have been mine, I thought, if I'd been able to put up with a man who adored me and doted on me—a gentle, loving man—for these past ten years. But, of course, I knew that *that* life would have looked quite different. This now—the horses, the country house, the classical music in a doorbell—this wasn't about what Braydon and Madeline had built, but rather what Braydon-after-Madeline had dreamed. And "putting up" with anything has never been a strong suit for me.

I didn't examine these thoughts with regret, but rather with an oddly detached curiosity. As though someone else were having them. But they captivated me for a few moments, these thoughts. And it was while thinking them that I became aware of voices, alarmingly close by.

Without considering my actions, I ducked into one of the open stalls. A ridiculous reaction. I knew that while my feet carried me into the stall, it was an action born entirely of instinct. Knew it while I ducked under the cover of a hayrack at the far corner of the stall. Still. It was as though my feet had little minds of their own and didn't care what the mind between my shoulders sensibly suggested.

Once I was hiding in the stall, there seemed no way of getting myself out of there without making things worse. So I stayed where I was while the voices and their owners grew louder and closer.

It was two voices, I decided quickly. Plus the clip-clop of a couple of sets of shod hooves.

One voice, high and merry, belonged to a woman. The other voice was a man's: deep and redolent and filled with affection and perhaps something else.

"I *knew* Algernon would be too much for you," the woman said cheerfully as they entered the barn. "You really did make yourself out to be a more accomplished rider than you are."

"Well, there you have it." There was laughter in this voice as well. "What man won't do something foolish for the admiration of a beautiful woman? And I think perhaps I am not so poor a rider as you indicate."

It sounded as though they'd stopped in the wide aisle and, from the activity I could hear and the course of their conversation, I figured they were likely in the process of cross-tieing the horses, stripping them of their tack and grooming them after a ride.

The aisle was fine for me. I knew they'd never see me from there. But once the horses were ready to be put away, would they come into *this* stall? I figured there was a two in six chance they would. Not the worst odds I've ever been up against, but I've certainly seen better.

"It's dangerous, though—that pretense," she was continuing. "I could have given you Sunny. He's a much quieter mount."

He laughed. "Ah, danger, my pet. I live for such things, as you well know."

I did not recognize her voice. I'd never heard Braydon's wife speak beyond a chilly "hello" at Bray's memorial service, yet it seemed likely that this calm, confident and proprietary voice would in fact belong to Mimi Gauthier.

I had no problem with the man. Especially since this

was a voice I'd often heard from behind closed doors, engaged in conversations not directed at me: Curt Foster. Though my mind fought against believing it, the syntax and the tone were unmistakable, as well as the gentle accent I'd always heard in Curt's voice but never commented on or asked about. But how could it be Curt? After all, I told myself, what business would he have here, in South Langley, riding with his boss's widow two days after the man's remains had been laid to rest?

The conversation, its content and timbre continued along the same vein. Curt's voice came from a steady spot I gauged to be perhaps twenty feet from where I crouched, hopefully hidden. Mimi's—if it was, in fact, Mimi's voice—moved farther away and then came back, as though she were doing the horse-related work. Which, to me, made sense. They were her horses, after all. And it was her barn. I'm no equine expert, but I do know that how the animals are taken care of is very important. She'd likely want to do it herself.

Confirming a couple of my guesses, I heard her say, "Be a love, Curt, and take the saddle you were using into the tack room? You'll see the empty rack where it belongs. I just want to quickly do Merianna's tail."

"Can I take something else into the tack room?" I heard him respond, his voice husky. "You're not in a hurry, are you, madam?"

The sound of a gently passionate exchange made my heart beat faster for so many reasons. Firstly, and of course, considering my position, I just wanted them to finish up with the horses and get the hell out of the barn so I could get out of there undetected. I mean, seriously—there was a big house just over *there*. Why not go find a bed?

Secondly—and no less naturally—I didn't know what it meant that Braydon's new widow was kissing his old friend and associate so close to the time of Bray's death, but I figured it couldn't be good.

And, thirdly, I did *not* want to hear anyone making love while I hid in the shadows. I have been many things in my life, but I'm no kind of voyeur, and that kind of action so nearby was more likely to make me lose my lunch than tickle my libido. It had been a gorgeous lunch and I was keen to hang on to it.

I heard a zipper, then a musical riff of giggles—hers—then the dull thud of what might have been a boot coming free from a foot and thudding to a rest on the concrete.

"Look at you! You're a stallion. How do you want to take me? Like this? Oh, yes—your willing mare!"

And more stuff like that. I felt like humming—honestly I did—to drown out their inane and breathless love talk. I didn't do it. Humming would have been a seriously bad idea while I cowered under a hayrack and while they had access to weapons like pitchforks and shovels.

Just when I was about to come to terms with the fact that—yes—I probably was about to hear Curt and Mimi do the nasty within ten feet of me, I could hear them move toward the tack room. I wouldn't have been able to say what I was more relieved about—the fact that I wouldn't have to listen to any more of their quasi-equine coupling or that I should now be able to slink away undetected. In either case, I was thankful that the comfy sofas in the tack room had provided a more attractive love nest than a scratchy and cold barn floor.

When all I could hear was the occasional equine stamp and snort of the real horses left in the aisles, and the pounding of my own stupid heart, I dared poke my head up to look around. Two lovely horses stood patiently in cross-ties in the aisle, with bits of tack and grooming equipment left more or less willy-nilly while their mistress had gone to answer her booty call.

I made soft clucking noises with my tongue as I approached the closest of the horses, knowing that my sudden appearance might startle him. The animal turned his head toward me, as though surprised by my presence but not shocked or startled. He had reason to know that humans, after all, do the most curious things.

It was lucky that I'd been around horses at least a little bit, since I had to duck under the muscular neck of the one closest to me to get out of the stall. I put my hand on his mane as I moved away, enjoying the rough feel of the hair beneath my palm. I wished briefly that I had the nerve to finish the grooming and tuck the horses into their stalls. *That*, I thought, would have been funny: for the lovers to finish in the tack room and come out to discover the horses had been put away.

Clear of the barn, I walked quickly, firmly and as

quietly as possible back to the car. Once there I sat in the driver's seat for a couple of seconds that seemed like half an hour while I collected myself.

At first I was concerned that Old Stinky's throaty sports car voice would attract the attention of the lovers, but I chided myself for that a beat later. As locked in passion as they'd likely be by now, there was little chance of that. So I started the car and made my way back down the long, beautiful driveway. My heart was still pounding firmly, but I didn't look back to see if anyone was following me. Not even once.

Canadian and U.S. cultures are very different. And I'm not talking yogurt. There are strong similarities between the two and they have roots that are somewhat similar, but the evolution of both has not been the same at all.

One thing, however, is not different in many places on either side of the border: urbanization has ripped the heart right out of a lot of small towns in both the United States and Canada. This has mostly come in the form of shopping malls funneling small-town inhabitants out of little hamlets and dropping them together at the mall, usually at what used to be the edge of town, leaving the old downtown an ill-loved shadow of its former self.

While some towns have let their old lifestyles slide into the past unmourned, in other places town fathers and mothers have gotten together to inject new life into their downtown cores, trying—sometimes futilely—to maintain some of the wholesome dignity that the town centers of old held for their residents.

As I fled north on 216th Street, away from the Gauthier estate, I discovered that the city of Langley was like that. I hadn't really known where I was going when I left there, I just knew I wanted to get away. Fast.

The road cut through gently rolling fields—more horses, more estates—then smaller properties giving way to subdivisions and, after a few miles, the town itself. The city of Langley looked like a town that had fought back in the culture war. The old downtown was not hugely populated, but it was very charming.

Though a drink of something strong would not have been unwelcome right then, I settled instead for the strongest thing I could drink in large quantity and still manage to drive a car: espresso. Followed by more espresso. I found a coffeehouse that seemed to reflect the town's recent infusion of charm, with a parking spot for Old Stinky right out front. Even with coffee at hand, with everything that had been happening, I had the feeling that there wasn't enough espresso in the world to get me through this day.

As I took a seat at the window with a large latte in a bowl-shaped cup, I thought about all that I'd learned.

Mimi and Curt were lovers. I hadn't seen the woman in the barn and I hadn't recognized her voice, but I couldn't imagine who else it might be. And the cadence of the lovers' voices, their level of comfort with each other and the tenor with which they'd approached lovemaking made me think this wasn't a new development. It made me think, too, about Curt: who he'd been when I knew him and who he had become. What had there been between him and Braydon? I tried to remember. What had been the dynamic when I'd known both of them well?

Curt had owned the restaurant in Bed-Stuy where Braydon had been executive chef. Although the term "executive chef" was a bit of an overstatement for a thirty-five seat bistro in what had still been a fairly rough neighborhood. They had, I thought, spent as much time dreaming and talking and scheming about food as they had serving customers. And, truly, the food at Quiver had been sublime. Really, really innovative and first-rate. Unfortunately, too few people had known about it—and, if they'd known, they hadn't wanted to make the trip out to Brooklyn—a fact that had rankled both men endlessly.

And I thought about our ill-fated trip to the Finger Lakes, none of which I ever got to see. Thinking about that day now—from the distance of a decade and in the context of a larger whole—even the race had meaning. Boys being boys? Sure, maybe that. But also, the whole incident seemed to me to highlight a competitiveness that both men had usually kept in fairly good check. Had they competed, also, for Mimi? Or had that been a competition Braydon had never even been aware of?

I thought about seeing Curt at WhyVeeAre, a restaurant as different from Quiver as could be imagined.

And though it was the flagship, WhyVeeAre was only the tip of the iceberg that had floated Braydon home. There were half a dozen restaurants all over the U.S. and Canada, and from all reports, every one was just as sumptuous and successful as Braydon's fledgling effort. What would that, I wondered, have done for Curt's competitive streak?

Before I could really stop and think things through and talk myself out of it, I fished my cell phone and Filofax out of my bag, dialing Anne-Marie's number as soon as I found it.

"Madeline," she exclaimed when she heard my voice, "what's wrong? Is it the car?"

"No, no, the car's fine," I said, realizing that wondering if Old Stinky was actually capable of a big trip wasn't so far off the mark. "It's just that…that something has come up. I'm going to stay in Vancouver another day. Is it all right if I spend another night at Bray's?"

"Sure, Madeline. Of course. Is everything all right?"

I thought briefly about telling her at least a bit about what I was thinking, then discarded the notion. The fact was, I didn't really *know* anything. Certainly not enough to tell. Anne-Marie and her mother had enough on their minds—and their hearts—without me adding to their burdens.

"Nothing really, Anne-Marie. A…a personal matter. An old friend of mine is in town." This, at least, was true. "I thought I'd spend an extra day with her."

"Well, of course, Madeline." If Anne-Marie sensed

anything was amiss, I didn't hear it in her voice. "Mother will be home all day. Just drop by whenever and pick up the keys. I'll let her know you're coming."

The next question, I knew, might be more difficult. "Anne-Marie, I was just wondering, how long has Curt worked for Braydon?"

"Curt?" Anne-Marie was clearly mystified. "Let me think. A year maybe. No, wait—closer to two. My parents were moving to the new house right around the time Curt moved to Vancouver to take the job. I remember because there seemed to be so much moving all at the same time. Why?" She sounded somewhat concerned.

"Oh, nothing really," I assured her quickly. "It's just that, I knew Curt back in New York. When Bray and I were together. And I wondered if he'd been part of Braydon's company all along."

"No," Anne-Marie said with confidence. "Definitely not. I hadn't heard his name in years before Curt came to Vancouver to work with Bray." Anne-Marie was quiet for a moment and I thought she was getting ready to say goodbye. I was wrong. "It's funny you should mention Curt now. Braydon never said anything, but I had the feeling that things hadn't been right between them for a while."

This was news to me. "What do you think it was about?"

"About?" Anne-Marie said, as though she hadn't considered the question before. "I don't know. Just forget I even mentioned it. Now that I've said it aloud

I realize it was nothing. Probably just some work thing. A menu issue or something."

After I got off the phone, I thought about what Anne-Marie had said. Things hadn't been right between them. There could be a lot of reasons for that, and Curt having an affair with Braydon's wife could certainly have been one of them. A menu issue? Mimi would *not* have been on the menu.

Next I called my mom in Seattle to let her know I'd be detained at least another day.

"Oh, kitten, I'm so sorry to hear that," she said. "I got mangoes! I don't know if they'll last."

"Mangoes," I repeated, not really understanding.

"You know—sort of oblong tropical fruits with a long hard stone inside."

"I know what they are," I told her. "Just not why you're mentioning them to me."

"I know you love mangoes," she said simply. "I got a case. They were on sale at Safeway. I thought we could have them for breakfast tomorrow. Now I'm not so sure."

I smiled, imagining my mother in her kitchen surrounded by ripe mangoes. "That's sweet," I said, "that you thought of me. And I'll just be a day or so extra. They'll probably hold." I had another thought. "Anyway, *you* have one. Tomorrow for breakfast, with your tea. You don't spoil yourself enough."

I could hear the smile in her voice when she replied. "You're right. I don't. I think I *will* have one tomorrow. Just for me. But I'll hold the rest for when you get here."

When I put down the phone, I felt a ridiculously sharp pang. I missed her. I missed her more than usual. Plus I had the feeling that, if she were here with me, she would make sense of all the disparate things I was seeing.

After a few minutes of sipping and thinking, I made the final call. The one I'd been putting off until I felt fairly confident they would have had time to finish playing in the barn and put the horses away.

I was relieved when she answered on the second ring.

"Hello, Mimi? This is Madeline Carter. I was…that is, I am…"

"I know who you are. What can I do for you?" She did not say, "Why are you calling?" but I heard it anyway.

"I have…that is, I'd like to come by and talk to you."

"Come by? My caller ID said this call is coming from California."

I was nonplussed for a moment, but only just. New technology does that to me sometimes. "Oh, I'm on my cell phone," I said, opting to try for levity. For charm. "My phone thinks it's in California, wherever it is."

"And you're not?" she asked, not matching the warmth in my voice.

"No. Actually, I'm in Langley. Having a coffee."

"In Langley?" It was obviously not what she'd been expecting to hear. Then she said again, "In Langley. I'm not quite sure what to make of that."

I ignored her question, since it was partly unvoiced anyway. "Would half an hour be all right?"

"For what?" she said.

"For me to drop by. In perhaps half an hour. Though I can get there sooner, if it suits."

"No, that would not suit. At all." And then, with more strength, "I would prefer you *not* come by, under the circumstances. I am…I am distraught. I think your presence would not help with that. And I'm on my way out the door, in any case. If you have any further requests, direct them to my lawyer. My brother can put you in touch."

While I drove back to the house on 216th Street, I thought about exactly how distraught Mrs. Mimi Gauthier had sounded. Not on the phone, but earlier, in her barn. Under different circumstances, I might have taken pity on the grieving widow and did as she requested: left her alone. But the thought of her laughter—young, carefree, abandoned—and her betrayal angered me on her late husband's behalf.

At that moment, I think I was half back in love with the memory of my ex-husband. Part of that, I guess, was feeling somewhat protective of him, despite the fact that he was beyond hurting now. I felt protective and, from where I was standing, I couldn't imagine a pair from whom more protection would be necessary.

On the other hand, I couldn't help thinking about the girl I'd met in the store on Robson Street, the one who had told me her friend had spent the night with Braydon. It was a sobering thought. Infidelity was not something I would have associated with Braydon. And yet. Suddenly I was seeing infidelity all around me.

I backed Old Stinky into a driveway opposite and just up the street from the one that led to the Gauthier's home. From that vantage I could see the drive that led to the Gauthier estate but, unless someone were looking for the pale blue cloud that was Old Stinky, I didn't think I would be noticed.

And then I waited. Mimi had said she was going out. I realized that might have been an untruth, but I sat there in any case, just thinking. It wasn't as though I had anything else to do.

Within twenty minutes—twenty long, slow-moving minutes—my wait was rewarded. The large Chrysler that had been parked in front of the house came into view, going a little too fast for the road that carried it, a dark, burly head on the driver's side. Curt. Alone in the car. He headed south, the direction I'd come from earlier in the day. Presumably, he was heading toward the freeway.

Still I waited. And probably less than seven minutes later, a dark blue BMW convertible popped into view, the top pulled down on this sunny day, Mimi's bright hair plainly visible as she turned the car northward, toward the city of Langley, where I'd enjoyed my coffee half an hour before.

I sat in the car a further ten minutes and thought about what I wanted to do. Truly, I reasoned, there was no reason for me not to pull the car back onto the road and head for the freeway myself, and from there, head south as I'd intended this morning. I still had time to get to my mother's before full night. Share one of her mangoes.

The thought of my mother's house in Seattle—a beautiful Victorian restored right down to its antique escutcheons—and her tea and welcoming presence almost persuaded me. And then I thought of Braydon and the games people play and the house lying empty and beckoning just across the road, and I knew there was only one thing I wanted to do.

I thought about leaving the car where it was and walking into the property, the better to run away undetected should someone come, but on a couple of levels, this didn't feel like a good idea. And the biggest reason was the car itself. You could leave a late model tan Ford at the edge of the road and no one would look twice. But a sky-blue 1962 Sunbeam Alpine Mark II? You didn't need to be a car expert to remember *that* ride. Especially since it was a vehicle Mimi was likely to recognize. Heck, she'd probably even ridden in it, maybe driven it herself.

Besides, I reasoned, Langley is a rural community. Even if she wasn't going far, she'd be gone for a while. The closest block of stores was fifteen minutes from the house, and with any luck, she was going farther than that. I'd have time.

When I parked Old Stinky in the same spot it had occupied before, I felt a tremendous wave of déjà vu. I brushed it aside. Of *course* this felt familiar, it was like the coffee-filled hours between hadn't even happened. This time, however, I knew the house was empty. I slung my messenger bag over my shoulder and headed in for another round of Pachebel.

The front door was locked, as I'd known it would be. But it had seemed logical to try it anyway, after I'd rung the bell for good measure. Just in case. But nothing stirred inside the house.

To my surprise, the French doors at the back of the house that I'd peered through earlier were locked, as well. I'd reasoned that, a big house down a long driveway on a quiet peaceful road in a country and area not known for its high crime rate would probably have fairly lax security. And I wasn't far wrong: no dogs, no gates, no security cameras. I couldn't even see an alarm system. But the door was locked and I wasn't prepared to do anything about it. There were doors in the walls of both arms of the U that framed the courtyard, however, and the first one I tried opened to my turn.

I stood on the threshold, the door open wide in front of me, a wave of household scents wafting past. I could smell something perfumey and floral in that wave. And something edible, like toast. Old coffee. Furniture wax. Laundry soap. All the smells that make a house a home were present in that quick taste.

What am I doing? I thought, putting a foot in the door and calling out, "Hello? Mimi? Is anyone here?" I didn't expect that anyone was, but it seemed better to be safe than sorry.

I stood in a large bedroom, though I figured it probably wasn't the master suite: not quite big enough, and it didn't have the over-the-top luxury that my glimpses of the rest of the house through the windows led me to expect of the master. This would be, I thought, a guest bedroom. A queen-size four-poster bed dominated the space, a thick rug covered the floor and the mirror at the back of the dresser reflected the image of a huge bouquet of fresh flowers along with my scared, pale face.

As I stood and looked around, I was aware that I'd crossed more than a threshold to reach this space; I'd crossed a line, as well. In the past I had done things that could be put down to trespassing, but this? This was breaking and entering, no two ways about it. Even if, as I rationalized to myself now, there had been no actual breakage involved.

Unaccountably, my grandmother's voice floated into my head: "In for a penny, in for a pound." I sighed deeply. What the hell? And moved into the house.

And it was a lovely house, new money or no. The kind of deeply upholstered joint most people wouldn't squawk too much about having to spend their days in. Or their nights.

Everything was beautiful. The floor space that wasn't covered with thick rugs gleamed warmly, and even the antiques looked new.

Oddly, I didn't feel the rush of adrenaline I would have thought would accompany my first gosh-honest-for-real break and enter. I felt detached and interested, as though I were touring a show home at a county fair. Only at the back of my mind was I thinking: *Where would she keep it?*

When I found the master bedroom, I checked both

nightstands, and while I did see a lot of valuables, I didn't find what I was looking for.

I found the junk drawer that everyone has in their kitchen, but it wasn't there, either. It was quite full, though. Of junk. Pens and pencils and twist ties and...not what I was looking for. I moved on.

In the other wing of the U—opposite the one that held the bedrooms—I found a very complete home gym, plus two rooms given over to office furniture. There was a computer on a desk in each of these rooms. From their decor, I could tell these were his and hers home offices. Hers was decorated in the French provincial style, the furniture painted a milky white and elegantly aged and distressed. I'd never asked what Mimi did for a living, but from the books assembled neatly on the shelves it was obvious—though perhaps it should have been before this, as well—that she was an interior designer. And, from the looks of this place, probably a pretty good one. Though I doubted she worked cheap.

When I bent to examine her desk, I noted that the computer was on, a screensaver blocking whatever was on her screen. I ignored it and continued on my mission.

I didn't have to look far. I found it in the wooden inbox on her desk between a cell-phone bill and a letter from a client: Braydon's suicide note. I shot a glance around the office; no photocopier. There was a fax machine, but taking the time to figure out how to use it to make a copy didn't seem like a good idea.

I sighed. Looked around helplessly, trying to think what to do.

In for a penny...

I folded the note carefully along its original crease and tucked it into the Filofax in my bag. I hesitated another second or two, then added the cell-phone bill to my cache.

...in for a pound.

I thumbed the mouse on the desk and the screen-saver instantly disappeared, displaying an e-mail program in its place. I could see that Mimi had sent Doug a message probably minutes before she left the house. I was about to look at it to see what it said when I heard something.

The garage door scraping open.

And, now, belatedly, here it was: the adrenaline rush I'd been wondering about when I entered the house arrived in one big push. It almost knocked me off my feet.

With a strangled sound, I was in motion instantly, heading back the way I'd come. Down the deeply carpeted hallways, past the beautiful kitchen with the toast and coffee smells, through the gorgeous master suite, into the flowery guest room and out the door into the courtyard by the pool, remembering to turn the knob so it would lock behind me.

I had just closed the door when the French doors that I knew led to the kitchen opened hard and fast. I heard a feminine voice behind me. "You," was all she said.

I pasted a smile on my face as I turned around,

hoping I looked less manic than I felt. Hoping, also, that it would look as though I'd been knocking—and perhaps peeking—but not actually coming out the door.

"Hi, Mimi," I said. I was pleased when my voice came out sounding calm and unfazed. I only hoped she couldn't detect the pounding of my heart, see the slight shake of my hands. "I was just about to knock on the door."

"You thought if I didn't answer the front door, I might answer at the back?" she said sarcastically.

I deepened my smile, ignoring her tone. "Something like that. And I was right, because here you are."

She was level with me now and I could see that her gray eyes were cold. Almost menacing. I wondered if that was how she always looked, but thought it likely it was something my presence ignited in her. Not that I could blame her.

"And I'm *not* pleased to see you. Look, whatever you want, Madeline Carter, I am completely uninterested. You should have saved yourself a trip. Seeing you here, I am even *less* interested in what you might have to say. As I told you on the telephone, if there is something you really feel I can help you with, I suggest you contact me through my lawyer. Now please, get back in that repulsive little car and drive away or I'll call the police."

And with that she turned away and, without a backward glance, went back into the house, closing the French doors with a firm thud that was just left of a slam.

I felt like sagging against the door in relief but did not. I collected myself as well as I could and marched, stiff-legged, back to the car—*my* car, I reminded myself. I got inside and drove away.

As I headed back to the city, I noticed a few black clouds lazing on the horizon. If I didn't miss my guess, it was going to rain. Seriously and soon.

Fourteen

Just to go over the facts—at least as I know them—there is nothing in my background that has prepared me for cat burglary. Or any other kind. I have an M.B.A. From Harvard. I spent, as I've said, a decade as a broker at a prestigious financial firm with an international profile.

My family background is modest and entirely American. I was born of the extreme middle class and so, unsurprisingly, it is in my upbringing and my education—if not my nature—to take the middle ground. And, despite all of this, as soon as I'd walked into Mimi's house uninvited, I knew I had crossed some sort of line.

So when my hands started to shake not long after I got back on Highway 99 and pointed Old Stinky toward Vancouver, it didn't exactly surprise me. Started to shake so badly I knew I'd better stop the car before I did some kind of damage to myself or other people.

It was a delayed reaction. I was able to tell myself this with an almost clinical detachment. And yet. That didn't make me feel any better. Nor did the tug of water I took from the bottle I always carry in my bag.

I'd stopped the car at a long, unbroken stretch of freeway, where there were cow-dotted fields on one side and an unbroken expanse of the Pacific Ocean on the other. As I watched, pink-tinged late-afternoon clouds were being overtaken by their darker, more violent looking brethren. It was beautiful. Even in my distracted state I had to acknowledge what I was seeing: the beauty of it. The majesty. Just watching seemed to calm my nerves somewhat, take me outside of myself. Which, at that moment, seemed a good place to be.

When the rain started I welcomed the change it brought. The air seemed suddenly thicker; you felt you could almost bite through it. And as the water pooled on the pavement, it seemed to glisten. For a heartbeat, the rain looked like bright jewels against the inky blackness of the road.

The biggest change in the environment was, for me, very immediate. Though Old Stinky seemed to have been flawlessly repaired and restored, and the convertible top looked perfect to the eye, the addition of hard rain added something new to the equation. Though I couldn't see the water coming in, after a very few minutes of rain beating on the roof, the moisture beaded thickly on the passenger side of the car and traveled craftily over to the driver's side, where it dropped on my head, one delicate bead at a time. It stopped being amusing quite quickly.

But a wet head was the final piece. It simultaneously annoyed and amused me and, in that state, I finally felt possessed enough of my self that my hands stopped shaking, the dryness in my mouth gradually ceased and I felt, finally, prepared to carry on.

It was true: I *had* crossed a line. But it didn't bother me so much anymore. I'd gotten over it. I was now pretty sure I was right: there was more here than met the eye.

Maybe a lot more.

My stop at Jessica and Robert's house was blessedly quick. The beating rain discouraged conversation. Jessica didn't even ask me why I'd decided to stay another night. Maybe she didn't care? But Anne-Marie had called her as promised, and Jessica had the keys waiting in the foyer when I rang the bell. When she handed them over, she greeted me brightly, but didn't ask me to stay.

Though I'd been pleased to say goodbye to Braydon's apartment in the morning, I was glad when I pulled Old Stinky back into its familiar stabling under the ground. It had been a long day and a lot had happened. Heck, I'd even been out of Canada for a couple of minutes. And then there'd been that pesky line to cross, the one that wasn't at the border.

And I was just plain tired and wet.

I grabbed my overnight bag, my laptop case and my

purse out of the car, as well as the folder of paper the border guard had found under the seat. Between that and what I'd lifted at Mimi's house, I figured I'd have a full evening of reading.

With my arms and mind so full, I frankly didn't notice the condition of the locks at Braydon's front door. Had the door been locked before I stuck my key in there? I couldn't be sure. What I *did* know was that the apartment hadn't reeked of cigarette smoke when I'd left, nor had the stereo been on when I'd locked the door in the morning. A local dance station: it created an entirely new environment in the apartment.

"Hello?" I called as I dropped my armload of stuff on the sofa.

No one answered me.

I wasn't afraid. I didn't know who else had access to the apartment. As far as I'd known, I was the only one, and no one had told me others might be using it.

Even so, I walked through the apartment carefully, looking for signs of occupation as well as occupants. I found the signs easily. The occupant would come later.

A light meal had been prepared in the kitchen. I noticed that a cutting board had been left out, and there were crumbs on the counter. A bottle of expensive-looking wine, open, the cork to one side. This all was new. In the morning I'd left the place as tidy as when I'd found it.

The computer was on in the little office.

Upstairs, I could taste bubblebath under the smoke

in the bathroom, where a soap dish had been used as an ashtray and left on the tub's wide edge. I looked at the two long filters on the plate; both rimmed in soft crimson.

By now my mouth was dry. I recognized it as the classic fight-or-flight response, which didn't help much with my mood. I've never been much of a fighter. In any case, I couldn't imagine I was in danger from an intruder who'd stopped to take a leisurely bath that included a couple of smokes. While wearing lipstick.

On the other hand…

Leaving the bathroom, I noticed that the door to the roof deck was open. I toyed briefly with the idea of going back downstairs and calling Anne-Marie or Jessica or the police or *anyone*, or doing anything other than going up those stairs to see who was there. Then I reminded myself about the food and the bath. And the lipstick. This was probably just some friend of Braydon's with a key; nothing to freak out about. I checked my tongue: my mouth was still dry.

I headed up the stairs anyway.

It was raining and her back was to me, but I had no trouble recognizing the dark cascade of her hair. She was sitting under the protection of a garden umbrella, wrapped in a deep green silk bathrobe that was so big on her I took it to be Braydon's. There was a glass of wine at her elbow and she was smoking furiously while she sat, as though in deep contemplation.

"Sonya?" I said.

She jumped up at the sound of my voice and spun around quickly enough to upset the wineglass, though she grabbed it in time to stop it from crashing to the ground. Reflexes like a cat, I thought wryly. Another thing that, oddly, did not surprise me.

"Madeline Carter," she said, her voice strikingly composed for someone who had just jumped and spun. "I didn't expect to see you here. I'd heard you went back to L.A." She relaxed into a chair facing me, but was still protected by the umbrella.

Her calm surprised me, and I suddenly felt as though I were the intruder here, not Sonya, who had been calmly drinking and smoking and bathing.

"I was going to," I said simply. "And then I didn't. But no one told me to expect anyone here."

"Well, they wouldn't have, would they? Who would have known I'd be here?" she asked, as though this were the most obvious thing in the world.

I had no answer. And it was raining hard enough that I was getting wet.

"I'm going inside," I said, sluicing water off my face as I moved toward the stairs.

In the bathroom—not the one Sonya had bathed in, but the downstairs powder room—I used one of Braydon's fluffy guest towels to quickly dry my face and hair. Then I went into the living room and just sat. I had a pretty good idea Sonya would be along soon enough.

Though she stopped off in the kitchen to grab the

open bottle of wine and a second glass, I didn't have long to wait.

In the living room she refilled her wineglass, splashed some wine into the other glass for me and put it on the coffee table closest to where I sat on the sofa with my stuff, then she dropped easily into one of the chairs opposite me. She stretched lithely, like a cat, the foot of one smooth leg caressing the other. Bray's silk robe clung to her damply, and her hair, so smoothly perfect at the funeral, now curled lightly as it dried. Sonya Foy was beautiful in her gentle disarray and she seemed to want me to know it.

"So you're staying," she said, pointing at my belongings.

"I'd planned on it, yes," I said. "Obviously not, though, if you're already staying here." I noted with irritation that my arms were folded across my chest in a defensive posture.

She laughed then, an oddly musical sound. "I do have a home, you know."

I forced my arms to my sides and looked at her evenly. Home or not, it was obvious she wasn't going anywhere for a while. Especially not in Bray's robe.

"Then why—" I indicated the bathrobe and her still-damp-from-the-bath hair "—why all this? Why are you here?"

It was her turn to shrug. "I don't know. I missed him, I guess. I thought this might make him feel closer." She paused, as though thinking about it. Then she sighed.

"It didn't, though." She was quiet so long that her voice, when she finally spoke, startled me. "He could be such a shit, but he was so special. I guess you'd know that better than me."

I looked at her without saying anything because what, really, could I say? The person she was describing was someone I didn't know.

"How did you get in?"

She looked at me with amusement. "How do you think?"

I ignored her. Said it again. "How did you get in here?"

More amusement. "With my key. Come now, don't look so shocked, Madeline. Surely you knew."

"Knew?"

"Braydon and I were lovers."

I sat there too long without saying anything. I could tell it was too long from the look on Sonya's face. Forgive me for borrowing a romance-novel phrase, but I can't think how else to describe it: she looked at me with sardonic amusement. Sardonic. I'd never really known what it looked like. I do now.

After a while, I felt as though I had to say *something*. I've never really given it much thought, but I guess on one level I consider myself to be something of a sophisticate. I've traveled extensively in Europe and a teensy bit in the Far East. I can drive a stick and even change my own oil or a tire when pressed. I can eat with chopsticks as though born to it. I've read Chaucer, Dickens and Tolstoy, including three different translations of *War and Peace*. I can, at a glance and without even the smallest reach, tell the difference between a Monet, a Chagall and a Van Gogh. I've seen—and even done— a lot of things that some people would think of as odd or weird or off, and I'd gotten to a place in my life where I thought there was very little that could shock me. But this little northern soap opera was turning out to be something that could.

"But what about…" I felt silly and naive even as I started to say it. But Sonya didn't let it drop.

"What *about* Mimi? Have you met her? She's hardly a consideration."

"She's his wife!" I said more indignantly than I'd intended, even while a mind picture of her and Curt in the stable floated unwillingly through my head.

"Oh, please. Don't go all Pollyanna on me. It wouldn't suit you, Madeline."

"What do you mean?"

"You're a big girl. And have you met Mimi? Do you understand her pedigree? She was never anything other than a convenience."

I shook my head, not understanding what Sonya was telling me.

"Don't look so dumbfounded, Madeline. Of course that's all it ever was. She was Doug's little sister. What better way to bind Doug to him than marry his sister?"

"But why would he need to bind Doug?" I said, feeling, as Sonya had hinted, like some sort of blind

Pollyanna. "Doug worked for Braydon. Then," I corrected, "for the company when they went public. I don't see why Bray would need to marry the man's sister. That's a little…" I searched for a word. "Well, it's just a little medieval, don't you think?"

"Did you know Braydon *at all?*" Sonya said scornfully.

I picked up the wineglass, swirled the maroon liquid before taking a sip. It was an amazingly good wine. Sonya had good taste or Braydon had a great cellar. Or both.

"Did I know him?" I repeated. "Maybe I did, a long time ago. Not so much anymore, I'm thinking."

"He can't have changed that much," Sonya observed. I didn't respond. It hadn't been a question.

"So, tell me your theory, Sonya. Because you seem to have one. Why did Braydon marry Mimi? Why did he feel the need to secure Doug?"

"It's not a theory at all. These are things I know. Things Braydon told me." She paused to top up her glass. She made a motion to do the same for me, but noticed mine had barely been touched. With a scornful sigh, she added another inch to her own glass before continuing. "Braydon thought of Doug as a babysitter. For the company. Doug would stay behind and look after the fort and Braydon could do whatever he liked." She paused and appeared thoughtful for a moment. "Though, honestly? I don't think there would have been a Braydon Gauthier without Doug." She stopped when she saw my face. "Oh, don't look like that. You know what I mean. There would have been a Braydon, of course. But no one would have known his name. No one would have cared," she said, as though to underline this thought. "Doug helped put Braydon on the map."

"And you," I said softly.

"And me what?"

"Well, you helped put Braydon on the map as well, didn't you?"

She looked at me with understanding. "Oh, that. That's much later. What I mean is, from the beginning of Gauthier Fine Foods. Doug met Braydon, ate at WhyVeeAre when it was brand-new and said, 'Aha!' Do you understand?"

"I think so."

"Braydon would have been happy spending his career cooking at WhyVeeAre and maybe writing a cookbook every five years. Doug offered…more."

"What kind of more?"

"Well…" Sonya spread her arms to encompass the whole apartment, and I understood that she was indicating a way of life and, perhaps, a way of being. "Everything. Doug made all of the connections, for starters. He put the package together, you know?"

I nodded. I did.

"He marketed Braydon to the television people. He started Bray thinking of other restaurants. He did the groundwork for the IPO. He was even the one who had the idea for the frozen food."

"Bray must have *loved* that," I said wryly.

Sonya smiled. "You *did* know him. But, yeah, Bray wasn't nuts about the idea at first."

"Okay, so Doug created Gauthier Fine Foods. And things were going well. Everyone was happy. I understand that part. But why did Bray feel the need to marry Doug's sister? It sounds like everything was going great."

"I think what really happened was Doug got tired of always being in Braydon's shadow. Remember, no matter what Doug did and no matter how successful the company got, it would always be *Gauthier* Fine Foods. And it was Braydon's face on the frozen foods. Braydon on TV. Braydon on the books…"

"Braydon, Braydon, Braydon," I offered quietly.

"Exactly. So, according to Braydon, anyway, a little over two years ago, Doug started making sounds like he wanted out."

"Out?"

"Yeah, out. See, he had this talented, beautiful sister, right?"

"Mimi?"

Sonya nodded. "And his idea was to create a company around *her* just the way he'd done it around Braydon. Only it would be all about him and his family."

"So Braydon married his potential competitor? How crazy is that?"

"Well, plenty, I guess, if you're looking for a happy marriage. But that was never Bray's goal." Sonya's eyes met mine. "I think he'd had enough of the idea of happily ever after."

Ouch.

"But it wasn't just neutralizing a competitor," she went on. "By marrying Mimi, Bray felt he was solidifying Doug's relationship with the company. And, in a way, giving Doug what he wanted. See, with Braydon and Mimi married, Doug wouldn't just be working for Braydon's best interests, but for that of his family, as well."

"Couldn't he just have given Doug money?"

Sonya laughed at this. "That would have been *my* thought, as well. Not something quite so…extreme."

"You're talking about Mimi like she was some kind of property. Didn't she have a say in the matter?" I realized as I asked this that I'd need to take Sonya's reply with a grain of salt. She probably wouldn't voice the most unbiased opinion on the topic of her lover's wife.

"Mimi was very young, Madeline. And I'm not necessarily talking years. She always struck me as…malleable. I think that's what Braydon felt, anyway. And what a life he offered her." I thought I heard a trace of envy in Sonya's voice and didn't discount the notion. Under the circumstances, it would be somewhat expected. "I don't think she was even twenty-five when they married. It would, I think, have seemed like a fairy tale to her. She had this look, around the time that they married," Sonya said thoughtfully, "this look of absolute bliss. Like all her dreams had come true. It didn't last long, that look."

"Were you…" I hesitated. Tried again. "Were you and Braydon…"

She saw my hesitation and laughed. "Were Braydon and I lovers then?" She took a sip of her wine. Smoothed the silky fabric of the robe over her flank. "On and off. Off and on. We've been that way as long as we've known each other. So I guess that answer is, yes. I was never very far out of the picture."

"That must have hurt," I said quietly.

"What?"

"Being involved with him. Watching him marry someone else."

"Oh, that." She waved her hand airily. "That was business. Business is business. He did the right thing. I told him so, not that he ever needed my reassurance. But mixing love and marriage never seems to work very well, does it?" This last seemed pointed, and I blushed accordingly. She was right; it certainly hadn't for me. "Now business and marriage? That makes more sense." She nodded, as though reassuring herself.

"So…did it all work out the way Braydon had planned?"

"Well, on the surface it did. It looked like it did. Doug stayed in place. Mimi got the fairy tale horsey cottage in the sticks and Braydon on the weekends."

"And what did Braydon get?" I asked.

"You already know the answer to that, Madeline." I just looked at her, waiting for her to continue. Finally she did. With a deceptively pleasant smile, she said, "Braydon got dead."

Fifteen

I'm loath to admit it, but when I was younger, everything made much more sense. You looked at the world and what you saw was what you believed; the two things didn't need to be so very different.

When I look back on it now, I sometimes think I'll never again possess the wisdom I had when I was seventeen. I knew *everything* at seventeen. I had opinions on politics and world affairs. More than opinions, I saw the mess everyone else had made of everything in the world and just couldn't understand how they could all be so stupid. If they'd known what *I* knew—I thought—the planet would be a much more sensible place.

The beauty—and perhaps the curse—of being seventeen is that you don't see the entire spectrum. You see the blacks and you see the whites, but you haven't developed the taste or the sensibility for all the subtle hues in between. Love was love and hate was hate. They were different and not related. And ambivalence? Empathy? Those aren't in a seventeen-year-old's palette and certainly not in her vocabulary.

When Sonya left, I continued to sit on the sofa. I reached over, grabbed the wine bottle and poured the dregs into my glass. And then I sat and sipped and tried to make my mind a blank. There was so much in my head right then—too many conflicting thoughts—and I wanted to create a quiet canvas where I could sort things out.

What, I wondered, would my seventeen-year-old brain have made of this situation? It seemed that every time I thought I knew something, I got another piece that all but nullified everything else. Braydon had been sleeping with Sonya—and perhaps others—but had been married to Mimi who had been sleeping with Curt who had been Braydon's good friend. It made my head spin. And Doug, who had wanted to go renegade but had been prevented from doing so by Braydon's marriage of convenience. To Doug's sister. Mimi, who, to hear Sonya tell it, had been deeply smitten with Braydon, at least going in.

Even while I struggled with all of this I realized that Sonya was not to be considered an unimpeachable source of information. And I hadn't even gotten around to asking her about her own involvement in all of this, beyond the Braydon connection, that is. By the time we'd come to that place in the conversation, I'd been on overload.

I was so tired that it felt like about a million o'clock, but when I glanced at my watch, I found it was just nine-thirty. Certainly early enough to be in under most people's cutoff, at least in the Pacific time zone.

I called Tasya in Malibu and, after we'd exchanged a few pleasantries, I asked her to duck into the guest room and get a phone number from my business card file—a phone number I didn't keep in my Filofax because I hadn't thought I'd ever need it again.

"We miss you, Madeline," Tasya said when she got back to the phone, her accent as always twisting my name into something that sounded very much like *Mad-A-Leen*.

"I miss you guys, too!" I said, meaning it. "How's my running buddy?"

"Oh, I think Tycho misses you most of all. Jennifer has been at her mother's all week and Tyler and I have been quite busy, so Tycho has had no one to bug. He's looking at me now. If he could talk, I think he would say 'Hurry home.'"

Home. I'd begun to forget what that felt like. I glanced out the window and saw wet on the pavement, the lights of the city, which I'd been able to see clearly at night since I'd arrived in Vancouver, were tonight obscured by a bank of wet fog. Despite the fact that I'm a Seattle girl, and so should be somewhat impervious to moisture, I felt the damp in my bones.

I knew I should probably leave the next call until morning, but it was in my head now and I wanted to get it out. Besides, I knew Anne Rand was about as hungry as they come—in so many ways—and I didn't think she'd mind a business call, even if it was Saturday night.

"Hi, Anne," I said when she answered. "I don't know if you remember me. Madeline Carter?"

"Madeline," she said effusively, "of course I do. You live in Malibu. We met south of Los Angeles, yes?"

Hearing her voice on the telephone surprised me. I'd forgotten her cultured British accent. It didn't go with the woman I remembered, driving a beat-up Honda, wearing a grease-stained house dress and eating at such a rate I had no trouble at all imagining why she practically needed two seats at a mall food court.

She'd said we met south of Los Angeles, as though it had perhaps been at a garden party or a premiere. What she didn't say was that she'd been hired to follow me and had botched it badly enough that I'd spotted her and bought her off. It didn't matter; I knew she would take a credit card for payment and that she worked cheaply. Besides, she was the only private investigator I actually knew.

"Right," I said. "That's me. Listen, I'm not sure, but I might have a little bit of work for you."

"Why aren't you sure?" she asked.

"Well, I'm in Canada at the moment and I need some information on someone who lives here."

"Ah," she said. "Whereabouts in Canada?"

"Vancouver. In British Columbia. Can you help?"

"I might be able to. Does the person have a British Columbia driver's license?"

"I…I don't know. I don't have driver's license information. But I saw her drive a car."

"Ah," Anne said noncommittally. "That won't help. What about date of birth?"

"Uh-uh," I said, beginning to realize how foolish this all must sound. "Not that, either."

"Well, what do you have?"

"A name. That's all, really. But it's a distinctive name."

"Shoot."

"Sonya Foy."

"You're right, that's fairly distinctive. Better than if it were a Betty Smith, if you see what I'm saying. Okay, and you said she lives in Vancouver?"

"That's right."

"Born there?"

"I…I don't know."

"Of course you don't." I chose to ignore the sarcasm in her voice. "Okay, and no date of birth. What about approximate age?"

"I'd say between thirty and forty."

"Well, *that* narrows it down." More sarcasm. "Actually, Madeline, I'm good, but no one is *that* good. I do need a little more to go on."

"Well," I said thoughtfully, "she's in a stock-related business. She's a promoter."

"A promoter?" Anne repeated.

"Yes. A stock promoter," I clarified. "And I'm not certain, but it's possible she may have been a broker at one time." This was a total shot in the dark on my part. No one had even hinted that might be true. But it was what I'd sensed from her in the beginning. And it was a pretty safe bet, since a lot of promoters take that route to get there.

"You think she might have been a broker? But you're not certain?"

"Right."

"Well, actually, if you're right, that really should help narrow things down. Professional associations and so on. I'll take a run at it, anyway, and let you know if I turn anything up. Meanwhile, if you *do* manage to get a driver's license number, please let me know. It would make everything much simpler. Would probably even save you some money in the long run. Less digging for me to do."

"Right," I agreed. "I will. And there's one more thing. But it might sound silly."

"*One* thing that might sound silly?"

"If you are able to determine who this person is," I said, ignoring her tone, "I'd like also to know what she was doing last Friday night and Saturday morning."

"You're kidding me?"

"No. I'm not."

"Madeline, it just doesn't work that way. You can't hire me to follow someone *after* the fact. It's against the laws of man and nature."

"Still." Even though I could see her point, I thought she was sounding a little dramatic.

"Still nothing. I *might* be able to find out who she is—*might*, mind you—but I'm not going to be able to find out where she was. At least, not without flying me up there and having me launch a full-scale investigation. And I have the feeling that's not what you meant, is it?"

"No…I guess it's not."

"Right then, Madeline, I'm honestly not sure I can do anything at all for you, but I'm not sure I can't, either. I'm going to need to charge you for at least a few hours' digging time, and a bit more if I actually manage to turn anything up."

Considering the fact that I'd given her practically nothing to go on, this didn't sound unreasonable to me. Nor did it surprise me when she told me the earliest I could expect to hear from her was Monday afternoon.

With the apartment empty again and my phone calls made, I remembered what had caused me to cross that line earlier in the day: Braydon's note.

I carefully made sure the front door was locked—not that it would do any good if there were untold keys floating around out there—and poured myself back onto the sofa next to the pile of stuff from the car I'd dropped there what now seemed like hours before.

I found the note carefully folded into my Filofax, just as I'd left it. Mimi's cell-phone bill was there, as well. I couldn't understand what had possessed me to take it, though in the moment, it had seemed important.

Without a second look, I stuffed it back into my Filofax and pushed them together back into my bag.

Braydon's suicide note was a different matter. At first glance, it looked exactly right. The handwriting was masculine though slightly loopy, the letters slanting as though created by someone who preferred their left hand. There was no salutation on the letter, just a date—the date Braydon had died—followed by a brief note:

> *Though there is much in my life that is good and rich, I find I no longer have the strength or interest to go on. I have given everything I have—everything I am—to the creation of perfect food. With one gesture, with the withholding of a single star, they have undone all of the good I had hoped to bring and to share.*
>
> *I send my love and apologies to my wife, Mimi, as well as to my parents and others of my family who love and care about me. Please know in your hearts that this is not a result of anything that you did nor from the lack of anything you could have done. But may the editors of the Vulcan Guide rot forever in a singular hell.*
> *Sincerely,*
> *Braydon Spencer Gauthier*

On one level, the note was beyond disappointing. I didn't know anymore what I'd hoped for, but I knew this wasn't it. There was also something vaguely unsettling about it. It was, in a word, passionless. And Braydon had been many things to many people, but no one would ever have said he was without passion. About anything. In fact, the opposite was true: to my knowledge, he'd brought passion to everything he ever did.

I no longer have the strength or interest to go on.

Granted, it had been years since I'd seen him, but the fact that he'd had all of these accomplishments in the interim told me that, if anything, his world had become wider, his passions more firmly fixed. And the Braydon I'd known would not have written the note I held in my hand. I knew that as well as I knew that he wouldn't want to eat duck with orange anything, or something that could be described as couscous risotto. And you can know a thing positively and also understand that you'd be completely unable to convince anyone else. Knowing a thing isn't like proof.

And proof of what, anyway? I wasn't even sure about that. It was feeling less and less likely to me that Braydon had killed himself. More and more probable that someone had either killed him and arranged things to look like suicide, or held his hand while he killed himself.

I went back to the loopy script. I'm no handwriting expert, but I began to feel sure that someone who *was* an expert would be able to see that Braydon hadn't written this note.

The first thing that confirmed this for me was the ink that had been used. When I'd known him, Braydon had insisted on brown ink in his pens. Always. It had given his writing an odd, slightly archaic look, which is one of the things he'd liked about it. "It's different," he'd told me when questioned about it. "I never like to be the same. Not if I can help it." It had meant that buying refills for his pens had required shopping at specialty stores, but it was a small price, he'd said, for exclusivity.

The ink used in the note had been everyday black, not Braydon's more exclusive brown. And you think: well, heat of the moment, right? Except what I saw all around me put a lie to this. I went into the kitchen and then to the little office and checked. Every single pen I found in the apartment held brown ink. The pen next to the pad by the phone in the living room? Brown ink. The copybooks in the office and the kitchen? All written in brown, brown, brown. The notes to himself on the refrigerator and on sticky notes on his computer? You guessed it: brown again.

And so I'd gained another completely contradictable fact: Braydon had used pens all the time and he scribbled even his hastiest note to himself in the mud-brown ink he favored. It was possible he'd just picked up the nearest pen—which happened to have black ink—in order to do his last bit of writing on this earth. It was possible. But I thought it damned unlikely. How conclusive was that? Not very. Still. It was another thing that bothered me.

That loopy, masculine handwriting bothered me, as well. And, again, it was something I couldn't quite put my finger on. I studied the note as well as various samples of his writing from all the sources I'd found around the apartment while I tried to clarify what was wrong. It was hard.

Finally it came to me. In his notebooks, in his messages to himself and other people, in every scrap of certifiably Braydon handwriting samples I found around the apartment, it looked as though he'd been writing in a hurry. That's not to say he was, but I knew that as an extremely synastral left-hander—Braydon almost looked as though he were writing upside down—cursive writing did not come easily. I knew that he'd had to practice and practice to come up with a personal style that didn't look messy. But it always looked like it had been done in a hurry.

Braydon's last note, when I examined it again more carefully, did not have that appearance. It didn't look exactly wrong but—with ample samples of Braydon writing around for me to study—it didn't look quite right, either.

Which meant…what? I was suddenly so tired I couldn't think. Tired due to a long day? Or tired because of all these conflicting thoughts? I couldn't be sure. I only knew that trying to wring more sense out of my brain before I slept was about as likely as making cheese out of stone.

I gathered my belongings, dragged them up to the bedroom with me, then made a few short preparations for bed. I don't remember falling asleep, but I don't remember my head hitting the pillow, either. My sleep was satisfyingly deep and utterly dreamless. I needed it.

Sixteen

I came awake with the feeling that something was wrong. And the phone was ringing. I checked the luminescent dial on the clock on the nightstand: 8:30 a.m. And it was light out. Morning, certainly. But still.

I checked the phone. Line two. Thinking it was probably Anne-Marie checking in with me, I grabbed the phone, barely pausing to clear the sleep out of my voice.

"Carter," I said reflexively. An old habit that's taking its time about dying.

The voice on the other end surprised me. Not Anne-Marie, but more: it was unrecognizable. Not feminine, not masculine and devoid of expression.

"I have information for you," the voice said.

"Information?" I repeated, not understanding.

"About the death of Braydon Gauthier. Meet me at the Dodge Hotel at three-thirty this afternoon."

"How will I know you?" I started to say, then realized there was no longer anyone on the line.

I held the phone a few moments longer, as though hanging up would end the connection fully. While I held the cold, dead plastic in my hand, I became aware of the pounding of my heart.

"Hello?" I said into the phone, knowing it was futile. Knowing there was no longer anyone on the line to hear me. "Hello?"

I replaced the receiver, then picked it up again, touching star-69 on the touch-tone phone. I knew it was worth a try, but was unsurprised when the automated voice told me that the last number that had called the line was "unavailable." Clearly, anyone up to using electronics to disguise their voice on the phone would think to block their number before making the call.

I lay back down just to think about what the call had meant. I could hear the light touch of rain on the window. A soothing sound. I knew if I listened to it long enough and I didn't have so much on my mind, I could fall back to sleep.

Someone had called me—or at least, called the person they expected to be here—with information, they'd said, about Braydon's death. What would that mean—information? I wondered if I should go. At least, I *thought* I was wondering about it, until I felt my feet on the fuzzy rug at the bedside. Then I headed down to Braydon's home office to find the phone book.

The Yellow Pages listing for the Dodge Hotel was

enough to clue me in: it wasn't a four-star establishment. The address, on East Hastings, told me everything. I didn't know a lot about the city, but I knew enough to avoid the downtown east side, which, I could tell, was pretty much where the Dodge was located.

I might not have gone had my caller suggested an evening rendezvous. The downtown east side is the worst part of town. The kind of area where you lock the doors of your car just to drive through. But three-thirty in the afternoon, I thought. On a Sunday. What could happen?

Still, it was hours away yet. Too many hours away to contemplate not filling them in with something. I'd go mad. But since it was Sunday, the number of useful things I could actually do was limited. I wanted to get back into the Gauthier Fine Foods offices and have another poke around, but that, I knew, would have to wait for the following day.

Meanwhile, I had some things that needed doing. One had to do with my personal and mental health. It had now been four days since my last run, which was some kind of record for me. Though it was wet outside, it was the kind of light drizzle that didn't concern me very much. Running in the sunshine is better, but I was born and raised on the wet coast; a little rain wasn't going to make me melt. Plus I knew that a good run would knock the cobwebs out and keep me from going stir-crazy until the afternoon.

I'd brought running gear with me from L.A.—I tend not to travel without it, just in case. So I pulled on track pants, trainers and a white T-shirt, adding a roomy fleece as a top layer to ward off any rain-borne chills. I poked through Braydon's armoires until I found a ball cap—I'd figured he had to have at least one somewhere. The single one I found was black with white letters. Team Food was stitched sedately onto the front of the cap. Whatever *that* meant, it would at least keep the rain off my face if the current threat turned into something wetter and more substantial. I secured my hair in a ponytail, jammed the cap onto my head and prepared to head out the door.

Before I left Braydon's apartment, I wrote the West Broadway address for DW Investments on a scrap of paper and tucked it into my messenger bag, along with the keys for the condo, my cell phone and enough loot to buy a coffee and pastry after my run. Without my Filofax, a hairbrush, makeup and some of the other junk I usually carry, the bag was light enough to run with.

I knew Broadway was, at most, ten city blocks from Braydon's apartment. I also knew Broadway was a long street, and I didn't know the city well enough to buy a clue from the address. Still, I reasoned, I had to pass the day somehow; I might as well do it running as anything else. Fun, for a change, to have a destination more or less in mind rather than the targeted runs—out and back—that I usually did in the Malibu hills.

Braydon's apartment was pretty much at sea level and Broadway is somewhat above, so the first part of my run was a fairly steady uphill. The gentle rain coming down was the kind that gets you frizzy rather than the variety that soaks you down and after a while I stopped noticing it at all. I just enjoyed the feel of challenging my body, as well as the novelty of hearing my shoes slap against the wet pavement, and the envelope of quiet that seemed to have come over the city with the rain. The wetness had subdued the sound somehow. I ran on the sidewalk and the cars that whizzed past me seemed to have a distant, muffled sound.

And the way the world smelled! Pretty much as it had when I'd stepped out of the airport, but more and more and more. The light rain seemed to act like sandalwood to perfume—it enhanced the separate components and blended them. As I ran, I felt as though I could smell the green of the grass, the salty warning of low tide and the scents of rubber and gas on pavement. That last doesn't sound pretty, but it brought me home. Brought me back to childhood in a way that even food seldom has.

I didn't see anyone following me. To this day, I'm not sure anyone ever was. It didn't take long, though, for the feeling of pleasure that comes to me with exertion to fall away. Before long, my good steady run had fallen to a trot and then to a firm walk while my head would swivel around to look at that car—had I seen it before?—or that pedestrian—was he looking at me oddly?

I tried to chide myself. Why was I jumping at shadows? And yet. Call it instinct if you will, but I knew I felt *something*. Something dark and unpleasant and just out of my reach. I didn't like the way that felt. As I approached my first destination, I tried to push the feeling of uneasiness aside and just focus on my search. It was hard.

Broadway is a busy main thoroughfare, four lanes wide, but the sidewalks were wider than normal there as well. With only a single false start, I determined which way the numbers were running, then discovered the address I wanted on West Broadway was farther east than I currently was. A few blocks in the right direction and I realized I'd be at my destination in just four more blocks.

I was almost a full block past the address I'd jotted down for DW Investments before I realized I'd missed the building. I felt as though I'd been looking for it pretty carefully, so not finding it where it belonged brought me up short. I backtracked at a walk until I found it, then understood instantly how I'd missed it in the first place. The address wasn't the office building I'd been expecting to find. Instead it was a mailing and business services place wedged between a coffeehouse and a used-clothing store. The kind of place where low-rent companies and small businesses rent "palatial offices" roughly twelve inches deep and eight inches wide, and where they can get photocopies and inexpensive Internet connections and buy postage stamps while they're at it.

It was Sunday and the main doors were locked, but I knew that, even if the place were open, any answers I'd hoped to get wouldn't be available to me here.

At the locked doorway, I turned around quickly and was sure I saw someone pull back into an entrance farther down the street. I kept my eye on the spot while I trotted toward it, my heart hammering as I got close.

At the last possible moment before I turned toward the entrance, I asked myself to judge the wisdom of what I was doing. If someone was following me, confrontation might not be my best approach. Still, I was in motion and my momentum seemed impossible to stop.

I braced myself, then prepared to meet whoever had been following me. I turned into the entrance and found…nothing. No one was there. There was a bench in the doorway and the kind of ashtray that's always filled with sand and dotted with extinguished butts. A doorway led, presumably, to apartments inside the building, the same apartments that could be communicated with via intercom. There were buzzers next to the names of the building's occupants to make this possible. The main door itself was locked, however. Either my mind was playing tricks on me—a fact I was quite willing to accept—or whoever was following had managed to buzz themselves into the building at my approach. Either way, I felt a tiny bit easier afterward, because in either case, wasn't I now safe from being followed? When I resumed my run, I didn't feel as light-hearted as I had when I'd started out, but at least I'd left the paranoia behind and didn't feel the need to constantly be darting looks over my shoulders.

Halfway back to Braydon's, the flinty rain gave way

to something more serious. The rain didn't exactly come pounding down, but it was suddenly doing more than making me frizzy.

Stopping off for a coffee was a mistake. Though the coffee felt good going down, I watched in dismay from a table inside the café as the serious raindrops turned into a wall of water. *This* was pounding rain. I heard it bouncing off a skylight, saw it dropping down the collars of the patrons who ducked into the shop for a break.

Running in this weather made about as much sense to me as swimming in a waterfall. I resigned myself to spending a peaceful hour sipping my latte, reading the local newspapers and trying hard not to turn quickly to look at whoever came through the door. Before I could get seriously into any of that, though, I remembered that I'd brought my cell phone along. I brightened; I could play with that for a while. Maybe catch up on some phone calls while uncovering some of the phone's secrets. And talking on the phone wouldn't stop me from keeping one eye on the door.

I decided to start by calling my mom and updating her on my whereabouts. I was now sure I wasn't going to make Seattle for at least another day, and anyway, calling her would help pass the time while I waited for the rain to ease up.

When I pulled the phone out of my messenger bag I cursed mildly; the phone was turned off, something I hadn't noticed when I'd popped it in there. I tried to think how long the phone would have been off and realized it was something I'd done after I left the coffeehouse in Langley the day before. Would I ever get used to having one of these?

Almost as soon as I'd turned the phone on, it let me know there were five messages waiting for me in voice mail. Another irritating thing, I thought: now I couldn't even call my mom without first listening to my messages. Or maybe I could have; it was getting my mind around doing things in a different sequence that was troublesome.

Two of the messages were from Emily. In the first one, she wanted to know if I was having fun in Seattle (I wished!) and to let me know she'd have to stay in Vancouver at least an extra two days. "Hope that doesn't mess with our T & L plans," she quipped. "Call me."

Her second message was less cheery and quite to the point. "Honestly, Madeline, the whole deal with a cell phone is you have to turn it *on* once in a while. Otherwise you miss the whole frickin' point." I grinned while I listened to the message. Emily knew me *so* well; it was obvious that no other scenario had even occurred to her.

There was a message from my mom, wondering when I was due to turn up at her place. "And I have to warn you," she said with a smile in her voice, "your sister's new passion is cooking, so you might be in for a scary treat." I didn't need her to tell me which sibling she was referring to. Any time there is a new passion involved, it is my little sister, Meagan, who does things large and briefly. Our older sister, Miranda, has built a beautiful life with a gorgeous husband and two equally gorgeous kids. She's a decent cook and has a Rolodex full of caterers' phone numbers for the times she doesn't feel like doing it herself. And certainly nothing she'd either cook or have catered would have my mother calling it "scary." Miranda does the hostess thing in a way that makes lifestyle magazines want to send a photographer. Meagan…well, Meagan does not.

There was a message from Tasya, wondering when I was coming home. It had obviously been sent prior to me talking to her the night before.

I called my mom and let her know that I definitely would not be making it to Seattle before Monday evening at the earliest. "That's wonderful, sweetie," she said a little too loudly. "And, guess what? Meagan is going to make mango chutney."

"She's there now, isn't she?"

"That's right, darling," Mom chirped back.

"And how scared are you?"

"That's exactly it, isn't it?"

"You're sad about your mangoes?"

"You could say that."

I couldn't help laughing. "You think that's the scary part, don't you, Mom? But it's not. What comes after mango chutney? Think about it before you answer."

"I haven't a clue," Mom said brightly.

"Curry, Mom. Miggs will be making you a curry next."

"That's right, dear," Mom said cryptically. "I'm looking forward to seeing you, too. You can't get here quickly enough."

"You think I'm going to hurry now? With Meagan standing by with semi-exotic ingredients? Am I crazy?"

"That's what relatives are for, dear. I'll see you soon. Just *as soon as you can*," she said cheerfully but emphatically before she hung up.

Emily sounded almost ridiculously glad to hear from me.

"Okay, get this—I fly up here to do this because *you're* here, right?"

"Right…" I said cautiously.

"Now you're in Seattle and Latencia has—and I quote—'the worst case of influenza her generation has ever seen.' How do you like that?"

"Who are you quoting?"

"Her doctor. Her nanny. Her mother. Her pet iguana's holistic gardener. *Somebody*. I don't know. That's not the point, Madeline."

"Does she really have a pet iguana?"

"*That's* not the point, either."

I'd known that, but I was still at a loss. "What's the point?"

"The *point*, my dear Sherlock, is that I came up here because you were here and I thought it would be fun. Now you're in Seattle preparing for lots of fun and I'm stuck here waiting it out because the race is on—the baby pops, the flu breaks, the project gets shelved because our leading lady has a personal life."

"Oh," I said quietly. "I have good news, then."

"Excellent. Good news is…good. What?"

"I'm still in Vancouver."

"You are not."

"I am. And I'm free for dinner. How 'bout you?"

Not long after I'd nursed my second latte down to the dregs, the rain let up enough that I figured I'd brave running the rest of the way back to Braydon's. It was two o'clock. I could get back to the apartment and clean myself up in plenty of time to make my mystery appointment at half past three and then meet Emily for dinner at six. Emily could have met me earlier, but since I had no clue how long my three-thirty would take, I'd thought it best to leave plenty of time between them. I mean, that's a problem, isn't it? When an anonymous caller makes an appointment with you at a mysterious location to give you information on the death of your ex-husband, how much time should you book? It hadn't, to my recollection, been covered in any of the manuals, so I decided to play it by ear and go long.

Back at the apartment, I collected all the towels Sonya had used for her bath the night before and bundled them into a big heap behind the door. I'd figure out what to do with them later. Fortunately, there were large stacks of clean towels in a cabinet in the bathroom. I chose a couple of these and set them aside while I started a big, steamy shower.

After my shower I put on a light application of

makeup, then pulled on jeans and a powder-blue tur-
tleneck. I thought it likely I wouldn't want to be dressed
up where I was going.

The Dodge Hotel proved to be an even bigger dive
than I'd feared, in a part of the city that was worse than
anything I could have imagined. In fact, I hadn't even
suspected that there were parts of any Canadian city as
bad as the heart of Vancouver's downtown east side,
which was exactly where the Dodge Hotel was located.

Even daylight didn't provide much of a shield, especially in the murky half-light of a rainy afternoon. I
parked about a half block from the hotel, right on
Hastings Street, hoping the car would be safe on a main
thoroughfare.

It was the longest half block imaginable. Between
my parking spot and the hotel I saw vagrants asleep in
the doorways of boarded-up businesses, and prostitutes
plying their trade openly, though I wouldn't have liked
to even imagine what sort of trade these poor women
might have. They looked undernourished—and not in
the fashionable L.A. party kind of way—unkempt and
just generally unclean. Even from where I was standing,
it looked like a horrid life.

Men shuffled about in unsavory little groups. Some
of them might have been the women's pimps, but
they couldn't all have been. Together, they represented a sordid tableau of some sort of culture about
which I had only the slightest idea. I walked toward

my destination hurriedly, and no one talked to me or even seemed to see me. It was almost as though I walked in a different dimension. An eerie feeling. I wondered if it would have been different at night, if the dimensional separation would have crumbled. But I knew I'd never have the courage—or the desire—to find out.

Inside the Dodge Hotel, things were better, but not by much. The lobby looked to me more like a convalescent home than a hotel. The furniture was shabby beyond keeping, the carpets so worn that there were spots where they'd ceased to exist at all. Rough men and women seemed almost camped out on the balding couches and chairs that ringed the lobby space. Though the lobby was relatively crowded, it reeked of must and damp and disuse. You could smell old cigarettes and booze and body odor. You could smell, in a way, desperation.

The front desk was protected by a cage, but it was empty. I hesitated between the front door and the desk, unsure what my next move should be, and fighting the urge to just run back to my car and forget whatever potential information might be waiting for me here.

A woman, seeing my confusion, seemed to take pity on me, and left her companions on their bare couches to come offer assistance.

"Who you lookin' for?" she asked. Her hair was limp and dirty, her nails broken, her teeth mostly gone. It was impossible to guess her age, but I suspected she was probably younger than she looked.

"I...I'm not sure," I said honestly. "I was supposed to meet someone here at three-thirty."

"*You're* supposed to meet someone *here?*" She looked not only surprised, but perhaps slightly aghast. It was apparent to her that I belonged somewhere else. The realization of that pleased me slightly, but it also made me a little sad. Clearly, her words and her tone said I did not belong here. But where did that leave her?

"Yeah. At three-thirty," I repeated.

"If you're meeting someone," she said helpfully, "it would probably be in the beer parlor." I must have looked blank, because she pointed toward a door I hadn't noticed before. "It's through there."

"Thanks," I said, meaning it. I fought the urge to press a dollar or two on her. I didn't want to insult her, but it really looked as though she could use it. Instead, though, I forced myself toward the ominous-looking door.

In the beer parlor, the first thing that hit me was an almost solid wall of sound. The classic rock was amplified through a sound system that had probably seen its prime around the time Jimmy Page was learning to shave.

In a city that was early to bring a smoking ban to bars and restaurants, the air was thick with cigarette smoke. A scarred bar followed one wall, the rest of the dimly lit space was filled with round, terry-cloth covered tables, and most of *those* were covered with thin-looking pilsner-style beer glasses and cheap, overflowing ashtrays.

Half a dozen heads lifted when I entered, then went quickly back to whatever they'd been doing before I arrived. It was likely, I thought, that I might look like some sort of law enforcement in a dive like this. Anyone clean probably would have.

Though there was no place in the beer parlor of the Dodge Hotel that looked like an inviting place to take a load off, I opted to hover near the bartender. He was well over six feet tall and more than half that across. He had a look of someone who'd been hired as much for his ability to break up a fight as he had for his skill at mixing drinks. If any trouble was going to erupt in this joint, I reasoned, it was unlikely to erupt in his vicinity. I glanced at my watch: 3:20. I decided I'd give my mystery caller until exactly 3:35. If someone hadn't approached me by then, it was back to Braydon's for me. And back to the shower to try and get the beer and stale smoke smells out of my hair.

I checked my watch again: 3:23.

I ordered a glass of draft beer that I had absolutely no intention of drinking. But it felt too prissy—even for me—not to at least *order* something. Plus, I reasoned, the whole process of ordering and waiting for my drink to arrive would help time pass.

I toyed for about three seconds with the idea of ordering a glass of wine. But this wasn't the kind of place where you asked for the wine list, and a glass of the house wine felt like it could be a dangerous proposition. How long would the bottle have been open? And what vintage would the wine be? Tuesday, I imagined, had been a good day for wine. So beer. I mean, if you came right down to it, what else would be correct to drink in a beer parlor?

"You lost or something?" the bartender asked when I gave him my order.

I looked at him closely to see how much he was mocking me, but didn't see a trace of it. I let a small smile escape. "I am not lost," I told him. "I'm waiting for someone."

His eyebrows shot skyward at that. "You're waiting for someone in *here*? This I gotta see." And he lumbered off to pull my beer.

After the huge bartender slid my drink across the bar to me and I slid my money—plus a tip that felt like a protection payment—back to him, I checked my watch: 3:26. I sighed, anticipating that the next nine minutes of my life might feel as long as waiting for Santa to come when I was six years old. Only that Santa wait had been exquisite. Being old enough to know what was coming—gifts and visiting and the love of a family spun near—yet young enough to give yourself up to it fully.

There was nothing exquisite about this nine minutes. I sat at the bar, my grimy glass of beer in front of me, feeling as out of place as a chicken at a badger convention, as exposed as a mushroom on a log. I sat there and *willed* time to pass, conscious of almost every second, conscious of wishing I was anyplace but there.

In the end, I gave it a bit longer than I'd promised myself. I gave it an additional excruciating five minutes.

But when by 3:40 no one had tried to make contact with me, I couldn't make myself sit there another minute. I gave the room a final scan, saw no one making their way toward me, and headed out the door, not the one I'd come through from the lobby, but another I hadn't seen on my way in that led to the street.

Outside, the scene, almost half an hour later, was completely changed. When I'd arrived there'd been a sort of skid row languor. No one had been in a hurry; the residents had nothing but time on their hands. Now, though, except for a few vagrants still passed out in doorways, most of the people I'd seen on my way in were either gone or ranged near the two police cars and ambulance half a block away, quite near my car.

They were finishing something. The emergency vehicles had, I decided, probably been here almost since I'd entered the hotel. That caused me a bit of relief because it meant that, with a strong police presence nearby, at least my car would probably have been left alone.

When I got closer, however, I felt badly about the relief I'd felt. Whatever crisis had been under way had already passed. The paramedics had a human-shaped burden on a gurney neatly zipped into a body bag. My car was safe, yes. But someone was dead.

As I got into my car, I could see that the police and the ambulance attendants were preparing to leave the scene. And one policeman, in addition to his usual police paraphernalia, had a purse tucked under one arm. I couldn't be sure, but I thought for a moment it looked as though it were shaped vaguely like an alligator or a crocodile. Something amphibian and quite green, anyway. I tried not to let that bother me.

Back at Braydon's apartment, I spent a full thirty minutes in the shower, willing the hot water to wash away the stench of the beer parlor of the Dodge Hotel. Willing, also, for my brain to empty. I had spent what was perhaps the longest half hour of my life in that beer parlor and nothing had happened. Yet I had the uneasy feeling that even going there had been a huge mistake.

I still felt uneasy, but somewhat better after my shower. And now, a dinner with Emily the largest challenge on my horizon, I started to relax a bit. In all likelihood what I'd seen was *not* a purse shaped like a reptile. And if it was, it had belonged to some street person. Surely those purses were more common than I'd first thought. How exclusive could they be? Sure, Gwen was a geek, but that didn't mean she was the only person who would have had access to equipment that could have disguised her voice on the phone. And what made me think she would have information she'd want to share with me, anyway? It hadn't seemed as if she'd liked me very much when she met me. If Gwen *did* have information, I'd probably be the last person she'd call. And so on. I tried to put emotional distance between myself and whatever had happened—and *hadn't* happened—at the Dodge Hotel.

It wasn't easy. As much as I love seeing Emily, I no

longer really felt much like dinner. I have lived a mostly sheltered and even somewhat cosseted life. I don't generally think in those terms, but spending even half an hour in that place had brought me up short. There is much beauty in my life. There always has been. Even the ugly things that have happened to me happened against a lovely backdrop. What if, when you opened your eyes in the morning, there was so much ugliness you couldn't see past it? And it wasn't even the ugliness. Not really. Rather, what it represented.

What if you had to live your life without hope?

Like the good friend she is, Emily had dutifully programmed her cell number into my phone when she gave it to me. Her number is in the first position on my auto dial.

"Emily," I began when she picked up.

"No!" Her voice was strident and it startled me.

"No what?"

"You are not canceling our dinner. I don't care *what's* going on in your life. I don't even want to hear it until you're across the table from me, you got that?"

"But Emily—"

"I'll see you at six," she said firmly. And then she was gone. I found myself staring bemusedly at the phone.

I looked through the scant wardrobe I'd brought with me with increasing alarm. I'd planned for maybe two days and nights in Vancouver. I was now heading toward day five, and even with the purchases I'd made on Robson Street before Braydon's service, pickins' were getting slim in the clothing department.

I settled on wearing the black Marc Jacobs suit again—because, I reasoned, you really can wear that almost anywhere—but this time with a shimmery champagne-colored blouse I'd bought the same day. With boots and a dark pashmina, I felt as though there was no place in most cities I couldn't go.

Emily was staying at a hotel that was geographically only a couple of miles from the Dodge, but, in real time, might have been on a different planet. She'd told me that the Vancouver Hotel was beautiful, and we'd agreed to meet and eat there. "The restaurants here at the hotel are gorgeous," she'd said when we'd decided to meet for dinner earlier in the day. "And I've been so busy running around looking for bad food, I haven't really had a chance to try it."

"WhyVeeAre was bad food?" I said.

"No. That was awesome."

"And that pub. The Sunset Grill?"

"That was great, too."

"Okay, so the bad food was…where?"

"Just call me from the lobby when you get here, all right? And we'll find someplace to eat in the hotel."

I felt an unaccustomed thrill of trepidation when the hotel valet took Old Stinky away. I stood under the porte cochere and watched with apprehension as my little blue cloud disappeared into the parking structure. And then

I smiled; the car seemed to be bringing out some latent maternal instincts in me. I'd have to watch myself.

Emily must have been waiting for my call on the house phone, because it seemed as though she joined me in the lobby thirty seconds after I replaced the handset into the cradle.

"Oh, good," she said when she caught sight of me. "You dressed for dinner."

I smirked at her. "You thought maybe I'd show up in jeans and Docs?"

"Do you still even have Docs?" she asked.

"You know what I mean." Doc Marten boots were a fairly constant threat between us. My threat, her vapors. "But you said we'd be eating in the hotel and I figured you wouldn't be staying at a dump." I looked around the carefully restored Victorian structure. "And you're not."

"No. I'm not. And I poked around earlier, to see which restaurant to pick," she said. "And I pick the lounge. It shares a kitchen with the main restaurant, 900 West, which is supposed to serve really great food. But the lounge is more casual. I thought it would be fun to just sit there for a very long time and eat and blab. Sound okay?"

"Absolutely. Sounds great."

Lounge seemed like sort of an overstatement to me. It was club chairs and elegant sofas and well-padded banquettes around lovely antique tables of varying heights; servers in black slacks and vests and white shirts with linen over their arms. To me, it seemed very Vancouver, though certainly not downtown east side. Kind of New World meets the Raj. You wouldn't for a heartbeat think you were in New York, but you knew you weren't in London, either. Emily and I picked a comfy-looking table for two on the opposite end of the room from the piano bar and settled in for a quiet but elegant evening.

"So tell me about your crisis," Emily said as we settled in.

"Crisis?"

"Yeah. The one you called about."

"Oh," I said. "Well. I'll tell you about it sometime. Not tonight, though. It's depressing stuff. And I don't want to be depressed again. I want to just enjoy your company. Maybe laugh a bit. Okay?"

Emily smiled and nodded. "Okay. I'm up for enjoying myself. We can get to the depressing stuff when we're back in L.A. Depressing stuff always goes better with sun."

We ordered an appetizer that had been proclaimed as a "flight" of caviar. It turned out to be a three-tiered concoction that made us feel very posh and special. Especially since, at our server's suggestion, we'd accompanied the appetizer with a modestly priced bottle of champagne. "Caviar is best with a sparkle," he'd advised, so sagely we hadn't thought to argue.

"Very grown-up," Emily smirked when we'd been served.

"Yeah. That's exactly it. All of this dining in beautiful places is making me feel very grown-up. I could get used to this."

"Well, don't get *too* used to it," Emily warned. "Or you'll *really* get grown-up. Remember what I said about the Film Industry Diet? The secret is a steady diet of food you don't like. I've been falling off of that with you." She looked at me steadily for a moment before she spoke again. "Actually, I forgot that I hate you. *You* never grow at all. What's your secret? Never mind. Don't answer that. All your damned running. You don't sit still long enough to eat."

"Yes," I said evenly. "That's it. Plus, I never eat when you're not around. Ever. It's why we have to go for dinner at least every two weeks. Otherwise I'd die."

"*Phhllt*," Emily said.

"Now *that's* ladylike," I pronounced poshly, and we both subsided into a fit of entirely un-grown-up giggles.

It was while getting said giggles under control that I caught sight of a familiar curtain of blue-black hair. The last giggle caught in my throat.

"What's wrong?" Emily asked.

I ignored her for just a second, looking at the table at the far side of the room through narrowed eyes.

At first I thought I couldn't be right—how can the world be that small?—but the cut of her expensive little suit—severe and sexy all at once—and the flash of her profile confirmed what I'd thought at first glance: Sonya Foy was in the house. It was a Sunday night, but there she was in full business gear. Three expensively dressed men were at the table with her—one in chinos and a golf shirt, the other two in suits. It appeared to be some sort of business meeting, and all three men seemed focused on Sonya's every word.

"Madeline, what is it?"

"Change places with me," I said hastily. "I don't want her to see me."

"Who?"

"Just do it, then I'll explain."

Emily and I exchanged places easily, though Emily's eyebrows stayed in the raised position while we slid around. "Listen, Mad, you know I love all this cloak-and-dagger stuff. But if you don't tell me what's going on pronto, my head is going to explode."

"I hate it when that happens," I quipped.

"Shaddup," she said cheerfully. "And tell me."

Where to start with Sonya? So much of what I knew about her had more to do with impressions and instinct than actual fact. So far. I went for it anyway.

"Well, for starters, I think she was Braydon's mistress."

"Seriously? Mistress?" Emily risked shooting another glance at Sonya. "Okay," she said when she had. "I can see that. And, believe me, those are *not* real."

"That's what I thought."

"Bray pay for them?"

"I dunno. Anyway, she's also a promoter. In fact..." I shot another quick glance in her direction "...I think she's promoting right now."

"Shaddup!" Emily said. "How cool is that?" Another peek. Then a sigh. "Madeline, what's a promoter?"

I hesitated, trying to think of just the right words. The right *fast* words. I felt as if I needed to do something. "It's like, sort of a salesperson. Of stock. But mostly unofficially, you know?"

"Not really."

"Well, you've probably gotten e-mails from promoters before. You don't play the markets, so it would just have looked like spam to you. You know— notices that XYZ Company is expecting super returns this quarter and will be going through the roof in the next two weeks so you'd better buy, buy, buy. You've seen those?"

"Sure. But what's that have to do with her?"

"It's the same principle, just she's old school. And a different level, too. See, promoters raise the value of a stock by talking it up. Sometimes it doesn't even matter if there's anything behind the talk. They just blab about it anywhere they can—on the Internet, in a boiler room, or like this—" I shot what I hoped was an unobtrusive thumb in Sonya's direction "—one on one."

"Or one on three," Emily offered.

"Sure. Whatever. One on fifty if you can get a roomful of investors to sit still. The idea is to get people buying what she's selling."

"I don't get it," Emily said. "What's in it for her?"

"Well, that depends. In the old days, companies sometimes had promoters on retainer. Even now, it can sometimes be a sort of consultancy position, like part of investor relations. Where the promoter is on staff and they get paid in cheap stock which they sell right into the hype they create. Sometimes, though not often, they're board members, and their business cards say something else entirely. Like vice president in charge of finance. Or vice president in charge of rubber ducks."

"Rubber ducks?" Emily looked confused.

"Okay. Sorry. Forget the rubber ducks. My point was, the title doesn't matter. What matters is what they do *unofficially* for the corporation. Sometimes there's no connection at all between the promoter and the company. I mean, if a promoter has a large enough block of stock on their own, they gain just by having the stock worth more. That's what they do in the boiler rooms. The brokerage will buy a large chunk of some fairly worthless stock and just sell the shit out of it. Stock goes up, brokerage sells their shares, stock tanks. Get it?"

"More or less," Emily said doubtfully. "One thing I *do* know—I'm *so* glad not to be in your business. It's very confusing."

"Tell me about it," I said. "But listen, I'll fill in the blanks later, okay? Right now, I want to figure out what she's doing."

"Why?" Emily asked, quite sensibly.

Her question brought me up short. "I'm not sure," I said. "I guess I want to know if she actually *is* a promoter. Because no one has come out and told me that. I just sort of sense it. And if she is, what's she promoting? I mean,

I think I know. But if I'm right, it'll clarify something for me. Listen, you've never met her before. Maybe you could go over there and sit at the table next to her and just sort of eavesdrop. See what you hear. While you're doing that, I'll slip out before she sees me and—"

"Why don't you just ask her?"

"Ask her what?"

"Ask her what she's doing," Emily said thoughtfully. "I mean, really—why not?"

"What? Just go over there and say, 'Hey?'"

"Yeah. Something like that. You'll know the right words. You know her, right? But in my life," Emily said sanctimoniously, "I've discovered that you get the best answers from people if you just ask the question. Politely."

I tried to think of one solid reason why I should *not* do what Emily suggested, but when you came right down to it, she was right. Ask the question. Why the hell not?

I picked up my bag and made as though to head to the ladies' room. I saw Sonya see me, and plastered a big ol' smile on my face, one of surprised but welcome recognition.

"Sonya," I said, approaching her. "Imagine. Hello!"

If she was uncomfortable, she didn't show it. Nor, I must say, did her companions. It struck me that, business meeting of a sort or no, the type of men Sonya worked would seldom be adverse to feminine companionship. Let's see, what was my clue? Well, the way she wielded those melonlike breasts as though they were weapons, for one. You didn't hoist cantaloupes like that and expose them if you weren't hoping someone—or maybe a lot of someones—would notice.

There are promoters who rely on technology to do what they do. The Internet, broadcast faxes, or banks of phones and cut-rate "brokers" to work them. Other promoters use facts and fictions—technical analysis, exaggerated claims—to bamboozle potential clients. Still others use charm and influence to "sell" their stock. To me, Sonya had the look of someone who could—and would—use all three. And more. Someone who would use every weapon in her arsenal, every tool at her disposal, to get her marks to do what she wanted. I looked at the three well-fed and expensively dressed guys sitting next to her and almost felt sorry for them. They didn't have a chance.

"Well, Madeline. This is a surprise."

"I'm here with a friend of mine for dinner." I indicated Emily across the room. "She's up from Los Angeles on business."

I glanced at the table surreptitiously. Sonya followed my glance but swept the papers spread out there into her bag in a single, elegant motion. Though not before I'd seen the Gauthier Fine Foods logo on the top of a couple of sheets of paper. One had looked like a financial report. A couple of others like press releases.

"I'm from Los Angeles, too," one of the men said. "Well, close enough. Pasadena."

Though I got the feeling Sonya would rather I stop

hanging around their table, it was obvious to both of us that introductions at this point were necessary.

"Madeline Carter," she said tightly, "this is Will Adams." She indicated the man who'd said he was from Pasadena. "And that's Chris Lippincott from Montreal and Walker Eng from Dallas." I shook hands all 'round, seeing interested eyes, pricey wristwatches and manicured nails.

Ignoring the fact that I hadn't been invited to join them—and the fact that I'd just noticed the food arrive at my table—I pulled up a chair from an empty table nearby and sat down with them, smiling sweetly. I saw Sonya's lips tighten, but she didn't say anything.

"Dallas, Montreal and Pasadena, huh?" I said pleasantly. "That's a long way to come for a meeting."

Lippincott laughed. "That would be a long way, even to meet with someone as charming as Sonya here. But we've only just met her. We're here for a convention."

"A convention," I said sweetly, but my eyes were on Sonya. "That's fun. What sort of convention?" To her credit, Sonya's expression didn't change.

"Dental health," Eng chimed in.

"We're orthodontists," Adams said helpfully, as though I hadn't already figured this out. Sometimes stereotypes work. These three *looked* like they spent a lot of time in people's mouths.

"But Sonya," I said lightly, "your teeth look perfect to me. Who would have thought you'd require the services of a trio of orthodontists?"

This earned me another tight smile, and if I wasn't mistaken, she was getting decidedly pale around the edges.

The men didn't look pale or tight. They looked positively jovial. In fact, my comment earned a hearty round of good-natured laughter.

"Oh, no," Adams said, "you're right about that. Nothing wrong with *this* girl's choppers. That I can see, anyway. No, Sonya here has been kind enough to point out some investment opportunities, right here in the city. And I must say, I've never met such a charming financial advisor," he said gallantly, beaming at Sonya. This earned both him and me another tight smile as Sonya signaled the waiter for a new drink. There was more I could have said, but I'd heard enough. As soon as I could politely manage it, I excused myself and went back to Emily and my own table.

"Okay," I said to Emily when I dropped back into my chair, "she is *so* pumping the stock."

"Your crab cakes are getting cold," Emily said.

"Why would she be pumping the stock?"

"You're not asking me, right?"

"Hmm? No. Sorry. Of course not. It's just...why?"

"How do you know that? That she's pumping the stock, I mean?"

"Well, first, the table was covered with Gauthier Fine Foods stuff when I got there. And those guys? They're not even local—they're in town for a dental convention."

"You're not serious?" Emily said, visibly aghast.

I nodded.

"Are you telling me she's working conventions?"

I laughed. "Well, yes and no. I didn't ask, but she probably either has some kind of go-between who hooks her up with people like that, or she already knows one of their colleagues or someone who would put her in touch with them. I don't imagine she just comes down here and hangs around the lobby."

"Well, *look* at her, Madeline. It wouldn't be such a reach, would it? Though if she was a call girl, she'd be a pretty well-paid one. I think that suit is Chanel."

"Do people even say that anymore? Call girl? What is that? Sounds like a customer service representative."

"Ha," Emily said tonelessly. "Ha. Ha. Anyway, I don't know. You put a hooker in a Chanel suit, and I think you've got yourself a call girl."

"Well, whatever you call it, she'll probably make more money tonight than any kind of call girl ever would. I'm serious. The question is—again—why?"

"That's pretty obvious, Madeline."

I looked at Emily closely. "Not to me, oh oracle of the stock market. Please, tell me, what do you see?"

Emily snickered at my shenanigans, but said, "No, seriously. It's all, like you said, in the name—stock *promoter*, right?"

"Right…" I said.

"Well, she's *promoting* it. She wants it to be worth more. Or someone does. Get it?"

"Well, sure, but, it's not a microcap, Emily. It's never been, like, a *cheap* stock. Or even a devalued stock. That is, it's always had value. It's just not the sort of thing that needs *that* type of promotion." I indicated Sonya on the other side of the room. Will from Pasadena was already gone. Sonya and the two who were left were now standing and shaking hands and generally looking as though they were making their goodbyes.

"And…" Emily said.

"And what?"

"I don't really see what one has to do with the other," Emily said, blissfully confident in her ignorance of the stock market.

"It's just that…" I'd meant to explain that well-financed, well-organized, well-backed corporations didn't stoop to those sorts of tactics. That was reserved for shady organizations. The kind that were more sizzle than steak. And then I realized something. Or perhaps realized the edge of something.

"Just that…what?" Emily asked.

"You're right," I said quietly, thinking while I spoke.

"I am?" Despite the fact that she'd been championing her theory, I could tell she was surprised that I was agreeing with her.

"Yeah," I said. As we spoke, I could see Sonya and the two men crossing the lounge, clearly saying goodbye to each other. As they went, Sonya shot a glance in my direction. She gave me a little wave and her face pulled into a smile, but it didn't reach her eyes. I waved back.

"It's so obvious," I said to Emily. "I just didn't see it before. Gauthier Fine Foods *is* a cheap stock, in all ways but price. The price hasn't had a big downward spiral *because* of Sonya Foy—and maybe others like her. She's been pumping it, but not up. She's been keeping it level by getting people to buy in at critical times. Maybe…maybe if she wasn't, it would have been going down."

"Really?"

I sighed and sat back in my chair. "I don't know. Maybe. I need to get my hands on the financials she was showing those guys."

"I thought you said you went through the financials that day at the office."

"Yeah. I did. But now I'm thinking… I don't know what I'm thinking. But I'd like to see for myself if what Doug showed me is the same as what Sonya's showing around."

"You might get a chance." At Emily's dropped voice, I looked up. Followed her eyes. One of Sonya's orthodontists was back. And he was heading toward us, a big shit-eating grin on his face.

I struggled for a second with his name. Lippincott from Montreal? No. Certainly not Eng from Dallas. No, this was, of course, the Californian. Will, I thought, from Pasadena. The one who'd left before the others. His name came to me just as he arrived at our table.

"Well, hello there, Will from Pasadena. This is Emily, from Huntingdon Beach." They nodded at each other. Smiled. I did not like the looks of him, not now that he was alone. Separated, as it were, from his herd of fellow orthodontists. Or maybe I just did not like the fact that he was standing at our table on a Sunday night, in a strange city, presumably heading back to his life the following day and giving off an odor of want and desperation so thick it was almost palpable.

Under the circumstances, I did the only thing I could do: I asked him to join us.

Emily's head snapped around so quickly I thought maybe she'd hurt herself. I smiled sweetly in response to her sharp, questioning glance and said soothingly, "Well, I think poor Will here is all alone and needs some company." When Will smiled broadly at that, Emily mimed sticking her finger down her throat and gagging when his head was turned. And, though it was difficult, I did not laugh.

There was nothing distinctly unattractive about Will Adams from Pasadena. No hideous scars, protruding growths or odd hair patterns. He was perhaps ten years older than either Emily or myself—midforties, I guessed, and not heading toward fifty particularly badly. He wasn't unattractive, but I was spectacularly unattracted to him. Even so, I sat in my chair in what I imagined to be a seductive fashion, batted my eyelashes at him kittenishly as I tried to ignore Emily's expression—confused and aghast—from beyond his clearly interested face.

"So, Will," I said, pitching my voice low, "tell us about yourself."

"Not much to tell, really," he said predictably. "I'm an orthodontist." He laughed self-consciously. "But you know that already. I'm flying home tomorrow. Not so much to tell," he said again. "What about you two? What do you do?"

Before Emily could interject—and from the look on her face, she hadn't been about to, in any case—I said quickly, "We're in pretty much the same business as Sonya."

"Wow. That's funny. I haven't actually met a stock analyst before. And now I've met three in one day. Are all analysts strikingly beautiful women?"

"Excuse me." Emily flagged our waiter, slightly more loudly than she needed to, I thought. "Can you bring me a sidecar, please?"

"A sidecar? That's fun," I said. "I'll have one of those, too. Will?"

"Make mine Crown and ginger," he said to the waiter. And then to me, "That's a popular local drink. Crown Royal is Canadian whiskey. Rye whiskey. With ginger ale," he laughed self-consciously. "And when in Rome…"

"Exactly," I said, "I agree. I'll have that instead of the sidecar, please."

Emily just rolled her eyes.

"So what was Sonya analyzing for you?" I asked as innocently as possible. Because I knew quite well that Sonya was no analyst.

Will looked mildly alarmed. "You're not competitors, are you? I wouldn't want to say anything out of turn."

To my surprise, I felt the toe of my shoe touch his calf lightly under the table. "And if we were…?"

I saw his eyes widen at the touch, but not with alarm. Then a grin came just as our drinks did. "I'd say," he said, picking up his lowball glass and tipping it to me lightly, "I'd say it wasn't a problem."

I leaned toward him slightly, intimately. "And…"

"And…?"

"Sonya's analysis?"

I tried not to flinch when I felt his hand touch my knee. It didn't stay there and I thought I might have imagined it. But I willed myself to stay where I was. I even managed another kittenish eyelash bat, but only by studiously avoiding looking at Emily.

"The analysis…oh yes. Well, would you like to see the paperwork she gave me?"

"I…would…love…that," I said slowly. Invitingly. An invitation I saw hit its mark by the look in his eyes. I wasn't sure if I should applaud my acting or hide my head. I dared a glance at Emily and had my answer: she was watching me with a horrified fascination. A look that intensified with Will's next words.

"I was just up in my room when I decided to come down and see if I could join you ladies. I left Sonya's paperwork up there. Why don't you come up? For a drink. I've already decided not to invest with Sonya. Now that I know there are so many…attractive… options. I'll give you the whole folder she gave me."

I swallowed deeply, trying again not to flinch when

I saw his eyes drink in the motion of my throat. There really wasn't a lot being left to the imagination here…and I had no intention of following through. On the other hand, I really, really, really wanted those financials.

How far are you willing to go? I heard a little voice ask.

I answered without hesitation: *Not that far.*

And yet. I could think of no other way to get what I wanted.

"A drink." I stopped and cleared my throat. My heart was pounding. "A drink would be…nice."

Emily's eyes widened, but she didn't say anything. Just sat in her chair as though she'd recently taken root.

I avoided Emily's glance while Will and I crossed toward the exit. He didn't touch me, not with his hands. But I could feel him enveloping me somehow, in any case.

Halfway to the exit I stopped and turned toward him. "I think my friend might be mad at me, leaving her here like this. Let me just have a word with her. I'll meet you at the elevator in a minute, okay?"

There was a look in his eyes so intense it took me aback. I think, just at that moment, he would have agreed to anything. It was frightening.

I stopped him with a hand on his shoulder just as he was about to move away. I could feel the heat from him in that single touch. "On second thought," I said, more calmly than I felt, "it might take a few minutes longer

than that. I'll meet you in your room, all right? Order
me another one of those Canadian drinks."

He gave me his room number, the heat I'd felt
from him reflected clearly in his eyes. "Don't be
long," he said.

"I won't."

"What the *fuck* is going on?" Emily demanded when
I got back to the table.

"I'm getting those financials," I said breezily.

"Are you going to *do* him in the process,
Madeline? Because if you're thinking about it, you
should be aware that if he's not married, I'm the
queen of the moon."

"I know he's married," I said. "And I have no intention of *doing* him. I'm just going to get the paperwork
and skedaddle."

"This is *so* uncool, Madeline. This is so not like
you." She seemed to have another thought. "And this
is *so* dangerous. You can't just play someone like that
and think nothing is going to happen."

"Listen, he gave me his room number. I'm just
going to go up, like I said, get the papers and get out of
there." I reached into my bag, pulled out my wallet and
dropped enough cash for my portion of the bill on the
table. I gave her his room number. "If I'm not back in
ten minutes, call security or something. Like, help me
get out of there. Okay?"

"Jay-sus, girl. I don't know how I let you talk me into this shit." She wasn't happy, but she didn't argue, and when I left the table, she stayed put.

There are moments in your life that you understand are significant. Times when you know full well that the thing you're doing is providing a turning point to your becoming the person you are destined to become. You don't get many of those moments in your life, and traveling up in the elevator to Will from Pasadena's hotel room, I realized that, despite all appearances, this wasn't one of them.

What sort of craven woman, I asked myself, deliberately plays a man she thinks has something she wants, with no intention of delivering what he desires? I had been drinking, but I knew I wasn't drunk. That is, I couldn't blame my actions on alcohol, as convenient as that would have been. And I also knew that a part of me was seriously enjoying playing this ancient—and potentially dangerous—game.

I told myself he deserved it. He most probably *was* married and trying to score a little action before he headed back to his regularly scheduled life. But two bad ideas don't make a good one—that bolt from the blue again. And two wrongs never, ever make a right.

When the elevator stopped on the floor directly beneath the one I was heading to, I almost got out along with two blue-haired ladies coming home from a day of shopping and seeing the sights. In my mind's eye, I could imagine myself getting off the elevator car, waiting for the next going in the other direction, and then heading back down to lobby level and the relative safety of the lounge, Emily and the crab cakes I'd abandoned.

When the door closed again, though, and the elevator continued its trip up, I was still on board.

How far, I wondered, was I willing to go to get what I wanted?

In the end, I wasn't required to find out.

"It's open," Will from Pasadena called out in answer to my knock.

"It's me," I said.

He called out from behind a closed door, "Make yourself comfortable. I'll be right out."

He was in the bathroom, presumably making himself all shiny clean for our tryst. I could hear brushing and gargling and water running. I didn't sit down. My eyes scanned the room, spotted the folder I'd seen in his hand when we were with Sonya. When I flipped it open, I saw the Gauthier Fine Foods logo. I stuffed the whole folder into my bag and headed to the door.

Will from Pasadena emerged—shirtless—from the bathroom just as a knock sounded.

"Room service," a voice called out. They'd gotten here so fast, I thought, Will from Pasadena must have bribed someone.

I almost bowled the guy delivering the room service over in my haste to leave the room; I saw him reinforce his grip on the tray he carried—a tray bearing our drinks, a split of champagne and a plate of oysters on the half shell. *Oysters*. Of course.

"I've changed my mind about that drink," I called over my shoulder as I headed out of the room, catching an elevator just as the doors were about to shut.

As the doors closed behind me, I thought I heard my name.

"Madeline," is what I thought I heard. Somewhat plaintive and a little hurt. I could have been wrong, though. But I was pretty sure that—shirtless and married as he was—he probably wouldn't follow me.

I didn't feel good about it, but I'd gotten what I came for.

By the time I reached the lobby, my hands had stopped shaking. And when I saw Emily, heading out of the lounge and toward the elevator, my heart rate was pretty much normal.

Emily barely acknowledged my presence. "Glad to see you survived," she sniffed, and kept on walking, a take-out container in her hands.

"Where are you heading?" I asked, falling into step beside her.

"Up to my room." I was hurt that she didn't ask where I was going.

"Can I come? I want to…I sort of want to hide out for a while."

Emily raised her eyebrows but not her voice. "I guess

you do," was all she said, but she indicated that I could follow her if I wanted.

I hadn't paid close attention to details when I was briefly in Will from Pasadena's room, but I had the feeling that Emily's suite was practically identical, though two floors higher up.

"The view is incredible," I said, peeking out the window at the dark, wet city spread out below us. "And your room is so pretty," I said. "I love the paisley chairs."

"Cut the crap, Carter," Emily snarked at me. "You're being all nicey-nicey now, but who was that down there? I don't think I even recognized you."

I plunked myself down on the bed, letting my purse fall to the floor next to my feet. "I dunno what came over me, Em. Honest. It just seemed like the thing to do."

"Sometimes, Carter, you scare the hell out of me. Was it worth it?"

I looked at her blankly for a moment, then realized what she meant. "The file!" I said, scooping up my bag and pulling out the folder. "I don't know yet. Let's see."

Emily gave me a whole thirty seconds of reading before she said, "Well?"

"Hang on. Give me a minute." I scanned in silence for a while, but I didn't really need even the minute I'd asked for. I had seen at first glance that these numbers had little relation to the ones Doug had allowed me to see a few days earlier. It just took me longer to believe it.

When I told Emily, she didn't get it at all. "How can

that be?" she asked. "Financials are financials, right? Why would these be different?"

"Well, that's the big question. Honestly? There could be a lot of reasons. The most obvious one would be that Doug showed me the real financials, and he's cooked up these ones to show potential investors what they want to see."

"Blow sunshine up their ass, you mean? How legal is that?"

"It is not legal. But it's also not necessarily the whole story. Like, neither of them might be right." I was thinking aloud now, but I went with it, a sense of excitement growing in my gut. "The ones Doug showed me might have been created just to appease the family, make them think things are more together than they actually are."

"Again, I ask, how can they do this?"

"Do it? Emily. It's just paper. It's easy. But you're right—at least one of these sets of figures is clearly cooked. Maybe both of them. Tossing shit like that around is bound to catch up with you eventually. And *that's* illegal."

"So why do it?"

"Something this obvious? *If* Doug had a hand in it? The only thing I can think of is that he's preparing to scuttle his boat." I thought of DW Investments. Even *that* was beginning to make sense.

"*Please* don't start with maritime metaphors, Madeline. Just tell me what you think is going on."

I tried to line up everything I knew and lay it out for Emily. In a way, of course, I was laying it out for me, as well.

"Okay, on the one hand, we have a company that we know—at least up until a year or so ago, two at most—had a lot of value in it. Like, *hard* value—money and the tools to make more."

"*Counterfeit?*" Emily squealed.

I laughed. "No. Sorry. My fault. Not actually *make* money. Just, you know, all the tools of good business. Solid positive cash flow."

"Oh," Emily said, looking subdued. "Right."

"Then Doug decides he wants out, Braydon doesn't want to let him go. Bray either marries the sister so Doug feels compelled to stay, or Doug throws his sister at Bray so he has more of a stake."

"Or both," Emily said thoughtfully. "Both of them thinking they're manipulating the other into doing what he wants."

I thought about that. "Possibly. Anyway, after a while, Doug decides it isn't enough. Or maybe the sister ends up unhappy. So Doug starts taking money out of the company in ways that aren't obvious to anyone."

"Extortion?"

"Maybe." Then, when I thought about it, the picture became clearer still. "Well, not exactly. Like, when Braydon wanted to build the new offices. Doug set up a company designed to overbill Gauthier Fine Foods for virtually everything. Braydon doesn't care what it costs—he's built a money *machine* and figures that Doug will take care of him in any case."

"Only Doug is pocketing money on the side?"

"Big wads of it, I'm guessing. And that's just one way. It's possible he was doing this from all angles, basically husking the value out of Gauthier Fine Foods without anyone noticing."

Emily was grimacing in the middle of her attempt to understand. "What about Sonya? Where does she fit in?" She pointed at the folder I'd stolen from Will from Pasadena. "What about that?"

"I'm guessing it was Sonya's function to keep the whole thing looking good publicly. See, if Doug was on the inside with a shovel taking money out, he wouldn't have wanted it to show up in a way that would cause the stock to go *down*. If nothing else, that would have been the ultimate tip-off to Braydon that something was up. But as long as the stock price continued pretty much unchanged, Bray wouldn't concern himself with it. Or that's what Doug would have thought. That's probably even why he 'accidentally' let things slide. He *wanted* the stock to get delisted because, once it was trading on the Pink Sheets, it would be easier to manipulate what was shown to the public."

"And to Braydon."

I nodded. "*Especially* to Braydon."

"So what happened?" Emily asked.

"What happened to what?"

"To Braydon. How does Braydon's death fit into all of this? Or does it?"

I lay back on the bed for a minute, thinking things through. I thought about the sheaf of papers under the car seat and the short ribs and *everything*.

"Maybe it does fit in," I said finally. "Maybe he found out."

I stayed with Emily for a couple of hours. We ordered two bottles of San Pelegrino and some cheesecake from room service, and we had that with the crab cakes Emily had rescued from our attempt at dinner. Then we sat and chatted for a while about anything other than the topic that had been foremost on my mind for the last few days.

We drank our fizzy water and talked about Emily's relationship, my new old car, the progress of the ADR Emily was in town for, and about a few of the people we both knew back in L.A. I guess we were trying to put things back where they belonged between us. It seemed like it worked okay, and when we parted, Emily gave me a big hug and said, "Don't be a dope, all right? None of this stuff will matter once we get back home."

When I collected Old Stinky from valet parking, I carefully checked the little car's flanks for signs of abuse, but they'd taken good care of things, despite the right-hand drive. I gave the kid that brought her back to me a pretty good tip before I wheeled her back toward the condo.

I was almost afraid to open the door when I got back to Braydon's apartment—afraid that the stink of cigarette smoke would come snaking out again and with it the wrath of a woman tricked. However, all was quiet on that front. If anything, the condo just seemed sadder and lonelier, as though the longer its owner was gone, the more neglected the place would feel.

I walked into the little office and picked up one of Braydon's cookbooks and looked closely at him smiling at me from the front cover.

"What did you get yourself into?" I asked pointlessly, though I was glad when he didn't answer.

I wandered about the place fruitlessly for a little while, touching a photograph here, a sculpture there, as though contact with the objects that Braydon had cared about would bring things into sharper focus. It did not.

After a while, I gave it up. I was beyond tired and had entered into a mental place where things were beginning to make *less* sense, not more.

Once I'd settled into bed, though, sleep eluded me. All of the delving I'd been doing came rushing back, presenting me with a lot of questions, but no real answers.

If I was right about the things I'd conjectured at Emily's hotel, I was in the center of a huge corporate mess. Though I was pretty sure I didn't have a fix on the whole thing, I knew that if even half of what I thought was true, police involvement at this point would not be inappropriate.

On the other hand, when I thought about what I

actually *knew* in a solid and provable way, there wasn't much that would hold water. There was, of course, the matter of the multiple financials, but someone would need to get both sets of books—and more, if there were any—to the police. And, I realized, possibly not even the police at this point; based on that alone, it would likely be more something for local securities investigators and the SEC to look at, not a criminal matter.

The *real* question for me at the moment: was what I had told Emily correct? Did Braydon get himself dead because he'd discovered that his company was becoming a writhing viper pit?

And, if that were the case—if Braydon *had* been killed—who was the viper? Who had done the deed? Doug? While there was plenty I felt Doug was capable of, I really didn't peg him as a killer. On the other hand, there's just no accounting for what some people will do for enough money. Or power. Or both.

The whole issue of DW Investments clouded things, as well. If I was right about everything, Doug certainly had been the one with the most to lose if Braydon found out about his plans while they were still unfurling.

Too, the nature of that final meal still bothered me. As I'd told Emily, that hadn't felt random. If someone *had* made Braydon that meal and either tricked him into eating it or forced him to do so, the choice of food had been deliberate. A sort of final thumbing of the nose at someone—Braydon—deeply despised.

Who could hate Braydon that much? Enough not

just to kill him, but kill him in a way that the victim himself would find odious.

Not that dying is ever a desired state, but it would have been possible, given the poison used, to do it in a way that was pain free. To do it in a way that the victim had no idea what was even happening. The addition of loathed food into the equation seemed to bring another dimension.

Did that mean that whoever had killed Braydon needed to be someone with the culinary skills required to prepare a dish that was both up to Braydon's standards and completely detestable? If so, that would narrow the field. And cooking at that level was certainly not something I thought Doug himself was physically capable of doing.

What of Curt? He certainly had those skills. And he would also have had knowledge of which foods Braydon really loathed. But did Curt have anything to gain from Braydon's death? And had Curt despised him enough to want him out of the way? Even forty-eight hours ago, I would have said no. But that was before Langley and the barn. Did what Curt have with Mimi outweigh whatever friendship he'd had with my former husband?

Then, of course, there was Mimi herself. But that didn't really add up for me, either. What, after all, did she gain from Braydon's death? And could she possibly have hated him so badly that she wanted him out of the way, whatever the cost? And what made me think she'd hated him at all?

I tossed and turned on these thoughts for most of the night. When I finally fell into a fitful slumber, a cool, gray light was just beginning to slant through the windows. I fell asleep when it was almost time for me to get up.

Seventeen

I woke to full, silver light. I could still hear the rain on the skylight, but it seemed to have slowed in the night. It wasn't really pounding anymore, just sort of beating steadily.

Like a heart, I thought uncomfortably.

In the bathroom, I started a big, steamy shower. Steamy enough that, when I emerged a full twenty minutes later, my skin was a bright, abused pink and the day a clean question mark beyond me. This clean, I knew, anything was possible.

In the kitchen I ground beans, then put the espresso machine through its paces. I didn't have a schedule today, though there were plenty of things I wanted to do. I'd need coffee—strong and good—so I could figure out what my next move should be. At the moment, still damp from the shower and with my morning coffee still in the future, I had yet to figure out that move.

It was Monday morning, so, naturally, once I had that coffee at my elbow, I thought about checking the markets and my place in them, but I knew I didn't have the spirit for it. There was so much on my mind—so much that was *here* where I was—that I didn't feel capable of doing a good job of trading for myself.

There's a certain amount of concentration required to do what I do, and do it properly and well. Fortunately, I'd had a good month thus far—more than good enough to cover my expenses—so I didn't feel as though I needed to worry about it overmuch. I'd be back in Los Angeles soon enough, I reasoned, without all of the distractions of being in a strange place and dealing with a stranger situation.

I went to Braydon's little office and turned on the computer, then used Google to search on how one would go about finding information on a privately held company in British Columbia.

The fact is, at the best of times and with a fair amount of information at your disposal, it can be difficult to find out much about a privately held company when the company in question doesn't want much to be known. In this case I didn't even know the company's legal status. Was DW Investments incorporated? Or were they a sole proprietorship? And, since I was in a foreign country where I didn't know all the rules, was there even such a thing as a sole proprietorship to contend with?

I started doing Internet research on the status of private companies in British Columbia and how one could go about getting information on them, but after about fifteen minutes with too much information and none of it very good, I gave it up. There just *had* to be a better way for me to use my time. I gave a thought to calling Anne Rand and adding this request to my order, but I decided against it. Better to wait and see what she turned up on Sonya, not to mention find out where my tab with her was after that.

Since I didn't know where I'd end up spending the night—back at Braydon's or in Seattle at my mom's—I packed the car the way I had on Saturday morning, as though I wasn't coming back. This time, though, when I shut the door, I didn't think about closing chapters or anything remotely poetic or prophetic. I just thought about making sure I'd locked up properly, and then about making tracks.

Without realizing I had a clear plan on where I was going, I headed Old Stinky east from Braydon's apartment, but I wasn't too surprised when I pulled the car smoothly into a spot at Gauthier Fine Foods. On some level, I must have known this was where all roads must lead.

Stina smiled when she caught sight of me in the foyer. "Hey, Madeline," she said cheerfully. "Doug didn't tell me to expect you today."

"He didn't know I was coming by," I said. Then, "*I*

didn't know I was coming by today. I just sort of ended up here. Is he around?"

"He is," she said, glancing at the multiline telephone system. "But he's on a conference call. It could be a while. Did you want to have a seat?"

I started to nod, then had another thought. "Is Simon free?"

"I'm not sure," she said with another glance at the phones. "I know he's here, but not what he's up to. I'll check for you."

After she'd spoken with him briefly, she smiled at me again. "He told me to tell you he's not free but he's cheap. You're to go up to the editing suite on the production level. He said you'd know how to find it."

The door to the editing suite was closed. I knocked lightly and, when I didn't get an answer, I pushed it open a few inches. The "hello" I'd meant to call out got stuck in my throat.

Simon was at a computer with headphones on—the reason he hadn't heard me—and every monitor in the place was lit up...and filled with images of Braydon.

I stood there in the doorway for a moment, undetected, and watched Simon work. He was confident and assured with the computers, pulling frames from here and plopping them there. You could see that confidence in the concerted way he focused his attention and the simple assurance of his hands. You could tell he'd done this a lot. But that's not what drew my attention. Or, at least, it wasn't the only thing. What caught my eye was a segment that showed Braydon first talking to the camera, then pulling a pen from a pocket on the right shoulder of his chef's whites and making a notation in a journal. After making a quick note, he addressed the camera again, popping the pen back into the pocket while he spoke, then turning his attention to the preparation of something lovely and edible.

Maybe Simon felt watched, or maybe he was breaking off because he was expecting me, but, just as the image of Braydon turned back to the food at hand, Simon turned in his seat and saw me standing watching him. He smiled while he pulled the headphones off and hit a few of his controls. I watched as the screens darkened.

"Still at it, I see," I said.

"Yeah. And lots more to do. Though I don't usually do this part myself anymore."

"You don't?"

"No. Today I just felt as though it needed to be me. This last time. And, honestly, the guys are better at this than I am. It's their job, after all. And I'll get them to fine-tune for me when I'm done. Like I told you the other day, though, it's therapeutic." He seemed to consider a moment. "Actually, seeing your face is therapeutic, too."

"It is?" I said, unsure of how to take what he said.

"Sure. I've been sitting here wallowing a bit, I think. Seeing you is a lovely surprise."

"I'm not interrupting anything?"

"Not at all," he said, stretching. "I needed a break, anyway."

"Gwen's not in today?" I asked, as nonchalantly as possible.

Simon looked at me closely anyway. "No," he said—carefully, I thought. "Why?"

I shrugged, as though it had been an aside. "Just that last time I was here—" I indicated the editing suite "—she was working away with you."

Simon sighed heavily, looking, I thought, a little sad. "Sorry for overreacting, Madeline. I'm a little sensitive about Gwen today, I guess."

"Why?" I said, swallowing the lump in my throat.

"I'm kind of worried about her. She was in on Saturday and said she'd be here first thing Monday. And she didn't show up and she's not answering her phone. It's probably silly of me. Likely something just came up. She's usually a very dependable sort. Well, you saw her. Doesn't she look dependable?"

I nodded, wanting to tell him what I suspected and *not* wanting to at the same time. "Dependable," I said after a while. "Yes. I guess, when you mention it, she does."

"That's why I'm worried. I mean, she'll probably just turn up with some very good reason. But this isn't the sort of thing she does."

I thought again about telling Simon that I feared something bad might have happened to Gwen, and why I thought so. Two things made me hold my tongue.

On the one hand, I really didn't know if it *was* Gwen that had called me and had intended to meet me at the

Dodge Hotel. Basing it on a purse sighting hardly seemed rational. Why cause Simon potentially needless grief?

On the other, I still wasn't quite sure about Simon. For all I knew, if it *was* Gwen who had been taken away in a body bag, Simon might have had something to do with it. If that were the case, tipping my hand now would *not* be a good idea.

"Anyway," Simon was saying, "it's just not a good time. I really need her right now. Ah, well," he said, rising, "I've decided that your purpose here today is to momentarily divert me from such thoughts. Come on," he said. "Let's get out of here." He picked up a few folders and led me out of the room, down the hall.

"Look at that view." He pointed out the big window in his office when we got there. "It looks different today, doesn't it?"

I nodded while I looked. It did. The rain that continued had rendered everything a dull, flat gray. I could see downtown, as I had a few days earlier, but now it was like looking at the same view through a soft focus lens. Exactly the same. Only different.

He joined me at the window. "You know, a lot of people not from here don't completely *get* Vancouver. You hear it when they talk about the place. They mention the rain or the grayness or how they miss the sun or whatever. But it's not really like that. Do you see it?"

"I'm not sure. What do you mean?"

"Well...look. It's beautiful. And it's changeable. Right now, it's raining hard, but it won't do this for long. In another hour, it might slow to a light drizzle. Or stop altogether. The sun might even come out. And tomorrow it'll start all over again."

Seattle is just a few hours south of Vancouver by car, so my hometown is in a very similar weather belt. When you're from a place like Seattle, you don't think about the rain or the gray. At least, I never did. Rain simply is. Until it's not. Simon's little speech—touching as it was—told me something about him.

"You're not from around here, are you?" I asked.

He smiled. "That obvious, huh? But, no. I'm not. I'm from Halifax, originally, by way of Toronto." Both places known for climates that are overall colder and drier than Vancouver's. Or Seattle's, for that matter. "But I've lived out here for about four years."

I smiled at him. "Long enough to fall in love, huh?"

"More than enough."

"How did you and Braydon connect?"

"Just as you'd expect, I guess, with someone like him."

Simon perched on the edge of his desk and told me he'd been the producer of the top food-related television show in the country. The show had won awards several years running and had been gaining an American viewership as well. He told me that was something a lot of Canadian shows—and not just those about food—aspire to because there are so many more Americans than Canadians. The U.S., he told me, was a much bigger market. Being successful in both markets with a single show, Simon told me, was a delicate and difficult thing. Every stage of production had to be carefully considered, not just for general excellence, but with this dual viewership in mind.

He obviously understood the challenges and, on seeing the show Simon produced, Braydon had understood that Simon understood.

"He courted me," Simon said now. "As much as he ever courted you, I'm sure. But I was happy at my old position. I had a lot of freedom. And other things—nonfood things—on the go."

"How did he convince you?" I asked.

"*More* freedom. More money, of course. And the promise to invest in my film work when the time came."

"He made you an offer you couldn't refuse?"

"Something like that." He nodded. "And he built the studio."

"And you built him the show he wanted."

"Pretty much." He hesitated, looking suddenly deep in thought. "Such a shame." And I could see he was referring to Braydon's death, not his life. "I really didn't see it coming."

"You didn't?"

He shook his head. "No. Not even a little bit. I think I was probably more surprised than anyone. I mean, I worked with the man. We saw each other almost every day. You'd think I *would* have seen it coming." Simon looked genuinely distressed.

"Did it ever occur to you that maybe he *didn't* kill himself?" I asked quietly.

"Sure. Of course. But that's natural, don't you think? Part of just denying, I guess, that maybe there was some way I could have helped if I'd just seen the signs."

"More than that, though. Like, did you ever think that someone might have killed him?"

Simon just looked at me for a moment, his eyes narrowed. "Who?" he said finally. "Who would have killed him?"

I shook my head. He had me there. Who indeed? "I guess someone who would have been better off with Braydon dead than alive."

To my surprise, Simon laughed at this. "But that was so many people. It's probably too big a number to work with."

"What do you mean?" I said, genuinely perplexed.

"Oh, Madeline. I'm sorry. It was a joke. Sure, Braydon pissed people off sometimes—that's really what I was referring to—but doesn't everyone? I think all really talented and creative people do. He was always very…single-minded in his vision of the way things should be. People didn't always get that. Did he make people mad? Sure. But *that* mad? I wouldn't think so."

"So, what I said—people who would be better off with him dead…"

"Madeline, there was just no hint of any foul play. If there had been, don't you think the police would have seen it? I think maybe you're in your own denial," he said gently. "I'm sorry. I hope you don't think that's a cruel thing to say. But maybe you just have to face it. If no one else ever suspected such a thing, why are you?"

I didn't take offense. I knew none had been intended. Even so, Simon's words bothered me more than I would have thought possible. What if he was right? Was my mind engineering something where no possibility existed? What would that say about me? About how I'd felt about Braydon? I didn't know the answers to those questions and I was suddenly unsure of how I felt about exploring them.

Simon and I agreed to meet for lunch later in the day. Not knowing the city well, I suggested the bar Emily and I had found the night of our walk. He knew it instantly and agreed to meet me there at noon.

I stopped the elevator on the executive office level, thinking to pop my head in to see if Doug was free. Doug's office door was ajar and voices floated out gently. Doug's baritone and a feminine voice I knew I'd be able to recognize anywhere, anytime, forevermore: Mimi.

I didn't mean to listen at the door. That is, listening was not my intention. I meant to back away, perhaps go off in search of Stina or maybe just hang in Braydon's office until Doug was available. I really did not mean to eavesdrop. But the sound of my name made me prick up my ears like a dog.

"I'll say it again," Doug said. "Madeline is harmless. Better than harmless. She told me herself she was going to get Jessica to back off."

"Are you even listening to me?" There was a

petulant whine in Mimi's voice, one I hadn't heard before. One she maybe reserved just for her big brother. "I had the creepiest feeling after I told her to leave. I went in the house and I felt as though someone had been *in* there."

"Oh, Mimi, please. Don't be silly. The doors were locked, right?"

"Of course they were."

"Are you suggesting she broke in?"

"I don't know what I'm suggesting. Just, I don't know, Doug, why was she poking around?" Her voice dipped below a level I could hear. I knew that if I put my face a little closer to the door, I'd be able to catch Mimi's voice, but I didn't want to risk being seen. I tried to look as though I were standing outside the nearly closed door, waiting patiently, as though perhaps Doug had asked me to chill outside his office before he could see me. That was, at least, what I *hoped* it looked like.

"It doesn't matter anyway, Mimi. There's nothing there for her to see. Right?" Then more strongly, "Right?"

"Yeah, yeah, right. Whatever. Fuck, Doug. I don't even know anymore."

"Then stop worrying about it, Mimi. I mean, look in the mirror. Do you have any idea what you're doing to your face when you scowl like that?"

"Fuck *off*. You sound like Mother."

"I'm serious, Mimi. Wherever this road leads, you'll want that face intact. You'll need it where we're going."

"Where we're going," she said again in just the same

tone. "I wish you'd give me some clarity with that. You say the same things, but nothing ever happens. At least *I'm* making things move forward."

"What do you mean by that?"

"Madeline?"

I straightened up so quickly, I almost injured my neck. Stina had approached silently. I glanced down at her feet, looking for soft soles; she'd been amazingly quiet for a woman in heels. "What are you doing here?" she said.

I moved deeper down the hall as inconspicuously as possible, trying to put distance between myself and Doug's office door. I really didn't want him to find out—from Stina or any other way—that I'd been listening. "I…I was trying to remember my way to Doug's office," I lied. I checked Stina's face for signs of doubt, but couldn't read her. I'd just have to hope for the best. "I didn't want to bother you again and I figured he'd be done his phone meeting by now."

Stina looked at me cautiously, as though trying to figure out what to do with me. After what seemed like a long time, she said, "Why don't you wait for him in Braydon's office?" She didn't hang around for an answer, but turned and began leading that way. "No one is using it and you can make your calls in there."

Calls? I tried to remember if my stumbling lies had included anything about calls. I didn't think so.

To my surprise, rather than ushering me into Braydon's office and then continuing on her way, she followed me in, then closed the door behind her.

She indicated I should sit on the sofa, then crossed to the desk and picked up the phone, punching in a three-digit in-house extension. "Hi, Bev? It's Stina. Will you cover me out front for a while? Yeah, something's come up."

My eyebrows shot up at this, but I didn't say anything. Stina obviously had something in mind. I decided to let it play out.

She crossed to a chair facing the sofa, folded herself into it gracefully and just sat there, regarding me benignly for a couple of beats.

Finally she seemed to make a decision. She sighed deeply, in a way that made me think she hadn't noticed it, then said, "Okay, Madeline, what's up?"

"Up?" I repeated.

"Yeah, up. Something is going on. With you. I want to know what it is."

I looked at her appraisingly, trying to read what her face and her body were telling me. I couldn't. But it was important. Was she on the verge of telling Doug she'd found me lurking—listening—outside his door? Or was she in a similar place to where I was, with more questions than answers? I had no way of knowing, but I *did* know I didn't want to share anything with her until I had a better idea. One thing, though: the fact that she'd gotten me quietly out of the hall and into Bray's office seemed like a good sign.

"I don't know what you mean," I said quietly, still undecided.

"I think you do." She looked at me thoughtfully. "More than that, Madeline, I think you're afraid to say anything to me right now in case I go to Doug."

I raised my eyebrows, but didn't answer.

"Okay," she went on. "Let me put this another way. I found you eavesdropping outside of Doug's door, yes?"

I shrugged as noncommittally as possible, but I had at least part of the answer now: she *had* known I was listening at that door.

"Okay. Well, whatever. I just wanted to let you know I'm not going to tell Doug."

I felt a flood of relief so acute, for a split second I felt light-headed. Hopefully, she was telling the truth.

"Why?" was all I said.

"Why?" she repeated. "That's probably a good question. And I have no intention of answering it fully. Let's just say that there are things going on at Gauthier Fine Foods at the moment that are not in my ultimate best interests."

"Why?" I said again, not really expecting an answer. Then, "Wait—were you one of Braydon's hires?"

She nodded. "And it's not just that. I was an early hire, Madeline. There were stock options. And I exercised all of them, plus bought more on my own. If Gauthier Fine Foods were to suddenly disappear, I'd not only lose my job—and it's a pretty good job—I'd lose the nest egg I've been building. For obvious reasons, I'd really rather that not happen."

"I can see that," I said. And I did. "But why would

you think the company would disappear? There's been no indication of that at all."

"Not to you, maybe," she said. "Not to most people. But I see things. I hear things. With Braydon gone…well, I'm not saying anything more, but it seems to me to be pretty convenient for some people." And she cast her eyes in the direction of Doug's office.

"Stina, do you believe Braydon killed himself?"

Stina swung her face toward me, wide-eyed. "Is that what you think?" she asked. "You think Doug killed him?"

"Whoa," I said. "I *so* did not say that."

"Yes, but…it's what you think, isn't it?"

Was it? I had to think about it for a moment. Had Doug killed his business partner—his brother-in-law? There were, I thought, other, easier ways of getting rid of an unwanted partner.

"Honestly, Stina, I don't know what to think anymore. But that wasn't on the top of my brain. No."

"But you do think someone killed Braydon." It wasn't a question.

"I think…I think it's a possibility. Yes. What about you? Was that something you ever thought about?"

"I guess it was the first thing I thought about when I heard. I mean, I worked with Bray every day almost. Every day he was in town. I even traveled with him sometimes, when he needed an assistant when he was on the road. Don't get me wrong, I'm not saying we were friends or anything. We weren't. But in some ways I was closer to him than most of his friends because he was my boss and he would let his guard down around me. Does that make any sense?"

I nodded. It made a lot of sense.

"So when I heard he'd killed himself, my first reaction was just shock. Because I'd seen him that very day and he was totally himself. There was no weirdness about him. And you'd think that on a day someone did something like that…well…you'd think they'd be a little weird at least. And Bray wasn't."

The short ribs sprang once again to mind.

"So you thought it didn't feel right?"

"I guess. But then everyone said it was suicide and there was a note and everything and I just thought, well…sometimes I guess you just really don't know someone, do you?"

"Did you ever see the note?" I asked her.

She shook her head. I fished my Filofax out of my purse and took the note from it, handing it across to her.

"Ohmigawd," she breathed when she read it. "Where did you get this?"

"Never mind. Just look at it, Stina. And tell me what you think."

She did as I asked and I watched as her eyes widened. When she looked back at me her face looked vaguely shocked. "Are you sure this is the note they found with him?"

I nodded. Considering where I'd gotten it, I was pretty sure.

"Bray didn't write this," she said without hesitation.

"Are you positive?"

"Absa-fuckin-lutely," she said with complete confidence. "I saw his handwriting every day. I mean, it kinda looks like his handwriting," she said, drawing the same conclusion I had. "Actually, it *looks* like it a lot. But it just…isn't. And not only that. It's the ink, too." I didn't say anything. I didn't have to. I knew what was coming. "He never wrote in anything other than brown ink. He didn't make a big deal about it, not in public. Like, it wasn't something people *knew*. But I knew. I once handed him a pen with blue ink in it—he was signing a book or a contract, I can't remember—and he just *lost* it. I made sure I had a supply of brown refills on hand after that. So, yeah, I'm totally sure. Bray did *not* write that note."

"Then who did?" I asked softly, almost not wanting to say it aloud. Because that was the big question, wasn't it?

Stina got the import of what I'd asked right away, and turned her attention back to the note, scrunching her face up thoughtfully while she examined it. After a while she said, "I really don't know. Whoever wrote it wanted it to look like Braydon's handwriting, so they disguised their own, right?"

I nodded. "That's what I was thinking. I just hoped that maybe, seeing it, something would twig."

She shook her head, a disappointed look on her face, as though she'd been hoping the same thing.

"Do you know what Braydon was wearing when they found him?"

"After...after..." Stina stumbled over the word. People do. It's so final.

"Yes."

"He was at the restaurant," Stina said. "He'd been working. I'm pretty sure he was in his whites."

"In his chef's whites?"

"Yes. I think so. Why?"

"Well, the ink thing again," I said thoughtfully. "If he *was* in his whites, then he'd definitely have had a pen on him, in the pocket on his shoulder...."

Stina saw right away where I was going with this. "And if he had a pen on him, it would have had brown ink. And he would have used it."

I nodded. "That's what I was thinking, yes. Did he always carry a pen?"

"Well, always when he was in whites, yes. Most other times, too."

"Okay, look," I said, "I gave you a big secret. I showed you the note. Now I want a secret from you. You said—what did you say?—that there were things going on around here that are not in your best interests. Things that might even make the company disappear. If you could just give me a hint of that, Stina, it might really help me."

"Help you what?" she asked.

"Oh, God, I'm not even sure anymore. Just go with me on this, okay? Why do you think the company is in trouble?" I asked baldly.

"There's a lot of stuff, really," she said thoughtfully. "A lot of little stuff. And some not so little. The stock thing bugged me. I mean, Doug is so careful about *everything*, I just don't see how the stock got delisted. Like, he's the guy who takes his car in when it's due for a service, and always makes sure he doesn't carry a balance on his Visa. His pants are always creased. His tie coordinates with his shirt and socks. He's a detail guy. For him to miss filing on important things…well, it just doesn't add up."

I nodded. I'd had the same thoughts myself.

"When the stock got delisted…it just seemed beyond odd. Then the whole thing with Sonya. I never really understood that. But it bothered me."

"How so?" Though I had an idea. Some of that had bothered me, as well.

"Do you know what she does? She's a promoter. Yet it seems like ever since she got involved with the company, things have been worse, not better."

"What do you mean?"

"Well, it just seemed like she showed up one day, and the next thing you know the stock is delisted. I mean, not overnight. But it seemed connected. And…well, this could sound silly. But I don't actually *like* her."

I smiled. It didn't seem silly to me at all. "I suspect she might have that effect on people."

"Well, maybe on women," Stina acknowledged. "But she does not have that effect on men."

"Braydon?" I said.

Stina nodded. "Sure, Braydon. But just about everyone, really. Guys dig her. I suspect it's part of what she does," she said cattily. "Dazzle 'em with her boobs."

I laughed. "Anything else?"

"Well…weird meetings lately. Not just since Braydon died, either."

"Who had weird meetings?"

"Doug. And what's weird? Just stuff you wouldn't normally think would be connected to the company. Rough-looking types, sometimes. From companies I don't know about." She shrugged. "But that could be anything, I guess. It's not like I know everything that goes on around here."

Yet we both knew that this wasn't strictly true. Stina was in a position to know, if not everything, then a lot of everything. And she'd also obviously concerned herself above and beyond in an effort to protect both her livelihood and her investment.

"And, okay," she went on. "We've both told secrets, right? You will not breathe this to anyone…but…the whole Mimi thing has always bothered me."

"Why?"

"Well, just Braydon and her never made a lot of sense to me. Like I said, I've traveled with the man. I know his type." She looked at me appraisingly. "You're his type, obviously. And maybe I'm his type, though we never had that kind of relationship at all. But Mimi? So not. There was always something…well, just wrong about it to me somehow. And since Braydon died, she's been here, with him—" a thumb sent

Dougward again "—a lot. Like a real lot. And it's making me nervous."

I weighed her words carefully. Not just their meaning, but the tone in which she said them. It was possible I heard a note of resentment around her not being one of Braydon's chosen ones. But I chided myself. Maybe I was reading too much into everything.

"Under the circumstances, though," I reasoned, "there are probably lots of reasons for Mimi to be here."

Stina shook her head. "I don't think so. It's just…well, it just smells bad to me."

"Listen, Stina, a lot of what I've heard about Braydon and Mimi sort of has that odor. I've heard Braydon married her to keep Doug close to him. And I've heard Doug wanted her to marry Braydon so he would have a family hold on the company. The only thing I *haven't* heard is why Mimi married Braydon. No one has said anything about love or a grand passion on either of their parts. And it just makes me wonder, what was in it for her?"

Stina considered my words for a while before answering. "It's funny, you know, I've never really thought about it in that way." She got up and crossed back over to Braydon's desk, where she retrieved a little framed photo I hadn't noticed before.

She handed it to me as she took her seat again. "Look at her. Look at *them*."

It was a wedding photo. Braydon was impressive in a tuxedo of such a dark brown, it was practically black.

It seemed to me he wore his success like an aura. His bride, I thought, looked like a part of that: a delicate badge of success on his arm. Her slender form was sheathed in an ivory gown, her head covered by a short veil. She was smiling, an expression I'd never seen on her face. She looked so young and hopeful, I had trouble reconciling the girl in the photos with the woman I'd gotten to know only slightly, but who had made such a strong impression.

"She looks like a princess," I said after a while.

"That's exactly it." Stina nodded. "That's just how it was. Like she was a princess connecting two great royal houses. I think she started out idealistic. She had some idea about what being married to Braydon would be like. The glamour of being married to someone who is essentially a star. The travel, the respect, not to mention the attention of this amazing man."

"So what happened?"

"Well, I'm guessing what happened is none of what she planned. They bought that big ol' place in Langley and Bray basically stuck her out there."

"Hardly stuck," I said, with more heat than I intended. "She had a car, right? It wasn't like she was a prisoner."

"Well, yes and no. Sure, she had a car. But he made it pretty clear he preferred her to be out there. He brought her out for the kind of gatherings where the wife is supposed to show up on your arm, but he spent most of his time in the city. I think he made it clear to her that he didn't want her here. It was his space. And aside from spending the occasional weekend out there with her, he just kept doing his life like he always had."

"'Doing his life,'" I said. "What does that mean?"

"Oh, come on, Madeline. You must know. You were married to him, too. He kept on playing his 'hautest bachelor' schtick. Lots of travel, great parties, women."

"Women?" I thought again about Sonya. And about the woman in the store who said she'd seen him in a club.

"Surely you knew? Everyone did. He didn't bother making a great secret of it. No one in particular, as far as I knew. More quantity than quality, was how it felt. I remember thinking that would have been hurtful to Mimi. You know—opening a magazine and seeing pictures of your husband with some model. Yikes!"

"Let me ask you something else," I said, going in a different direction. "DW Investments. Do you know that name?"

"Sure. They were the company that contracted a lot of the construction on this building."

"Really? Who heads the company?"

Stina looked confused for a moment, as though trying to think about it hard. "That's funny. Now that you mention it, I don't think I ever met an actual DW Investments person. Is that even possible?"

I nodded. It was all too possible.

"I met lots of the subcontracts," she said. "Too many of those to even sort them out. But I guess all of our actual business dealings were done with DW. Weird."

"Not as weird as you think. Stina, do you know

how I could get a phone number for DW? Or a contact person's name?"

"Sure," she said, walking back to the desk. "I'll call accounting."

She punched in another extension and I listened to her half of a five-minute conversation while she tried to get the information I'd asked for. I could tell it wasn't going as she'd thought it might.

When she got off the phone, she looked perplexed.

"That's really weird," she said. "No one in accounting has that information. How can that be?"

I shook my head. I really had no idea.

"And it didn't feel like a runaround, either. They checked files and everything. Checked our contact database. We don't have contact information listed, beyond an address where the checks go. Do you want that?"

"No. I've got it."

"Aside from that," Stina said, "they just referred me to Doug. I'm not quite sure what to make of it."

I thought I did, but I wasn't saying anything. Though in reality, I could have. DW Investments. He hadn't even gone to the trouble of hiding the connection. Who else would DW Investments be other than Doug Withers? Or, just as likely, Doug Withers's personal enrichment fund, because wasn't that what it had amounted to? It was certainly beginning to look that way.

I knew there was at least one more thing that Stina,

since she worked inside the company, might be able to help me with.

"The paperwork you brought me when I was here, Stina—did you have any idea what it was?"

"No. I didn't look it over. Just basically delivered it to you from Doug's office. Why? What was it?"

"Lotta stuff," I said, "mostly financials. But I'm thinking they weren't what I needed to see."

"I don't understand."

I hesitated, unsure of how much to tell her. She'd seemed forthright enough during our conversation, but I thought I might have detected the occasional calculating note in her tone. I chided myself again for jumping at shadows. I was, it seemed, seeing conspiracies everywhere I looked. Besides, if I really did want to find out more, what other choice did I have? She was the best game in town.

I took a deep breath, then plunged in. "I have reason to believe that the financials Doug gave me might not have been actually reflective of what the firm has been doing."

"What? Madeline, what you're saying. That would be huge."

"I know, Stina. That's why…I guess that's why I'm being as careful as I am. I mean, it's a pretty big accusation."

"You got that right."

"What I really need is access to all of the firm's financial information for the current fiscal."

"That's impossible. I mean, it probably *isn't* impossible, but it's certainly not my area of expertise. I wouldn't even know where to begin to look."

"I might," I said thoughtfully. "I could tell you what to look for. What to remove."

"I'm sorry, Madeline. I've probably already told you more than I should have, but stealing financial information? I can't do that."

"It wouldn't be stealing," I assured her. "More like borrowing. We would put it all back. Or not even remove anything. We could make copies."

When she got up and took a couple of steps toward the door I was pretty sure she didn't even know she was moving. "That's beyond what I can do. Again, I'm sorry. I don't know what else to say."

I had another thought. "Okay, you won't do it, I understand that." She stopped moving. Looked at me. I pressed on. "But how about this—could you get me in here? After hours, I mean? With keys or whatever for doors that might be locked?"

She looked hesitant, but I could see I had a better chance on this tack than I'd had with getting Stina to do it herself.

"I mean, theoretically? It's possible," Stina said hesitantly. "With the studios and the magazine, we have people in and out of here 24–7. And security isn't even on-site at night."

"So there aren't any armed guards or anything in the building?"

Stina shook her head. "Not at all. It's not like we're a bank or anything. Or even like we have gold or jewelry lying around. There's a security system, of course, but everyone has the code. So yeah, I guess I could get you in pretty easily, when I think about it. But, honestly? I'm not sure I want to. I have a lot to lose," she said frankly. "I don't see that you do."

"No, you're right. I don't have as much to lose as you do. But I think you might have something to gain. Look, if even part of what we've been talking about here is true, the company is in serious trouble. If you *do* get me in, I could let you know what I find out. You'd know before anyone else, Stina. At least, that way, you'd have a chance to act."

She looked at me for a moment without saying anything. We both knew what I was offering: absolute inside information. When faced with it, not too many people will say no to that. I could tell by the expression on her face that she would do it before she said the actual words.

"But, Madeline, it *so* couldn't be traced to me."

"It wouldn't be," I promised.

"When would you want to get in?"

I thought about what I had proposed. And I could still avert it. I could just tell Stina thanks but no thanks and head down to Seattle and then back to L.A. and never give another thought to Gauthier Fine Foods and the web of intrigue that surrounded it.

"How about tonight?" I said finally.

Stina considered this. "Okay, here's what we'll do. I'll work late. Can you get here at eight?"

I nodded.

"I'll let you in and then take off. That way I don't even have to give you the codes. And it's early enough that, if you *did* get caught, there would have been enough ways for you to have gotten in that it won't necessarily be trackable back to me."

That sounded reasonable enough. I told her I'd see her at eight.

Eighteen

I arrived at the Sunset Grill fifteen minutes early for my lunch appointment with Simon. In reality, it wasn't so much an appointment, but I was reluctant to call it a date. And I wasn't so sure that Simon would have been likewise reluctant.

The Grill was just as it had been on the night Emily and I had visited, only the proprietor wasn't in evidence today and there was a larger crowd at midday than there had been late on a weeknight. The lunch fare and the feel was lighter and brighter, too. More restaurant than bar with daylight showing through the windows, even if it was the gray light of a rainy day.

I relaxed into the pub-ish atmosphere. There was music playing, its nature indiscernible under the lunch-time chatter all around. I felt safe here. Protected somehow. And I exhaled a breath I hadn't realized I'd been holding.

Vancouver was getting to me. Not the city itself, but the unexpected turns my northern trip had taken. This was my sixth day in the city—I'd been here much longer than expected—and it was getting difficult to remember what expectations I'd had for this visit before I got there. I'd imagined a tearful reunion with Braydon's family and a final quiet goodbye to the man I'd briefly called my husband.

And now? Now I was actually contemplating—more, had committed to—gaining illicit entry to a place of business with the sole purpose of maybe stealing but certainly reading documents. I shook my head as though to clear away the cobwebs that must be growing between my ears. Honestly, what was I thinking?

It had all come upon me so quietly, small piece upon piece. The plea from Jessica, the growing suspicion that Braydon hadn't actually killed himself, the understanding that everything was not what it seemed with Gauthier Fine Foods and, in fact, with Braydon's whole world. And what, I asked myself, did any of this have to do with me? Nothing, I told myself. Everything. Old debts, new curiosities and the curse of a personality that seldom lets me leave well enough alone.

Simon arrived exactly on time.

"I haven't been here in ages," he said, looking around as he took his seat. "And I can't remember why that is. I really like it. I just don't get to Kits much these days, I guess."

"Kits?"

Simon smiled at me. "This area is called Kitsilano. In fact, this close to the beach it's called Lower Kits. How could you recommend a restaurant and not even know where it is?"

I shrugged and smiled back. "Well, I knew *where* it was, I just didn't know *what* it was, I guess. My friend Emily and I found it by accident the other night."

"Well, happy accident," Simon said. "And, if I remember correctly, they make a mean burger."

Despite the gray day, both of us ordered iced teas. Presumably, Simon had to go back to the office at some point, and I felt I wanted my head as clear as possible. Simon decided to try for that mean hamburger and I got the special: a steak sandwich with a Caesar salad. I felt the need for some serious red meat.

Since I wanted no misunderstanding about why I'd agreed to have lunch with him, I didn't waste a lot of time on pleasantries. While we waited for our food, I launched right in.

"Earlier today, you said you thought there were a lot of people who would have benefited from Braydon's death."

To my irritation, Simon looked amused at the question. "Did I say that? I'm sure I did *not* say that."

I looked at him evenly. "I'm sure you did."

He shrugged, taking a sip of his iced tea. "Ah, maybe I did. But it sounds…different when you say it in that way. I guess what I meant was, I really don't think anyone tried to kill him."

"Not tried, Simon. He's dead."

"Okay. I don't disbelieve he killed himself. But, that being the case, there are probably some people who are not entirely sorry."

"Like…" I could see this was going to be like pulling teeth. And yet I had the feeling that there were things Simon could tell me. Things he maybe even wanted to tell.

"Well, okay. His wife, for one."

"His wife?"

"Yeah. Don't misunderstand. I am *not* suggesting Mimi killed him. On the other hand…" He shrugged. "Doug's been talking to me about producing a show that she's going to be hosting."

"She's taking Braydon's place?"

Simon actually looked perplexed by the question. "Well, that's the part I don't get. I mean, that's what I thought at first, too. But that's not it. It's a whole new show. And I guess I really should not be talking about this. But it's just so odd."

"A cooking show?"

"Some. But more like lifestyle. Food and fashion and design."

"That's pretty much outside of the Gauthier Fine Foods realm, right?" But even while I said this, I remembered the mock-ups I'd found under the seat of the car.

"Well, yes and no. Braydon's mandate was always as much lifestyle as food. So that in itself wouldn't be odd. Or even continuing Braydon's shows *and* doing another one. That would be stretching things, but not unthinkable. But, no—this would be separate. And I've had no word on what we're doing with Braydon's existing shows."

"And they were both successful?"

"Oh, absolutely. Before Braydon died they were both picked up in half a dozen new markets for next season."

"When would you normally have started shooting for the new season?"

"Well, not immediately. Braydon would have been working on stuff, of course. He always was. But we wouldn't actually be going into the studio together for a couple of months. But still. If we're going to be working with a new host…well, we really have to get cracking."

I put this information away to think about later. "Okay, so who else do you think would benefit from Braydon's death?"

"Well, his family, of course. There's a lot of money at stake here."

"But he was spreading that around, anyway. And none of them look like they're hurting."

"True enough. But you asked. What about Curt?" He seemed to be warming to the topic now that I'd gotten him started. Getting into the spirit of my game. "He can't have been happy seeing Braydon be so successful when he couldn't make that happen himself."

I shook my head. "That's more like a motive than a

benefit. And anyway, from what I've seen, Curt has a very good job. Probably makes a lot of money, too."

Simon nodded. "Still," he said.

"Still," I agreed.

"What about competitors?" he asked, as though thinking aloud.

"He had competitors?"

"Of course he did. Everyone has competitors." He seemed to think for a moment before quashing that theory on his own. "Though honestly, in Braydon's case he'd done so much to create the market—blazing trails and everything?—I don't really see that. It's not like anyone else could just step in and do what he did. And in this business, if he does well, then he attracts a bigger market share, and the networks start signing more shows that they hope will keep the same viewers from switching stations. So, in a way, everyone wins."

"Right, on the TV end. But what about other aspects? Other types of competitors?"

"You mean like other chefs?"

"Sure. Or anything."

"I don't know. I mean, chefs are pretty competitive. But I don't think they go around offing each other. Not that I'm giving credence to your theory," Simon added quickly. "But if we're just tossing ideas around…"

"We are," I said.

"Okay, then. In that case, what about me?"

"You?"

"Yeah. If we're being fair, we have to look at everyone. I could have done it."

Our meals had arrived. They looked great and I wasted no time in cutting off a nice slice of rare steak and popping it into my head. I chewed thoughtfully before I answered. "Well, you liked Braydon, for one. I can tell."

Simon shook his head. "He could be an awful prick sometimes, Madeline."

"He could?"

"Sure. Don't tell me you didn't know that. He could be petulant...."

"Braydon?"

"Absolutely. And moody. And he worked everyone very, very hard." He looked very satisfied with himself for pointing all of this out.

"Even so, Simon. I don't see how you would have benefited. You told me yourself he made you an offer you couldn't refuse. And lots of creative freedom. And," I said, remembering, "he was going to finance your film, or something like that."

"Right. That was the deal. But we talked about it last month and he told me he couldn't get his hands on the money right then. That was how he put it. And I'd just have to 'cool my jets.' That actually pissed me off, because we *do* have a contract."

"You don't look very mad."

Simon smiled. "Aw, I knew he was good for it. And I knew how he was. I took his advice—I cooled my jets.

I knew he'd get whatever money he was waiting for and then things would be fine again."

I looked at him for a moment as though considering. "Yeah, sorry. Not you. I just don't think you're good for killing him."

Simon smiled again. "Ah, well, I tried."

Something he had said dawned on me. "But back up a second. You said he was waiting for money?"

"That was how he put it. I had the feeling he was expecting some type of cash infusion."

I thought about that. It didn't jive with anything I'd been given to understand by either the family or any of the financials I'd seen for Gauthier Fine Foods. Money had been coming in, sure. But it had been going out, as well. It didn't seem to me that any large payments had been expected. Still another piece that didn't mean anything. But another piece, nonetheless.

"You going to take him up on it?" I asked after a while.

"Take who up on what?" For the moment, more of Simon's attention was on his hamburger than on me.

"Doug. Producing the new shows."

"I'm not sure. Frankly, he's being a little cloak-and-dagger at the moment and that's bothering me. That's probably why I mentioned it to you in the first place," he said thoughtfully. "And then there's the whole Mimi thing." He grimaced a bit. "I mean, she's lovely. But I think she's also a bit of a potential loose cannon."

"How do you figure?"

Simon seemed to consider his words carefully before

he answered. "I don't think she's ever thought of me as anything other than the help. Like the guy who does the gardens, you know? Only, in this case, I was the guy who did the shows. Which isn't exactly inaccurate, but still. Because of that, though, she pretty much acted like I wasn't there a lot of the time. And I saw her just trash Braydon a few times."

"Trash him how?"

Simon appeared embarrassed. "Well, it was usually something to do with other women." He looked apologetic. "Sorry, but you asked. Mimi seemed sure Braydon was sleeping around."

"Was he?"

"Gosh, I don't know. It wasn't the kind of thing we talked about." I had the feeling Simon knew more than he was letting on, but didn't feel it was an entirely appropriate topic of discussion with Braydon's ex-wife.

"It's not the first time I've heard it, Simon. Someone told me there were a lot of women and that Braydon wasn't exactly discreet."

Simon didn't meet my eyes and, though the restaurant was not brightly lit, I thought I saw him blush slightly. "Well, there might have been. Sometimes he'd bring some girl to an industry party. Did he leave with them? I don't know. I didn't watch for that. It wasn't my business what Braydon did in his personal life. But he was a brilliant chef and, in so many ways, an exceptional human. I was proud to work with him."

I was touched by Simon's loyalty to Braydon, as well as his obvious—though in this case pointless—care for my feelings. We finished our lunch over less provocative topics. Simon seemed relieved to ask me about my work, and he told me about his. I found myself liking him more and more, and knew that, under different circumstances and at a different point in our lives, he was the kind of careful, sensitive guy I would probably have been attracted to.

And he made me laugh. I've always been a sucker for a man who can do that.

My cell phone rang just as I was getting into Old Stinky.

The way I've just said that makes it sound all calm and organized. A cell phone rings, you answer it with a dignified "Hello?" That's how it's supposed to go.

But here's what actually happened: my purse started making an awful electronic shriek. I dropped it on the street, a bunch of my stuff came pouring out, which, since I was parked on a little hill, was sort of a problem.

By the time I'd collected my hairbrush, my lipstick, two tampons and Simon's business card, the shrieking had stopped. Fortunately, the phone has caller ID and I actually know how to use both that and the voice mail, so I could tell that the call I'd missed had come from Anne Rand.

There was a coffee joint within eyeshot and just across from the beach, so I opted to nip in there, get a latte and return my call from within sight of the surf. I am, at all times, a sucker for both lattes and beaches.

I chose a bench right on the seawall, with a large chestnut tree to protect me from the light drizzle that still fell. I would get frizzy again, but I decided I could handle it.

"I am the goddess überfinder of all things," Anne said with typical understatement when I got her on the phone. I could tell from her tone that she'd probably met with some success and my credit card would be lighter by the end of the day.

"I take it you found something?"

"I did! Despite the fact that you gave me almost nothing to go on, I was able to put together quite the little dossier on your Ms. Foy."

"How did you do that?"

"Oh Madeline, don't be silly—that would be telling. Trade secrets, you know. Let's just say I used all of my resources and called in a favor or two."

"What have you got?"

"Well, I've put together a little report that I can fax or e-mail to you, if you like. I present quite an official report, you know. I'm rather proud of it."

"Swell," I said. "I'm looking forward to it. You can e-mail it to me. Meanwhile, though, would you mind hitting the highlights while I've got you?"

"Well, your Ms. Foy *does* hold a British Columbian driver's license, but she's not a Canadian."

"She's not?"

"No. She's a Yank. Born near Chicago, thirty-nine years ago."

Close to forty. I'd been right.

"She was a stockbroker in New York City until about seven years ago when she—ahem—ran into a spot of trouble with the National Association of Securities Dealers."

"She got into trouble with the NASD? For what?"

"It's quite complicated, but I've put it all in the report," Anne said primly. "It will suffice for now if I tell you that she was charged with excessive buying and selling within a client's account."

"Churning," I said. Which meant she'd been excessively trading client accounts without their instructions in order to generate commissions. She'd probably been using other people's money—and putting clients at risk—to create the appearance of action in the portion of the market in which she was trying to create interest. Not something nice girls do in the financial world. That is, not if they wanted to stay in that world, which she obviously hadn't.

"Is that what it's called? Well then, your Sonya was churning. There was also another matter that included some question of misrepresentation, but that was never proved."

There was more. Details of her life, where she'd lived, where she'd worked and gone to school, who she'd been married to. None of this interested me very much. The churning and misrepresentation had confirmed everything I'd suspected about Sonya Foy. And more.

I thanked Anne and was about to say goodbye when she stopped me.

"Wait, there's something else. You asked me specifically about Friday and Saturday night, a week ago."

"You've got something?"

"Well, it's not much. But then I didn't have much to go on. I can't tell you precisely what she was doing, but I can tell you where she was doing it."

"And where was she doing it?" I asked, playing the game that Anne was obviously enjoying. After all, how often could it be that she got to play the "goddess über-finder of all things"?

"Portland, Oregon. At least, that's where her credit card was. From, near as I can tell, Thursday morning until Sunday night. Gas stations, meals and hotel rooms for that time period put her there at any rate, which covers the time you asked about. Does that help at all?"

"Actually, it does."

"Good," she said, sounding pleased with herself, "because I'm charging you an extra two hours for it."

When I got off the phone with Anne, I sat on the bench for a while, watching gulls swoop over the low waves, and dogs and their owners playing on the wet sand. These, I knew, would be impressions of Vancouver I'd take away with me.

I thought about Sonya Foy.

Anne's report confirmed my suspicions about

Sonya's professional life—it was shady. But, if Sonya had been with her credit card on the weekend Braydon died, it also put her far, far from the scene of the crime. If she'd killed Bray, she certainly hadn't done it with her own hands.

I realized, also, that Sonya and I had been stockbrokers in the same city at the same time. It was possible we'd known some of the same people, perhaps attended some of the same parties, and certainly shared some of the same concerns. I might even have heard stories about Sonya relating to her misconduct. You always heard things—tiny blips on the radars of our financial existence. We wouldn't, however, have heard stories about her exile. Once the deed was done—the career ruined—we lost interest. We never thought about those who had violated the code we lived by. For us, those people simply ceased to exist. We didn't think about them off in some financial backwater, churning smaller accounts. Or cruising dental conventions for potential marks.

So I felt it was possible our paths had crossed sometime in the past. Crossed, but never intersected. Nor had they ever been likely to. Until now.

Nineteen

By midafternoon, I was in a state of mild anxiety. It was, I knew, anticipation and—just a little bit—plain old fear.

Time was counting down.

Even though I'd packed up Old Stinky in the morning, I still had the keys to Braydon's apartment. I opted to go back there and try to relax in private for a while. Try to get a grip on the reasonably nutty thing I was planning.

Back at Braydon's, with the door locked and my feet up, I still couldn't relax. I could almost feel the elevation of my blood pressure and a certain heat behind my eyes. My mouth felt dry and I sipped at my water. But I didn't feel thirsty.

With more than five hours before I was due to meet Stina, I knew there was plenty of time to call the whole thing off. I even came close a couple of times, the hard plastic of the phone in my hand grounding me in a way that nothing else at that moment could. I visualized myself calling Stina, telling her to forget it. Then getting in my car, heading to Seattle and shutting this whole Vancouver episode out of my mind. Out of my life.

Half a dozen times, I started to dial the phone. One time, I punched in all of the digits, but it wasn't the number for Gauthier Fine Foods.

"Hey, Mom," I said, when I got her at the golf course where she works. "It's Madeline."

"I know who it is, sweetie. You don't have to identify yourself to me. You're my favorite middle child. I always recognize your voice. Where are you?"

"Still in Vancouver."

"Still? What's wrong? You sound funny. Funnier than before."

"I…oh, Mom. I don't even know where to start. So I'll save it all for when I see you. Probably tomorrow now. I don't think I'll get out of here tonight."

"All right," my mom said carefully. I could almost hear her restrain herself from trying to pull more out of me, her respect for me and my choices warring with her take-care mommy instinct. I love both of those parts of her.

"But, Mom, can I ask you something? Something hypothetical, I mean."

"Of course," she said evenly. "Shoot."

"Okay. Let's say you're in a position to find out a truth about something that maybe won't impact your life, but will impact on the lives of other people. What do you do?"

"Too hypothetical," she said reasonably. "Bring it closer to home."

I thought for a minute and thought also about just discontinuing the call. What, after all, did I expect my mother to do?

In for a penny.

"Well, let's say you're in a situation where you feel pretty sure that everything that everyone thinks is incorrect. And you don't even know what *is* correct, but you can do something that will help everyone find out. Do you do that thing?"

"Is the thing dangerous?"

"No. Not dangerous. Not entirely legal, but certainly not morally wrong, and there's no danger involved."

"Oh, kitten, you know hypothesis isn't my strongest suit. That was your dad's area. But, okay, let me see. The power to find the answers is with me, is that what you're saying?"

"Right."

"And there's a thing I have to do—that maybe only I can do—that will put things right."

"Yeah."

"Well, obviously, you've only given me enough facts to give you the answer you want to hear, is that right?"

I laughed. I couldn't help myself. My mom is just *that* smart. I could be so full of bullshit I couldn't see, but my mom could wipe it all away in a heartbeat. I could remember having this feeling at sixteen, and I had it again now.

"Okay. Maybe that's sorta right."

"Well then, based on these vast amounts of information, yes. Of course I'd do it. As long as, you know, it didn't endanger me or—and listen closely to this please, Madeline, because it's the most important part—as long as it was in no way likely to worry my mother or otherwise cause her concern."

I dressed carefully. That sounds ridiculous, but it's true. I gave careful thought to what I would wear to illicitly poke around the Gauthier Fine Foods building after dark when there would be no one around.

The pants I wear to run in: Lycra and spandex, mostly black yoga pants with a white stripe at the seam. A black T-shirt. Cross-trainers. And my messenger bag, because I hoped to find things I'd want to take away with me.

I pulled my hair into a high ponytail, examining my face in the mirror as I did so. I looked too pale, I thought, and I could see the pulse at my throat. I seemed to be holding my eyes too wide and my mouth was slightly open, my breaths coming in teeny, short bursts. And I hadn't even left the apartment yet.

Again, what was I thinking?

I drove my car around back of Gauthier Fine Foods and entered the building by the side entrance, as Stina had instructed. The door had been left propped open. Stina had said she'd be there to let me in and then she'd leave. I decided she must have changed her mind and left the door open for me instead, keeping herself completely in the clear. That was fine. I let the door close behind me and even waited for the double-click sound that indicated it was locked.

One thing I'd miss Stina for: I'd thought to ask her to point me in the direction of where I might find financial documents. I didn't even know where in the building I'd find the accounting department. I figured I'd ferret it out, though. It was only 8:00 p.m. If it took me six hours to find what I needed, I'd be tired, but it would be okay.

I hadn't seen any cars in the parking lot, but both Stina and Simon had said that some people at Gauthier Fine Foods worked funny hours. Though it was most likely that anyone moving around the building at this hour would be attached to the creative end of the business—and I wasn't planning on going near those floors—I decided to avoid the elevator. It just seemed less likely I'd run into company on the stairs.

Since I didn't know where accounting was I decided to start with Doug's office. Before he was CEO, he'd been chief financial officer. It figured that he would keep a lot of key financial stuff near him, especially if he was twiddling the books.

Even though the building was new, the stairs were creepy. Stairways in office buildings just generally are. There tends to be an air of disuse and passive neglect. I could smell the newness of the building, plus a gentle accumulation of dust and debris. The cleaning staff, I could tell, did not go out of their way with this area.

When the stairwell disgorged me on the third floor I discovered I was on the side of the building opposite Doug's office. I moved down the hallways quietly, listening for signs of occupation. I didn't hear any. Just the scents of toner and stale coffee, the feel of industrial carpet under my feet.

Outside of Doug's closed office door, I hesitated. Even this near, there was still time for me to back out, but when I seriously considered it, I couldn't come up with one good reason why I should.

...in for a pound.

I was here now, after all. And I had so many questions. I'd keep going, I told myself, if for no other reason than to satisfy my curiosity.

The lights were off in Doug's office when I entered. I thought about leaving them off—the half-light that filtered in through the door was vaguely comforting— but finding my way through files in a dark and unfamiliar office was beyond me. And I hadn't thought to bring a flashlight.

When I flicked them on, the lights momentarily seemed too bright. I had to fight the urge to turn them off again. I hesitated by the light switch for a good half minute, my hand hovering. There was still time for me to get out of there. Still time for me to cast aside this ridiculous, half-baked plan.

In the end, though, I decided to just go for it. I was there, wasn't I? Dressed in dark spandex-Lycra. It was, in a sense, too late to go in any direction but forward.

There was a lateral file cabinet behind Doug's desk. It was needle in a haystack time, but I had to start somewhere and this seemed a likely place. Better, I decided, than the vast possibilities of the accounting department. Incriminating information would best be secreted near the top. And here I was.

I scanned the folder labels before I looked more closely at the contents of files. All of what I was looking at seemed like run-of-the-mill, day-to-day Gauthier Fine Foods stuff. What had I expected? I chided myself. A folder labeled "Madeline! Don't Look Here"? Clearly, that wasn't going to happen.

I moved to another cabinet and then another, unaware of time as it passed me, tightly intent on my quest.

Oddly, it was in a bookcase, not a filing cabinet at all, when I finally found something of interest. Behind a row of beautifully bound first edition works of fiction, I found a low stack of file folders, hidden more or less in plain sight. Had I not moved a book and peeked behind, I would have missed the files altogether.

"Bingo," I said softly as soon as I looked at the folder labels. He was a methodical man, all right. Even his illicit material was neatly identified. "Foy" on an especially thick folder; "DW Investments" on another. I got very excited when I noticed one of these was marked "Final Financials 1" and the very next one "Final Financials 2." A cursory inspection confirmed what I suspected. The "final financials" I had here were anything but. Rather, they were differently skewed versions of the same thing. Precisely what he would have given Sonya in file 1, while the second file gave the type of "final financials" he might have supplied to the Gauthiers or other board members.

My instinct was to sink into the cushy leather chair behind Doug's desk and pore over the documents. I glanced at my watch; it was already 10:30 and I wasn't sure I'd even done all the digging I wanted. There was no time for reading. What I needed was a photocopier so I could copy what I'd found, before spending maybe another half hour looking around. And then I'd need to get out of there before I pushed my luck and someone discovered me poking around in places I wasn't supposed to be.

I was pleased though unsurprised to find a photocopy room between Doug and Braydon's offices. Unsurprised because it stood to reason that anyone who did this kind of fudging would always want to know there was a photocopier close to hand.

While the photocopier warmed up, I ducked down the hall to where I'd seen a lunchroom. I stopped partway there, feeling, as they say, the hairs raise on the back of my neck. Such a cornball expression. And yet. That's how I felt standing in the empty hallway of Gauthier Fine Foods: as though each of the tiny, blond hairs on the back of my neck were craning themselves in an attempt to turn into antennae.

I stopped, of course. Stopped dead in the deeply carpeted hallway. And I stood perfectly still. I could hear...nothing. Or at least as close to nothing as possible. I could hear the low hum of the air conditioner, the white-noise buzz of electricity, the peaceful sound of the rain hitting a window nearby. I could hear my heart. Nothing else.

I made the remainder of the trip to the lunchroom even more quietly, ever alert for the slightest movement, the quietest noise. I heard more of the same nothing.

When I returned to the photocopy room with a new bottle of water and a chocolate bar I no longer had an appetite for, the photocopier was warmed up and ready to go. It took me a couple of minutes to figure out how to make the document feeder work properly, but I knew the time I lost here would save a lot in the long run.

Once that was done, I didn't bother sorting through the material to see what I wanted to copy. Rather I just pushed everything into the document feeder, then let the machine hum, trying not to cringe at the sound the working copier made as it seemed to rip through the night.

My plan was to replace the original documents and take copies of everything with me to peruse at my leisure once I'd left the building, something I planned on doing as quickly as possible. But, I thought, everything had gone pretty much like clockwork. I grinned to myself, trying not to feel smug. It was hard. I was almost there.

The lights were off in Doug's office when I went to replace the files. I could have sworn I'd left them on. And yet, they were off. And, I could suddenly feel the hair on the back of my neck again.

I stood there in the doorway, rooted to the spot, trying to think about what it meant if the lights were off when I'd left them on. Nothing, very probably. I convinced myself that I must have turned them off when I left the office. It was a difficult job, that convincing, because turning lights off when I leave a room is not one of my habits. Still. I was about to reach for the light switch when I became aware of a sound that almost stopped my heart.

Breathing.

Someone else's breathing. Not mine.

I started to leave, to back out the way I'd come, but the lights came on just as I felt something cold behind my ear. It felt evil, and some instinctive part of me knew it was a gun.

"Easy now," said a feminine voice, as though she were settling a high-strung horse. It was a voice I recognized without any trouble at all.

"Mimi," I breathed. "What are you doing here?"

"Nice question," she sneered. "Considering. I'd ask you the same thing, but I already know."

"You do?" I turned my body ever so slightly so that I could see her a little bit better, standing behind me with her arm extended, the barrel of a gun to my head.

"Of course I do, Madeline," she said, her voice a parody of concerned sympathy. "You've been distraught ever since Braydon died. It wasn't until he killed himself that you realized you still loved him. Then staying at his apartment, driving his foolish car, seeing his family again, it came to you." Her voice here took a tragic, melodramatic dive. "You didn't want to live in a world that didn't have him in it. So you came here under cover of darkness, in order to end your life near where he spent so many of his final hours."

At first her words made no sense to me. I didn't feel any of those things. My brain felt stupid and sluggish just listening to her. Then I got a glimmer of what she had in mind.

"You're going to kill me," I said, surprising myself at the calm in my voice and my heart. No use, I thought, for panic. Not once the worst has happened.

"Oh, Madeline. No. You're going to kill yourself."

"So it was you. All along. You killed Braydon."

I could feel an impatient motion from her. "That sounds stronger than it was. I think it's more accurate to say I hastened the inevitable."

Yeah, I thought. *By forty years.* Though I didn't say it aloud. Considering the fact that she had a gun to my head and the deadliest weapons in my possession were a bottle of spring water and a tampon, making quips seemed like a really bad idea.

"But why, Mimi? I don't get it. Why didn't you just divorce him?"

"Divorce him. Like you did? And what did that get you, Madeline? Nothing."

"He had nothing when we split up. There was nothing for me to take, even if I'd wanted to."

"But he gave you things, didn't he? Even after he was

dead, you still got his stupid car. That's because he loved you, Madeline. He never loved me." If there had not been a gun to my head, the venom in her voice would have made me step away. With all things considered, though, I checked the instinct and didn't move an inch.

"And all those girls. He rubbed my *nose* in all those girls. So I divorce him? Then what? Oh, he loses some money. But would he even care about that? There's more where that came from. But he killed himself. So what am I now, Madeline? What am I now? Not the scorned wife. No. Not anymore. Now I'm the poor widow. The poor, young, beautiful, rich widow with the world by the fucking balls."

There was, I thought, something like madness in her tone. I did not think, however, that Mimi was insane. What I was hearing, I knew, was the fury of a woman scorned, determined to be scorned no more. No matter what the cost.

It all made me think of a story I'd read about a woman who found out her husband was cheating on her. As the philandering husband left his hotel after a tryst with his lover, his wife attacked him with her well-built luxury car. Once he was on the ground, she drove over him. Then she drove over him a couple times more, for good measure I guess.

When I'd read the story I'd thought: Yeah, right. How does *that* happen? Standing here with Mimi Gauthier's gun to my head, I understood. It was *this* anger. *This* energy. *This* pure fury that had gotten that man flattened by his wife's car. That had gotten Braydon dead by his wife's hand. That was about to get *me* dead, if I didn't think of something quickly. And, frankly, at that point, I had no idea what my next move should be. I knew that staying alive was at the top of the list, but I wasn't quite sure how to accomplish that.

"But why me, Mimi? What did I ever do to you?"

"Well, that's a problem because, of course, you haven't. But you've been asking questions. You've been snooping around. You broke into my house, stole Braydon's note. And you're here, aren't you? Preparing to walk out of here with what you probably figure amounts to some sort of evidence. The way you've been going, you're *this* close to figuring it all out and going to the police. And, Madeline? At this point, that is just unacceptable." The sorrowing widow was gone now, so rapidly I could almost believe I'd imagined her. What I heard now was all business and tight calculation. I suddenly missed the anxious, jealous wife. I guessed I stood a better chance with her.

"How did you know about the financials?" My voice surprised me. It was a rough little rasp. My throat had gone dry. If she was saying what I *thought* she was saying, my goose was cooked. There was no hope for any kind of cavalry. I was on my own.

"Oh, *you* know, don't you, Madeline? I know about them the same way I know about the note. *You* know how I know."

"Stina." It came out in a whisper.

"And really, Madeline, this could have gone either way. From the look of her this afternoon, Miss Stina put a lot of thought into deciding which horse she was going to back. And she chose the right one, didn't she? She *knows* who puts the butter on her bread. Who *will* put the butter on her bread. And I will reward loyalty. She knows that, too."

"And Doug?" I didn't want Mimi to stop talking. It seemed to me that, the longer I prolonged whatever she had planned, the better chance I had to figure something out, or—still dreaming of the cavalry—for someone—anyone—to come by. I remembered the empty parking lot. Rescue didn't seem likely. But it was the only hope I had. With a gun pressed to my head, all the power was on Mimi's side.

"Doug doesn't know anything. Oh, the financial stuff, of course. He was doing his part to pave the way for a brave new company, killing this one in the process. And he doesn't know it, but I was doing my part at the same time. He wouldn't have had the balls to do what needed to be done with Braydon." She gave a short laugh. An unpleasant sound. "There are some things just better left to us girls."

"Mimi, this will not look like a suicide. You can't kill me. If you do, they'll know I didn't do it myself."

"You're not going to shoot yourself, you stupid bitch. You're going to hang yourself from the overhead lights in the studio. Think how dramatic that will be! They'll find you swinging in the morning. Poor, poor Madeline.

She just couldn't go on living without him, so she hanged herself near where the world saw him work every week." Mimi sighed, as though infinitely pleased with her solution. Then she dug the gun more firmly into my neck. "We're going up there now. I will be *right* behind you with this thing. If you make *any* funny move, I will not hesitate to splatter your brains all over the place. And I know what you're thinking—that would not look like a suicide. But an intruder shot by an unknown person here in this building? Sure, that would look suspicious. And the police would *not* come looking for *me*."

There was no quaver in her voice. No hesitation. I think that frightened me more than anything. And she seemed perfectly capable of doing precisely what she'd threatened. Despite that, I could feel the minutes counting down as we made our way slowly down the hallway, then waited for the elevator, then rode up to the studio level. The more time passed, the closer I was to death. That's true for everyone, of course. But most of us don't see our end coming toward us by the minute. It's not a sensation I recommend.

Though I'd had a teeny hope of finding the studio level awash with light and people and noise, the elevator doors opened on dim lights and silence. My only hope was that somehow, in the process of getting me from standing to hanging, I'd find an opportunity to get away. I was a good five inches taller than Mimi and probably outweighed her by twenty or more pounds. If it came to it—and if she didn't have a gun in her hand—I was confident I could take her. But she seemed to have a pretty firm grip on that gun.

When we entered the studio proper, relief washed over me when I saw Curt sitting on the counter of the set kitchen, the photographic sunset looking odd behind him now that it wasn't illuminated.

"Curt!" I said, the relief apparent in my voice.

"Hey, kiddo," he said easily, getting to his feet. And I noticed a coil of rope on the counter next to him, and oddly, even more frightening to me, gloves on his hands.

"Oh, Curt. No." Understanding his purpose for being there washed me in unexpected grief. It's not that I'd thought of him as a friend. At least, not for a long time. Braydon certainly had, though. And now it all made sense. The perfectly prepared food. Curt. The vindictive choice in those foods. Mimi. Together somehow in this awful thing.

"But Curt," I couldn't stop myself from asking, "why? He was your friend."

It was Mimi, however, who answered. "Braydon was no one's friend. Braydon took and took and the only helping he ever did was when he helped himself. I *love* Curt. Curt knows that. And when all of this is over, the restaurants will be Curt's. *He* will be the head of one of the most successful chains of restaurants in North America, just as he should be." I couldn't tell if she was saying this for my benefit, or to reinforce something she and Curt understood between them. Maybe both. "*We* will be the power couple of lifestyle and food. We will, Curt," she said almost pleadingly, and I understood at that point that Curt was perhaps not as committed to their course as was Mimi. "It will all be just as I've said. We just have this one teeny obstacle to overcome."

I was not enthusiastic about being an obstacle. Though I was even less so about the idea of being their fait accompli.

"Now let's just get that over with, okay? The sooner we get this part behind us, the sooner we won't have to think about it anymore."

I saw Curt square up his shoulders. He offered me a weak smile, then looked away, perhaps from the fear and fury in my eyes. I knew I could expect no help from that quarter.

He began to move toward me. "Do you have the note?" he said to Mimi gruffly.

"In my bag. I don't want to take my eyes off her, Curt. Come get it from me and give it to her."

He did as she asked—crossing to her carefully, extracting the note from the bag slung over her shoulder without ever compromising the hold Mimi had over me.

When he handed me the note with one gloved hand, it felt like a ritual, though one I didn't yet understand. I took it and read it quickly. It was uncanny. I *knew* I hadn't written it, yet only those closest to me would suspect that it wasn't in my hand. And maybe, I thought with alarm, not even then.

*Time passes, but doesn't heal all wounds. I'd forgot-
ten that. I never stopped loving Braydon Gauthier.
Now that he's gone, I can't bear the thought of living
without him. Please tell my family that I'm sorry and
that I love them. But I think they will understand.*

The note brought emotion close to the surface. The
thing that swam up felt distressingly like panic.

I knew now, as Mimi did, that no one would ever
suspect I hadn't written it. I also knew that, to duplicate
my handwriting so precisely, they had to have had something to work from. My mind went to the night I'd
gone back to Braydon's apartment and had felt
as though someone had been there, perhaps going
through my things, looking for samples of my handwriting. I thought to ask, but realized, suddenly, I didn't
care what the answer was. I was going to die. I understood
that now. I wasn't prepared for it, but who ever really is?

After I'd held the note for perhaps a minute, Mimi
said, "All right, Curt, that should be enough." When
Curt retrieved it from me and crossed over to place it
on the counter in the set kitchen, I understood. Fin-
gerprints. That's why they'd shown it to me. Why also,
at least in part, Curt had worn gloves. Now my finger-
prints were on the note and his were not. I wondered
if Mimi's were, then realized, with the other details so
carefully handled, they would not be.

I felt the arrival of the elevator before I heard it. And
I could tell from Mimi and Curt's reaction that I wasn't

the only one who wasn't expecting it. The overhead lights came on at almost the same moment, and the three us blinked rapidly as our eyes adjusted to the new brightness.

"Hey." Simon stood in the doorway, looking at us in confusion. His was the face of a man who had not been invited to the party and wonders what he did to be left out. "What's going on?"

This, I knew, would be the only moment. I would not get another chance.

I took it.

I launched myself at Mimi in the split second she took her gun off me, surprised by the presence of an unexpected other.

The gun went off just as I propelled all of my body weight into her, knocking her off her feet. I heard the explosion of sound, but didn't see the result.

Mimi and I fell in a heap on the floor. I could hear the gun spin away from her, the hard thud of its distant landing making me hopeful it was out of reach for the moment.

Everything happened so quickly then, I can't credibly report it. I knew there was blood, but whose I couldn't at that moment say. I felt nails raking my cheek, was aware of a handful of hair in my hand and a sharp pain in my left elbow as it connected with the floor. Perhaps there were punches going both ways, but I don't recall, though the bruising I'd have later would support this.

What I do recall: Simon, moving while he dialed his

phone, calling 911, then finally separating us. Mimi a bedraggled mess, blood and bruises and scratches. Me beside her, probably the same. Curt, the source of all that blood, on the floor, unmoving.

I looked at Simon, but he shook his head.

"No. He's gone."

Gone. What could that mean? *Gone.* I could see Curt, right there, on the floor. He hadn't *gone.* I felt something like hysterical laughter trickling up out of me from some untended place and knew then that I was probably in some kind of shock.

Simon wanted me to go down and let the police in, but I couldn't do it. The desire to laugh had passed, but now I was shaking so badly I couldn't imagine making the trip.

I stayed, instead, with Mimi, while Simon went down to let them in. He'd retrieved the gun and propped it in my hand to keep Mimi cooperative. I doubted very much I could have used it, but it didn't come up. It was over for her now; her lover was dead, her secret well and out. There was nowhere left, really, for her to go. And, like I said, I'm bigger than her. She wasn't going anywhere.

The Vancouver City Police arrived quickly and in large numbers. And other emergency personnel, though I didn't pay much attention to them. Even when a paramedic looked me over, examined my scratches and my bruised elbow and gave me a tetanus shot. Even when they zipped Curt into a body bag and wheeled him away.

The police took statements, asked a lot of questions.

They were thorough. We were there for hours. At one point, someone pressed a cup of tea into my hand. I don't remember anything ever tasting so good. With the passing of time and the tea, my hands steadied after a while. And my heart stopped racing.

I answered all of the questions as well as I could—to the best of my ability—but, when I look back on it, I realize I'd shut off my emotions by that point. Put all the feelings away in a place where I could look at them later. I know I sounded dispassionate when I gave my statement. I doubt that the cop knew I was just trying to keep my hands from shaking. Trying to keep from being overwhelmed by shock and sadness and fatigue.

At one point, Doug showed up, his eyes wide and alarmed. There was no sign of Stina, though that didn't surprise me.

By the time the police were done with me, light was spreading across the Vancouver skyline and, with it, a hint of gold. The rain was gone and the city looked beautiful.

In my car, I rolled down the window, put my hands on the steering wheel and just sat there for a while, enjoying the feel of the cool air on my skin. Enjoying, in a very basic way, just being alive.

"You were right, then." It was Simon. I hadn't noticed his approach, but for some reason, I didn't feel alarmed.

I considered his words. "I guess I was. I'm sorry I was. It would have been better if I was wrong."

"Would it have?" His eyes looked tired, like they'd seen too much.

"I don't know, Simon. It's just sadder this way, somehow. I mean, it was sad when I thought Braydon killed himself, sure. But I guess I just hate to find all this badness. I hate seeing the worst in people confirmed."

"His family will be relieved, Madeline. They felt bad about the way he died. It's human to feel as though you haven't done enough. And it's just good, I think, that the truth be known. Better, always, than a lie."

I made a mental note to call them, from the road. Perhaps ditch off the interstate at a rest stop on my way to Seattle, and spend some time filling Anne-Marie and Jessica in. He was right: they'd feel relieved. It wouldn't bring him back, but it might make their hearts hurt a little less to know for certain it was nothing that they'd done, and that there was nothing that they *could* have done. No, it wouldn't bring Bray back, but it would make a difference.

"The truth is better than a lie. I know you're right," I said, looking up into Simon's kind eyes. "But. Still."

"And Gwen." I looked at him closely, then. Saw he was close to tears. "It's why I was at the office tonight. She died of a heroine overdose, Madeline. I just found out. It made me so sad, I couldn't sleep. I thought I'd come to the office and work."

"Where did they find her?" I asked quietly.

"What?"

"Did they find her on the downtown east side?" My voice was calmer than I felt.

"How did you know?"

I told him, then, about the phone call, about my trip downtown and my fruitless wait. Mentioned the purse shaped vaguely like an alligator.

"Was it them, do you think? Did Mimi do this, too?"

I shook my head helplessly. I honestly didn't know and maybe never would. But it was one more thing to be sad about. One more thing in what now felt like a mountain of hurt.

The sensible thing for me to do at that point would have been just to drive back to Braydon's apartment and crash for a few hours. Or, failing that, I could have gone to Emily's hotel or Jessica's house, or Anne-Marie's for that matter. I had options. But I didn't want to do any of those things.

I knew, also, that Simon wouldn't have been averse to comforting me and letting me rest at his place for a while. That was a tempting thought. He was a good man and part of me felt as though I needed goodness close to me just then. I could imagine a bed somewhere—somewhere that was probably warm and slightly messy but nice, nonetheless—and me in it, Simon's arms around me, protecting me from dreams that were bound to be frightening. Bound to be bad.

In the end, though, I realized that what I wanted most of all was a ridiculous thing for a woman in her mid-thirties to desire. Right then, there was only one person who could comfort me properly. Right then, I just wanted my mom.

The police hadn't told me I couldn't leave the country. And I knew I'd probably have to come back at some point; that there'd be inquiries and trials and a lot of other stuff I was too tired to think about now.

Mimi had killed Braydon. Mimi and Curt. And they'd tried to kill me, too. Doug, I could see now, had been guilty of many things, but not that. I supposed that he'd been hollowing out the company he had mostly built, perhaps self-righteously trying to take back the value he felt had been created with his own energy.

Mimi had known what Doug was up to and had, in her own twisted way, thought she'd help her brother reach his goals. Goals that, if successful, would have seen her created as a star in the way that her husband had been. That, I thought, would have been Doug's plan.

The funny thing was, Doug's plan had been well on its way to working. Without his sister's intervention, everything would have probably gone off just as he intended. Doug would have continued to take large amounts of money out of the company by various measures, covering Gauthier Fine Foods' dropping value by keeping the stock off the exchanges that would have required that it be monitored more carefully. Embezzlement is what they call that. Not murder.

At the same time, he had Sonya working to promote the stock by any means possible. Sonya's promotion had kept the stock price buoyed beyond what it would have been under normal circumstances. And Sonya had been selling a shell of a company. A gorgeous, well-polished shell, but a shell nonetheless. By the time Doug had gotten through with it, Gauthier Fine Foods would have been less than a shell. It would have been a husk.

If left to the course he had set—and if Braydon had not died—I could see Doug continuing on for another year, perhaps more, carefully diverting value out of Gauthier Fine Foods before finally walking away, finally leaving the company while it floundered in the throes of death.

He had stolen money from the company while the building was under construction; I was fairly certain about that. What about the real estate the building sat on? Hadn't someone told me that Doug had once owned it? Had he flipped it to the company at immense profit? And who supplied the raw materials for the frozen food line? Who owned the factory where it was packaged? The trucking company that moved things around? The linen suppliers for the restaurants? There were so many ways that Doug might have been funneling cash straight out of the company and into his own pocket. I had a feeling securities investigators or police—perhaps both—would spend months unraveling it all.

But Braydon had died. That had focused attention on the company in ways that Doug couldn't afford. It had, for instance, brought scrutiny from Braydon's family. And that, of course, had brought me.

And bringing me. What had that done? As I said goodbye to Simon and pointed Old Stinky out of the city, I thought about that. As far as I could tell, my presence hadn't done much. What had been wrong at Gauthier Fine Foods had been so deeply wrong, I couldn't help but think that the rot would have come to the surface sooner rather than later. It would have been exposed one way or another.

Nothing I could have done would bring Braydon back. Nothing would put things right. Make things the way they once had been.

A chapter closed. I could feel it. A door clicking shut softly behind me. I was glad to get Old Stinky on the highway, the sun glinting off her hood as we drove. My little blue cloud.

We headed south. I didn't look back.

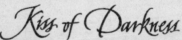

The first in a sensational new series from the bestselling author of *Intern* and *Killer Body*

BONNIE HEARN HILL

IF IT BLEEDS, IT LEADS.

It's a newspaper mantra—the most gruesome stories always run on the front page to get people's attention. When the body of the city's first woman mayor is discovered in a dusty vineyard, California's Valley Voice investigative reporter Corina Vasquez lands the bloody lead story.

But she also attracts the attention of a killer.

"Engrossing, provocative and haunting, *Intern* is a riveting combination."
—*New York Times* bestselling author Mary Jane Clark

IF IT BLEEDS

Available the first week of September 2006, wherever paperbacks are sold!

MIRA®

MBHH2339

True Confessions
of the
Stratford Park PTA

by Nancy Robards Thompson

The journey of four women through midlife;
man trouble; and their children's middle
school hormones—as they find their place
in this world...

Available October 2006
TheNextNovel.com

LINDA L.
RICHARDS

32240 THE NEXT EX   ___ $6.99 U.S. ___ $8.50 CAN.

(limited quantities available)

TOTAL AMOUNT	$ _____
POSTAGE & HANDLING	$ _____
($1.00 FOR 1 BOOK, 50¢ for each additional)	
APPLICABLE TAXES*	$ _____
TOTAL PAYABLE	$ _____

(check or money order—please do not send cash)

To order, complete this form and send it, along with a check or money order for the total above, payable to MIRA Books, to: **In the U.S.:** 3010 Walden Avenue, P.O. Box 9077, Buffalo, NY 14269-9077; **In Canada:** P.O. Box 636, Fort Erie, Ontario, L2A 5X3.

Name: _____
Address: _____ City: _____
State/Prov.: _____ Zip/Postal Code: _____
Account Number (if applicable): _____

075 CSAS

    *New York residents remit applicable sales taxes.
    *Canadian residents remit applicable GST and provincial taxes.

MIRA®

www.MIRABooks.com

MLLR0906BL